Praise for V

"Milchman is the Swiss Army knif[...] is partly a who-is-my-husband-rea[...] [...] [...], p[...] [...] [...] wilderness story, and partly a Manhattan-family drama, all rolled up in elegantly propulsive prose, and shot through with sinister suspense. The real mystery about Milchman is why she isn't already huge."

—Lee Child, *New York Times*
bestselling author of the Jack Reacher series

"On a honeymoon gone terribly awry, two newlyweds battle for their lives in a powerful story of survival told by one of the richest and most riveting voices in today's thriller fiction. From start to finish, *Wicked River* twists and tumbles and roars, carrying readers along for one hell of a thrill ride."

—William Kent Krueger, *New York Times*
bestselling author of *Ordinary Grace*

"*Wicked River* is an intriguing mix of hopes and fears. A tale fraught with danger, but loaded with place and character. It's spicy, smart, and entertaining."

—Steve Berry, *New York Times*
bestselling author of the Cotton Malone series

"A contemporary *Deliverance*, and a terrifying thrill ride into the darkest side of human nature. With a breakneck pace and shocking twists and turns around every bend, *Wicked River* will keep you up late at night—and haunt your dreams long after you're finished."

—Chevy Stevens, *New York Times*
bestselling author of *Still Missing* and *Those Girls*

"Riveting. A hybrid between John Fowles's classic *The Collector* and Erica Ferencik's *The River at Night*, this novel will appeal to fans of psychological suspense as well as those who enjoy trips to the backcountry."

—*Library Journal*

"Suspense oozes like blood from a wound on every page of Jenny Milchman's *Wicked River*. As scary and tense a book as I've read this year."

—John Lescroart, *New York Times*
bestselling author of the Dismas Hardy series

"From time to time, I come across an action manuscript that shares my high regard for the [action] genre and the intensity it can achieve. One such book is Jenny Milchman's *Wicked River*, which I urge you to experience. It thoroughly gripped me, not only because of the excitement it creates and the inventiveness with which it does so, but also because of the subtext about a honeymoon in which the various stages of a marriage are condensed in a wilderness that's both physical and psychological. *Wicked River* is a wild ride."

—David Morrell, *New York Times*
bestselling author of *First Blood*

"Jenny Milchman's characters jump off the page... *Wicked River* is compulsive reading—I kept holding my breath and turning the pages faster and faster. It's a book that should cement Jenny's place as a must-read thriller writer for fans hungry for domestic suspense in the style of Gillian Flynn."

—M. J. Rose, *New York Times* bestselling author

"Chock-full of suspense and danger, *Wicked River* by Jenny Milchman takes you on the journey of a lifetime, canoeing fast-moving rivers and hiking through tangled forests where humans have seldom trod. This is the story of Natalie and Doug's honeymoon. They wanted natural beauty and adventure; they get both, in abundance. You'll be glad you joined them. *Wicked River* is wicked thrilling!"

—Gayle Lynds, bestselling author
of *Masquerade* and *The Book of Spies*

"*Deliverance*, meet *Into the Wild*. Jenny Milchman knows how to construct a tautly wound, raw-boned thriller that will keep you up like the howl of wolves outside your tent."

—Andrew Gross, international bestselling author
of *The Blue Zone* and *The Dark Tide*

"A story about passion and betrayal on the high stakes stage, *Wicked River* is intensely gripping and perfectly paced—a real standout that pushes the domestic thriller category to its very edge. With her usual mastery of setting and character, Jenny Milchman has outdone herself."

—Carla Buckley, international bestselling
author of *The Good Goodbye*

WICKED
A NOVEL
RIVER

JENNY MILCHMAN

sourcebooks
landmark

Published by Sourcebooks Landmark, an imprint of Sourcebooks, Inc.
P.O. Box 4410, Naperville, Illinois 60567-4410
(630) 961-3900
Fax: (630) 961-2168
sourcebooks.com

Library of Congress Cataloging-in-Publication Data

Names: Milchman, Jenny, author.
Title: Wicked river / Jenny Milchman.
Description: Naperville, Illinois : Sourcebooks Landmark, [2018]
Identifiers: LCCN 2017040810 | (trade pbk. : alk. paper)
Subjects: LCSH: Psychological fiction. | GSAFD: Suspense fiction.
Classification: LCC PS3613.I47555 W53 2018 | DDC 813/.6--dc23 LC record available
at https://lccn.loc.gov/2017040810

Printed and bound in the United States of America.
BVG 10 9 8 7 6 5 4 3 2 1

*For Josh, who was there on our own honeymoon in the woods,
and every joyful, beauty-filled, wild day since.
Thank you for making this journey possible.*

ONE YEAR BEFORE

Twigs and branches tore at her arms like razor wire, so fast was she running. Breath coming in bull puffs, stinging her nose, drying out her throat and mouth. Her feet churned the soil into clouds of dust. It hadn't rained in weeks, the driest August on record.

If rain had been predicted, Terry wouldn't be here right now, caught in this mad race to a nonexistent finish line. She always checked the Weather Channel assiduously before a hike. Five-day forecasts were relatively accurate, and Terry didn't backpack for more than three. That way, she only had to take two days off, brackets around a weekend, including time for travel. As with everything else, Terry was practical in her outdoor pursuits. She didn't push herself to cover long distances, nor deal with things like bad weather. Trying to get a stove lit under a drumbeat of rain, slick outer gear humidifying the inside of your tent. Who needed that?

What she wouldn't give right now for the annoyances of a drowned-out expedition.

He was right behind her.

Huh, huh, huh came the breaths she fought to drag in. She could feel their pulse in her eardrums. She couldn't keep going at this pace much longer. She'd had a head start, but the man was taller and fleeter than she, made strong by all the work entailed in the shelter he was starting to build.

He had asked Terry if she wanted to see the shelter, and for a moment, she'd been tempted. With horrified regret, she recalled the keen insight and interest the man had exhibited in her approach to hiking and equipment preferences. His attention had been compelling. But coming to her senses—just go off with a strange man in the woods?—Terry had declined, and then he had gotten angry.

That was when she ran.

Woods surrounded her on all sides, both cape and canopy. She broke through another pincushion of sticks, shutting her eyes to protect them, hoping the ground would stay level before her. Fat, fleshy leaves slapped at her face; then, she realized that the leaves were actually flying through the air like missiles.

Terry twisted, shooting a look over her shoulder as she raced on.

The man was hacking at trees with a machete, reducing their protruding branches to stubs. Whereas Terry had only her body to use as a blade, which was taking its toll on her. Bubbles of blood dotted her arms; welts stood up on the exposed part of her chest. Her shoes relentlessly beat the clods of earth, stirring up that crematorium wake of ashy dirt behind her.

She had told the man her name. That was the thing Terry couldn't let go of now—how susceptible she had been to his charms. "Terry," he had echoed. "A solid, capable name." If he had said her name was beautiful, or even pretty, the connection would've been lost. Terry herself was neither of those things, and she knew that her name wasn't either. Its full version—Theresa—felt too fancy and she'd adopted the diminutive in girlhood. Terry lived alone, cooked herself solid, nutritious meals, and assisted a pool of doctors during the week, while hiking solo on the weekends. The man seemed to recognize all of this about her, and be drawn to her despite it.

Or because of it.

A meaty stick caught her in the back, thrown like a javelin by the man. Terry nearly went down, but stumbled and regained her footing. She was close to giving up, just stopping like a kid in a game of tag. *Okay, you got me.* He would in the end anyway, wouldn't he? But no, she couldn't die out here in her beloved Adirondacks. The man was close enough now that she could hear the hissing slash of the machete blade, feel a rainfall of slender pine needles when he sliced through the air with the weapon's steel edge. She drilled down and found a final spurt of speed, not daring to take another look behind her.

But the woods were opening up at last, giving way to some other sort of terrain. What was it? Her brain was too oxygen deprived, too terror fueled, to process the change in landscape.

The man hurled his machete in a great, soaring arc of rage, its silver spear turning end over end, headed right for her.

They were at a gully. That was what explained all the sudden space.

Terry dove just before the blade hit the rim of earth and plunged into the ground.

He would expect her to roll all the way to the base of the ravine, use the creek that rushed there to make her escape. Instead, Terry threw both hands out, clawing her nails into dirt, stones, and grit, arresting her fall halfway down the hill. Scrabbling on her belly in panic, praying that her movements were invisible from above, Terry made her way to an overhang of rock and slid beneath it. The stone ceiling protected her from sight. Terry tasted soil, felt some creature of the earth—a worm, or maybe a small snake—squiggle away, its sinuous body cool against her bare cheek.

The man bushwhacked past the new, wobbly trees that clung to the ravine, maneuvering downhill through brittle, rain-deprived brush, and coming within a few feet of Terry. Upon reaching the bottom, he entered the water and went splashing downriver. After a while, she could no longer hear his churning feet.

Enough time passed that Terry began to picture her getaway. She'd only be half a day later than expected, and who was there to expect her, really? Just the doctor who worked Mondays. Terry pictured signing the Turtle Ridge trail register, her hand shaking so hard that her entry would be nearly illegible, although she would still follow protocol, do the right thing; that was Terry's way. She could actually feel the wooden lid on the box that protected the log, too heavy to hold, given her compromised state. It would fall, catching her bruised and scraped fingers, and she would bite back a bleat of pain.

But at least she'd be safe.

She had saved herself. Calm, capable Terry, far too prepared and competent to wind up in trouble in the woods, would be out of this mess soon.

Then a pair of arms as strong as winches slid beneath the rock and pulled her out.

PART ONE

LOST

CHAPTER ONE

We deceive ourselves.

Those were the words in Natalie Abbott's head when she woke up the morning of her wedding.

It was a terrible thing to think, especially when you were about to get married, and Natalie immediately rolled over in the lofty bed and tried to fall back asleep. Today would be a huge day, and tomorrow promised in some ways to be even bigger.

But sleep refused to come, forestalled by the prospect of this afternoon's ceremony, and last-minute preparations still left to make for their honeymoon. Sunlight streamed through the gauzy curtains that hung over the windows across from her bed. The country inn where she and Doug were getting married dated back to 1812, and amenities like blackout shades had been sacrificed in favor of historical detail. The glass in the windows had warbles in it that had been blown there two centuries ago.

Apprehension began to turn into anticipation. Natalie wrapped her arms around herself—this inn did have air-conditioning, at least—and shivered in pure delight. What a beautiful place to be married. If you were going to start a new life, this was the setting for it.

There was a knock on the door, and Natalie threw back the flowery sheets and padded across the floorboards, wearing only a baby-doll nightie. She had hoped that Doug might make a middle-of-the-night excursion to her room, despite the ban against them seeing each other until this afternoon. A final romantic interlude with her fiancé seemed worth shucking some old-fashioned superstition. Most of the married couples they knew had bent other rules, agreeing to a "first look" for convenience's sake, for instance, while Natalie and Doug had decided to opt for tradition and take wedding photos after the ceremony.

Tradition was important to both of them, and for much the same reason: neither had had a lot of it while growing up. Which meant there were gaps, big holes, when it came to talking about their pasts, but Natalie never blamed Doug for going stony and silent. There were parts of her own upbringing that she avoided thinking about as well.

"Doug?" she whispered, cracking the door.

"Doug!" came the retort as her sister pushed her way through the opening. "You get to spend your whole life with him. But this is the last day I can take care of my baby sister." Claudia gave an exaggerated sniff, then smiled at Natalie.

Natalie took a step backward, allowing Claudia inside and offering a smile in return. Doug was maintaining the custom, her older sister was keeping the promise she'd made back when Natalie was just a toddler and Claudia already crossing the threshold to teen status, and the faint trace of foreboding, with which Natalie had woken, was finally receding, like a wave on the beach, before the wonder of this day.

Claudia held out a tray. "The inn sent breakfast since Doug's in the dining room eating his," she said. "And Dad wants to know if there's anything he can do to help."

They exchanged smiles, Natalie knowing that the blend of ingredients she saw on her sister's face must be mirrored on her own. Indulgence, regret, annoyance.

"My mani?" Natalie suggested, displaying ten ragged nails. It was about as likely that her father would take on the task of grooming as anything else—which was to say, not very likely at all.

Claudia acknowledged the comment with a wry nod, then set the tray on an antique desk and whipped a cloth napkin off a plate. She poured coffee from a carafe, its fragrance filling the room. "The girl is coming in a few hours with her kit," she said. "She'll do your toes too."

Natalie wiggled her toes against the wood floorboards. She walked over to the desk—though the motion felt more like prancing—and took a bite out of a muffin. "Then I guess we won't need Dad's assistance."

They traded smiles again. Claudia fingered a strand of Natalie's hair while Natalie explored the interior of an omelet. "I think you should wear it up after all," Claudia said.

Natalie looked up at her big sister, and nodded.

Later that afternoon, Natalie glanced at the porcelain clock in her suite, an analog relic that actually ticked. Just past two o'clock, with her hair and makeup already completed. Less than two hours to go.

Natalie gave the woman laboring over her scruffy hands an apologetic look before casting her gaze toward the view outside. As dictated by custom, she and Doug had parted just before midnight last night. Right now, he was probably hanging out in one of the outbuildings scattered across the generous grounds of the inn, or maybe playing a game of tennis or basketball on the far-off courts.

Absurdly, Natalie missed him. Until this moment, she hadn't realized how accustomed she had grown to having Doug by her side. It'd been easy to allow the distance between herself and her friends to draw itself out because Doug filled a void inside Natalie that no one else ever had. From the night they'd met three years ago, stumbling into each other—literally—at the bar where Doug drank with his buddies, a gaping hole inside Natalie had closed over like water filling in a space.

"Hold still," the woman doing Natalie's nails cautioned.

Natalie hadn't even realized that she'd flinched. She felt a pang of loneliness, incongruous on this day when she was going to pledge herself to be joined to someone else forever.

Her sister had left to see to the host of last-minute tasks—checking on the floral arrangements, making sure the fruit gummies were tied up in their taffeta bundles—while Natalie had filled the remainder of her morning with a long, luxurious bath. Then came the arrival of the three beautifying women, like Sleeping Beauty's trio of fairies: this one who did nails, another who had applied a painterly palette of makeup, and a third who'd looped Natalie's hair into a series of curlicues, then added a dozen slender braids, securing the whole thing with a rafter of vines. Natalie felt a bit silly being tended to so richly, but even she had to admit that the effect appeared to be worth it. Doug would hardly recognize her. They could let out her hair like a pleated cloak around them when they had sex for the first time as a married couple.

Natalie glanced down at her lap, then at the floor. Her manicure was nearly done, and her toenails glistened like tiny peach seashells.

Claudia was to be her maid—make that *matron*—of honor, and Natalie also had two bridesmaids. Not her closest friends from the city—there'd been tension with Eva and Val ever since Natalie had met Doug, and it'd come to a head after the engagement. Natalie had been forced to reach out to a pair of old college friends, with whom she had largely lost touch, but who rallied when Natalie explained that she was getting married.

Most of Doug's boyhood crop of friends had also dispersed, but the two who remained in the city, Mark and Brett, got drinks or ate lunch with Doug fairly regularly. Natalie was glad she had at least matched her fiancé's set of groomsmen. It would have been all too easy to have nobody standing up there besides her sister, an uncomfortable reminder of the way her own friendships had disintegrated.

A rap on the door and Claudia reentered, Natalie's wedding gown in its plastic sheath slung over her arm.

"Doug's mother just arrived," she announced. "I helped unload her bags and showed her where her room was on the map." This last said with just a touch of perplexity—helplessness puzzled Claudia. She added, "She seems to like the inn."

Natalie gave her sister a smile that felt a trifle wistful. "I was hoping she might come over here to say hello. You know, before the ceremony."

"I'm sure she will," Claudia replied briskly. Problem presented, solution imposed—that was Claudia's way. Often, she even had the power to enact said solution. Only not in this case. "Give her a few moments to settle in."

When Natalie first met Doug, she had hoped that she and his mom might become close. In Natalie's view, almost any mother who was still alive held that warm, thriving potential. But Gail Larson seemed too overwhelmed by life to have much to offer anybody else, and this extended to her own son. She puttered around her overlarge apartment—three bedrooms in New York City!—assisted by a phalanx of friends, several of whom had been invited to the wedding.

The woman doing Natalie's nails reinserted her bronze-coated brush into its bottle and dabbed on a clear top coat. Then she stood up, waggling a finger in Claudia's direction. "Don't come anywhere near her with that dress for at least thirty minutes, you hear?"

"We'll just chitchat till she's dry," Claudia agreed, setting a timer on her phone.

When it chimed a half hour later, Claudia helped Natalie into her dress, shimmying the ivory silk down over Natalie's hips, then sucking in a breath.

"Oh my goodness," she said. "Will you just take a look at you. My baby sister, who could believe it?" And she rotated Natalie toward the mirror.

Natalie was surprised to feel a pinprick of tears. Claudia flew across the room for tissues, dabbing carefully at Natalie's eyes to avoid smudging the color on her lids.

"I know you must miss Mom," Claudia said. "Especially today."

Natalie gazed at herself in the glass, trying to conjure the face she'd stared at so many times in her parents' wedding portraits.

"I wish I missed her," she whispered. "I don't even have that."

Claudia adjusted the silken threads that held the dress up until they formed a rippling line across each of Natalie's shoulders, then walked her around the bridal suite so Natalie could get a feel for her shoes and the long sweep of her dress. As they passed the bank of windows, Claudia halted abruptly enough that Natalie's toes bit the hem of her gown. Claudia steadied her, then crouched down to peer outside.

"Natalie," she said, her voice sharp. "What are those guys doing?"

CHAPTER TWO

Natalie and Doug had chosen the Blooming Garden Inn in upstate New York because its idyllic, pastoral setting seemed the stuff of wedding dreams. The bridal suite occupied a wing of the Victorian structure, painted sage, adorned by violet shutters. The suite had its own separate entrance looking out over the wildflower meadow where the ceremony would take place.

Standing beside her sister, Natalie bent down too, and looked.

At the end of the winding stone walk that led away from the suite, white wooden chairs had been set up. None of the rows were filled yet, but it was still a bit early, plus Natalie and Doug had known that their wedding would be on the small side. Both of their family trees were so fractured, with breaks and jogs along the lines. It was another of the things that bound them together.

"Are those Doug's groomsmen?" Claudia asked, sounding slightly annoyed. She leaned closer to the window. "They're going to be late."

Beyond the meadow lay an empty field, which marked the boundary between the inn's property and the road running alongside. And standing in the midst of that field were two men who from this vantage point did look a lot like Doug's best friends.

Natalie twisted to look at her sister over her shoulder, feeling the glide of ivory silk against her. "Why would they just be standing around over there?"

"They're not even dressed," Claudia replied, still with that tinge of annoyance. Her sister didn't like unexpected disruptions or changes in plan.

"And I don't think they're just 'standing around,'" Claudia added. "It looks like they're upset about something."

Natalie dropped to her knees to get a better look through the glass, her skirt forming a puddle of silk on the floor.

"Let me go see what's happening," Claudia proposed, straightening up from the window.

But Natalie was the one getting married, growing up in some sense after today. She gave a quick shake of her head. "I'll do it."

"Natalie!" Claudia burst out. "You can't go out there like that."

Natalie began heading for the door that opened onto the meadow. "It's early. No one's even seated yet."

Except for the musicians. Standing in the doorway, Natalie could see them unfolding chairs and propping sheet music on metal stands, an elderly foursome that she and Doug had had constant trouble working with. They didn't even return texts. Natalie hoped they wouldn't be as clueless when it came to the program she and Doug had put together. Natalie had wanted music playing while the guests began to gather, and during rehearsal, the quartet seemed uncertain about the right time to start.

Natalie took a step outdoors, Claudia behind her, still protesting.

Mellow afternoon light lay over the grounds. Natalie and Doug had decided to forego an evening ceremony because they wanted to get an early start the next morning. Well, Doug did anyway. He'd given Natalie a bunch of details about the route they'd be taking and why leaving first thing mattered. When Natalie suggested pushing their honeymoon back a day—the idea of twenty-four unscheduled hours to lounge around the inn alone together feeling like the height of luxury—Doug had balked, saying that honeymoons always started the day after the wedding. Natalie wasn't sure if that was Doug sticking to time-honed ritual again, or if he was just eager to get going. Their honeymoon destination had been his idea after all.

A trellised gazebo stood in the midst of the meadow, awaiting the moment when Natalie and Doug would say their vows. Was Doug inside it already? Flowers draped the entrance, making it hard to see. An aisle had been mown between the tall, waving meadow grasses, and Natalie's father stood at one end, shifting from foot to foot as if he wasn't quite clear about his role in all this. None of the other members of the wedding party had come down from the inn yet.

Claudia shielded her eyes, squinting. "That's definitely them."

Sunlight shone right into Natalie's face, and she could hardly see. She visored her eyes, moving closer. Mark and Brett presented an odd sight, huddled together, wearing shorts and ratty tees. Natalie supposed men didn't need as much time to get ready, but this was cutting it close even so.

The two did appear to be arguing, their mouths open as they gesticulated with their hands, although their voices weren't loud enough to carry.

Doug emerged from the gazebo, squinting out at the field, and Natalie's heart leapt inside her. Her fiancé looked so stunningly handsome in his wedding garb—linen pants and a broadcloth coat, a single rosebud at his breast—that the sight momentarily distracted her from whatever might be taking place in the field.

Doug began to cross the meadow, tall flowers tickling at his legs. It could've been a photo shoot in a magazine, except for the expression of anger plastered across her fiancé's face. He joined his friends in the adjacent field while Natalie took another step toward it. All three guys became embroiled in discussion, Doug's gestures also effusive. One of his hands was balled into a fist, the other raised and out-turned as if in protest.

Protest over what? Claudia was still trailing her, and Natalie shot her sister a brief look of confusion before hurrying forward on her own.

Mark withdrew a phone from his pocket and swiped his thumb across the screen, frowning. He shook the device as he walked in a circle, holding it up toward the sky.

Cell signal was spotty in this little country town. It would be nonexistent where Natalie and Doug were headed on their honeymoon tomorrow.

All three guys turned around at the same time to face the road. It lay, one lane and spooling, barricaded on its opposite side by a thin strip of forest. A dark, late-model sedan came gliding along the asphalt, like a shark slicing through the gray-black sea.

Natalie picked up her skirts, fighting to close the distance between herself and Doug.

Her fiancé's voice became audible. "No way. Not now."

A few early guests must have emerged and caught sight of Natalie; from behind she could hear whispered *oohs* and *aahs* gathering force like a wind. She felt her freshly manicured nails dig into her palms as her hands formed panicked fists.

Natalie hurried past the last of the prettily arrayed chairs and into the field, her path sending her across a portion of aisle.

The string quartet launched into the preamble Natalie and Doug had selected to play before the processional began. Natalie knew they should have hired someone else. Notes from Beethoven's Ninth soared toward a cloudless blue lid of sky. Triggered by the strains of music, Natalie's father raised his head and took a few halting steps.

Claudia went running over, stretching out an arm to stop their dad, whose glossy shoes caught a loose clod of earth. He tripped, righting himself as he looked around for Natalie in the dazzling sunlight. Claudia dashed forward, holding up her dress, and signaling the musicians to stop with a guillotine motion to her neck.

The instruments abruptly cut off.

Mark and Brett and Doug all looked up at once with identical expressions on their faces. As if they'd been suddenly jarred out of whatever had been preoccupying them, jolted back to the here and now. They grew flustered, brushing at their clothes, edging sideways until they were out of sight of Natalie's father, the musicians, and whichever guests had begun to assemble.

At a distance, Natalie followed their progress across the field.

Mark began shaking his phone as if a small animal had latched itself onto his hand. He swiped at the screen, a goggle of dismay distorting his features.

Natalie's skirts tangled, and she came to a stop.

The *thunk* of twin car doors could be heard from the road. Two men emerged from the vehicle, dressed in cheap, slick suits and square-toed boots, which chewed up the field as the men began crossing it.

Mark and Brett exchanged looks, while Doug gave them a merciless glare.

The two men were heading straight for them. One was brick-faced with sullen features, mottled, ruddy skin, and an elongated head. The other seemed to have a handicap. The heel on his left boot was a good three inches higher than the one on the right, and he walked with a plodding, relentless hitch in his step. The first man broke into a jog as his friend struggled to keep up.

"Mark—" Doug warned. He didn't appear to have noticed Natalie, now standing a little ways behind him.

His groomsmen pivoted in the direction of the two men, leaving the bower of blossoms, partially trod-upon aisle, and thankfully still-empty chairs. Mark and Brett walked casually toward the road, at a slightly faster clip than a stroll. When they reached the men in a broad sweep of grass, Mark and Brett sandwiched the pair, guiding them away from where the festivities were set to begin.

Natalie spun in place, fighting to understand what had just happened.

Claudia could be heard shushing their father: "I don't know, Dad. I'll find out."

Doug headed back toward the gazebo, the look on his face the antithesis of a party: a poisonous brew of knit eyebrows and carved-out hollows in his cheeks forged by clenching his jaw.

Natalie reached out to him. "Doug?"

He looked surprised to see her there, his vision clouded.

Then his face folded. "Did you see those screwups?" he asked, voice so low and thunderous that Natalie had trouble making out what he'd said. "They ruined our day—"

"Doug, no!" Natalie interrupted. She felt a flicker of fear. Things couldn't be ruined as easily as that. It didn't matter who those men were, or what connection they had to Mark and Brett. Anything like that was peripheral, outside the confines of the union she and Doug were about to enter into. Natalie took her fiancé's face between her hands. His cheeks felt heated, fiery. "No," she repeated. "It's going to be perfect."

Doug looked down, as if only now truly parsing her presence.

"All that matters is us," Natalie whispered, holding his gaze.

Gone were the music, those men, the guests who would soon be getting situated in their seats. Natalie's sister, just itching to fix whatever had happened, and their father, ambling about and bewildered. Nothing and nobody existed except for Natalie and Doug. Amber late-day light shone down, enveloping them in their own golden halo.

Natalie rose on tiptoes, unsteady in her heels, and Doug caught her, one arm upon the small of her back, strong enough to keep her from falling.

Then he learned over, just an inch or two, and they looked into each other's eyes. Natalie had to blink from the sheer overwhelm of their stare. Passion had always been a spark in dry grass between them, instantaneously ignited. Yearning, reaching, Natalie made up the difference between their two bodies until she could brush Doug's mouth with her own. It was fevered like the rest of him, and tasted of anger.

Doug caught her lips between his own, kissing back hard, biting her almost. Natalie moaned, the sound lost to all the space around them. She drank Doug in, a bloodletting only she could absorb. Doug pulled her closer, flattening her breasts against his broad chest until Natalie could no longer tell where he ended and she began.

There was a stirring from behind, and dazed, Natalie and Doug parted. The pastor hurried toward them.

"Hey, I think you folks might be jumping the gun," he said, settling himself into place at the gazebo and straightening his tie. "The wedding hasn't even started yet."

CHAPTER THREE

b est wedding kiss ever Mia texted after the long, boring ceremony
was finally over. She looked down in frustration at the line that
stopped halfway across the screen. Five words appeared: *Message could
not be delivered.*

She bit her lip, and felt her annoyance ease a little. Mia's braces had
just been taken off last week—she'd begged the ortho to make sure it
happened in time for her aunt's wedding—and the silky feel of her teeth
amazed her every time.

Mia stuffed her useless phone into the clutch her mother had loaned
her. Aunt Nat and Uncle Doug were running back down the aisle, a
shower of rose petals tossed at their heads. Mia got up and reached into
the basket placed at the end of each row of seats so that she could throw a
handful. A breeze lifted the velvet scallops and scattered them across the
grass. Pretty. Mia decided to do the same thing if she ever got married.

What were you supposed to do at a wedding after the wedding part
ended? Eat, of course, and dance, but neither seemed to be an option just

yet. If her dad were here, she'd at least have someone to talk to, but again, not an option. Mia decided to go in search of her mother and grandfather.

They were nowhere to be found. Not standing in the field with the other clumps of guests, or near the little structure where the ceremony took place. Mia figured her grandfather must've had some need he couldn't figure out on his own—maybe he wanted a drink, or a phone that actually worked—and her mom was attending to it. That was kind of her mom's way, taking care of everything for everybody, whether they wanted her to or not. Although there were plenty of drinks right here, Mia observed, as she wandered around in the bright sunshine. A waiter passed by, tray held high above his shoulder, and Mia reached for a glass of champagne.

The waiter looked down as she took it. "You of age?"

He looked pretty young himself. Cute too. "Everybody's of age today, cowboy," Mia replied, then danced off with the glass tipping in her hand.

She decided to go ditch her phone. If she had it on her, she would only try to use it, and that was a losing battle. Guests looked down and smiled as Mia tripped past. Her borrowed shoes weren't easy to walk in. Mia didn't recognize any of these people, and still couldn't find a member of her family. Actually, she thought she saw one person who might be related—distantly—in part because he saw fit to snatch the nearly full glass out of her hand. Mia didn't really care. Champagne tasted sour, plus she was already feeling a little fuzzy in the head.

After making a quick pit stop at her room, Mia came back out of the hotel and finally spotted her aunt and uncle. They were standing beside a tree with leaves partially cloaking them, kissing in a way that made Mia's cheeks burn. She looked away, and when she took a second glance, they had stepped deeper in between the branches, although they could still be overheard.

"Are we going to talk about what happened?" Aunt Nat asked.

Silence, until Mia wondered if they were kissing again, but then

Uncle Doug spoke. "You don't have to worry about it. Call it a blast from the past."

Mia crept closer to the tree.

"Mark's and Brett's pasts, you mean?" Aunt Nat asked.

They were talking about the two hot groomsmen, but other than that, Mia couldn't make sense of a single word. Still, she did know that a conversation this tense didn't belong on your wedding day, and her skin began to prickle. Her mom and dad used to sound like this. Before they stopped talking to each other at all.

She should leave, go in search of her mom, but Mia couldn't bring herself to turn away from the tree. Far across the lawn arose a sudden plume of laughter, glasses clinking, the buzz of a party really getting started. The dull, old-timey musicians had left, and now a DJ was playing something by some hip band.

"Okay, I get it," Aunt Nat said after a pause. "They're your friends, you're protective of them. But can you at least tell me why you got so ticked off?"

Mia frowned. She knew something must've happened before she came down from the hotel—her mom had been all rustled and upset as she took her place at the head of the aisle, plus Uncle Doug's groomsmen had almost been late, still adjusting their ties when they appeared—but Mia herself hadn't been there to see whatever it was. She was always missing out on stuff other people were right in the middle of.

"Do you?" Uncle Doug said.

"What?" Aunt Nat responded.

"Get it," Uncle Doug said.

"What?" Aunt Nat asked again.

"Come on, Nat," Uncle Doug said, and though his voice sounded gentle, something in it warned Mia that what he was about to say wouldn't be. "We both know that friends haven't exactly been your strong suit in life."

There was a silence. Something in Mia's chest plopped with hurt for her aunt.

She began to back away. Fast, almost falling in her loaner shoes. She shouldn't have been here in the first place. The kissing had been private, not for anybody else's eyes, but this was secret in a different way altogether. No wonder her parents were getting divorced. If this was what marriage was like, then Mia would skip it completely, even if the rose petal part had been nice.

But then Aunt Nat answered, cool and strong. "Don't turn this around on me, Doug. I have a right to ask. Who were those men?"

Mia practically let out a cheer.

Uncle Doug snorted. "You mean Lefty and his partner?"

"Doug!" Aunt Nat said, protesting and laughing at the same time. "Way to make fun of the handicapped guy. He had a *limp*. That isn't what made him shady."

Feeling better somehow, Mia began to drift in the direction of the band. Maybe she'd get another glass of champagne, drink the whole thing this time. The taste had become less gross on her tongue, like chilled honey and lemon.

But then Uncle Doug spoke again. "Shady," he repeated. "Look, Mark and Brett are big boys. They can handle things on their own." A second or two ticked by. "I'll tell you more about it. Just not today, okay?" A pause and he added, "Today is for us."

Mia saw her aunt and uncle's bodies merge behind the leafy boughs before she finally turned away for real, racing off across the lawn.

The wedding had begun to wind down—outdoor dinner eaten, dances danced, and speeches made—before Mia realized she'd barely gotten to see her mother all night. She'd caught glimpses of her flitting form, ducking here, pausing there. Everything had been such a bustle, her mom seeing to a zillion tasks and demands, but as the guests began to head over to the pool or the bar, Mia decided she'd better return to their shared room.

She passed a waiter clearing empty plates and glasses from a long plank table. Another waiter dipped a taper into a tub strewn with flowers, igniting a flame for the lingering partygoers still milling around. Twinkling candles had been scattered all over, even though it wasn't full dark yet. Night was descending in that slow, lazy way it did in summer, as if it might decide never to arrive.

A path wound through the grounds, forming a shortcut to the steps at the front of the hotel. Mia jogged left to take it, her heels sinking into soft dirt. Mountains rose like hooded shoulders, making Mia feel claustrophobic, like they could close in around her at any second. She missed the towering skyscrapers back home in New York, fixed in place by foundations and cement.

Shouts and calls arose from the pool area and floodlit tennis courts, too distant to provide much comfort. Mia had been unprepared for how spooky it would feel out here alone in the blue half-light of evening. The moon hadn't yet risen, and there were no stars. Mia went to fish out her cell phone, then remembered she didn't have it on her. She felt like she'd been suddenly paralyzed or struck blind. What was she supposed to do with her hands and eyes without a phone? She sped up, grasses nipping at her bare legs. Some kind of nocturnal bird took flight with a great rush of wings.

Mia hurried on. The parking lot lay between her and the hotel, and the sight of the cars was somehow reassuring, so man-made and of this world. Nature by itself was intimidating. Not for the first time, Mia wondered why Aunt Nat and Uncle Doug had chosen to get married in the country versus someplace romantic like a castle in Europe or on a beach. She stepped out of the field, grateful for the feel of asphalt beneath her feet.

Mia ran past the first row of cars, swatting at a bug that landed on her neck. Her hand came away bloody, and she looked down at it with distaste. She'd have to wait to find a sink at the hotel; she couldn't very well wipe off her hand on her fancy dress. Luckily, the building was visible now, casting its shadow across the hunched vehicles. She rounded a corner and came upon two people standing on either side of a car.

"Hey there."

Mia stopped in place, facing Uncle Doug's friends, the ones who'd been in the wedding. They were both so hot, they made the cute waiter look ugly.

"Hi," Mia said shyly. Just the one word caused her cheeks to fire. No lines about cowboys coming out of her now. "What's up?" she added stupidly.

The first friend—she was pretty sure his name was Mark—gave a hard tug on a rope, making muscles ripple beneath his rolled-up sleeves.

Mia only registered then that there must be a reason they were here at the car. She felt like she was drugged—the lingering effects of the champagne maybe—as she lifted her head and spotted a long boat on the roof. It was a beautiful contraption, made out of some kind of highly polished wood. Mia had never seen anything like it. Of course, it wasn't like she went around boating all the time.

Both guys followed her gaze. Then the one named Mark explained, "Got to make sure tomorrow gets off to a good start."

His words brought back a bite of memory. Not only had Aunt Nat decided to get married way up here, she was also heading into the woods for her honeymoon. Again, Hawaii or Paris would've been way better choices as far as Mia was concerned. No matter where Aunt Nat went, though, it still meant that Mia would be stuck all alone in the city for the next week, her friends' schedules booked up with camps and sports and get-a-head-start-on-school programs. Mia's parents were no use in the company department these days. Aunt Nat was all she had.

The hot guys were looking at her, their eyes glinting in the night.

Mia studied the top of the car again, trying to come up with something to say. "Nice boat." Was that a canoe? Or a kayak?

The second guy looked at Mark. Brett? Derek? He had a hot guy's name.

"Wedding present," he explained.

Mark chuckled, giving Brett-slash-Derek a playful slug on the arm. "Groomsmen," he added. "It ain't all about the bachelor party and chicks with whipped cream."

Mia felt her face flare again. Not because of what Mark had said, but because he was staring right at her. Mia dropped her eyes, but she could tell that Mark kept right on looking. She lifted her gaze, and he smiled. Mia smiled hesitantly back.

"Hey," he said again, walking around the car in her direction. He stopped within a foot or so of her, close enough that she could sniff faint sweat on his body, along with an overlay of clean deodorant. He smelled like a man. "Pretty dress."

"Thanks." Her face must be a mask of red by now. She could feel it, like paint. Thank God she'd gotten her braces taken off.

Mark held her eyes with his. "I'm not so sure it's a good idea for you to be out here all by yourself." He took a look around the shadowed lot and gave a mock shiver.

That made her nerves loosen their grip. "I think I can handle it," she retorted.

Mark looked down at her again. Droopy eyes that said he was thinking way more than he ever would say, skin so smooth it gleamed. Just a bristle of hair on his chin, but still, a man's growth, not a boy's. He was more gorgeous than any actor. Mia cursed her comatose phone for like the thousandth time that night. She was missing the selfie that would've redeemed her whole summer, made every girl in school jealous next year.

"It's not you I'm worried about," Mark said, and his voice became genuinely caring. "It's whatever else is out here." Another look traded with his friend. "Can I walk you back to the inn?"

It wasn't like the hotel was far away, but still, Mia felt her whole body begin to tingle. Alone time with the legit hot guy. She cocked her head up at him, taking a step forward. Mark shot one more look over his shoulder, then settled a hand lightly on her waist, igniting a strip of flame. Mia wasn't sure she'd be able to walk. She didn't know if he could sense the effect he was having, but Mark steered her gently out of the parking lot, headed in the direction of the building.

The other guy called, "Tell Doug good night from me," before rising on the soles of his shoes and leaning over the car.

CHAPTER FOUR

Natalie stood on tiptoes, T-shirt riding up and exposing her stomach to the predawn chill. She was trying to make sure their new canoe was lashed on securely, but if it didn't warm up soon, she was going to have to stop and dig her fleece out of her pack.

Their wedding gift from Mark and Brett was a study in polished woods, lying like a glossy brown beetle on the roof of the car. Natalie went higher on her toes, reaching to stroke the canoe's smooth finish. In just a few hours, this vessel would become of the utmost importance: Natalie and Doug's primary mode of transport as they paddled through the most untouched stretch of wilderness the Adirondacks had to offer.

Doug and his mother came walking down from the inn, Doug holding on to his mom as if she were a brimming glass, about to spill. Gail Larson wasn't exactly the maternal type—in fact, Doug seemed more inclined to protect her than the reverse—but still, Natalie watched their progression with a pang of jealousy.

Her mother-in-law came to a stop just before the parking lot. "I think

I'll say my goodbyes to you now," she said. "It's a bit early for me. I'd like to get some more rest."

Natalie stepped forward for an embrace, Gail hugging back weakly.

"Sure you can make it okay on your own, Mom?" Doug asked.

Gail was already turning to go, picking her way across the grasses growing at the edge of the lot. She lifted her hand in a small wave.

Doug came over, did a couple of things with the ties around the canoe and the roof rack on which it lay, and suddenly the boat didn't budge so much as an inch. Doug turned and wrapped his arms around Natalie's waist. "Ready to go?"

She settled into his embrace, grateful for the transfer of warmth from her husband. *Her husband.* Doug's ability to see a problem and fix it, the way he had of setting a course and steering things, gave Natalie the feeling that she had finally come home. She grinned, nodding assent. "As ready as I'll ever be." The words came out darker than she had intended. Natalie suppressed a flicker of apprehension, focusing on the sensation of her husband's firm, unwavering hold.

Mark and Brett had volunteered to bring Natalie and Doug to their put-in spot on the lake. This was to be a somewhat elaborate endeavor, requiring two cars. After dropping them off, Mark and Brett would drive separately to the spot where Natalie and Doug were going to emerge from the woods just over a week from now. They would leave Doug's car there before driving together in Brett's back to the city.

Doug's groomsmen had really stepped up, Natalie reflected, despite whatever weirdness had gone on before the wedding. They'd just barely made it into the processional on time, but any lingering resentment on Natalie's part was eased when Claudia told her that Mark had escorted Mia back to her room last night after the girl had gotten turned around on the sprawling grounds, returning her red-faced and giggling.

It had turned out to be a wonderful celebration in the end.

Doug loosened his arms, letting Natalie out of his grasp, and walked around to the rear of the car. It was Mark and Brett's turn to emerge from the inn, yawning and sleep-drugged, scrubbing at their faces as they lugged along suitcases and garment bags.

They'd all partied pretty hard last night, and Mark and Brett looked as tired as Natalie felt. Given the place she and Doug were headed, such a state seemed not only unwise, but potentially dangerous. They needed their wits sharpened, to be on the lookout for things. What kind of trip had they planned for their honeymoon? Natalie wondered suddenly. A period of time that was supposed to be spent relaxing and simply enjoying each other, but would instead require navigating dense reaches of forest, grappling with equipment, and providing for themselves.

It was too late for such thoughts, although a small shudder took hold of her. Here in the mountains, the sun hadn't yet penetrated the sky, and the morning remained tin-colored, chilly for July. Back home in the city, the heat would already be mounting its assault on the day.

"Everyone feeling good?" Mark shouted as he trudged across the lot, Brett following at a dawdle. "A hangover is what every backcountry trip should start out on."

"Let's get this show on the road," Doug called out, clearly impatient. He held up his phone. "You have the location in your GPS? Our phones won't work up there."

"They barely work here either. We've been kicking it old-school for three days," Mark called back. "That's why I stopped at a gas station and bought this." He held out a wedge of paper, whose neat accordion folds would do nothing, Natalie knew, to assist her in making their way. She and maps spoke a different language.

When they had begun to plan this trip, Doug had asked Natalie if she was sure she would be up for it. She'd never been a big outdoorsperson, although Doug had taken her rafting and they'd camped out a few times. Still, Doug had voiced concern that Natalie couldn't survive a whole week without creature comforts. Had it been pride—a need to prove herself to her then-future husband—that had gotten Natalie into this mess?

Not a mess, she chided. In fact, it was the ultimate in romance: two people on their own in nature at the start of their lives together. Living life pared back to basics. *Think about it*, Doug had said when he first proposed the idea. *Skinny-dipping. Sleeping beneath the stars. I don't want some waiter coming up and taking our drink orders*, he'd concluded. *I just want you.*

We can always order the daiquiris back home, Natalie had joked, although no self-respecting New York City bar had blended a daiquiri in a decade, and Natalie had actually been looking forward to the lack of affectation that would come with a good, old-fashioned stay at a tropical resort.

But Doug had said, "That's the future Mrs. Larson," in a tone of such approval—he might as well have said, *That's my girl*—that Natalie was helpless before it. Even as she also looked down at herself with distaste, observing her tendency to acquiesce, go along with whatever Doug wanted.

It's not just that you don't have time for us anymore, Eva and Val had once told her. *It's like you don't even wish you did.* No wonder Natalie had had to dig up bridesmaids from the buried time capsule that was college. Meeting Doug, the prospect of their marriage, had woven a cocoon around the two of them, protective, but also isolating and alone.

As soon as Natalie had approved the honeymoon, Doug got right to work, purchasing gear and hiring a guide to plan out their route. And now they were ready to embark, too late for second thoughts or regret.

Natalie shivered, her arms sandpapery with gooseflesh. A momentary signal blip allowed her phone to ding an alert, and she grabbed for the device. Before climbing out of bed this morning, Doug still asleep beside her, Natalie had uploaded a stream of photos from last night—or tried to. They must've finally appeared. She glanced down at the screen, hoping for a comment from the ashes of her friendships with Val and Eva.

Not even a *like*.

A few months ago, Natalie had begun a position in medical HR, recommended to the head of the department by her sister, who was a nurse in the same healthcare system. She hadn't grown close with anyone at her new job yet, and none of her coworkers had been able to make the trip up for the wedding, although one had texted sorry I missed such a fun night beneath a selfie of Natalie and her bridesmaids on the dance floor.

Natalie suspected those college friendships were going to dwindle away again, even though they'd all promised, sloppily, drunkenly to keep in better touch.

Would it be just her and Doug from now on? On the river, and in life?

Another alert sounded. Mia, probably benefiting from the same lift in signal, had texted u were the most beautiful bride along with six exclamation points. Natalie felt a warming flash of love. Natalie had been more than a sister to Claudia, a trial daughter almost, and in much the same way, Mia felt like more than a niece to Natalie.

She noticed Doug staring at her, a smile on his face that looked loving, excited, and nervous, all at once. He mouthed a *let's go*, and Natalie shoved her phone into her pocket as she hurried over to the car.

She paused.

She could at least get her fleece out of her pack. She might've acceded all thoughts and preferences of her own when it came to this honeymoon, but she didn't have to be cold, damn it.

"Just a sec," she said to Doug, hoping that chattering teeth didn't cause her voice to tremble. "I need to get something first. It's freezing out here."

She flipped open the trunk, and had just begun to dig through the contents of her pack, when a shout assailed her.

"Aunt Nat, don't go!" The voice was heaving, out of breath. "Don't leave yet!"

Natalie spun around to see her niece flying down the inn's drive, all overlong legs and waving arms. Claudia followed in Mia's churned-up path, and their father brought up the rear, blinking and stumbling under the load of bags he carried, which prevented him from joining the scrum Natalie and Mia and Claudia formed as they all hugged goodbye.

The sun broke like an egg over the horizon, rendering the entire world a blushing, new-bride pink.

CHAPTER FIVE

In hindsight, Kurt Pierson wished he'd had some idea of his location when he went into the river. That way he could've climbed back up and pillaged the left-behinds of their disbanded group. Tools, gear, even the chickens would've helped him begin some sort of subsistence living, although Kurt quickly came to understand that he would've slaughtered every last one of those birds, rather than wait for them to lay eggs. The hunger that attacked when you didn't have a single bite to eat was like a kind of madness.

That had been two years ago, give or take—Kurt had no access to a calendar—but the memory of his suffering was as acute as if he were still experiencing it.

His belly had been empty, gnawed apart by a thousand teeth, although his head was stuffed full of knowledge. The people with whom he'd come into these woods, intent on starting some sort of utopia, and armed with strategies for wilderness survival, had been forced to admit failure. The starry-eyed group of philosophers had met online, yearning after a mythical Walden, but didn't even last one season, leaving Kurt to carry out their plan by himself in the woods. Doing anything alone was its own special brand of hell to Kurt, but for once in his life, solitude had been the least crushing of his burdens.

His very ability to survive was in jeopardy.

During those initial months, hunger undermined what had always been Kurt's greatest asset: his mind. So he'd doubled down, dousing himself with cold creek water whenever wooziness took hold, locating vines to build a snare as he'd been shown. When he couldn't tie the green strands tightly enough, he sacrificed a pair of laces from one of his boots, letting the lip flap around his ankle as he strode off to hide in a makeshift blind.

By then it was fall, the carnival of color on the trees allowing for a fairly accurate estimate of the passage of time. A month or more since he'd separated from his group. He had lost perhaps twenty pounds, he figured, ten percent of his body weight.

The first animal he trapped—a chipmunk or possibly a mole, something small and brown and skittering—was so close to life that had Kurt released it, it would've scampered away. Instead, Kurt pounded it into a mash with a rock, his arm growing more feeble with every strike, before he ate the creature raw, spitting out bits of fur. Without a single match, Kurt didn't have any way to cook his kill.

Because of how things ended, Kurt had chosen not to accompany his group out of the wilderness. Just call it a loss, and return to civilization? He couldn't do that; he suspected what would await him there. Still, despite having mined his companions for knowledge, Kurt was finding that theoretical understanding stood far apart from actual application. Before too much time had passed, life proved itself sufficiently difficult that he began to consider an exit strategy.

After snaring the chipmunk, he decided that if ever he was going to have the vigor to trek out of the woods, this would be the time. It took a full day of walking, but eventually Kurt came to a trail and followed the path to its outlet. There he jumped back, concealing himself behind a tree, hoping that his hunger-addled sight had been wrong. Kurt snaked back through this more trafficked region of the forest to find a second winding path. Then a third. One trail after another, in a kaleidoscopic whirl, expending calories he couldn't spare only to confirm what he'd already guessed would be true.

Posters were tacked up at every trailhead, each bearing a recent photograph of Kurt, along with two that had been doctored to show what he would look like with longer hair and a beard. Blocky letters demanded *Have you seen this man?* Surely they'd barnstormed the surrounding towns too.

Kurt Pierson was a badly wanted man, and having emerged, dripping and reborn from that river, he had to confront the facts. If he couldn't make a life for himself in this wilderness, then he would spend the rest of it in a prison cell.

Things had gone wrong for their troupe in the woods, yet only Kurt had acted, and if he slunk back to the real world as his compatriots had, he would be leaving to face murder charges. He owed the fact that he hadn't yet been captured—for surely his former group members had given him up without a qualm—to the impenetrable density of this region, the low likelihood of locating a target within it.

That first fall and winter, staying alive was Kurt's only goal. He made do with dry, crackly leaves spread across the bare ground during the remaining clear days, then boughs strapped to the trunk of a tree with pond grasses to keep out the autumnal rains, and a snow cave forged after the first blizzard.

The bout of hunger Kurt experienced once everything froze made the one that had hit before he'd trapped the chipmunk seem akin to skipping a midday snack. He could hardly stagger to his feet in the mornings; during the nights, his body contorted itself into the shape of a fetus.

There wasn't a single animal to snare, no grasses to suck green juices from before spitting out a rough mat of stems. The snows came unceasingly, without the sky pausing to catch its breath. The worst moment arrived when, while gnawing at his nails, Kurt accidentally bit a piece of flesh off the tip of his finger. He chewed and swallowed it, savoring the morsel. A plan occurred, making sense in the state he was in. He would cannibalize himself until there was no more of him to be had.

If an off-season hunter hadn't arrived, Kurt would've died that day or the next. Alerted by the clap of gunfire through the silent snow, Kurt first trudged, then fell to his knees and crawled, winding up near the hunter who was dressing his illegal kill.

Kurt crouched, undetected, beneath an overhang of branches until the hunter left. Then he emerged to scoop up each clump of innards left steaming on the snow. Kurt parceled them out, knowing he would throw everything up if he ate it at once. He consumed the leavings like bloody ice pops until they ran out some days later, at which point Kurt was spurred onto his feet again for a second shamble through the woods.

If he'd had the energy, he would've jeered at himself for how little distance he had to cover in order to change his destiny. An abandoned ranger's cabin had stood nearby in a thicket all along. The tiny structure was windowless and falling down, but a few items—tinned food and kitchen implements mostly—had been left behind. These and some Swiss-cheesed wool blankets enabled Kurt to endure long enough for spring to poke its mossy snout out of the ground. At that point, snowmelt collapsed the cabin he'd called home for the last days, weeks, months—he had little idea of time by then—and Kurt barely crawled out in time to avoid being crushed.

He was so shrunken and frail that he lay blinking on the wettened soil, not registering for a while that a deer, also winter weakened, had stumbled into the trap Kurt had never dismantled, and which was now exposed by receding snows.

Kurt knelt beside the animal, gnawing at its hide until he bore down to a heated swath of flesh. He tore a hunk off the deer's body with his teeth while it still lay expiring, and as the deer's life ran out, Kurt felt his own begin to return.

Spring turned out to be a lazy man's banquet: all those helpless, mewling young. Kurt feasted on minute birds in their nests, baby gophers that he consumed in one bite, even a litter of bobcats. He had to kill the mother when she appeared—more feasting—but by that time he'd pilfered a machete in addition to other essentials from the first backcountry hiker of the season, who had strayed too close to Kurt's lair.

The hiker returned from a dunk in the creek to find his pack lighter, thinned out, and as he stomped off—cursing about there being no place left where a man could be alone anymore, and since when did backpackers steal from each other—a nearly forgotten hunger awakened in Kurt.

He had always fueled himself, satisfied the deepest portion of his appetite, with succor derived from other people. That was why he'd chosen to enter the woods in the first place—what better source of study than living in a small pack of people utterly dependent upon one another? How Kurt had enjoyed those initial days spent together, a time of intimate wonder during which he'd borne witness to the ways in which a flock of differing folks adapted to having their entire lives dismantled, and adjusted to a life devoid of possessions and creature comforts.

It was something Kurt had come to miss back home: that close surveillance of others. Kurt's son was getting older, eleven then, less needy and dependent. Bizarrely enough, he'd begun to express an inclination to spend time on his own. That one had come out of nowhere, and Kurt had been ill-prepared for it. In addition, his wife had filed for divorce, saying she'd always felt held at a distance by Kurt, a claim that was patently absurd. Kurt had never observed anyone as deeply as he had his wife. The chance to live in the sort of proximity that building a new society would require served to appease Kurt, allowed him to get past the loss of his family.

Exposing people's most intimate aspects, sucking on their skinned meat as he did the wildlife that were restoring him to health, gave Kurt a depth of satisfaction, one that made him pity men who didn't have the same. And with the physical deprivations of winter relieved, Kurt needed his other form of nutrition more desperately than ever. He was alone out here. No wife, nor son, not one member of the group with whom he had originally come to these woods.

Why had he not thought to take the hiker along with the pickings of his pack?

The more terrain Kurt covered, the greater his risk of discovery. It'd be safer to remain still, wait for somebody else to come along.

In this new life of his, Kurt didn't have a good way of marking time, and granularity finer than big chunks of months, the passing of the seasons, eluded him, an artifact of the world he had lost. Rain had washed clean the char marks Kurt had slashed onto a boulder for a rudimentary calendar, and the cabin wall he'd carved a tally into during the winter collapsed. But as the days began, undeniably, to pile up, Kurt started fearing that another hiker might never venture this far off the beaten path, into this particular pocket of wilderness.

Spring had turned to the flesh of his first full summer before he was given an opportunity. A female hiker, making her lone way through the woods, businesslike and methodical as she traversed the difficult terrain. She stopped and spoke when Kurt approached her, not unwary—nowhere near as blithely unaware as the utopians had been—although Kurt did catch the faintest hint of a smile beginning to bloom on her face while they conversed.

For a few blissful minutes, the woods held the prospect of becoming the Brigadoon Kurt's fellow woodsmen had imagined but failed to create. Bushes clustered with berries, a laughing, crystalline stream, the crackle of a freshly lit fire—all should've combined to seduce Kurt's new companion, the source of lasting study he needed to procure lest he perish from loneliness.

Although Kurt was typically able to predict moods, thoughts, and behaviors in others with unerring accuracy, he hadn't anticipated how fiercely this woman would try to leave. How much of a fight she'd put up.

Or what he would have to do to stop her.

During the yawning emptiness of the days to come, Kurt had ample opportunity to debrief, rehash, figure out what had gone so terribly wrong.

He had tried to keep the hiker here by dint of brute force, instead of relying on what had always been his truest skill set, his special talent. Which was digging out—like a dentist did rot in a tooth—the weak, sore spots people had, then positioning himself to fill them. That kind of finesse had nearly been lost to starvation and cold, but it could be regained. And although such maneuvering took time, time was all Kurt had now.

When next somebody came along, he would be prepared to make them stay.

CHAPTER SIX

It was supposed to be a three-hour drive. Not terribly many miles, but the roads were slow and winding, and they'd been warned of construction along the way. The window of time during which roadwork could be completed in the Adirondacks was brutally short, thanks to the length of the winter season. Every half hour or so, Doug either had to grind along at an even slower speed than was warranted by the crooks and bends in the roads, or else stop altogether and wait for the other lane of traffic to clear and the DOT worker to twirl his sign, allowing them to progress again at a crawl.

After five such pauses, during which Natalie managed to leaf through each of the guidebooks they had brought, perusing pictures of edible plants and methods for starting a fire in the rain, she began to take the signs figuratively as well as literally. Something was slowing them down, trying to prohibit their arrival.

This was a different world from the one they had left behind in the city, or even the mannered wedding-in-the-country scene to which they had just bid adieu. The inn had offered a polished sort of rural, prettied-up and—insufficient cell signal aside—made workable for people who were used to instant gratification and delivery in a thousand different forms. But the region into which Natalie and Doug were now travel-ing was the real deal. Shacks sinking low in the soil, abandoned farms, places that achieved the status of *town* without benefit of a school, a post office, or even a grocery store. Darkened, empty buildings so completely devoid of hope that no *for sale* or *for rent* sign was thrust into the ground outside. Here was a land where survival was not a given.

Natalie reached out and touched Doug's hand on the wheel.

"You hungry?" he asked, a smile opening up on his face although he kept his fingers locked around the steering wheel and his eyes on the road. "I found a diner on Yelp. Home cooking, our last for a while. Should be coming right up."

"Diner breakfast, yum," Natalie murmured. They were bargain-basement foodies in the city. Doug loved to find sources of cheap eats, which they would review together. Their profile name was WRFF: *will review for food*. The joke was a bit insensitive actually. Natalie wondered why that hadn't occurred to her till now.

Doug shifted then. "Anything wrong?" he asked, his forehead creasing.

After a moment, Natalie replied, "Maybe we're not cut out for this."

Her husband's frown eased. "A little late to be having cold feet, isn't it?" he said. "It's already like our sixteen-hour anniversary."

"Ha-ha," Natalie responded absently. "I didn't mean our marriage."

Doug reached out and squeezed her hand. "I know you didn't," he told her, his tone still humorous. Then his attention was required by the road: a spiral turn around a chiseled cliff. When the route straightened out, he adopted a Cockney accent to ask, "It's the canoe trip you'll be referring to then?"

"Unless you have tickets to Tahiti hidden in there," Natalie responded, pretending to pat the pockets of her husband's cargo shorts.

Doug placed one hand over hers, giving it a nudge. "Watch it, Mrs. Larson," he said mildly. "Or I'll have to pull over, and Mark and Brett will have no idea why we're late."

"Oh, I bet they'd have some idea," Natalie replied. Her voice was breathy, and for a moment their gazes met and didn't release.

Then Doug looked back at the road. "Nat, the trip's going to be great," he said. "Really. The guide made sure it's totally manageable even for a novice. No whitewater over Class II or III, and not even any very long portages."

Natalie glanced away. They had gone rafting together before, so it wasn't the prospect of paddling or the carries that was throwing her. They'd also camped out a few times. Outdoor adventure may not have been her natural bent, as it was Doug's, but wasn't that what marriage was all about? Sharing pieces of yourself, trading them back and forth, until you became another person in a way, some sort of merged being? The notion struck her as suddenly disquieting. What did she know about marriage anyway? By the time she was a toddler, her father was already a widower. She let her gaze rest on the window, keeping her face averted from Doug's.

The landscape at the Blooming Garden Inn had been lovely: bucolic and pastoral with sloping meadows that surrounded the canting structure like long skirts. But the terrain into which they were traveling had changed, become mysterious and tangled. It was all sharp dips, causing Doug to tap the brakes repeatedly, and tall columns of trees. Tunnels into forest so deep, their outlets could hardly be imagined, much less glimpsed.

Off Road Adventures, the outfit Doug had enlisted for help planning their trip, had a storefront in a town with a peculiar, menacing name. Wedeskyull. Doug had to pronounce it for Natalie. *Weeds-kill.* She suppressed a grimace. She was seeing omens, when in fact this day had taken on an almost-paradisiacal quality. Her handsome new husband's arm looped across her shoulders as he drove one-handed into the town, sun shafts shining down through the trees, spilling like lemonade over the streets.

The countryside they'd just driven through was vanquished by this place, a village out of a storybook, charming and quaint. Peaked shop rooftops, main street running alongside a sparkling lake, curbside plantings bright with blossoms. Natalie stared out the window as Doug spun the wheel, easing into a parking space—no endless circles around traffic-choked blocks, or fifty-dollar price tags for garages—and felt peace settle over her like a parachute. For the first time, she understood why people decided to live up here. For the briefest of flashes, she couldn't imagine leaving.

"Nat?" Doug said.

He was looking at her from the driver's seat. She hadn't even noticed him shift into Park. She felt embarrassed somehow, drawn in so instantly by a land to which both of them were mere visitors. She pointed to a café with a pretty blue awning, letting out a grateful groan. "Caffeine."

It was already lunchtime. The home-cooking place Doug had found on Yelp wound up being shuttered—literally: a hand-lettered sign hanging askew on the slats that barricaded the window sadly deeming the place *closed for business*—and they had left too early this morning for the inn to be serving coffee.

Doug glanced at the dashboard clock before turning off the engine. "How about I brew you a pot over our campfire tonight?" he suggested. "You know how good coffee tastes made outdoors. And we've still got an hour to our put-in. We'll need to make some miles on the water today if we want to stick to our route."

"Doug." Natalie heaved a sigh. "This is starting to sound more like training camp than a honeymoon."

Her husband spotted something outside the window then, and Natalie followed his gaze. A guy about their age was just opening the door of the structure that housed Off Road Adventures, which stood a few doors away from the coffee shop. He emerged onto the porch and took a look up and down the street.

Doug was staring at the guy, but just as Natalie started to voice another protest—something along the lines of not realizing she'd married the coffee Nazi—her husband reached over and unlatched her belt. "Come on," he said. "Let's meet with this dude, then I'll buy you the biggest grande they sell up here."

"Up here, it's probably still called a large," Natalie said, cheered, and followed her husband to Off Road Adventures.

Fortified an hour later by not just coffee but lunch as well—the café turned out to have a full menu in addition to cups with comfortingly pretentious names for its sizes—Natalie felt imbued by a sense of promise, ready to head to their put-in on Gossamer Lake. The spot seemed prettily, even aptly, named, considering that Natalie and Doug had just come from the frills and flowers of a wedding.

It wasn't just the dark roast or the pleasantness of the town causing Natalie's mood to rise. The guide had comforted her as well. He fit the part of wilderness outfitter as if created for it: river rat with a touch of hipster Brooklyn. He had short blond dreads caught in a ponytail and what appeared to be permanently tanned skin, plus a closely cropped beard that seemed to glisten with damp. The wings of a tattoo—it might've been an eagle, or a hawk—sprouted from beneath the collar of his worn tee, and he wore shoes Natalie had seen advertised in outdoors magazines, the kind that fit the feet like second skins. Even his name, which Doug had stumbled over at first, worked. Forrest.

Natalie had sent her husband a daggered look. *Don't you dare make a joke.*

Forrest picked up on Natalie's nervousness right away, suggesting they all take a walk away from the shop to sit on the banks of the sunny lake.

"On a scale of one to ten, all the trips Off Road puts together," Forrest had said, grinning at Natalie across a stretch of glowing green grass, "the one we set up for you has a difficulty level of, say, one point five." He gestured to the flat sheet of sun-dappled water to their right. "We teach folks to paddle out there on Lake Nancy. That'd be a one."

Natalie let her eyes travel in the same direction. "We're awfully far north," she said. "It feels like we're in another country."

"You're in Franklin County, deep in the Adirondack Park," Forrest said. "The land within the Blue Line covers six million acres."

Natalie looked at him blankly.

"The Blue Line," Forrest repeated. "The boundary around the biggest protected region in the lower forty-eight. Five national parks could fit inside."

Natalie nodded. "So, um, do you ever go along on trips? Instead of just laying them out, I mean?"

Forrest exchanged a look with Doug that Natalie didn't have to work hard to interpret. Something about how frustratingly adorable women could be. It made her want to punch the two of them—not playfully either—and remark, *Oh, but we take your inflated Match.com profiles and game day superstitions very seriously.*

"Sure," Forrest said at last. "That's probably 75 percent of what we do." He looked at Doug again. "But not usually for honeymooners."

Natalie felt Doug's hand on hers. "Come on, honey," he said. "Solitude, remember? We haven't had enough of that lately, with all the wedding planning and your new job. And a one point five?" He glanced at the guide. "I'm almost tempted to ask for more rapids."

Forrest chuckled and got to his feet. Natalie rose too. Doug had accomplished his purpose, although she would've bet that her husband didn't have any idea how he had done it, what he'd said that had worked.

But Natalie's worry had been flushed away by one single word. *Honey.* Doug had never called her that before. *Nat*—the shortening of her name, its diminutive—was as far as he'd go. And for Natalie, terms of endearment carried the distant, warm echo of memory, whether real or assembled. The vague, idealized sense Natalie had was of a mother who used sweet words, bought toys, filled the house with delicious scents. Certainly there were none of those things after she died.

Forrest handed Doug a yellow pouch with the jagged cliff logo for Off Road Adventures on it. Inside was a sealed ziplock bag containing two thick folds of paper, zigzagged all over with lines, unintelligible symbols standing out here and there. Natalie blinked under the bright warmth of the sun, trying to make sense of the maps, but failed.

"Just for backup," Forrest explained, picking up on her worry again. "If your GPS happens to die out there, it's no problem. Sometimes analog gets the job done even better."

Real, paper maps seemed like relics from an ancient world to Natalie, but Doug tucked the ziplock back into its pouch agreeably enough. "That's it?"

"Assuming you stuck to that list we emailed you," Forrest said.

Doug ticked items off on his fingers. "I packed neutralizers for the iodine. Even if we never need them."

"Better safe than sorry," Forrest agreed. "And remember, in case of emergency, there are a couple of resupplies along your route. I marked them on the map. You'll never be more than a two-day paddle from shelter and other people."

Doug nodded.

"You should be in good shape," Forrest said, and Doug nodded again. "I think that we are."

The guide clapped a hand on Doug's shoulder, reaching the other out to Natalie for a polite shake. But when Natalie offered her own in return, he grasped it harder than she'd expected, and held on.

"Something you're gonna learn out there," he said.

Natalie sensed Doug's gaze resting on her from behind.

"There's a beauty to what you're doing," Forrest said. "Something I could never explain from here." He glanced at the blue arc of sky overhead. "In the end, everyone paddles their own river. Now. Go paddle yours."

CHAPTER SEVEN

Everyone paddles their own river?" Natalie chortled as she seated herself in the car beside Doug.

He glanced at her and smiled, but distractedly.

"Come on," Natalie said, still boisterous. She traced a finger along Doug's cheek while he pulled away from the curb. "You know what we should do now?" Another laugh escaped her. "Go paddle ours."

He patted the pouch, which he'd placed on the console between them. "Want to put that in the glove for now?" he said. "I'll transfer it to my pack when we arrive."

"Doug," Natalie complained as she complied with his instruction. "Why are you not laughing about our guide's Zen and the art of honey-mooning?" She reached out to stroke her husband's face again, the smoothly shaved line of his jaw.

He caught her hand, but the action seemed less about touching her in return than putting an abrupt halt to Natalie's caress. She pulled free, hurt.

Doug checked the map on his phone before making a turn. "Sorry," he said. "Maybe I'm having a few start-up nerves myself. I'll feel better once we're on our way."

"Honey?" Natalie said, trying on the term. It felt like syrup on her tongue, viscous and warm.

Doug rotated the wheel.

"I'm actually starting to look forward to this trip," she went on. "Being alone out there, time just to talk and be together."

"I'm glad—"

"But it's not going to work if we're tense," Natalie went on. "I mean, the wilderness—all that space—will just magnify tensions, right?"

Doug kept both hands steady on the wheel. The road curved and he swung with it, both their bodies leaning. Then he made a sudden, sharper turn, onto a sandy shoulder beneath a skyline of pine trees. He looked at Natalie.

She stared back.

"I want this to be fun," Doug said. He stroked the line of her sleeve, the hairs on her upper arm standing antenna-straight in response. "No, I want it to be more than fun."

Natalie looked at him questioningly.

"It's the start of our lives together," Doug explained, his voice throaty. "Nothing can go wrong. It has to be perfect."

Natalie shook her head once, hard. "That can't be," she said, and he aimed a similar questioning look back. "Real life isn't perfect. Of all people, we both know that. This trip just has to be the two of us, coming together. Like we're going to do forever."

Doug stared out the windshield, sunlight glinting off the glass. "You're right. Of course you're right." He unlocked his seat belt and lifted himself in the seat. "And don't think I don't realize that you've told me the same thing before."

"Just once or twice," Natalie said dryly, eyeing Doug to gauge his response. Things felt charged between them. She wasn't sure how he'd take being teased right now.

Instead of answering, Doug leaned over Natalie, catching her lower lip between his own, and drawing her into his arms in the cramped space. They kissed so deeply that Natalie lost her breath. Doug's mouth scattered kisses on her throat, then her chest as he gave her room for air.

"I thought you were worried…" Natalie said when she could speak. "About getting on our way—"

Doug nosed her shirt up, exposing the skin on her stomach to the warm glow of sun in the car. "I'm not worried about anything anymore," he said, and dipped his tongue into the crevice of her belly button before traveling lower.

He made her wet for him, and she climaxed with a cry so sharp, it startled a bird outside the car into flight.

When Natalie and Doug arrived, Mark and Brett were standing at the edge of Gossamer Lake, water lapping their bare feet. The put-in spot deserved its picturesque name. Tendrils of mist rose from the surface of the lake, otherworldly and beautiful. Natalie and Doug wrestled the canoe down from the top of the car and placed it on the shore. Then they unloaded their packs and slid them as far into the bow and the stern as they could go, protecting them from splashes.

Because they'd gotten on the road so early, it was still only five minutes past one. Most of the day still lay ahead, not to mention the rest of the trip to come. Natalie felt a tingle of excitement.

Doug took out a small amount of emergency cash, then stashed their cell phones and wallets in the glove compartment, twisting the lock with a seldom-used key. "Feels weird," he remarked, looking at Natalie through the triangle of space made by the open car door. "When was the last time you didn't have a phone on you?"

It did seem strange. They were shedding the accoutrements of their everyday lives, as if by getting married they had become completely new people. But their phones would be of no use on this trip. They were safer stowed in the car.

For a moment, Natalie was struck by the same feeling about all of it—not only their possessions, but their jobs, their apartment, the bars and restaurants in which they spent so many hours. They all seemed meaningless suddenly, as if she and Doug had everything they needed right here and were leaving nothing of value behind.

Doug checked the trunk one last time, then called out, "I guess that's it."

Mark and Brett had taken a last quick dunk. They came walking up from the lake, shaking water out of their hair, wringing their swimsuits to dry them.

"Great spot," Mark said. "Really sets everything right, being up here." He sent Doug a look, veiled and secretive, as if referencing a private joke between them.

Natalie glanced away, recalling the interlude she and Doug had just shared in the car. Who knew what he'd told his friends, the jokes they had made about outdoor sex.

Doug handed the car keys over. "Leave 'em on the right front tire, okay?" He pulled the canoe toward the water, dragging it along the sand with a soft *shushing* sound.

"Thanks, guys," Natalie said. New day, new marriage, new chance to be close to her husband's best friends. "For everything."

Mark and Brett aimed smiles at her, then Mark stooped down for what felt like a totally normal hug, as if the strangeness had never taken place—no sleazy men in a car, or conflict with the groom. Brett deposited his own embrace once Mark released her. Guys were great at acting like nothing had happened, and in this case, Natalie figured she could learn from the approach.

She settled herself inside the boat and picked up her paddle.

"Need a push?" Mark asked, leaning over.

"I got this," Doug replied, and shoved the boat into the water, wading in a few feet before hopping inside and getting seated.

His paddle broke the even surface of the lake with hardly a ripple.

Mark and Brett waved at them, and then they were off.

CHAPTER EIGHT

Kurt heard the noise at noontime, sun shining down directly from above, the one way he had to set the clock of his day. The sound came from the creek, which ran close to camp. At its most roaring, the creek nearly became a river, but summer tended to lessen its flow.

For a second Kurt froze, uncertain what to do. He'd been preparing for this moment ever since he'd had to sacrifice the strapping female hiker—a year or so ago, as best he could judge by the passing of the seasons. In the intervening time, Kurt had put all but the finishing touches on his structures and had organized his scant supplies. Yet with opportunity finally facing him, he felt unprepared, and young, boyish, like a kid who never thought his mother would give permission, or even hear what he had asked.

Kurt cocked his head to listen. Silence was a rarity in the woods; even now, in the thick middle of a warm summer's day, branches soughed in an oppressive wind, and the nearby creek moved along slowly at a disconsolate trickle.

Standing still, Kurt tried to tease out whatever had alerted him.

Something heavy and deliberate, its rhythmic, recurring pattern suggesting human involvement. Two lengths of wood being banged together? *Thwocking*, repetitive knocks, but not light, like a woodpecker would make.

Backpackers in bear country were told to make noise, clang pots. But a solo hiker might not have two pots. This one was clapping sticks instead, imagining himself to be warding off bears, when in reality he had no idea who was about to greet him.

Kurt followed the sounds, his heart leaping as joyfully as the water when the creek was running at its highest. Already starting to build an impression of the man he would soon encounter: cautious, rule-bound. It had to be a man—the pieces of wood must be formidable in size for their sound to carry.

Kurt entered an ivory grove of birches, limbs scattered like bones across the forest floor. The hiker moving fast, amputating branches? Or gathering firewood for later? There was no need. Kurt had a woodpile that would keep them both warm.

The *clocking* noises grew louder, wood against wood, as Kurt moved toward the water's edge, a cry of *hello* perched on his lips. After that would come the suggestion that the hiker join him for a night's protection from the elements. Overhead, the sun had suddenly vanished and the sky looked thunderous, laden with rain clouds. His invitation should be welcome.

Kurt broke through a final scrim of branches.

His call of greeting withered like a spent balloon. Disappointment rained down on him as he finally spotted the cause of the sound.

Kurt strode into the shallow water, impervious to the strike of stones against his flesh. They bruised his feet as he kicked them aside: smooth, egg-shaped pebbles as well as bigger, roughly surfaced rocks.

Two branches had fallen into the stream and gotten stuck between rocks. The recent dry spell had exposed their top halves, while the lower parts were still submerged. The force of the water, even running low, was sufficient to bring the sticks into contact, over and over again.

Kurt let out a bellow of nameless, faceless rage. He needed names; he needed faces. Only fellowship would enable him to survive this exile.

Leaning over, he heaved the limbs free, like tearing two arms out of their sockets, splinters of wood daggering his fists.

CHAPTER NINE

When Mia and her mother got back to the apartment the day after Aunt Nat's wedding, Mia's father was waiting for them inside. Mia's mom put a hand to her chest. "Oh," she said. "I didn't expect you."

Mia's father apologized. "Maybe I should give you back my set of keys."

"Don't be silly," Mia's mom said. "I should've called when we left the inn so we could make plans for the day."

They were both so primly, perfectly polite with each other, Mia could hardly stand it. She spun around on the heels of her dressy shoes—her flip-flops had disappeared somewhere by the hotel pool—and stomped off down the hall.

"Mi?" her dad called.

She stopped. "Yeah?"

"I thought we could go grab a late lunch." Her dad eased himself off one of the kitchen stools and began walking toward her. "The phone signal was so poor up there, I never got to hear about the wedding."

"We?" Mia echoed, and there was silence.

Then her mother spoke. "I ate so much yesterday, I'm still full." Her voice sounded brittle, merry. "You and Dad go out," she instructed. "Bring me back some kung pao."

"I hate Chinese," Mia said, hearing the sulkiness in her voice. "I want pizza."

"Since when do you hate—" her mom began.

But her dad interrupted. "Pizza sounds great."

In her room, Mia traded the heels for flats and shucked off her T-shirt as well, grabbing a tank top. It was like a hundred degrees in the city. She wished she were back in the mountains, at the hotel, or with her aunt and uncle on their kooky canoe trip—anywhere but here.

When she returned to the kitchen, her dad was hanging his keys on the hook where they stored the extra pair, and her mom was pretending not to see.

The line at the pizza place was out the door, and there weren't any spots at the counter, so Mia was forced to agree to Chinese after all.

Over lunch specials—chicken with cashew nuts and General Tso's—her dad pinched a nut between his chopsticks and asked, "How was the wedding?"

Mia had requested a fork. She stabbed a piece of chicken and began to chew.

"Look at those teeth," her dad said. "Worth every penny. I mean, every dollar."

Mia flashed a smile for display. "It was awesome," she said around another mouthful. "Aunt Nat and Uncle Doug are such a great couple."

There'd been that weird exchange between them under the tree, but Mia didn't have any reason to go into that.

"Where'd they go on their honeymoon?" her dad asked. "Europe? A cruise?"

"No." Mia frowned. "They went on some camping trip. I thought you knew that." Her parents really must not be communicating.

Her father held out the teapot in her direction, but Mia shook her head. She hated the tea they served here. It tasted like old bathwater.

Her father drained the tiny cup he held, almost hidden by his cupped palms. "That's an interesting choice. Up there, you mean? In the Adirondacks?"

Mia nodded, poking around in the gloppy sauce for more chicken.

Her father pushed his plate aside and took out his phone.

Mia couldn't tell whether he was checking the time, or looking to see if he'd gotten any texts. She hunted for something to say to draw back his attention. "Something kinda weird happened at the wedding. Before the wedding, I mean."

Her dad placed his phone on the table. "Oh yeah? What was that?"

Mia's face felt hot. She didn't know what had happened really. And any reference to it not only exposed how out of it she was, but also resurrected the memory of those two hot guys, and what one of them had told her when he and Mia walked back to the inn.

"Um, I don't exactly know," she mumbled.

Her dad's gaze had wandered. He held up a hand, signaling for the check.

"I think one of Uncle Doug's groomsmen, like, freaked out or something," Mia said hurriedly. Could that have been why he was almost late to the ceremony? "Something in his past," she went on, cobbling together pieces from what Uncle Doug had told Aunt Nat.

Mia's dad gave a distracted nod as he fished around for his wallet.

"He didn't exactly tell me details," Mia added, talking so fast now that she felt a little breathless. "The groomsman, I mean. I guess maybe he felt embarrassed. So we talked about other stuff when he walked me back to my room."

Her dad looked at her then, brows drawn together in a frown. "Wait… What?" he asked. "Who walked you back to your room?"

Mia felt a flush of pride. "Uncle Doug's friend," she said. "Who was a groomsman in the wedding. That's what I've been trying to tell you."

Her dad's frown deepened, cutting into his face. "You spent time alone with Uncle Doug's friends at the wedding?" he asked. "Aren't they, well, Uncle Doug's age?"

Mia nodded. "Maybe even a little older." Hey, it was possible, right? The hot guy had never actually told her his age. And the look in her father's eyes now made the announcement, wrong or right, worth it.

He spoke under his breath, but Mia could make out what he said.

"So now's the time your mother decides to stop supervising everything."

His tone was so bitter and brutal that it made Mia's heart clutch. "It wasn't like that!" she protested. "Uncle Doug's friend acted perfectly normal." Boring even, except for when he'd said that last thing to her. "And Mom didn't do anything wrong. It was a *wedding*. Everyone was having fun." Unexpectedly, tears came to Mia's eyes. They flew off her face as she shook her head back and forth, refuting her father's accusation.

A waitress came darting over, holding out a handful of white cloth. "Extra napkins for you."

Mia sniffled and took the bundle. "Thanks," she said, and the waitress maneuvered away between the tightly spaced tables.

Her dad visibly suppressed a breath. "You ready? Do you want any ice cream?"

"No," Mia said, staring down at the table. "No ice cream."

At that moment, she heard a voice at once startling in its sadness and as familiar as her own. Mia twisted around in her seat, stretching to see.

"Yes, just one today," the voice said.

The waitress who had brought the extra napkins hustled by again, a woman fighting to keep up behind her. Mia's mom.

She stopped when she got to their table.

"Oh, hello," Mia's mom said. "I thought you two were going to Famiglia's."

Mia's dad turned around in his seat, hunting the waitress.

Mia pictured him asking for an extra chair to be dragged over to their table, the three of them putting up with cramped quarters while Mia's mom ate her dish. Three had always been kind of tricky when they'd gone out to eat as a family—restaurant tables were geared to four, or two. But Mia had never minded squeezing. She'd just decided to order ice cream after all when the waitress arrived.

"You can add her charge to my card," Mia's dad said, pointing to her mom as he stood up. "And she can have this table." He took a look around the crowded restaurant. "Isn't everyone supposed to have cleared out of the city by now?"

"I can take care of my bill," Mia's mother snapped. "And find my own table too."

Mia's father dropped the pen he'd been using to sign the check. It clattered on the glass-topped table. He gave Mia's mother the coldest look Mia had ever seen. "Of course you can, Claudia. You can do everything."

"Elliott, please," her mom said. "Not in front of Mia."

Her dad had been starting to steer Mia toward the exit, but when her mom spoke, he stopped and went back. "Speaking of whom…"

Mia's mother looked up from her menu.

"Why was our daughter hanging out with thirty-year-old men at the wedding?"

Mia's mom gave a dismissive shake of her head and let out a huff. "I wouldn't call it *hanging out*," she said. "One guy escorted Mia back to our room. He was just doing us a favor."

Like the hot guy had been babysitting her or something. The General Tso's started to sizzle in Mia's stomach. She burped and tasted a bitter orange flavor. "He was not!" she burst out. People at the surrounding tables looked up. "You don't even know what we talked about," Mia flung at her mom. She knew she should stop talking, but something red-hot compelled her, and her next words rushed out in a lava flow. "He didn't tell anybody else!"

Mia's dad blinked. "He didn't tell anybody else what?"

Mia's mom held up one hand in her I'm-in-charge-here gesture. "Mia?" she pressed, her voice sharpening. "What are you talking about?"

Mia squirmed. "Nothing," she said at last. Only it came out sounding a lot like *Something*. Which it had been, hadn't it? The hot guy had steered her out of the parking lot double time, like the PE teacher urging them around the track at school, while asking Mia to keep his secret. Her parents didn't have to know it was a stupid secret, one nobody would really care about, especially not now.

At least her parents weren't fighting, for the first time in forever. Instead, they were looking at each other without glaring, deciding what to do, her dad signaling a message that Mia recognized. *Pick your battles.* While her mother wore an expression that Mia couldn't identify at first, because it looked so weird on her mom's face. After a moment it came to her. Her mother looked uncertain.

Mia settled her arms triumphantly across her chest.

CHAPTER TEN

The leaves overhead made dappled patterns, like lace upon the amber water, as Natalie and Doug crossed Gossamer Lake. Dip, pull, dip, tea-colored droplets landing on Natalie's arm as they fell off the blade of her paddle. The water felt warmer than the air, which Natalie knew meant that her stroke was too shallow. Only the surface inches of the water got heated by the sun. After that came depths no summer rays could touch.

She made an effort to sink her paddle deeper—*remember to dig*, the guide had said back in that picture-perfect town—so as to spare Doug doing the brunt of the work in the rear. Natalie twisted around on her uncomfortable perch, more of a bar than a seat. Doug's hair hung over his eyes as he repeated the same sequence over and over in a seemingly effortless swirl.

"Get down on your knees," Doug advised. Her competent husband, always knowing what to do. It was so quiet out here that he hardly had to raise his voice to be heard. "Use that bar to lean back against, not sit on. It's different from a raft."

Natalie lowered herself as instructed, instantly feeling more comfortable, then peered around again. Doug had worked hard to keep them streaking along at a good pace while Natalie got herself resituated, her own paddle scarcely skimming the top of the water. Doug's biceps strained with exertion, the tendons in his forearms standing out.

He looked hot, Natalie thought, and suppressed a grin.

"What's funny?" Doug asked.

I could say anything out here, Natalie realized. There was no one to hear. "I was just thinking how sexy you look while doing all the work."

A grin took hold of Doug's face. "I love doing your work."

"I could get used to that," Natalie called back, picking up her paddle and attacking the water with renewed vigor. In truth, it felt good to be contributing, one part of the engine steaming them along.

But when Doug momentarily lifted his paddle out of the water, taking a break, the canoe immediately slowed down, trees changing from a blur of greens—hunter, forest, teal, even a few early shades of apple-gold—to distinct trunks and scallop-shaped leaves.

Natalie paddled harder—*dig*—but she couldn't get them up to speed again. "No fair!" she shouted. "All the power is in the rear!"

"Yeah, baby," Doug said in his Austin Powers voice, and Natalie had just let out a groan of protest when a sheet of water hit her in the back.

She shrieked, then jerked around.

Doug sank his paddle into the lake and began to pull hard, his muscles rounding. The canoe sped up as he blinked back at her innocently.

Natalie held her soaked shirt away from her body. "Turnabout is fair play," she said, rising to make her way toward Doug across the wobbly canoe bottom. "Literally."

"Watch it!" Doug said, flinging one hand out to steady the boat. "You'll tip us!"

Natalie immediately dropped back down.

"Paddle, Mrs. Larson," Doug said, grinning. "I'm sure you'll find an opportunity for revenge before too long. It's not like we'll be leaving the water any time soon."

They left it a mile later when the water began to shallow out, the blades of their paddles striking sandy bottom until the canoe rode up on a wash of brown leaves. Forest loomed over them, deep and impenetrable. It was cooler here by at least ten degrees, and Natalie's wet clothing had become a clammy coat against her. She shivered. She could fish out a change of clothes from her pack, but it might be better to let the sun dry her rather than start accumulating laundry so early on in their trip.

Doug pulled out his backpack and started rooting around in the outer pocket. He unzipped the little black case that contained their GPS device. "This is our first portage."

Natalie reached for the device. "How does it work?" she asked. Maps she wanted nothing to do with, but something akin to a cell phone seemed all right.

Doug showed her the screen. "This is us," he explained, zooming in. "And look, see where the river starts again?"

"It's not that far," Natalie replied, studying the tiny display.

"Only a quarter mile or so," Doug agreed. His tone was coach-like, encouraging. "And then we're on the water with no interruptions for a while."

Natalie handed the GPS back so it could be secured in its case. It was amazing how reassuring such a small piece of technology could be, like the tether that attached an astronaut to his spaceship.

She climbed out of the canoe, tea-colored lake water sloshing into her Norlanders, best water shoes on the market. She helped Doug drag the canoe onto higher ground, then got out her own pack and shrugged into it.

"Count of three?" Doug suggested, clipping his pack's cross strap on his chest.

Natalie lifted.

"This can't be a quarter mile," she huffed after fifteen minutes of trudging along. It might even have been more than fifteen; it was hard to keep track of time without any signifiers—phone or computer screen, mealtimes or appointments—especially while working out this hard. Too bad both of them tended to keep phones pinned to themselves all day and night and had never worn watches. Natalie wondered why Doug hadn't suggested getting one. It seemed the kind of detail he'd usually have been prepared for: the need to keep track of time in the outdoors when there wasn't any cell service. Unless schedules and hourly counts were just two more aspects of life back home that Doug wanted to put on hold for a while.

Natalie panted, the canoe a long, sagging weight, her fingers fighting to get a good grip on its rim. Her hands were slick, sweaty despite the chilly temperature. The straps of her pack hugged her like a straitjacket, cutting off breath. She and Doug were deep in the woods, and there didn't seem to be any hint of a river nearby. Not a single trickle, let alone a rushing sound, no dip in the landscape. It actually felt as if they were climbing. "Are you sure we're on the right path?"

"Well, it's not really a path," Doug said, prompting a flash of annoyance in Natalie. The line between knowledgeable and pedantic sometimes blurred in her husband. "We're essentially bushwhacking with a little help from our guide."

"But is the GPS saying we're in the right place?" Natalie asked. "I mean, it feels like we're going uphill to reach water."

Doug frowned. "I don't think we're going uphill." He gestured for her to take a break, and Natalie lowered the canoe to the forest floor with a grateful grunt. Doug dug out the device, and she came over and looked. "This is right," he said, pointing.

Natalie couldn't tell if she detected a faint note of relief in his tone.

"How about this?" he said. "We have another two-mile paddle to reach the world's most romantic camping spot, on the shores of our very own island."

Natalie raised her brows, impressed.

"So listen," Doug went on. "Why don't you take off your pack and rest for a sec. I'll run up ahead, check out how long the rest of the portage is."

Natalie glanced around. A breeze came up and slapped leaves on the trees back and forth, the foliage large and leathery this time of year.

"It's really just up ahead?" she asked, gesturing for another look at the device.

Doug handed it to her. "You'll be able to see me the whole time."

Natalie gave a nod, then unclipped her pack, letting it fall to the ground with an exhalation of relief. Must from the moldering leaves rose in a cloud, tickling her nostrils. She sneezed, and the sound was a loud bark in the thick, sleepy silence.

Doug strode away while Natalie got down on her knees to unzip her pack, its shrill whine jarring in the afternoon hush. She took a look around. Doug could be seen a little ways off, loping along between the trees, his feet sure despite the hills and furrows of the forest floor. At least he'd mat down a path they could use for the rest of the carry.

Her clothes hadn't dried fully due to the shade in the woods. Natalie pulled out a fresh shirt, making sure she was alone before pulling her damp one up and over her head. The only creatures that would've been treated to her peep show were some birds and small mammals, but the trappings of polite society were hard to lose.

Branches swished and swayed, a sudden wind picking up.

A piece of wood split with a smart crack, and she jumped. Had Doug broken that somewhere up ahead where he was walking? This wind didn't seem strong enough to sever a branch.

Suddenly self-conscious, Natalie wrenched her head through the collar of her dry shirt, bare skin goose-pimpling as she took another quick look around. She peered in the direction where she had last seen Doug. The vista ahead was clear.

Natalie got to her feet. The sodden garment she'd just taken off fell to the dusty ground, and she snatched it up again, stuffing it into her pack. She glanced down at the GPS, verifying her location. Looking at the land she was actually occupying didn't feel good enough, as if the device did more than orient, but rooted her in space.

Natalie walked forward, trying to spot Doug.

The woods appeared empty, and they felt empty too. The wind had died down as abruptly as it'd arrived, and the stillness was so complete that not even an insect buzzed.

No sign of her husband among the trees.

CHAPTER ELEVEN

Kurt's belly was full of berries and wild onions and tough, stringy meat, his body made strong by the capture of the game, and by the hauling and building required to finally complete the structure in which he would pass his third winter.

But Kurt was weaker and hungrier than he'd ever been in his life.

Mentally weaker and hungrier.

The vicious season arrived early here, and though it was still some months off, judging by the foliage and abundance of wildlife, Kurt knew that if he died this time, it wouldn't be because he lacked sustenance or shelter. Solitude would be what felled him.

The woods bore personalities, unless Kurt in his lonesomeness had created them. He didn't think so, though. They felt too real. One side the woods displayed was threatening, a cacophonous din of rustling leaves and branches whipping in the wind, cawing birds and clawing feet, and the evil chuckle of the creek. While the second, seen less often, was a cold parent. Oppressive in her silence: a shrouding cloak of quiet so thick that Kurt sometimes screamed aloud just to break it, mauling his eardrums to get at the cotton padding he was sure must be filling them, blocking out the sweet song of voices he craved.

He was going mad. Sometimes he saw faces in the ruts and lines of tree bark. He wondered what would happen if he spoke to them, whether they might answer back.

Kurt hadn't spied a trace of a human being in so long that he was becoming inhuman himself. Nearly four full seasons since the business-like hiker had refused to stay in his camp. The water-lodged sticks Kurt had mistaken for the presence of a visitor the other day didn't count, even though he had dragged them back to camp, carving crude faces into the wood until their sight offended him. Such paltry impersonations of the real thing, their only indications of emotion those that Kurt was able to deliver with the tip of his blade. He'd burned them in last night's fire.

With the tasks of daily life whittled down to a manageable load, Kurt lacked sufficient diversion to occupy himself. Boredom combined with isolation posed the worst pain he'd ever experienced.

One day, though, a different sort of pain presented itself, saving him from the brink of suicide—or worse, living out an untold number of years, demented and gibbering, alone in the forest.

He got injured.

Kurt had been stomping around the woods in wider and wider radii, in search of a flash of color that might signal a piece of clothing or a tent. Even a dried-up footprint would offer a morsel on which he could nibble, despite carrying with it the proof that he had been too late, missed his chance yet again. How deep was the imprint of the foot? Did it signify a heavyset man, or a lighter sprite? What did the footwear's sole reveal—an experienced trekker in good boots or an unprepared novice in sneakers?

So intent was Kurt on his aim that he failed to notice the hole an animal had dug, over which a burden of leaves had fallen, concealing its depths.

Kurt pitched forward, only just able to pull his leg free in time. Before he did, he heard the phantom snap of a bone, felt the cold, pure pain of it. Bathed in sweat at the imagined horror of what a break would mean out here, he lowered himself, panting, to the ground and let his heart rate settle.

He had strained something, but there was no significant damage, and as he limped back to camp, Kurt favored the ankle to hasten its healing. He couldn't be hobbling around now, or even less than at his strongest and most able, for a possibility had suddenly occurred to him.

Why couldn't he ensnare bigger prey than the chipmunks whose flesh he routinely chewed?

Human prey.

What if a perforation similar to the one into which he had just stumbled wasn't haphazardly dug by an animal, but deliberately placed? So that if a backpacker did chance to come by, he might break a bone and be stuck here, incapacitated?

A thru-hiker might be knowledgeable enough about wilderness first aid to take measures to go on, of course.

In which case, could a hole of the kind Kurt was envisioning be deepened, widened, made to catch a target and keep it there?

And to up the chances of successful capture, could Kurt plant more obvious obstacles, minor impediments left just visible enough that a trekker would steer clear of them, unaware that he was being guided toward an ambush, and wind up exactly where Kurt wanted him?

Tripwire fashioned out of vines, strung between trees and wrapped with thorns for good measure, sharp enough to slice an Achilles tendon. Skull-clobbering rocks perched on branches and set to fall at the slightest disturbance.

The whole of these woods could become a trap.

CHAPTER TWELVE

Natalie's teeth chattered, and she felt cold despite the dry clothes she'd put on. Abandoning her pack beside their canoe, she held on to the GPS and darted up the path Doug had forged, calling out loudly enough that her cries split the silence of the woods.

No response.

The sky dimmed up ahead. Were they losing daylight already?

Worst-case scenarios started to spark in Natalie's head. There was a cliff, and Doug had fallen off. A bear had attacked him, even though black bears were fairly amicable and fat with food this time of year. Her husband had tripped and hit his head. Suddenly, the woods seemed freighted with horrors. Natalie didn't know if she could haul the canoe all that way back to the lake on her own. How would she go for help?

She squared her hands on her hips and forced herself to breathe, turning around beneath the umbrella of leaves and considering. The GPS didn't show any sort of mountain. It wasn't detailed enough to display every feature of the terrain, but what she saw looked manageable, and there had to be a logical explanation for Doug's absence. Strong, young people didn't just up and die.

They do, something young and weak whimpered inside Natalie. *All the time.*

Not Doug, sure and capable as he was. Anybody but him.

She licked her lips nervously and was shocked to taste salt. Not sweat. Tears. "Doug!" she shouted, her voice higher and more hysterical than she would've liked.

She heard stamping in some brush to her left and swiveled on the uneven ground. Her ankle buckled, and she nearly went down. Something that big had to be a bear—and how nuts had she been to think of bears as *friendly*?

Then the top of a human head appeared—that was Doug's dark hair, wasn't it, stirred up by the rising wind?—and Natalie realized that despite the assistance of the device, she'd been looking in the wrong direction.

Her knees went limp with relief. She couldn't believe she'd let a little nature and solitude get to her like that.

Doug skidded to a halt in a clot of leaves beside her. "You're not going to believe this," he said, snatching her hand.

He didn't seem to notice she'd been scared, and Natalie saw no reason to tell him. Doug already worried that she was ill-equipped for this journey.

They walked forward until the trees parted, then mounted a slope that indeed looked over the banks of a river. Minuscule motions hinted at the power beneath the water's long, flat back. A whorl on the surface. How fast a twig was pulled downstream.

"Believe what?" Natalie asked.

Doug pointed, a glower forming on his face.

Ahead in the distance, but traveling fast, was an elephant herd of storm clouds.

Natalie released a sigh, a stream of pent-up breath.

They had talked about the weather when they were planning this trip, of course. Even Doug had to admit that as idyllic as pancakes might smell sizzling over an open fire, little was as miserable as camping in the rain. They had selected their wedding date predicated on an outdoors honeymoon. June might be the most popular month for brides, but it was black fly season in the Adirondacks. By August, the nights would be getting cold. July was the best month. Aside from the occasional freakish hailstorm, all you had to watch out for were thundershowers. You might avoid rain altogether if you got lucky.

We did not get lucky.

Her thought suddenly seemed to apply to more than a temporary spell of bad weather, as if the broad, all-encompassing sky would never lighten.

"We're going to have to pitch our tent under a downpour," Doug said. His voice was glum, and he looked as disappointed as a child.

Doug's certainty and competence came at a cost, Natalie realized. He shielded his soft spots, the weaker aspects of himself. Suddenly, her new husband seemed to contain as much below the surface as this river did beneath its own. Natalie felt as if she'd made her personal subterranean depths far more visible. Doug knew Natalie's deepest sources and vestiges of pain. But where did Doug's lie?

"It'll be okay," she told him softly. "For better or worse, richer or poorer, in sunshine and in rain. Isn't that how the vows go?"

Doug seemed to rally then. "Neither snow nor sleet... Wait, that's something else," he said, bracing his shoulders and giving her a grin. "Come on, let's go back and get the canoe. Maybe we can beat the storm."

Trees bowed over hunchbacked, their branches like long, dangling arms, as Natalie and Doug entered the water. The current took their canoe, swift and sure, while stone-colored clouds slid by overhead. The light overhanging the land began to change; the storm holding off, at least for now. Natalie let green beneficence bathe her as she probed the depths of the river with her paddle.

The boat started to speed along, as if hardly even touching the surface. Minute splashes, like watery hiccups, were the only audible sound. Natalie and Doug stroked together, more in unison than they had been since setting off.

CHAPTER THIRTEEN

Doug pitched the tent on a sandy hump of land just big enough for a patch of forest and a fortress-like ledge of rock. The tent they used was the one Doug had had forever, a battered orange and gray affair, roughly pentagonal in shape, with an entrance you crawled through in order to straighten up inside. At five foot five, Natalie could stand nearly upright; a shade over six feet meant that Doug had to stoop. Still, there was plenty of space for their sleeping bags—slick new ones that zipped together—and packs.

Natalie set about gathering wood, which she assembled in a ring of rocks on the shore. She started with brush and twigs for kindling, then constructed a tepee of thicker sticks and logs, the shape Doug had demonstrated to catch fire quickest. Ministering to the flicker of flame while hunting items in their food sack, Natalie had assembled the trappings of their first meal by the time Doug emerged on hands and knees from the tent.

"Hey, I think it missed us," he said, gesturing to the sky.

Natalie smiled, glad to see her husband's mood restored.

Doug slapped at a mosquito. "All that paddling works up an appetite."

Natalie held up the block of cheese she'd unwrapped and a baggie of noodles.

Doug pantomimed gusto. His skin was glowing, tanned from their day in the sun, and he'd traded clothes for swim trunks, revealing his broad chest and planks of muscle on his stomach. Natalie felt a low churning in her belly that had nothing to do with hunger. Desire, pure and simple, heated by the sinking sun.

Small waves from the river licked at the shore. Natalie got to her feet, the tasks necessary for the coming night vanishing from consciousness as she started to pull off her grimy, day-worn garments.

Doug's gaze traveled over her, an almost physical force. He scooped Natalie into his arms and headed for the water.

"Bath for two, Mrs. Larson?" he asked, his voice husky and deep.

"Sounds blissful," she murmured. "I never want to leave."

Doug bent over to deposit a kiss on her lips. "Have I finally made a nature lover out of you?"

Natalie felt herself relax in his hold. "Well, I don't know about moving to a desert island. But that town was pretty nice."

Doug grinned. "We'd probably run out of restaurants pretty quick on this island."

Natalie laughed.

Then Doug set her back down on the ground. "Damn."

She looked up at the sky, then all around. "What's wrong?"

Doug strode back in the direction of the fire. He crouched, hastily rewrapping the block of cheese and shoving food into the sack. "Why don't we just invite the bears?"

Natalie groaned. "I'll try to remember we're not in Kansas anymore. Although this *is* an island." When Doug didn't reply, she added, "I guess bears swim."

Doug got down on his belly and blew into the blaze. The flames shot higher, bits of orange flying into the twilight. "Nice job with the fire," he said. "Another log, and I'll bet we can keep this baby burning while we—"

"Doug…" Natalie groaned again.

He got to his feet. "Am I overdoing the Boy Scout?"

"Oh, believe me," Natalie said, walking toward him. "I love your Boy Scout."

For a second, Doug remained focused on the shooting sparks. Then he reached for her hand and began steering Natalie toward the water. A chill took hold, and as they cast their gazes skyward, it became clear why the temperature had dropped.

Clouds lay like a black canopy across the heavens. In the Adirondacks, the weather was as changeable as a teenage girl's moods. A loud crack split the silence, unleashing a drenching rain. The downpour soaked them, rendering Natalie's underwear sheer against her body, and dousing the flames Doug had just coaxed to soaring.

"Oh no—" Natalie cried before it struck her that her husband was laughing.

"Fool me once," he spluttered, shaking rain from his hair like a dog.

Dripping, Natalie started to smile.

Doug snatched her hand. "Come on!" he yelled, and they ran for the tent.

Rain made a battering shadow as they crawled inside, flecking Natalie's near-naked form. Watery damp enclosed them, sealed out by their tiny shelter.

Natalie ringed Doug's neck with her arms. "I love you."

"I love you too, Nat," he said, voice rough with desire and eyes hooded by wanting. "I always have."

But he didn't strip off his wet clothes, nor rid Natalie of the last items she wore. She let go, suddenly self-conscious, her skin stippled with goose bumps.

"Is something wrong?" she asked.

Doug's gaze was fixed on the mesh panel that allowed them to see out. "Doug?"

Rain continued to pound, while lightning hurled itself across the sky and thunder lashed, lassoing the planet. Doug reached for Natalie, pulling her so close that it seemed he was trying to pull her right through him, then entered her without laying her down. Natalie gasped, immediately starting to shudder against him.

Doug bore down, waiting for her climax to subside before beginning to move inside her. It felt as if the whole world was shaking them back and forth in its fist, although at a certain point the motion might have been no more than their bodies rocking against each other, over and over in fierce pursuit of the same glorious goal, which each one signaled with a shout of sheer and spontaneous release.

Natalie woke in the night to blistering moonlight. The skies had cleared, and everything was as bright as noonday. Doug lay prone on his stomach, both hands fisted, as if he'd been taken unawares by sleep, forced into it rather than indulging in a well-deserved rest. Natalie snaked as soundlessly as she could from the tent, before rising and padding, barefoot and nude, to the edge of the river.

She waded into a perfect cylindrical pool.

The trees lifted their arms blackly against the sky, draping leafy shadows as she started a slow, easy breaststroke into deeper water.

She had grown overheated in their sleeping bags, which were rated for three seasons, and lying as she and Doug had been, so close and intertwined. The frigid water felt delicious upon her. Natalie stopped swimming to see if she could touch bottom, but her legs dangled freely in the current.

She treaded water, gazing back at their island. *Their.* She'd come to think of this place possessively already. It would be difficult to paddle on when morning came, even though Doug had assured her that even greater natural wonders and more majestic scenery lay ahead. Still, Natalie couldn't help feeling as if nobody else had a right to tarry here besides the two of them. Had any other couple ever come together in the way that they had before sleep stole in, experienced such heights of passion riding out a storm that in the end felt perfectly timed, delivered like Mother Earth's own wedding present?

Natalie swam back toward land, covering just enough distance that her feet could find purchase atop a pair of slippery rocks. Then she threw back her head and rinsed her hair in the clear, pure water, droplets cascading over her shoulders and down her spine.

A ways off on shore, there was a hint of movement, and then a sharp crack.

Natalie's heart began to throb; she felt it cast waves through the water, turning the entire river into one giant, beaten drum. She started swimming as fast as she could for the shoreline, aware that when she got there, she was going to have to emerge with no clothes on. But that didn't matter; she had to get out of the water, this circular, glistening target into which her body was thrust like a dart.

She kept her gaze focused on land. The tiny island appeared motionless, untouched save for their tent and still-smoldering fire.

The water grew shallow; her knees scraped bottom.

Natalie climbed out, wrapping her arms around her bare body, and ran.

A whine as the tent zipper raked upward, and Doug crawled out.

"You heard it too?" Natalie shouted.

"Heard what?" her husband called.

CHAPTER FOURTEEN

Hiker's midnight," Doug said with a yawn as he strolled toward Natalie, holding out a set of clothes. "Or paddler's, as the case may be." He took a searching look around. "You only fall asleep that early out in nature."

Doug handed Natalie the clothes before shucking off his own. He waded into the water, dove without making a splash, then swam a few strokes before surfacing and standing waist deep.

"Doug, did you hear that noise?" Natalie asked from shore. She was glad for the clothing, self-conscious as she yanked shorts over her damp legs and wriggled into a tee.

Doug resembled a work of art come to life, standing with water grazing his hips, while moonlight cast its glow all over his exposed body.

He shook his head. "What noise?"

"It was loud as a shot. You must've heard it," Natalie protested. She wrapped her arms around herself. "Something banged. Or crashed down."

Doug walked forward, rising out of the river like a Greek god. Silvery drops of water fell from his skin. "Well, there're always noises in the woods," he said, his tone of voice logical. "Was it a bird maybe? Some animal stepping on a stick?"

It was Natalie's turn to look around. "I guess it could've been." She shivered.

Doug began to use his shirt to towel off. "Let's get the food and have something to eat."

"You came out of the tent at the same time as I got out of the water," Natalie said, allowing herself to be steered toward the tent's entrance. "I thought you heard it too."

Doug frowned. "I came to look for you. I woke up, and you were gone."

The explanation was simple—it made sense—yet Natalie felt something lacking behind it. She held back, her eyes scouring the nearby woods, the curve of the shoreline.

"We never got to talk about it, did we?" Doug said suddenly.

"Talk about what?"

He began combing his fingers through his glistening hair. "What happened at the wedding. With Mark and Brett."

Natalie looked up sharply. She was glad Doug had brought this up, yet did there seem to be something just a little off in his timing? Not off—perfect. This might be the one topic that would serve as a distraction for Natalie, lead her to look the other way from whatever had startled her back in the lake.

But what could have startled her that Doug wouldn't want her to know about?

"Okay," she said, ducking low to climb into the tent, then rising to greet him challengingly. "What *did* happen at our wedding?"

Doug's face puckered. "You don't have to sound like that," he said. "And actually, I realized that in order to explain it to you, I have to go a ways further back."

"Further back," Natalie repeated.

Doug stooped down and began gathering up the sleeping bags in his arms. He knee-walked to the opening of the tent, fabric pooling around him.

"Yeah," he said. "A lot further."

They dragged the food pack and their sleeping bags out of the tent and settled down beside the campfire, which crackled back to life once Doug struck a match. Natalie distributed the fresh fruit they'd brought, along with a hunk of bread and some sliced cheese, and they munched contentedly for a while before reclining on the cushy ground. The sky was densely packed with stars. It resembled a clove-studded orange, just enough space between each pinprick of light for a mere sliver of black. Natalie and Doug lay on their sides, fingers threaded, blinking up at the firmament.

"After my father walked out, he left us with that giant apartment, not nearly paid off," Doug began. "My dad used to go on these manic binge buys, way overextend himself. Actual repo men would come. And you know my mom… She can't do anything for herself. She almost lost the one thing that hadn't been taken away a dozen times. By the time I was in high school, we were most of the way to homeless."

"I'm sorry, honey," Natalie murmured. She'd thought of her mother-in-law as a bit silly and helpless, but not completely incompetent. "I didn't know it was that bad."

"I didn't want to tell you," Doug said, rolling away from her onto his back. "Your husband, a bum on the street."

"You were just a child," Natalie said sharply, her voice an intrusion into the blanketed silence of the night. She sought her husband's hand again, but Doug didn't reach back.

"Which brings me to Mark and Brett," he said.

A few flecks from the fire floated by Natalie's face, insectile, wandering. She batted at them, raising herself on one elbow and looking at her husband.

Doug rubbed at a piece of ash that had landed on his arm. It left behind a dark smudge. "We were all—the three of us, I mean—like a pack of wolf cubs wandering the city. We each had our individual deals. My dad you know about. Brett's was a gambler and a coke fiend. Still is, as far as I know. Brett saw him even less than I did my own father after he hit the eject button. And Mark never knew he had a dad at all. Seriously…till we were ten, I don't think Mark knew one was required."

Natalie swallowed, picturing the Oliver Twist–like group of urchins on the street.

Doug continued to stare upward without blinking. "Mark and Brett are good guys, though. They really are. I'm not sure what exactly is going on with them right now, and it might be a little misguided, but I know it can't be something really bad."

"Misguided?" Natalie echoed. "Do you even know who those two men were?"

Doug turned to face her in the darkness. "No. I swear. I never saw them before in my life."

"You didn't ask Mark or Brett?"

Doug's Adam's apple twitched in his throat. "When there's crap like we all had in our lives, you kind of learn not to, you know? We don't necessarily ask about stuff. We just know that we're there for each other."

Which wasn't a yes or a no. And not having seen the men before wasn't the same as not knowing what role they had played in whatever went on before the wedding. Doug's explanation felt vague, somehow diffuse, yet there was truth to it as well. Her husband was staring right into her eyes, and Natalie could feel the need he had for her to understand.

"You were right," she said after a moment.

"Always," Doug agreed solemnly. Then he smiled, though it looked more like a slash across his face. "About what?"

"What you said after the ceremony," Natalie replied. "I don't get it. I never had friends like that…who protected me from whatever I needed protection from. Claudia was the closest I got."

"She ain't bad," Doug said in the same joking tone. "I'd let Claudia put herself in front of a truck for me any day."

"Yeah," Natalie said. "The truck would stop just because she told it to."

They both smiled in the dark.

"Doug?"

"Yeah?"

"What made you tell me this now?" Natalie asked. She didn't want to feel on edge—let alone all the way to suspicious—when things were so close and warm between them. But she couldn't suppress the nagging feeling that she still wasn't getting the whole story. "About your mom… and your friends?"

Doug shrugged; she felt his shoulders lift against her. "I don't know. Something about being out here, I guess. Totally on our own."

He began to rub the fleshy web between Natalie's thumb and forefinger, and she felt her skin come alive. Her husband could ignite sensation in the most humdrum of body parts. She began picturing a take two, making love beside the fire, and the muscles in her legs weakened in anticipation.

"That's Snowshoe Mountain," Doug said gruffly, still stroking. "See it?" He let go to trace the outline of a hump in the air. "We'll be at its base this time tomorrow."

From somewhere to their left, a branch broke off a tree, clobbering the ground.

"Now that I did hear." Doug got to his feet, balling a fist. If he'd still been caressing Natalie's hand, he would've crushed it.

He seemed nervous, on edge somehow, but Natalie couldn't imagine why. Despite her earlier scare in the water, she felt more relaxed than she had in years. Between the demands of planning a wedding and starting her new job, it had been a tense time lately, and it felt good to have both things behind her. But that wasn't the entire explanation. Something about being up here kindled a state of calm she'd never experienced in the city.

Doug broke through a nearby thicket, swiping at brush so violently it must have left scratches on his skin. Then he came back, displaying a length of fallen wood. "Lucky this didn't fall on our tent."

Natalie stood up too. "Maybe a lightning strike weakened it."

Doug examined the branch. "I don't see any scorch marks."

Both their gazes left the piece of wood to track a slow trajectory around the copse of trees that made up the rest of the island.

"We're alone here, aren't we?" Natalie asked.

"This place is twelve miles downriver," Doug replied. "With no way to hike in. And it's maybe an eighth of a mile in circumference. We'd see another boat."

Natalie nodded.

Doug placed an arm around her. "It'd be easy to get spooked," he said comfortingly. "We're not used to isolation. But do you know how much safer we are right now than just crossing a street in the city?"

Natalie nodded again.

Then another crash disturbed the nighttime silence.

CHAPTER FIFTEEN

Much as a snake charmer calls forth a serpent from its basket, Kurt had summoned a newcomer to his camp. The plan he'd formed after stepping into the hole had succeeded like a charm, an incantation. It hadn't delivered a human sadly; Kurt's traps had yet to yield such spoils. But one ambush had been put to use, road tested, so to speak, and had worked exactly as planned.

Over the course of the past few days since he'd been injured, Kurt had managed to perform at a fever pitch of activity. He felt no pain in his ankle. And who cared for sleep, or his usual daily routine of chores? Long summer days and brightly moonlit nights allowed him to transform the woods just as he'd envisioned.

Now he lay flat on the ground, staring into the yellow eyes of a coyote.

He'd been apprised of the coyote's fall by a series of guttural yelps. It had landed at the bottom of Kurt's deepest hole, a natural depression in the land, widened and deepened with a shovel left behind in the ruins of the ranger's cabin. Kurt had to lower his own body down, then squat to hoist the coyote out. The beast had wept and mewled with pain, Kurt's grunts of strain merging to compose the sweetest imaginable ballad. Kurt had worried that the beast would limp away while he chinned himself back out of the pit, but he needn't have. The coyote lay, flank heaving, awaiting Kurt's ministrations.

It had broken its left hind leg. The break would've made the beast easy prey in the wild, but still—Kurt understood that the coyote had saved him far more than Kurt saving it. He figured out how to forge a splint out of sticks and immobilize the limb.

Kurt had lived in these woods for almost two years now. It was high summer, the leaves fleshy and green. He had begun speaking unabashedly to them. Looking for expression, shadings of humanity, in their veins.

No need for that anymore. He had a companion.

At first, Kurt kept the cur captive—tying it to a stout tree with rope belonging to the female hiker he had failed at taming—but after hours of studying the animal, learning its nature, Kurt realized his mistake. He didn't have to be frightened of this creature. The coyote was slinking around the tight circle Kurt had allowed it, looking up with humble gratitude, but not because of its injury nor the treatment Kurt had administered. Even in a robust state, this animal would be abasing itself on its belly versus growling and nipping at a man-sized human.

It didn't want to dominate Kurt; it wanted to be dominated by him.

The ingot of understanding returned to Kurt in a jolt. Coyotes were pack animals, and this one was in need of an alpha.

Kurt's body rigidified with a singular joy as he continued to examine the beast, hearing it as clearly as if it had spoken. More clearly, for with speech, people had a tendency to obscure their purposes, either out of a desire to deceive or because they didn't comprehend what they wanted themselves.

The nourishment Kurt had always derived from other people could be gleaned in a different way. This coyote posed an option he had never considered.

Kurt's recently completed shelter had been built using a method one of the members of the utopia had shown him, requiring neither materials nor tools. Stick and daub, the approach was called. Water from the creek had turned dirt into a mud that dried beneath the sun. Kurt salvaged boards from the cabin, while second-growth forest provided spindly logs for the walls of an additional adjacent room. Two rooms! He had a palace, a whole kingdom, but no subjects to populate it.

Kurt kept his eyes pinned to the coyote. Animals had a long history of serving as servants, companions, and proxy for kin.

He had always counted his appeal as mental rather than physical, but recent exertions had rendered Kurt's body strong, as rippled with muscle as a racehorse. His uncut hair was long and flowing, his skin copper, and his beard had grown bushy with health. He could be a real king now— and this coyote seemed to know it.

The animal squatted, licking the wiry fur on its broken leg. Kurt could see the spot where the bone was fractured. Though overall he thought he had done a pretty good job, there was a clear jog in the limb.

Kurt got down on his haunches too.

The animal lowered its eyes, then started to crawl backward, away from Kurt, sticking close to the ground.

"Stop!" Kurt said, a ringing shout, and the coyote paused and looked up at him.

Gooseflesh peppered Kurt's whole body. "I know," he said, in a quiet, firm voice. "I know who you are." He bent down, finding the spot on the animal's leg.

The cur let out a small whimper.

Kurt pressed on the bone, gently at first, then harder. The limb jerked in response, and the coyote whined. Sweat gathered at Kurt's temples; his body tingled all over. Could he split the bone without getting bitten? Create a compound fracture while remaining untouched himself? What treasures there were to be mined here, animal nature nearly as complex and multifaceted as what Kurt had observed in the human world.

He probed the wound, and the coyote yelped.

"Yes, yes," Kurt murmured. "I know. It hurts." He paused. "But you aren't going to stop me, are you? Even though you could sink those fangs of yours into my flesh, cripple me, and change your lot in life in an instant."

He felt a shudder of satisfaction—not at hurting the coyote but at understanding it—when the animal let out a helpless, pained yip.

When the alpha showed up, it proved to be a whole different creature from the one Kurt had mastered. Growling menace, bloodlust in the glow of its eyes.

"No," Kurt snarled back. "You can't have him."

His words were bravado, an act of sheer show. Terror of a sort he had only experienced once before in his life began to return. The fear didn't arise from the prospect of being savaged by the alpha. It arose from the dread of being alone again.

As a younger man, Kurt had been incarcerated, and though he hadn't liked it particularly, the real punishment had been the constant, ever-looming fear of solitary confinement, which the guards had quickly learned to use against him. Its mere threat would cause Kurt's mind to race like a rat in a cage, sweat to lather his body. Two human hands would be all the contact he'd get each day. Kurt would try to talk himself down from panic, imagining what he could've gleaned from those hands. Were they paper white or coffee brown? Did they bear tattoos or age spots? Retreat instantly or take their time after sliding in a tray?

Crumbs. He would starve to death in days.

The alpha coyote had brought with him the return of solitary.

Upon its leader's arrival, the coyote Kurt had come to know raced out of camp, awkward and clumsy, claws scrabbling against the dirt as it ran.

While the alpha began to descend on Kurt, teeth audibly snapping.

Kurt fell to the earth, assuming a position akin to the one he had noted during the time he'd been granted company, such that it was, the chance to learn the makeup of another being. He lay, chest rising and falling, curled into a shrimp-like C as he imitated the whines of the stinking cur he had lost. The alpha circled around him.

Kurt kept his gaze averted, staring at the humpbacked mountain whose shadow loomed to the west, until it felt as if his eyes would bleed.

The alpha sniffed him, and Kurt licked his own naked belly, repulsed by the taste of his flesh. And yet, something leapt inside him when he read identical disgust, contempt in the gold eyes of the alpha. He had anticipated how the alpha would feel.

The alpha came so close that Kurt could feel the riffle of its coat in the breeze, smell its gamy odor. At last, the coyote turned, controlled by Kurt even as it believed itself to be in control. As the enormous beast began to lope away, Kurt remained still, breathing hard and thinking, *You're no different from the first. I know you too.*

And at that moment, circulating air currents, the direction of a rising wind, or the beneficence of a generous god caused Kurt to smell something that hadn't been there a second before. The scent was far off, and high in the sky, so Kurt rose to his feet, forgetting to check on the alpha's progress. It turned when it sensed Kurt's motion, and started to sprint back toward him, baring black lips that exposed its fangs.

Kurt ignored it, and the alpha paused, mid-charge.

Kurt didn't care whether it jumped him. If it did, he would fight it, throw the coyote aside as easily as he might a limp rag. For he was imbued with hope, enough strength to go on.

This was no longer the innocent land that had lured Kurt and the merry band of utopians. These woods were outfitted, Kurt having worked with the intrinsic topography until it suited his needs and desires. He had built a maze, the prize at the end his camp.

Which had suddenly become relevant because the odor Kurt had just detected represented mankind's greatest accomplishment and the dawn of civilization. It signaled human presence in a way that nothing else could.

Smoke from a campfire.

CHAPTER SIXTEEN

Branches snapped, and twigs broke off and rattled to the ground. Suddenly, the whole island was alive with sounds. Some nocturnal animal skittered, and a trio of birds exploded into flight. Thank goodness for the starlight, which made it bright as day when it had to be eleven o'clock or later. Natalie saw the outline of the man clearly when he emerged from the stand of trees a few yards away.

It was Forrest.

"Ahoy, paddlers," he called, walking toward them.

Natalie turned to Doug and frowned. He looked as confused as she felt. No, not confused—Doug actually appeared to be a bit annoyed.

But he said, "Hi there," in a genial enough tone.

Forrest was dressed in the same clothing he'd worn when they met earlier at Off Road Adventures. Could that have been just today? It felt as if eons had passed, as if Natalie and Doug had already been married for years, journeying downriver forever.

Forrest swung a bright plastic paddle in a gesture of hello. "Just wanted to see how you two were doing."

Doug took a few steps closer. "You always check up on your clients at night?"

Don't be so confrontational, Doug, Natalie wanted to tell him. *Discretion is key, because am I the only one getting that this is a little strange?*

But she didn't say anything. From the moment she and Doug had fallen in love, Natalie had known she could never be two things to him: neither as fragile and dependent as his mother, nor as strong and in control as Doug was used to being. It left Natalie a narrow and constricted band in which to function. She was walking that high wire now.

"You seemed a little...uncertain," Forrest replied, focusing on Doug and speaking in a careful tone. He probably didn't want to offend Natalie since of course it was she who had been nervous. "So I wanted to make sure everything was as expected. That you were keeping the course."

Doug gazed at him levelly.

Forrest strolled over to where they'd pulled the canoe up on shore and ran his hand over the hull. "Boat looks good. Untouched. You must've had an easy paddle."

Doug still didn't say anything. He was deciding what to do, Natalie thought, computing different courses of action. And she was waiting for him to act.

But their guide didn't seem threatening in any way. Just a little overzealous. Maybe he was going for a promotion. Or maybe someone had been hurt on an Off Road expedition, and all the employees were on high alert.

Once the silence had gone on long enough to fray, Natalie ventured, "How did you know we'd be awake? It's practically midnight."

"I have a group paddling just a little ways west of here," Forrest said easily, pointing in the right direction. "We saw the smoke from your campfire. I figured you must be staying up late, enjoying the privacy."

Doug's voice finally seemed to return and he said, "We were enjoying it quite a bit. Till you showed up."

Now Natalie couldn't keep from crying out. "Doug! Don't be so rude. I, for one, appreciate the extra care and attention."

After a moment, Forrest looked away from Doug and smiled at her.

Natalie tried to smile back. *Weird, this is weird, even if I'm trying to pretend that it's not.* Then she thought to ask, "How long have you been here?" Had it been Forrest she'd heard from the water? Wandering around on this tiny divot of land for long enough that Natalie and Doug had had time to cuddle by the fire, trading mutual confessions?

Forrest frowned. "Not too long."

Doug switched his gaze back to him.

"I mean, I did paddle around for a little while," Forrest said after a moment. "Pretty spot."

It *was* a pretty spot, and yet Natalie had a cold, alien feeling then—as if she were missing something, that there was more to this encounter than she could fully parse. But she had no idea what it might be. And then a possibility occurred.

Had Doug *asked* the guide to check on them? Maybe her husband was concerned about their ability to accomplish what they had to out here, but didn't want Natalie to feel insecure. It would explain Doug's air of distance, the sense of something unsaid that had been troubling Natalie all night. He'd been expecting Forrest's arrival, and clearly the guide had gotten delayed for some reason to have arrived this late.

Forrest began backing away into the copse of trees, paddle lofted high and resting on his shoulder. More branches split in two and leaves flew free as the blade struck them.

Doug turned to gaze off at a distance, where a globule of moon trembled in the sky, so it was Natalie who bid the guide goodbye. "Thank you!" she shouted as foliage and tree trunks swallowed Forrest's form. "But we're fine!" She gave a little wave, then walked over to her husband, tilting her head so that it rested on his shoulder. She looked up at Doug and spoke in a softer tone. "We're really fine."

They fell back to sleep in the pearlescent light, Doug explaining drowsily that they had an easy paddle to Snowshoe the next day.

"Great," Natalie murmured. "We can sleep in."

"No alarm clocks in the wilderness," Doug said, rolling over and kicking his legs free of the sleeping bag.

Natalie hooked her calf over his. She'd expected to drop off immediately, but thoughts and questions nibbled at her fatigue. Did it matter if her husband kept small, inconsequential details from her, especially if his reasons for doing so were well-intentioned? What if he hadn't revealed every aspect of his past? No one liked to dredge up painful memories, especially not men who'd had to deal with things at way too young an age, as Doug confessed tonight that he had.

Still, it took until her husband had lapsed into a steady stream of snoring before Natalie was finally able to drift off to sleep as well.

Coffee brewed over an open fire tasted like heaven, just as Doug had said. Natalie drained her camp cup and polished off the last peach while Doug positioned their packs inside the canoe. You couldn't take much in the way of fresh fruit or veggies on a camping trip. From now on, it'd be freeze-dried nuggets from pouches, unless they found a patch of wild raspberries or blackberries, ripe early in the season.

Natalie kicked soil over their fire, making sure the final ember was dead, then checked their route for the day on the GPS. She made her way to the river through strands of grasses and broken sticks, detritus that had settled in the wake of last night's passing storm.

Condensation freckled the glossy wood of their canoe, the

consequences of a dewy morning. Each leaf bore its own silvery web, and the whole shoreline glittered.

Natalie crouched to rinse out her cup before stowing it inside the pack. They had a decomposable bag for trash, and she dropped her peach pit inside, this trip's first offering. Last night, they had eaten every scrap, preserving the rind of cheese for chili tonight. Natalie handed Doug the GPS so that he could tuck it away in its case, then settled herself in the front of the canoe and picked up her paddle.

As wild and tumultuous as last night had been—the storm, her swim, and then that unexpected visit from their guide—today was calm and still. A faint apricot glow lit the sky, and the day ahead had a comfortable, almost predictable quality to it. Natalie could imagine life out here taking on the semblance of routine. Paddle, eat lunch outdoors, make camp, sleep beneath the stars. It made sense in an elemental way. Every act was motivated, had a reason, unlike a lot of things back home.

The surface of the river was like glass when they entered; their paddles broke it with a crystalline plinking.

They began hearing the whitewater a half mile before they saw it.

CHAPTER SEVENTEEN

That's Class II or III?" Natalie shouted over the river's rush. "Really?"

"It sounds worse than it is," Doug called back to her. And then, "Stop paddling."

Natalie obeyed instantly, turning to snatch a peek at Doug before facing front again. It sounded like Niagara Falls lay up ahead, and she wanted to be able to throw herself out of the canoe, swim for the bank before they went over.

Doug thrust his paddle deep into the water, positioning the canoe laterally and keeping them still. "Let me give you a few pointers."

Natalie gave a single tremulous nod. The roar of the river had become constant white noise in her ears, although it alarmed her anew each time she focused on it.

Doug grinned. "You're going to laugh at yourself when you see what we're up against. The rafting trips we've been on were ten times wilder. Well, two or three times anyway. Class V."

His math didn't seem quite right, but as if for proof, Doug unzipped the pouch from Off Road and withdrew the little black case, powering on the GPS device.

He showed Natalie the screen.

She shrugged, though the tiny dot displaying exactly where they were at this moment was oddly comforting. "That thing only shows macro topography."

"My point exactly," Doug replied. "If there were some huge water-fall or something up ahead, we'd see it on the screen. An upgrade from flat to riffles, no." But the effort required to hold them in place against the current was clear. Doug gripped the paddle so tightly that his hand leached of color.

"So how do we do this?" Natalie asked. "I mean, when we went raft-ing, there were like eight of us in the boat. Plus a guide."

"Your job is just to keep paddling," Doug said. "I'll steer from back here, and the river will do the rest. Sound good?"

Natalie sunk her paddle into the water again, her hands sweaty upon the handle. The current instantly tugged the blade forward, and she had to lunge in the canoe to make sure the paddle wasn't sucked away down-stream. Natalie grabbed for it, bringing it back under control. Same stroke she'd been doing then, only a lot swifter.

"Okay?" Doug called as he loosened his grip. The canoe strained like a racehorse at the gate.

"Okay!"

They struck out.

It was more fun than Natalie could've imagined. Better than rafting because she had so much power, such control.

In the sunlight, the river sparkled like the silvery, speckled back of some great fish. And Doug had been right—the whitewater wasn't over-whelming. If not quite riffles, then ruffles. But there were boulders that formed narrow chutes, shunting their canoe along at a good clip. At one point, the body of water took a downward jog—the canoe staying level for a splinter of time, with the prow hanging over nothing but air—and then they were past it, a swirl of water catching Natalie clean in the face.

"This is great!" she shouted, blinking to clear her vision.

There were just one or two more rolls up ahead, spitting out glistening drops. After that, the river returned to its former, carpet-flat state. Natalie braced herself, submerging her paddle. The current moved so fast, it was as if she were pulling the blade through something thick, with substance. Bread dough or solidifying cement.

The back of the canoe spun out, a carnival ride wiggle-waggle, and Natalie laughed with sheer delight. "Doug, you've got us, right?" she shouted, facing intently forward. She wondered if there would be more rapids, if not on this stretch, then on the next, the one that led to their put-out. Oh, but she didn't want to think about this trip being over; it'd been even better so far than Doug had led her to believe.

The canoe straightened out, and Doug yelled loudly enough that she heard him over the rollicking water.

It didn't sound like a shout of happiness.

The whitewater required focus; Natalie could only twist around for a second. Just long enough to see Doug clutching his paddle in one fist, while his other palm lay open and he stared down at the river with an expression of stunned horror.

As soon as Natalie caught his eye, Doug attacked the current again, wrapping both fists around the paddle. But in the second that he'd stopped controlling the canoe, they'd gotten too close to a rock, which loomed like a mottled, rising moon just ahead.

"Doug!" Natalie screamed. "Steer!"

Her husband shifted course expertly, the canoe sheering off with a mere foot between it and the boulder. Natalie shuddered, suppressing an image of the collision that would've serrated their boat's glossy coating, splintered its wood. But Doug made the maneuver appear effortless, outwitting the river's obstacles with apparent ease.

Only his face told a different version of things.

No time to ask what had happened. Behind the rock, a final roll of water hurtled itself forward. They caught the spray at an angle, and the canoe threatened to tip. Natalie threw herself to the side that was about to lose contact with the surface of the river, and the boat righted itself. Whitewater broke over the rim of the canoe, putting two inches of sloshing liquid into the bottom, and then they were through the rapids and floating gently downstream.

"Doug," Natalie said, her teeth knocking together. She was too shaky to try to make it back to him in the stern. Her clothing was soaked, her Norlanders submerged on the floor of the canoe. They were going to have to paddle over to the bank, overturn the canoe to get the water out. "What happened back there? What did you see in the river?"

"I didn't see anything," he said stonily. "I dropped something."

They weren't lost, Natalie kept reassuring herself, after Doug revealed the item that had fallen out of his hand. The worst possible thing to lose. Not cash, or the credit card, matches, or their knife. The GPS.

Still, they knew exactly where they were, only had to retrace their steps to return to their starting point and find their way out again.

Not their steps. Their strokes. And of course, you couldn't paddle upstream. Which meant she and Doug were going to have to wend their way back on foot, a route that wouldn't come close to mirroring the one they had just taken by water. A knot of panic cinched inside Natalie's chest, and she made herself turn away from her husband, lest he see the expression in her eyes.

They paddled over to the lower depths, their canoe scraping bottom, and stared despairingly upriver.

Doug got out first, pulling the canoe onto shore with Natalie still inside it.

"Let's try and look," she suggested, a high, artificial note of brightness in her voice as she climbed out.

They trudged through the shallows by the riverbank. How many millions of gallons of water were plummeting by right this very second? Even if the river hadn't been moving so fast, spotting a small object in it would've been impossible.

Natalie got down on her hands and knees, combing through the mud on the river floor. She had to take some kind of action, even if it was pointless.

Doug's hand dropped heavily down upon her from above. "Nat."

She kept digging.

"Nat," Doug said. "Stop it. It's gone."

He turned and headed back to the boat, where he busied himself with tasks. He laid their packs on top of two sun-warmed rocks to dry out. Then he overturned the canoe, fighting its weight until water spilled out with a gushing sound.

"Why did you have it out anyway?" Natalie asked as neutrally as she could. "There was no navigating to do."

"I know," Doug groaned. "It was stupid of me. Idiotic. I must not have zipped the pouch all the way. And everything loose got jogged around in that first big roll. I saw the case as it went over."

I thought you said there weren't going to be any big rolls, Natalie thought but kept from saying out loud.

Suddenly, Doug clapped his hand onto the bottom of the overturned boat, striking it with a thud. "Wait a minute!" he cried. He turned around fast, kicking up splashes as he climbed onto the bank.

Doug went for the nearby rocks where their packs were sunning themselves, and revealed the pouch from Off Road. Natalie's heart sparked. He had remembered something, there was a secret, sealed compartment, the GPS wasn't gone after all.

But instead of the device, her husband came out with a ziplock bag. "The maps," he said triumphantly. "The guide said we could use these just as well. He said the GPS sometimes doesn't even work out here at all."

"It was working pretty well for us," Natalie replied, knowing she should've bit back that comment too. But the GPS had, in a short time, become something she depended on, like a cardiac patient would his pacemaker. Its loss felt monumental. This trip was going to take on a whole different quality now, the two of them no longer linked to civilization by a single artifact of the modern-day world.

Doug gave her a look. "It might've stopped. Or lost charge."

Natalie couldn't tell whether he was trying to gloss over what he had done—cast the mishap in a less catastrophic light—or if he wanted to make her feel better.

"I can't read maps," she said. This hadn't been something she'd talked much about with Doug—who had done the navigating on the couple of camping trips they'd taken—but it was actually a near-phobia for Natalie, some kind of learning disability, like map dyslexia. Her former friend Val was dyslexic, and the way she described sweating, being completely unable to focus, when faced with text was a lot like how Natalie felt about maps. "I actually failed geography in sixth grade."

"Lucky for us, I didn't," Doug replied distractedly. He had unfolded the sheet to its full length and spread it out on the ground, making sure to keep the paper a safe distance from the water. Crouching, he traced his finger along a thick, red line drawn in marker. "This looks simple enough."

"We're gonna party like it's 1999," Natalie muttered. She *liked* technology. GPS was so superior to this paper labyrinth that she was surprised anyone used to be able to find their way anywhere. Still, she dropped down beside her husband on the shore, water tickling her toes. "Do you really think you can get us the rest of the way with this?"

"Sure I can," he said. "This map is perfectly clear."

A breeze picked up, and with it, a flurry of last year's leaves. Natalie and Doug both swung around. A bird squawked in protest over something in the woods.

Doug frowned and got to his feet, starting to head toward the trees.

Natalie reached for his arm. "Doug? Where are you going?"

He removed her hand gently. "I'm sure it's nothing."

Then he walked off.

Natalie remained crouched on the riverbank. She watched the water sweeping by, experiencing the sensation of being carried along by something she could neither name nor identify. The force of her relationship with Doug. Where it had brought her, and why.

"Honey?" she called out. She flipped the wet ends of her hair out of her shirt and began to wring them out. Silence from the woods. If Doug disappeared again, as he'd done during their first carry, Natalie didn't know what she was going to do. Fifteen or twenty miles deeper into the wilderness. No GPS. Her heart began clanging in her chest.

But her husband came back, breaking through a barrier of branches. "Nothing," he repeated. "We should have some lunch and go."

Natalie fixed peanut butter sandwiches, while Doug studied the route with a seriousness that seemed worthy of such navigation. The sun shone down overhead, and Natalie knew they should take advantage of the light, the long summer's day. Still, she took her time, methodically arraying foodstuffs on the ground, repacking the bag. She felt hesitant to leave this spot, to depart for points unknown.

Doug came up and gave her a squeeze from behind. "Time to set out."

Natalie continued her painstaking preparations.

"Nat?" Doug said.

She twisted to face him. "That's just a lot of open space out there." What had Forrest said? Six million acres in the Adirondack Park.

"I know what I'm doing, Nat," Doug said, so sure, so certain, that it was easy to rise, like a puppet being drawn up by its strings.

CHAPTER EIGHTEEN

Mia sat on her bed cross-legged, commenting on her aunt's latest Instagram uploads, all from before Aunt Nat had left on her honeymoon, of course. Aunt Nat's account had been totally quiet the whole time she'd been gone, two long days already. Her Instagram feed looked like the city after a zombie apocalypse.

Another weird thing about Aunt Nat's account: Mia's were practically the only comments on it. Aunt Nat had uploaded a bunch of pics from the wedding, and aside from one lone, wish-I-could've-come type thing from somebody Aunt Nat seemed to work with, there were no replies. Not even any likes.

Mia began to scroll back up through her aunt's posts. She didn't tag anybody, except for Uncle Doug and Mia herself. Mia had to go back more than a year to see the usual comments and likes, mostly from the same two friends, who had super-pretty profile pics.

Mia checked her own account—also pretty quiet, now that school had ended—then dropped her phone on her bed. She and Aunt Nat were both friendless.

The hot, hip camps where Mia's friends were all going required at least a month's enrollment, and because of the July timing of the wedding, Mia couldn't find a session that worked for her schedule. Not that she could've afforded those camps, not this summer anyway, with her parents living apart. Supporting two households in New York City didn't come cheap, as Mia's mom (who paid all the bills) liked to remind her. And neither did trapeze training, filmmaking, and wakeboarding, activities the pricey camps boasted. They were located in what Mia would've once called the country, before she had been to the town where Aunt Nat got married. Now Mia knew. Her friends hadn't traded urban for rural this summer. They had gone away for two months to play in a park.

She felt older than all of them suddenly. It was as if the wedding had taken her off for much longer than a weekend, a voyage in the old-fashioned sense of the world. Sailing ships and uncharted destinations.

Mia padded barefoot into the kitchen, seating herself on a stool by the counter.

"Hey, you're up," her mom said, sending her a look of surprise.

"Can I have some of that?" Mia asked, pointing.

Her mother's eyebrows flared. "Coffee, Mi?"

Mia shrugged defensively. "It's decaf," she muttered.

Her mom continued eyeing her, then reached into the cabinet for a mug. "No more than half a cup," she instructed. "And put milk in it."

Mia hadn't been expecting a yes. She filled the mug joyfully, although the mixture tasted like crap. This was the same stuff that went into a Frappuccino?

"Mom?" she said, taking another quick swig. "I have a question."

Her mother sat down. "What a coincidence," she said, blowing on her drink. "I have one too. But you can go first."

Mia looked at the counter. At the Chinese restaurant the day they'd gotten home, she had referenced the dumb secret Hot Guy had told her, when in truth, weren't her parents the ones who really hid' stuff? Mia didn't even know why they were getting divorced. But she couldn't ask that. "What happened before the wedding?"

"Oh." Her mother shifted on her stool. "I'm not really sure. Doug's friends had an argument about something." She refilled her mug from the carafe.

Mia hesitated. "Did it have to do with the two shady characters who showed up?"

The words didn't sound like anything Mia would say—she was basically quoting Aunt Nat—and her mom caught it. She looked up, her face concerned.

"Shady?" she repeated. "How do you know about those men, Mi?" Her brows drew together. "Which brings me to my own question. Is this what Mark talked with you about when he walked you back to the inn?"

Mia's cheeks fired at the memory of her late-night stroll, but she shook her head. Mark hadn't mentioned any sketchy guys. The thing he'd told her had been about that gorgeous canoe. "I heard Aunt Nat asking Uncle Doug," Mia explained.

Her mom nodded, looking relieved. "Well, Aunt Nat married Uncle Doug, not his friends. Neither of us needs to concern ourselves with those men." She carried their mugs over to the sink as if the matter were settled. "What did Mark say, though?" Her mother's phone chimed then, and she reached for it. "Darn, Mi, I have to go into work. Shelley just called in sick, and they need someone to cover on peds."

Mia nodded. Her mom was a nurse in the NICU at Mount Sinai.

"Stay home, and I'll ask your father to get here as soon as possible."

Your father. Not Dad. Since when had that life edit gotten made? Mia bit her lip, turning away so her mother couldn't see her face. As if it'd kill her to be here alone. All her friends had been allowed to stay on their own for, like, two years.

"You and I will talk more later," her mom added in an informing way.

An idea struck Mia. "Hey, Mom?"

Her mother was plucking a pair of ducky-flecked scrubs out of the stacked dryer, which stood behind the kitchen door. She nodded over her shoulder.

"Do you know Mark's last name?" Mia would have some time before her dad got here. And she needed something to do.

"Um, no," her mom replied. "With everything going on before the wedding, I didn't even have a second to look at the program. Harding maybe? Harmon?" She paused to pull her uniform top over her head. "Look, Mi," she said, muffled through the fabric. "I know you're a bit at odds and ends this summer, and I know that thirteen is a bit of an odds-and-ends age anyway. But I don't want you focusing on some guy twice your age."

Mia blinked fiercely. Like her mom could control even her thoughts.

Her mom placed a finger underneath Mia's chin. "Promise me," she said, and Mia stared up at the ceiling, willing tears away. "No matter how cute he is."

"Mom!" Mia shrieked.

Her mother smiled at her innocently. "What? You think I don't notice things like that anymore now that I'm an old lady?"

Mia smiled back, and it wasn't as fake as most of her smiles had been lately, if not quite all the way to happy. She'd be by herself for at least a little while, in charge of things for once, which made all the stuff that had come to annoy her about her mom recede. She recalled the time, ages ago, when they'd been best friends practically. It was like that'd been two other people entirely.

She wondered if she could find Mark and Brett on Uncle Doug's Instagram account. Uncle Doug's groomsmen had stuff going on that nobody else knew about. Just the mention of them got Mia's parents all worked up, and Aunt Nat had been curious about whatever happened before the wedding. If Mia could figure out the deal, then she'd finally be the person who knew something first.

But when she got back to her room to look, she learned that Mark and Brett weren't following Uncle Doug. He didn't have many followers and wasn't on Instagram all that much. Probably Mia should try Twitter, maybe even Facebook, since Uncle Doug and his friends were pretty old. She decided to start with plain old Google.

The number of hits that came up when Mia typed in *Mark Harding* and *Mark Harmon* was overwhelming, like the worst school research project ever, and a lot of them appeared in multipage articles that would take forever to scan on the tiny screen of her phone. There was an actor by the second name, and his IMDB profile and a million other mentions jammed up Mia's feed.

She got up and wandered in the direction of her mother's bedroom. She hated going in there now that her dad had moved out. The room was at once still his—a shared space—and so completely changed by her mother's taking it over that Mia didn't even recognize it. She scurried to the night table and snatched up the laptop—her mom didn't want Mia having a computer of her own—before going back to her room and flopping down on her bed.

Even on the computer, the task wasn't easy. Mia's eyes stung from reading so much text. There were hundreds of *Mark Harmons* in the world, and dozens of *Mark Hardings*. If either of those was even the right name. Mia got distracted by a Marcus Harding who appeared to be a designer and made the coolest shoes she had ever seen. Straps strung together with jewels, heels as thin as toothpicks. This guy's profile pic didn't look anything like Uncle Doug's friend, though. Mia kept clicking on shoes, shocked when a price was displayed. Made Barneys look like Target.

She hoped her mother wouldn't discover this site and freak out about Mia shopping for totally inappropriate footwear. She knew her mom tracked her search history. Mia couldn't even be alone in cyberspace.

She went to try and find the page she'd started from, clicking the back arrow robotically, but had trouble because she'd navigated so far away. This must be what her teachers meant when they complained on her report cards that she lacked focus.

There had to be some way to find out more about Uncle Doug's friends. She decided she'd even be willing to try Facebook—what a loser site—but she had to friend Uncle Doug first to see what *his* friends were up to, and Uncle Doug was in no place to accept Mia's request. Literally.

Mia stared at the computer screen, at a total loss.

Then it came to her. What if she didn't just go online? Her dad was always saying how his students used their phones first, second, and last, without ever considering other sources of information.

It was pretty good advice actually. She should tell her dad she was taking it.

Kicking things old school. IRL and all that.

Because wouldn't Uncle Doug have info about his own best friends? An old phone that had them in the contacts maybe? Their business cards or something?

Her mother had told Mia to stay home, but Aunt Nat and Uncle Doug's apartment was practically like a second home to Mia. It barely counted as leaving.

Mia climbed out of bed and got dressed. She was about to go and grab the extra set of keys from the hook on the fridge when her phone trembled, caught in the folds of her comforter. A text from her mom read Your father's on his way.

CHAPTER NINETEEN

The trip had a different feel to it now. This pristine setting had a new menace; there was something sharp in the strike of their paddles as they sliced through the water.

They had more carries than Natalie had been expecting, although Doug didn't seem taken by surprise. The river kept petering out in swampy masses of bracken, causing Natalie and Doug to shoulder their packs and hoist the canoe with grunting, soldierly resignation. Doug called out assurances—the river's next leg lay just up ahead; they were about to come to a lake—and he was right every time, the symbolic rendering of their position on paper clearly no mystery to him. Whereas when Natalie forced herself to examine the same sheet, her vision went blank, and her pulse rate began to climb. She longed for the GPS as she might a missing pet.

She had to rely on her husband now, trust him completely.

But hadn't she been doing that all along?

Perhaps because Natalie had been on her own since she was so young—effectively parentless given her dad's deficits and difficulty functioning, Claudia's efforts to step in notwithstanding—it had been easy to let Doug set their course as a couple. He'd filled a gulf in Natalie's life whose depths she hadn't allowed herself to face when she was single. Now Doug was steering things quite literally, and having him in that role should've felt comfortable and easy and perfectly right.

But it didn't. Something was off, in the emotional realm as well as their physical reality. The woods had an eerie hollowness to them.

They made camp that evening beneath the chin of Snowshoe Mountain, its bulk reassuring, despite the presence of clouds. Doug had gotten them where they were supposed to go, the spot he had pointed to in the distance the night before.

The clouds scattered before any rain fell, and their evening passed unblemished, a whiskey-colored sunset bathing the landscape while they roasted strips of jerky in the fire—the meat sizzling and smoky—and chased them with marshmallows for dessert. Natalie and Doug fell asleep beneath a nearly unbroken canopy of stars.

Rain clouds had amassed again the next morning, and when Natalie went to brush her teeth, she saw that their supply of fresh water had run out. It seemed a milestone of sorts, a reaching of some frontier. Natalie filled both bottles from the river, rereading the instructions from the UV kit. A waterborne infection out here would be no joke.

Doug emerged from the tent, giving her a little wave as he stumbled down to the water's edge and doused his face.

Natalie waved back, pointing. "Coffee's ready."

Doug polished off the pot before going to dismantle the tent. Muscles worked in his upper arms as he yanked out the tent stakes; life out here made you stronger than any prepackaged workout in the city.

Her husband seemed antsy after all the caffeine, and Natalie hustled to load the canoe while he put out their fire. Once on the river, Doug took out the map, letting Natalie paddle solo as he studied the sheet of paper spread across his lap.

The map remained a muddled morass of streaks and blotches when Natalie looked at it, and she wasn't as strong a paddler as Doug. The canoe kept slowing down, and she bit back a grunt of frustration.

Doug thrust his paddle into the water, and they picked up speed before coming to another carry Natalie hadn't anticipated. The next body of water to appear was a lake.

"Are we on track?" she asked, once they'd set out. She lifted and dipped her paddle in what she forced herself to think of as a soothing rhythm. "You're looking at the map an awful lot."

Doug let out a laugh that didn't sound terribly mirthful. "Well, I'd better be," he said. "But yeah, we're on course. This lake ends there"—he pointed to the outermost confines of the body of water visible in the distance—"and then the river should pick up again almost immediately. May be shallow at the mouth for a few hundred yards. We might have to wade and push the canoe."

The topography went exactly as depicted, and Doug's air of relief seemed palpable. But Natalie found it hard to duplicate his feeling. The thought of making dinner from their stash of staid supplies, purifying water, then pitching their tent, only to repeat the same sequence for another four days, suddenly seemed about as appealing a prospect as housecleaning or going to work.

But Natalie couldn't say such a thing. Doug was holding up his end of their early marital bargain—navigating them safely through the wilderness—and she needed to offer support. Besides, what choice did they have? They were miles and miles from anywhere.

Resupplies. She suddenly heard the word in her head. Their guide had mentioned two such spots, both marked on the map. Doug could get them to one of those as easily as their designated put-out, couldn't he? They could emerge from the wilderness sooner than planned.

Except that her husband would never go for this scenario. It would feel like an admission of failure, if not for their whole marriage, then certainly for its adventurous start. Best to squelch the idea before it could take hold in her mind.

As they continued paddling, though—the sun moving steadily across the sky, Natalie and Doug's arms stroking back and forth with the unending repetitiveness of pump jacks—the idea kept tickling at the corners of her mind. Finally, she spoke up. "Doug?"

She twisted to face him in the canoe, and immediately wished that she hadn't.

Doug was paddling one-handed, staring down at the map with an expression she'd never seen on his face before. Fierce and dark and desperate.

"What?" he said in a voice that matched.

She opened her mouth to respond, but couldn't.

"We're not lost," Doug told her, leveling out his tone. "I swear. We're fine."

"Okay," Natalie replied, so softly that she wondered if he could hear. She began to paddle again, applying more force to spare Doug some of the labor as he continued to study the map. "Okay, that's good, I'm glad."

The river grew suddenly deeper, its current picking up strength, a dark, eely mass of moving water that carried the canoe along.

They were still at it three hours later.

Natalie shifted uncomfortably against the rigid bar at the helm of the canoe. She was ready to stop for the day, and it was only mid-afternoon.

In back, Doug suddenly began stroking harder, pulling the canoe through the water at a fast clip. The boat skimmed along, hardly making contact with the surface, as Natalie fought to keep up. She was panting by the end—although *end* seemed a strange concept out here in this vast expanse of land, as if there were some invisible finish line—while Doug paddled furiously, water coming off the blade of his paddle in veils. The canoe slid across a final stretch of water, entering the reaches of an ivory forest.

The sight was breathtaking, nearly enough so to restore Natalie's spirits.

Doug let out an audible breath and called, "Paddle over to the bank, Nat. Let's take a breather."

Once they had pulled the canoe safely out of the water, Doug took a walk around before collapsing on the ground and letting out another exhalation.

Natalie gazed down at him.

"Beautiful, huh?" Doug said. "I've been waiting for this spot the whole trip."

A strange, satisfied smile crossed his face, vanishing so rapidly that Natalie wondered if she'd imagined it. She took a look around and felt pretty awestruck herself. Golden-green birch leaves shivered on their limbs, while the stalks of the trees shone like tusks in the sunlight. It looked as if moonbeams had planted themselves in the earth.

"Nat?" Doug ventured as she positioned herself beside him on the ground. She laid her head on his chest, feeling a bristly new growth of beard along his jaw. "I've been thinking about something."

Natalie lifted herself on one elbow, examining her husband's face.

"Look," Doug said, his voice gathering strength. He got up and went back to the canoe, returning with the ziplock bag. He unfolded the map and spread it out for her. "You were right about the navigating. It's harder than it looks."

Natalie's chest cavity went cold. She was as blind as some underground creature out here, and if Doug was having trouble—

He settled the pad of his thumb on a wavering line, speaking with growing confidence. "But there's a trail here, see? Just a mile or so from where we are right now. A real, marked trail. We can pick it up and hike out in two days' time."

"Hike out?" Natalie said, disbelieving. Her voice blasted through the sun-haloed woods, and she took a furtive look around, convinced somebody might be there to hear.

"Don't you see?" Doug returned calmly. "This is a good spot to cut our losses. The birch forest was a real pinnacle of the trip. We can enjoy the area for the night, then hike out at first light. Maybe we'll even make it in less than two days."

Natalie sputtered. "But—what about our canoe?"

"That's the thing," Doug went on. "If we continue paddling, then we have to finish our trip as planned. I've gotten us this far, but what if I can't stick to the route? Waterways are harder to navigate than land. All the portages—if we can't find the right spot to reenter, we could be in real trouble."

"Well, then how about the resupplies?" Natalie asked. "Forrest said we would never be more than a two-day paddle from help."

"Same problem," Doug said, speaking patiently. "I'd have to locate them by water. And since we're not more than a two-day hike out, I don't see what paddling buys us. It seems riskier to me than a marked trail."

The woods were changing under the force of her husband's words. Natalie saw a different sort of forest closing in—not the idyllic shade of this spot, nor the places where they'd made love and frolicked and paddled. But barbed branches, trees with claws. And no discernible means of escape.

"We haven't seen one other person this whole time," Doug continued. "And it's not like anybody who might happen along would want to steal a canoe. Once we get out, we'll let the Forest Rangers know we had to abandon ship. Literally." Doug's face broke into a grin. "I bet they can truck out our canoe or paddle it back for us."

"I guess that could work," Natalie said. It was something very like what she'd been wishing would happen earlier that morning.

"I'm just trying to err on the side of caution, honey," Doug said.

There it was again. That magic word, slippery and unctuous, which could make her go along with almost any idea.

"Okay," she said at last. "As long as you don't feel like we're giving up. You know, on your dream trip or the perfect honeymoon or something."

"I don't feel like we've given up on anything," Doug told her. "In fact, I think only better times lie ahead for us from here." He bent to kiss her forehead, a chaste peck more suited to people celebrating their golden anniversary than newlyweds. "Let's get the canoe up on higher ground. We want to find that trailhead, make camp before nightfall."

CHAPTER TWENTY

Men died from gold fever, traipsing through jungles, getting bitten by disease-carrying bugs, or mauled by bigger creatures, in search of filthy lucre. While other men committed suicide or murder when love proved evasive. Still others fought duels in order to protect their honor, or that of a family member.

Kurt cared nothing for wealth or passion or principle. But as he searched for the source of the smoke from the campfire, he understood all those men and what it was like to be driven by an obsession so fierce that death paled in comparison.

Smoke could be smelled from some distance, depending upon the conditions. But after walking half a day in the direction he deemed likely to have been where the fire was lit, Kurt's initial fervor was replaced by a sick, rolling feeling of defeat. He hadn't found one sign of human penetration, still less the ashen remains of a blaze or a smoke-charred ring of rocks. Had desperation and loneliness led him to mistake an accidental combustion—a small and fleeting forest fire, say—for one that was man-made?

Man-made. What a pleasing pairing of words. What an urgent, desperate need Kurt possessed to find something out here made by somebody besides himself.

Back at camp, he grew increasingly frantic, climbing trees to unsafe heights so as to gaze toward the point where he'd scented the fire, scouring the land beneath the dense canopy of leaves for any sign of trespass or occupation.

By then it was evening, an impossible time to spot smoke. Sparks died out too soon to be seen; the builder of the fire would have to be within twenty feet of Kurt. Every passing minute while he waited for dawn to break was like a bite taken out of his skin. When the first glow of light illuminated the sky, he could stand it no longer. He headed out of camp, hunting the highest tree he could find. Upon coming to a particularly towering monster, he scaled it, then crawled out along a topmost branch to where the foliage grew more sparsely.

Not so much as a flicker of ash from another fire. It was as if whoever had lit the first one had vanished into thin air along with the smoke from his blaze.

Kurt squinted, feeling the limb he knelt upon dip beneath his weight but ignoring the danger, intent only on trying to spy a rise of flame off in the distance. Just a faint whisper of smoke would satisfy him. He sniffed so deeply that he felt his nostrils flare. Clean, green air and nothing more, yet his throat felt as raw as if he'd indeed breathed in blistering, toxic smoke.

Then he realized what had irritated his throat. Kurt was screaming aloud, and had been for some time. Shouting for the lighter of the campfire, or bellowing at him in abject rage, either one of which was sure to scare off anybody in the area.

Kurt slid backward along the branch, his heart gonging so hard he thought it would cause him to fall. When he reached the juncture of the tree where he could begin his descent, he had to pause and wrap his arms around the trunk. The sheer force of his desire felt like it might timber this behemoth, his bare hands sufficient to pull the tree's roots out of the ground.

And from this vantage point, Kurt glimpsed something in line with where he thought that fire must've blazed, though closer to his current position. Alive with want, clinging to the tree, he leaned out to get a better view.

He lost hold of the trunk. Kurt had time to envision his deadly plummet to the ground, now, when he had discovered a way back to the camper. His arms flailed as he fought to fling them around the trunk. Hoary bark scraped his face. Then he was clutching the tree again, safe and steady and still.

As cruel a foe as nature could be, so did she occasionally bestow great bounty, mercies upon her inhabitants. Her topographical features presented barriers for those who tried to invade her, but opportunities for those who sought to live in concert with her.

Like Kurt.

Assuming the builder of the fire remained in this area, the wilderness had just delivered an excellent means of rounding him up.

CHAPTER TWENTY-ONE

Natalie and Doug crouched beside the canoe, sorting through the contents of their packs. They'd be able to carry less weight on their backs than could go in a boat, plus the rest of the trip would only be two days now, not four. They could get away with halving their food supply and cutting down on clothes.

"No more swims," Natalie remarked with a note of sadness, tossing her bathing suit into the canoe along with two T-shirts and a pair of shorts. Not her favorites at least. This wasn't the kind of honeymoon for which you packed the cute results of a shopping spree. She went to top off their water bottles by the river's edge.

Doug stayed back, assembling the essential items that he'd offered to pack out. First aid kit, knife, matches, rain gear, tent. They chose to forego the comforts of camp pillows and sleeping pads, and also left behind the tarp. Doug took the UV wand from her, securing it in an outer pocket along with its replacement battery. Despite the last-minute change of plans, he was outfitting them properly, taking time to be prepared. That moment in the canoe, when he'd seemed like someone else entirely, had vaporized, returning to Natalie the husband she knew.

Doug added his own pared-down bundle of clothes to their stash, while Natalie went to wrap her arms around him, giving him a smile.

"Come on," Doug said, extricating himself and taking a shifting look around. "Let's get going."

They each hoisted a pack and shouldered into it, clipping the chest strap for extra support. Doug indicated a spot on the map, Natalie leaning over and fighting to see what he so clearly did. At last she gave up, and Doug pointed through the woods, indicating the direction they had to take in 3-D.

They flipped the canoe over, a count of one-two-three that Doug rushed, so the boat dropped to the ground lopsided, till Natalie let go and it settled into its new position.

Doug took a step into a thicket of trees, their white boughs and trunks like ghostly apparitions around him, while Natalie gave the canoe's sleek underside a final pat of goodbye.

The hike took over two hours, the terrain tricky and difficult enough that Natalie wondered if they were up for the challenge of the remainder. The bulk of the distance lay ahead of them, although it should get easier once they were walking on a trail. Still, this was an utterly untrammeled landscape, nothing like the places where they had camped before. Undergrowth as sharp as wires, trees packed together like arrows in a quiver. Doug appeared to make progress somewhat more easily, but they were both struggling.

The sun was low enough in the sky when they finally spotted a blue metal tag on a tree, indicating their arrival at the trail, that attempting further miles seemed incautious. Natalie fixed dinner while Doug pitched the tent and laid their sleeping bags inside, interlocking them with a high whine of zipper that was by now as familiar a sound as the sirens and horns playing all night long on the streets outside their apartment.

Doug crawled out of the tent, and she displayed the meal she'd made: sticks of jerky tucked into the last of their bread, dehydrated berries plumped back up with water and placed on squares of chocolate.

Doug eyed the spread with distaste. "Hold on, I have a contribution."

Natalie raised her eyebrows, mouth already full.

Doug strode over to his pack and poked around inside, coming out with a flask.

"Bulleit?" Natalie cried, delighted. "You've been packing that this whole time?"

"A wedding toast," Doug agreed.

"But why did you wait till now to bring it out?" Natalie protested, thinking of that first night on the island, other romantic moments along the way.

"Just seemed like the right time," Doug said. "And, you know, otherwise we'd either have to carry out the weight for the next two days, or leave it behind."

Natalie nodded agreeably before settling herself on the ground. She tore off a hunk of bread and jerky with her teeth, and reached for the bottle. Her husband's answer didn't feel quite satisfying—would a full flask versus an empty really add appreciably to the load in his pack?—but she realized she didn't care. They were getting out of here tomorrow, and thanks to the whiskey, had a fun evening ahead. "Well, I'm glad you waited," she said. "We can fortify ourselves before our trek."

Doug grinned at her. "There's the Mrs. Larson I first met in a bar drinking Bulleit over rocks," he said, accepting the bottle she handed back.

It was one of those summer nights that seemed to hold off forever. The sun remained stubbornly in the sky, casting shadows, turning bushes into man-sized humps, while Natalie and Doug drained the bottle of its amber contents. She kept sending him off to check on noises she found suspicious, unlike anything they'd heard on the river. Still, despite nerves, every bite of their meal got eaten—and a thing of crackers besides—before Natalie thought to stop them.

"We have to make sure we have enough for the next two days," she said, a statement that struck them both as funny at the same time. Their laughter shook and echoed through the woods. Tree branches swayed overhead, seeking, reaching.

"Come here, you," Doug said, making a grab for Natalie that felt sexier for its awkwardness. The forest finally grew silent, just the brush of their lips, intertwining tongues, and an undulating moan Natalie lost all control of.

"Doug," she whispered urgently. "Let's go in the tent."

She felt exposed in these woods as she hadn't in other equally vast stretches. The host of different sounds to get used to: scuffing, clangs, things Natalie knew couldn't really be there, and indeed never materialized when Doug jogged off amicably enough in search of their source. Nonetheless, she wanted a lid of fabric above her, walls all around, when her husband delved deep inside her body, taking it for his own.

Natalie began to head for the tent on all fours, triggering another bark of laughter from Doug at her clumsy crawl, which caused her to swivel around.

"Shh!" she hissed, and then she was laughing too, flat on the ground without quite knowing how she'd gotten there. It was a puzzle she forgot once Doug joined her, sliding his hands beneath her shirt, and freeing her breasts from their bra. He cupped them, not anything like gently, and Natalie groaned with unguarded pleasure, thrashing her head back and forth on a mat of leaves.

In this new position, something caught her eye. A flash of color—artificial, neon bright—from a distant section of forest, as low down as she.

"Doug?" she said, stopping his tantalizing, near-violent touch. "What is that?"

They got up, tripping a bit, unsteady on their feet, and made their way through the trees. Their path meandered at first, a halting succession of steps during which the swath of color vanished, slipped out of focus, causing them to blink and stop in place in order to bring it into sight again.

"There," Natalie said, and pointed, one finger indicating a wavering line.

Doug pushed in front of her, shoving branches back roughly enough to snap them. After a second or two, his footfalls came to a halt and he screamed.

It was a high, catlike noise, utterly unsuited to her strong, commanding husband. Not the sloppy sound of a drunk—this was a voice shrill with shock and overlaid with an emotion Natalie couldn't quite pinpoint. Despair?

She went cold all over, as if the river on which they'd been traveling had followed them here, a trickling trail, and forced Natalie to plunge back in.

Did you think you could leave me? the river asked. *You can't get off the water just like that, just because you decide to.*

"Doug!" she shouted back. "What is it, honey? What's wrong?"

Her husband had remained in place while Natalie continued stumbling forward, so at that moment she saw for herself.

Sprawled out at Doug's feet, his outdoor gear accounting for those bright wings of color, like a tropical bird's plumage, lay the body of a man.

CHAPTER TWENTY-TWO

Natalie watched her husband stumble backward, hand clapped over his mouth to stifle that awful scream. It was easier to look at Doug than at the discovery he had made on the forest floor. Although the sight of her husband in such duress, weakened and vulnerable, was almost as shocking as the vision of the body.

Was Doug still feeling the effects of the alcohol? His walk was more of a stagger, following an unclear line that barely skirted branches and boulders. While for Natalie, the man lying on the ground had sliced as cleanly as a scalpel through any lingering buzz, rendering her sober as a five-year-old girl.

"Doug!" She let out a cry. "Watch out for that tree—"

But her husband wasn't watching out, reeling backward as if incapable of any form of directed action, so the trunk caught him in the spine with an audible thud and sent him sliding to the ground.

"Doug!" Natalie cried again, and ran to her husband.

He got to his feet, and they both turned to focus on the fallen figure.

All was soundless: not a rustle of leaf, nor whisper of air, nor even the tread of an animal. There was an absence of any breeze or stirring through the trees, and the river was far enough away that its rush was muted entirely.

"He's dead, right?" Natalie asked. "Not just hurt? Or unconscious?"

Doug extended one hand wordlessly. Night had finally begun to descend in earnest, but still, Natalie could see what her husband was pointing to.

A hole on the man's forehead, open and gaping, like a single tarnished coin.

Doug let out another strangled cry, and this time, Natalie couldn't stand it. She hurled herself forward, hissing, "Stop that!" What a dreadful sound, like a child who couldn't comprehend what it meant to be hurt. "Oh, honey, it's horrible, I know, but we'll figure out what to do."

The shadings of a plan, their next several steps, began to occur to her. They would hike out double time. Darkness fell late this time of year, which meant they should be able to make the road by the following evening. Their flashlights would pick up blue trail markers until the sun rose. It wasn't as if they could spend another night in these woods. Then they would stop the first person they saw, go into the first home or business they came to, call the police and the Forest Rangers, or whoever Doug had said was in charge.

Neither of them had touched the body. That was good. Although it struck Natalie that maybe they should check for a pulse, hole in this poor man's head notwithstanding. They had a first aid kit; some type of rudimentary treatment might not be beyond them.

Stupid, she told herself. *He hasn't budged an inch since you found him. His chest is motionless, and he isn't even bleeding.*

She began to rise, pulling at Doug's hand. "Come on."

Time enough later to examine the shards of their honeymoon. Once they had procured help. She'd watched enough TV to know that they shouldn't stomp around here, destroying evidence. The fresher the crime scene, the greater the likelihood of capturing the killer. She and Doug couldn't help this man, but at least they could give the police a chance at tracking down whoever had murdered him.

"Come *on*," she said again, impatience creeping up on her. Her husband continued to sit so stilly. If he didn't snap to pretty soon, Natalie was going to have to go on alone, send back aid both for her husband and the dead man. But how could she possibly do that? She couldn't even follow a trail map. "We have to get out of here."

At last, Doug began to struggle to his feet.

"We came from that way," Natalie said, hands on Doug's broad shoulders, trying to turn him. "Let's go get our packs."

Doug took a step in the direction she indicated, then stopped. The silence was destroyed by a sound as sudden as a stick of dynamite exploding, which after a moment resolved into a crackle and crunch of leaves.

Footsteps, but cautious ones, each separated by a pause, their maker clearly trying to muffle noise, conceal his own trace.

Too deliberate for an animal, some creature of the woods.

Thoughts arrowed through Natalie's head.

This wasn't anybody they could turn to for help.

How could they have been so slow and stupid? Shock? Right until this very second, Natalie hadn't considered the person who had done this. And now it was too late. He had come back, needing to do something with the body, make sure the man was actually dead—or worse, because he'd found evidence of Natalie and Doug's presence, their tent or diminished dinner, and intended to do away with them too.

Natalie began pushing at her husband's back, forcing him into motion, making both of them head in a direction, any one at all, so long as it took them away from the pendulum beat of those slow, dread footfalls.

And then the pace of the steps changed.

Whoever had come was no longer moving with care.

He must've figured out that they heard him, and he started to give chase.

"Doug!" Natalie cried, the one word a claw in her throat, desperate and sharp.

She saw a glimmer in the trees, something metallic, unnatural amidst the brown-green woods. The barrel of a gun, thick as a man's finger.

Sighting on them, beginning to take aim.

Seizing Natalie's hand, her husband broke through a barricade of branches and finally started to run.

They ran as if catapulted from a slingshot, not taking care to avoid whipping brush or lashing twigs, let alone able to avoid making noise. Sticks split underfoot; leaves were torn off their perches with a sound like ripping skin. Shorts and T-shirts rendered their bare limbs vulnerable, exposed, yet Natalie and Doug raced on, impervious. They forged a weaving, twisting path, seeking only to leave behind the man with his gun.

A jutting branch sliced Natalie's cheek, and she cried out.

Doug jerked her arm hard enough that she pitched forward; he caught her and she righted. They ran on without faltering. Blood trickled from the wound on Natalie's face—more than a trickle maybe—but she couldn't think about that right now, how much blood there was, the warm, salty gulp of it.

She spat red and pushed on.

Doug edged in front of her so that he could take the brunt of the weapons of the woods, Natalie following the path that he broke. She ducked beneath branches that her shorter height rendered deadly, leaping over debris that Doug kicked aside. They kept going until their sprinting pace finally began to wane, hearts clopping like a herd of horses in their chests, at last settling into a jog, intent on putting as much distance as possible between themselves and the man who had infiltrated these woods.

A sudden wedge of rock loomed up, and Doug hoisted Natalie into his arms, swinging her around the wall of stone. He dropped onto the ground, pulling Natalie down as well. Their breaths came in loud, rattling gasps; they would be overheard if the man were anywhere nearby.

Doug pressed a finger to his lips, getting onto his knees and crawling forward to check, while Natalie rested for a moment. She placed her face against the rock, momentarily forgetting her injury. The rough surface abraded her flesh; it was as if she'd lain down on a wasps' nest. Natalie managed not to scream, although tears rolled helplessly down her cheeks in a scorpion sting of fire.

I think we lost him, Doug mouthed, glancing back at her.

Natalie's balled fists began to loosen.

Doug rose.

The woods appeared to be still.

Natalie stood up too, checking out their surroundings, searching for any indications that they had been tracked. Another set of equally fierce breaths. The shadow of a limb that belonged to a human. Footfalls on the forest floor.

Their own trail was already being lost to the detritus they'd stirred up, leaves shifting in a light breeze, covering their tracks.

Violet light penetrated the trees, the last, lingering remains of the day. Then darkness lifted its shoulders, blotting out the sky and woods until Natalie could hardly discern Doug's form beside her, let alone anybody who might have followed them, especially if he was keeping himself hidden. At last the stars began to wink on, and a manic smile of moon appeared in the sky.

No man. No one here at all besides the two of them.

"We lost him," Doug said again, a little louder this time.

Natalie inhaled raggedly, taking another look around. "That's not all we lost," she said, also low, but not because she feared anybody overhearing.

The reality of their situation had stunned her into shock, damped her voice.

They had no idea where they were. Their twisting, turning journey had taken them miles away from their original location. Spurred only by panic, their rash, heedless tracks would be lost to the night, and everything looked different by daylight anyway. The distance they had just covered would be impossible to re-create.

Understanding settled over Natalie like a slow, strangling net.

They were on their own in the wilderness now. Without any of their belongings.

No water, food, maps, or gear.

Nothing but a memory of the trail that was to have gotten them home.

PART TWO

FOUND

CHAPTER TWENTY-THREE

They used the huge rock in lieu of a tent, lowering themselves down beside it for the night. Doug wrapped his arms around Natalie; she leaned the good side of her face against him, and felt the machine-gun fire of her husband's heart start to settle down.

"He wasn't just a hiker who got into trouble," Natalie said after a moment. Inching up to the reality, bit by bit, so that it couldn't overtake her. "Or a paddler like us."

"No," Doug said, so quietly she could hardly hear him.

"He was shot," Natalie went on. "Intentionally murdered. By that man—the one who chased us."

This time, Doug didn't respond.

But Natalie couldn't stop herself from vocalizing the slow, steady crawl of this catastrophe. "Why would somebody deliberately kill a man way out here?" The answer was obvious—wilderness as vast as this made an excellent place to hide a body—although all Doug said was, "I don't know," in a stilted, wooden tone.

"I guess someone might bring a gun into the woods for protection," Natalie continued. "Or to hunt." But you didn't hunt with a handgun. "Maybe they were friends who came to blows?"

"I don't know!" Doug said, and now his voice seemed ready to split.

Natalie turned her face to look at him—the simple motion caused nearly unbearable pain—but then questions swept her up again. "A fight that bad though, out here in nature? It's supposed to be so peaceful. Where people come to get away."

For just a second, an image of that town filled her head, a welcome blotting out of this whole disaster. Wedeskyull. It had been so pretty. So picturesque. If only they could be back there now, before they had ever started out.

Doug uttered a hoarse laugh, the barking of a seal. "Like the Garden of Eden."

Natalie couldn't tell if he was agreeing with her—or scoffing at her.

"What's savage out here isn't the land, Nat," Doug said. "It's what people do to each other in it. That's always been true. Wherever you happen to be."

Her husband might not have meant the words to reassure her, but somehow they did. Natalie shaped her body to fit Doug's sloping form, and though she didn't expect to sleep, the sun was shining by the time she next opened her eyes.

Doug must have shifted her while she was out cold, for she was alone behind the rock. She got to her feet so abruptly she stumbled, light-headed and stiff from sleeping that hard. Doug stood a little ways off, shading his eyes as he took a look around.

He became aware that she had wakened, and turned. His face looked ravaged, his eyes dull with disbelief. A whole night hadn't been sufficient for him to make the transition. From blissful honeymoon to guns, to murder.

To the fact of them being lost.

He began to walk back toward her.

"Okay," Natalie said, the word gummy and thick on her tongue. She licked her lips, then tried again. "Let's figure out what we're going to do."

They took stock of their situation, talking in brief spurts, voicing hesitant ideas, while resting on the ground with the sun circling overhead. They hadn't just slept, but slept late. Reaching the road by nightfall would've been impossible given the hour, even if they had known where to go. Food wasn't a problem—yet—but even one full day without water would be. And the normal degree of thirst created by such conditions would be worsened by the alcohol in their systems.

"We came from that way," Doug said, pointing. "I'm 100 percent sure that this rock was in front of us. We nearly ran straight into it."

"I remember too," Natalie agreed. "But you're not suggesting we just head in the opposite direction, are you? We'll lose our bearings within a few yards."

Doug was looking at her funny.

"What's wrong?" Natalie raised her hand haltingly. "My cheek? Is it bad?"

She didn't dare touch the spot. The skin felt tight and sore, but at least it had crusted over. There was no more blood, aside from the Jackson Pollock scatter of drops that stained her shirt, and would, she supposed, till they had access again to that first-world luxury of laundry.

Doug looked down at his lap. His bare shins were skinned and abraded, the effects of last night's barreling run. "It just needs time to heal," he said at last.

His attempt at reassurance was more damning than if he'd expressed revulsion or squeamishness. Natalie felt the bite of tears behind her eyes, and the pain in her cheek flared anew. She struggled to change the subject. "If you're lost in the woods, you're supposed to stay in one place—"

"Only if there's a chance of someone coming along," Doug interrupted.

It was the same kind of logical thinking he had applied when suggesting they hike out of the woods instead of paddle. Except now, instead of using the calm, patient tone that had ultimately convinced Natalie, Doug's voice grazed hysteria. He wouldn't make eye contact, kept casting his gaze around.

Rather than causing Natalie to feel vulnerable and alone, Doug's fear actually had the opposite effect: coalescing in her a will to act and a slow, steady clarity of vision. They would stay put, she decided, conserving energy and resources. Luckily, they were starting out well-nourished and healthy, had plenty in the bank from which to draw.

"Natalie," Doug said in a high, teetering tone. "Come see what I was looking at before you woke up." He got to his feet, then extended a hand.

Natalie grasped it.

They left the protection of the rock to wend a path through the leaves, which crisped and crackled underfoot. Natalie turned back a few times, keeping the rock in sight, although Doug took no such pains.

She frowned. You were supposed to stay in place if you got lost. Every Boy Scout knew that. Even wandering this far broke the rule.

The earth began to curve in front of them, and then the whole of the wide, sunny sky appeared, a silvery yellow vista. At least the weather was holding, a lucky break for them.

Luck, she thought, not for the first time on this trip.

"Careful," Doug warned. "It's a steep drop."

"What did you want me to see?" Natalie asked.

He walked her forward a few more steps.

"This," Doug said, and pointed.

It appeared as if the whole of the Adirondack Park opened up before them, the view unveiling itself as they stared. Natalie had no idea what six million acres amounted to, but she would've sworn that every one of them was here on display. The spot Doug had led her to allowed a vista of miles. It looked as if the rest of the world had been eliminated, wiped neutron bomb clean, and replaced by wilderness. No people, or cities, or towns, or buildings, or cars. No swipe of road cut between trees. Not a single cell tower nor an electric wire.

No sign that civilization had ever existed at all.

Hunched mountains showed their backs to the sky, so far off they might as well have been on the moon. They continued on in concentric, overlapping arcs, an array endless enough to be dizzying. Before them was an aerial sweep of green, more shades than a crayon box held, broken only by the occasional shock of premature scarlet or gold. The view so unending, it tired the eyes. Spread out on three sides, like a tufted cushion big enough for God and all in His heavens, with the coming season predicted in the tableau. By the millions, these trees were going to give themselves over to color, before foliage abandoned them altogether, along with all heat from this part of the world.

The sight was hideous in its beauty, in what it meant for them.

Natalie turned to Doug, her eyes rounding with fear.

"The likelihood of anyone finding this spot is virtually nil," Doug said, her horror captured by his tone. "We don't stand a chance if we stay here, Nat. Not a chance."

"Okay," Natalie said, taking a step back from the ledge. "Okay." She began picking at the flecks of blood on her shirt, sending up a fine, red spray of grit. "What do you think we should do instead then?"

Doug walked a few paces off. "We have to find that trail. It's the only way."

The woods closed in on them from behind, and Natalie swallowed, or tried to, her throat pasty, as she turned toward the trees. Dark and inscrutable, hundreds of them, thousands, all undifferentiated, and every inch of forest floor identical too.

She felt fear begin to choke her. "A day," she got out. "Let's give it one day. If nobody comes along, then we'll decide what to do."

"Unless that bastard is the one who comes," Doug said harshly. He shot another look around. "And even if he doesn't, that's one more day when we'll be getting thirstier. And more hungry." He grabbed Natalie's wrist, tugging her in the direction they'd come from. "We have to find that trail while we're at our best. Don't you see that?"

Natalie let herself be pulled, then stopped and dug her Norlanders into the dirt. Water shoes for bushwhacking through terrain rougher than any she'd known could exist. She hadn't put her boots on back at the tent last night. Why would she have? She'd thought they had plenty of time to prepare for today's hike.

You're in this mess—and it certainly qualifies as a mess now—because you agreed. You always agree. To hike instead of paddle out. To come into the woods on your honeymoon.

To marry Doug in the first place.

That wasn't true. That was revisionism talking in the wake of last night's disaster, which wasn't even Doug's fault. But maybe if she'd opposed him more. Let more of herself out. She needed to do so now. This might be the last chance she'd have to effect their fates.

Natalie turned away from her husband so fast that air burned the left side of her face. Her wound pulsed like a live thing now. "We'll never find a trail in all this space," she said firmly.

She expected a confident *Yes, we will* in response, but Doug sounded desperate when he said, "That trail can't be more than three, maybe four miles from where we are right now. And even if the way we came last night isn't completely visible, we should be able to detect signs of it. Branches we broke. The sight of the—"

Body, Natalie mentally filled in. It was true, she thought, cold and focused. If they could find that body—assuming the man with the gun hadn't returned to drag it away—they'd be in good shape. A corpse made a hell of a landmark.

"Okay," she agreed at last. "But we walk slowly. Carefully, not in a frenzy. We look for indications that we were there."

Doug nodded.

"And we conserve resources," Natalie went on, issuing instructions in a way she never had before. "It feels like it's going to be warm today. We should avoid working up a sweat, burn as few calories as possible."

Doug nodded again before taking her hand and leading Natalie back toward the place where they'd spent the night.

The rock felt like a dinghy, the only source of safety they had in the world. She didn't want to leave it behind. As they passed by, Natalie reached out to stroke stiff fronds of lichen on the rock's surface. She had trouble letting go, lifting her hand reluctantly before taking a breath and striking out into the deep-green sea.

CHAPTER TWENTY-FOUR

It took two more days before Mia got the chance to make the trip to Aunt Nat and Uncle Doug's apartment. Her dad was in curriculum-planning meetings all afternoon, while her mom was so stressed about the extra shifts she'd had to cover—that woman Shelley was still out—that she actually agreed to let Mia spend time alone.

Avenue C was a whole other world from the Upper West Side where Mia lived, and she had always appreciated its frenzied nature when visiting Aunt Nat. Aging buildings no one bothered to fix up; bodegas that sold burner phones and cashed checks and spewed out Lotto tickets instead of having salads and bottled water on offer. One man wore what looked like a squirrel suit, even though it was like a thousand degrees out. Another, handing out flyers, was dressed as an enormous red pen.

Mia took one of the pieces of paper just to be nice. Didn't these guys get paid by how many they gave away? She didn't get why they didn't just throw them all into recycling bins then. She crumpled up the flyer as she approached Aunt Nat's apartment.

Even the climate was different down here, warmer and more humid. Maybe because there were fewer blasts of chilled air from stores and apartment buildings. In this neighborhood, doors were propped open to try and get whatever breeze there might be, circulating hot air for hotter. Mia's skin grew slimy during the walk from the subway.

Cars were crammed along every inch of street, some borrowing space from the sidewalk, and honking for no apparent reason. They didn't seem to want to go anywhere. One guy sat scowling on the hood of a slick, dark sedan that was parked so close to Aunt Nat's stoop, it looked ready to drive into the building.

Mia pushed past a man hanging out on the steps, more rudely than she would've done uptown. The man sent her an annoyed look, stumbling a bit as Mia brushed by. He clopped back down to the street as if one leg was giving him trouble.

"Sorry," Mia called out. She felt bad now, jostling the man with special needs. There was a kid in her class who walked like that. He had one leg that was shorter than the other. Marshall, his name was. Other than the leg issue, he was actually kind of cute.

Mia dug out the keys from her pocket, then found the one that opened the front door. She climbed the steps to the fourth floor, huffing a bit in the sweltering stairwell, unlatched all three locks and let herself inside, before falling onto Aunt Nat's couch with a huge exhalation of air. Actually it was Uncle Doug's couch, big and rough and beige. Mia let out another sigh. The apartment was stuffy and hot, providing hardly any relief from outside.

She went over to the fridge and got out a bottle of fruit-flavored water, letting the cold liquid refresh her as she took a look around. This apartment was, like, schizophrenic, Mia thought, crossing to a little stand of drawers and examining the objects placed on top. A vase with silk flowers, a plaque with painted swirls and inspirational words, and a small painting of an angel, all right next to a super-high-end wall-mounted

TV. Aunt Nat and Uncle Doug's tastes were so different. That couch with its feedbag upholstery alongside a cherub that was supposed to be flying but looked to Mia like it had a skewer stuck through its butt.

The cherub had been set on a pile of papers to hold them down. Mia riffled through each one. Mostly reminder notes about the wedding—*call caterer, change shrimp!*—but also a brochure for something called Off Road Adventures, which planned trips in the Adirondacks. Maybe the one Aunt Nat and Uncle Doug were on right now.

There were tons of photos scattered around, mostly of Aunt Nat and Uncle Doug. Their heads poking out of an orange tent, grinning maniacally at whoever was taking the picture. The two of them getting splashed on a raft, oars held high, water dripping. Standing on a cliff at sunset with their arms around each other. Eating at a restaurant—six photos at six different restaurants actually. Mia could just imagine what this place would look like once the wedding photos had come back. She spotted one picture of herself when she was younger. And there was her mom, looking awfully young too, nothing like her usual commanding self. Mia stared at that shot for a while.

No picture of Uncle Doug with his besties, though.

She turned and headed for the bedroom. If there was anything to be learned about Mark or Brett here—and it was striking Mia as increasingly unlikely that there was; her idea seemed pretty stupid now actually—it would be in the apartment's other room.

The living room was a mix of her aunt and uncle's things, but the bedroom had stayed pretty much the way it'd been before Uncle Doug moved in. A Shabby Chic duvet on the bed; framed posters with sayings hung on the walls. Aunt Nat liked painted words of wisdom.

Sometimes the end is only the beginning written in script across a scene that showed a path through the woods dead-ending at a view of the ocean.

Blech, Mia thought.

She opened the drawer in the bedside table on Uncle Doug's side, but there was no old phone in there—just some pens, a paperback, and, *eww*, a box of condoms. Mia shut the drawer as if it were a hot pot handle, gingerly, using just the tips of her fingers.

Aunt Nat's night table drawer yielded better results—there were some photos that balanced the whole Natalie-and-Doug show in the living room at least. Mia picked one up, feeling a bolt of recognition. Aunt Nat with the pretty women who used to comment on her Instagram account. They were standing in front of a store with the most amazing dresses in the window. And there was a selfie of the three of them, faces sunburned, toasting with bottles on a beach. Plus a few more, nights on the town kind of thing. Aunt Nat looked sadder in these pics. Kinda lost. She looked like a little girl.

Mia wandered over to the closet, fingering the hangers before crouching down. There was a cardboard box on the closet floor, its flaps slotted shut, and a message scrawled in marker across the top.

Doug, don't open!

Mia picked up the box and carried it over to the bed.

Inside, there was a cellophane-sealed package of ivory wrapping paper and one of those clusters of ribbon that looked like a little girl's ringlets. Underneath sat a leather-bound album. Aunt Nat hadn't finished it yet, a few trimmings and a drugstore envelope of photos remained loose, but there were pictures and mementoes affixed to the inside pages. Aunt Nat and Uncle Doug on various outdoors expeditions and eating at more restaurants, plus receipts for things whose importance Mia couldn't determine, greeting cards, a matchbook cover, even bits of shellacked shells pasted to seascape stickers for a cool 3-D effect. More sayings written in Aunt Nat's twining script.

Love is what was missing. Love is the glue. Love is what I found when I met you.

Mia hoped Uncle Doug would like his album despite the gloopy poem. She herself loathed scrapbooking.

She hit the lottery on the next page, though.

If at first you don't succeed, Mia thought.

Ugh. She was the one thinking in sayings now.

There was a picture of Uncle Doug, Mark, and Brett standing in a bar, arms slung around each other's backs, overflowing glasses raised. Aunt Nat clearly didn't mind photos of friends—she had preserved this one for Uncle Doug. So why were all of hers shut away in a drawer?

Mia dug her phone out of her pocket and snapped a shot of the photo. She took a close-up of Mark's face and another one of Brett's.

They were both so good-looking. Mia imagined scrolling through pics on her phone at school next year and pausing at this one. "Oh yeah, those were just some guys I hung out with at my aunt's wedding," she'd say, and all her friends would squeal and press her for details.

Mia nestled everything back in the carton exactly as she had found it and got up to leave the apartment. As she walked through the living room, she came to a sudden halt.

Something had changed.

She hadn't made a mess, left anything out of order, but as her gaze roved over the furniture, Mia saw what was different, and her skin broke into a thousand needle pricks. She felt like she had that time her mother had taken her to an acupuncturist to help with a truly grody headache.

Mia snatched another look around, but the apartment appeared to be empty. There was a clear path between her and the door, which Mia chose to walk toward now, fast, almost running. She took out her phone. She should've texted her mom before she'd left home. Then she would at least know where Mia was right now.

Mia took a second to engage the lock before racing down the stairs, sweat breaking out all over her body. Nobody lurked in the stairwell— she made sure to check each time before taking the next flight of steps.

Still, there was no denying what she'd seen. One of the ugly beige couch cushions, slowly rising up, returning to its full loft, as if somebody had only just gotten up off of it.

Had someone come in, then gone out again while Mia had been examining the scrapbook?

Her skin still felt covered in scaly prickles; despite the disgusting heat of the day, she shivered. She didn't want to enter the relative cool of the subway; she would feel safer aboveground on the packed street under the blazing sun.

Mia stood outside the door to her aunt and uncle's building, thumbing in a text to her mom, with a few minor adjustments to camouflage her timeline.

> think i left something at aunt nats going to get it
> then will come right back home

She was about to press Send when two men sandwiched her, one sliding her phone smoothly out of her hand, the other contributing a soft, spiraling hiss.

"Shh," he murmured. "Just be quiet now. Then we'll give you back your phone."

CHAPTER TWENTY-FIVE

By dusk, Natalie and Doug had to accept that they weren't going to arrive at the trail or their original starting point. They'd walked all day—which had indeed been hot, even worse than Natalie had feared, the sun drilling through the canopy of leaves in sharp spikes, slicking their bodies with sweat—and at first it seemed as if they were on the right track. They kept arriving at trees whose leaves looked shorn in a way that only their racing bodies could have produced. The route felt familiar: its switchbacks, twists, and turns.

They even found a branch broken off at exactly Natalie's cheek height. She and Doug had taken a few moments to line the protruding stub up with her face, Natalie biting back a screech of agony when her skin grazed the wood. Doug's mood after that had made the pulsing pain worth it, though. He'd been excited, swinging her hand as they trudged through underbrush, climbed over stones, and ducked beneath leaning logs, expecting to come to their tent or their packs at any second. They were going to be all right. A little thirsty and hungry and scratched up, sure. But Doug's decision to set out walking had been the right one, as Natalie must see now.

Around the time twilight began its slow, grudging ascent in the sky, that mood was gone, erased along with any feelings of familiarity toward the landscape. They were in a wood that seemed at once different from anywhere they had trekked before, and terrifyingly the same—the whole of the wilderness as featureless and indistinct as a Stepford wife.

"The man with the gun might've moved the body," Natalie said. They had both sat down to rest on a fallen log. Brush on the forest floor scratched their bare skin. Their legs were a mess, Natalie observed. Red and covered in welts, bug bites too. "That would explain why he came back in the first place. And maybe he took our stuff—he wouldn't want that spot to stand out in any way. So that's why we haven't seen anything."

"Possible," Doug replied.

He hadn't spoken much for a while now. Natalie wondered if his mouth felt the same as hers did: dry and fuzzy with fear.

Not fear.

The thought was delivered to her brain as if by a spike.

Her mouth felt fur-lined because after just one day, Natalie was already experiencing the effects of an unquenchable thirst. While the wound on her face contributed its own high, shrill note to the song of discomfort and dismay. Bringing her hand anywhere near her cheek was akin to touching a glowing coil on a stove. And yet the injury took a back-seat compared to the direness of the situation they were confronting.

"It'll be dark soon," Natalie said. "We'd better find a place to lie down for the night." She took a look around, and hot as she felt—oh, for a way to cool off, clean up, wash out her wound—she shivered. Low lavender light penetrated the forest, lending everything an eerie cast. What creatures lived in these woods so far from any trail? Who, or what, might be out here besides them?

"We have to stop anyway," Doug said, averting his gaze. "I have no idea how we're going to deal with *that*."

Natalie turned in the direction her husband was facing. She swayed for a second on her feet, then closed her eyes.

Whatever geological event had produced the chasm from which they'd set out hiking earlier that day—the place where they had scanned the view and seen what seemed to be the whole of the Adirondack Park—had continued wreaking havoc, lo these many miles away, creating a gully, a gutted-out cleft in the earth, which looked impossible to skirt or descend or in any way bypass. Trees as sharp as skewers filled the rift, the sides of which pitched at a slant that had to be forty-five degrees or steeper. They would've needed ropes, not to mention climbing skills.

Natalie looked at Doug. "We'll find a way around it in the morning," she said, through lips that felt like caterpillars, puffy and fat.

Doug looked away from her, his expression bleak.

"There's got to be one," she said, and after a long time, he nodded.

Natalie woke before light began to creep into the eastward sky, hunger biting at her belly. The need for food had nibbled at her throughout their long day of walking, but now that need had teeth, sharp and uneven.

She and Doug had fallen asleep against the log. Moisture from the ground had seeped into their shorts and dewed the backs of their legs, but the temperature was still high enough that Natalie didn't feel chilly. She tried to wipe her skin dry, sluicing wetness off with her palms.

Greedily, she licked her hands.

Natalie got onto her knees. The tops of ferns and nearby forest leaves were dappled with drops. She crawled forward, lapping up the scant beads of this moisture too, before forcing herself to stop and reserve some of the blessed liquid for Doug.

As she sat and blinked up at an acre of stars, growing inured to the sounds around her—crickets chirping, frogs cheeping, the sinking footfalls of nocturnal creatures—she became aware that Doug was starting to wake.

His breathing sounded uneven; when he first opened his eyes, they glowed like embers, threaded with red.

"How far do you think we walked yesterday?" Natalie asked.

"Hard to say." Doug's voice came out raspy.

Natalie gestured to the dewy leaves, and Doug's eyes sparked. He bowed his head, licking the green surfaces thirstily, almost panting.

"We probably walked for at least nine hours," he said once he'd imbibed all there was to be had. "It was almost dark by the time we stopped. Figure we made three miles an hour, maybe a little less, since we were bushwhacking—"

Natalie turned to him, aghast, in the lingering dark. "We covered more than twenty-five miles?"

The specific cant of Doug's features was impossible to make out, his face like marble in the last vestiges of the moonlight. "That's what I would estimate. Yes."

Natalie kept silent.

"But we were headed the right way back, judging by the sun. Due east, I think."

"You think?" Natalie said carefully.

"The sun isn't a compass, Nat," Doug replied. "I did my best."

Natalie stared up at the sky, now beginning to lighten. Day two had arrived.

"We weren't just going in circles," Doug said. "We followed the same rough direction as the trail. But assuming we were walking parallel, I have no way of knowing whether we would've been north or south of it." He licked his lips as if the act of talking had parched him.

"Don't do that," Natalie said tonelessly. "You're wasting saliva."

Doug's head dipped. "Speaking of. I think we should look for a stream."

"To follow out, you mean?" Surely not to drink from. "I thought that was a myth. An old wives' tale."

"Not a myth," Doug corrected, getting to his feet and brushing dirt and grit from the backs of his legs. "It can take a while. It's not as fool-proof as some think. But I don't see that we have any better option."

Natalie matched the faint sense of resolve her husband had mustered. "First, we need to figure out a way to cross this monster."

CHAPTER TWENTY-SIX

During the two years he had eked out a living in these woods, Kurt had never gotten a glimpse of what he'd just seen from his high-up perch, although in retrospect it seemed impossible to have overlooked or missed. A canyon so wide and deep and gaping, it looked as if Mother Nature herself had taken a bite out of the ground. Kurt, who had some experience digging holes of late, had to admire what nature had wrought. A geological calamity so massive that no one for miles around could hope to avoid it.

The sun began its sharp ascent in the sky, boding temperatures seldom seen in these woods, as Kurt descended from the Goliath of a tree and set out walking. Despite his stampeding hunt the day before to try to locate the camper, then the rigors of tree climbing, his muscles felt lithe, supple with optimism and hope.

The brush and undergrowth were too dense to take the most direct route, cover the distance as the proverbial crow would've flown. Kurt had to twist and turn quite a bit, navigating around impediments. Still, after a few short miles he came to the sight he had spied from the tree-top. He wiped a slick of sweat from his forehead.

Swinging his arms, Kurt began walking up and down along the edge of the canyon, looking for a place where a hiker might cross. Even Kurt would've been hard pressed to traverse such a beast, although at last the gap in the earth began to narrow, presenting an opportunity for passage. He'd had to stray some ways from its rim due to the roughness of the terrain, and as Kurt pushed past trees to observe from up close again, he suddenly stopped short.

Kurt felt his hand extend, seemingly of its own accord, disembodied. With a feeling of wonder, he studied the surface of the tree in front of him.

Deep in the creviced runnels of bark was a faded trail marker.

CHAPTER TWENTY-SEVEN

By daylight, the gully looked more challenging, not less. Its downside was too sharply tilted, and slippery with dry husks of leaves, to offer any means of a controlled descent, while the angle of the uphill would have prohibited scaling even if they made it to the other side.

"Walk alongside it till it ends?" Natalie questioned. "At least we'll know we're staying true to a route."

Doug shook his head. "That could take us miles out of the way. We can't spend energy like that."

"We'll waste a lot more on an impossible climb," Natalie replied. "And since we're not 100 percent positive which way we were walking, it might not even *be* out of the way." She regretted the words as soon as they were out of her mouth, each one a dry, hard pellet of accusation that even she knew undermined the skill Doug had applied.

But Doug didn't get angry—perhaps he lacked the energy for a quarrel—and instead began looking around, scouring the banks of the gulf. "What if we used that?"

Natalie let her gaze travel in the same direction. The part of the gap to their right narrowed significantly. Although no less steep, a mossy tree had fallen over that section, bracing the sharpest incline of the vee. If they could make it a few feet down the slope, the trunk would prevent them from sliding any farther, and then they could—

"You want us to walk across that log?" Natalie asked. Her heart started to scurry in her chest. "Use it as a balance beam?"

Doug stared at the rift in the earth, like a sailor looking out to sea. "You weren't as bad at gymnastics as a kid as you were at reading maps, were you?"

Natalie almost smiled, the movement unfamiliar on her mouth. "I never took gymnastics," she said. "But, Doug…that fall has to be—"

"Don't think about the fall," he told her. "And don't look down."

He reached for her hand, and they started toward the pitch.

"Want me to go first?" Doug offered. "Or should I trail you?"

The question sparked tears, which Natalie knew she didn't have to lose. But she couldn't help it. This crisis wasn't Doug's fault—he'd been trying to err on the side of caution when events had spiraled completely out of control—and yet here he was, still trying to make things as easy as possible on her. Doug always took the harder task, the lesser piece; it was the flip side of his tendency to steer things and chart their course. Maybe this was what marriage was really all about—learning the upside to every down in your spouse, and vice versa.

She swallowed, aware that no liquid went down her throat. "Let's get to the log together. I might need your help climbing onto it."

Doug nodded.

"And then I'll cross first. But I think I'm going to go on my butt."

Doug gave her a wan smile. "Lucky tree."

Natalie's fist felt weak, but she managed to punch him.

They positioned themselves horizontally with the rim of the chasm, wedging the sides of their Norlanders into the earth and using their hands to keep from sliding. If they'd had to descend any deeper in the gully, they would've slipped, tumbling into the spiked valley below. But the fallen tree met them a few feet down, and they let their bodies sag against its girth, unable to wrest their gazes from the perilous drop over which they hovered.

"I told you not to look," Doug said. He was white-faced as he spanned a cross section of log with his hands and chinned himself up. When his knees were level with the trunk, he swung one leg over. Then he leaned down to help Natalie.

She wouldn't have had enough strength without Doug. The rutted bark dug into her elbows and knees. She was panting by the time she'd gotten herself situated atop the log, the whole of the gully falling away beneath her. The air rising up felt thick and humid; sweat plastered her body, making a slip feel dangerously imminent. She wiped her hands back and forth across the fabric of her shorts so roughly that they rasped.

"Twenty feet," Doug said, his tone reassuring, bolstering her. "You won't be up high for much longer than that. And then if you had to drop, you could climb to the top on the other side same way as we came down over here."

If Natalie's mouth had felt dry before, now it was a crinkle of old newspaper, an attic cloaked with dust. She was afraid that she would start coughing with such force that she'd pitch right off the log.

"You go before me," she got out. "I need to see how it's done."

Doug hesitated for the barest of seconds. Then he sprang to his feet atop the tree trunk, paused to get his balance, and strode forward. He stopped only once in the middle—his strong, lean body seeming to float a hundred feet in the air, above a million treetops—before thrusting one arm out to each side like a tightrope walker. A few more steps and he was across, standing on the end of the log above where the ground began to level off. The whole maneuver had taken only seconds.

Her turn now. Natalie's heart was thrumming.

"It was a cinch," Doug called across the space separating them. "Even easier than I thought. Come on, Nat. You can do it."

Her legs hung over opposite sides of the log. If she had stretched one down, lowered herself just a bit, her toes would've scraped the steep side of the gully. But as soon as she moved forward a few feet, she wouldn't be able to do the same thing. And another foot or two after that, the ground would fall away altogether.

Natalie remained seated. She couldn't bring herself to stand up, knowing that drop was coming. She began pulling herself forward with her hands, then scooting on her butt to catch up, inchworm-style. Once. Then again. And again. Her legs now dangled freely, over thin air and an endless assemblage of trees, the spears of an infinite army.

"Nat!" Doug shouted. "That isn't going to—"

"Shut up!" Natalie hissed, so fiercely that she did start coughing, and had to lean over, gasping and retching and hugging the log till the spasm passed.

She opened her eyes.

The swath of trees Doug had crossed so glibly, seeming to float upon their tips, looked different from this vantage point. They were tall creatures, reaching hungrily for her, hoping she would fall into their clutches.

She stifled a scream; she didn't want to start coughing again.

"That isn't going to work, Nat!" Doug called, and this time she saw what he did.

Or felt it.

The width of the tree had been increasing while she'd pulled herself out over open space. Her thighs were spread at a sharper angle now, their muscles stretched to aching. This tree grew so broad at its center that her legs wouldn't be able to span it.

She started scooching backward, planting the flats of her hands behind her, then pushing up and reseating herself. Bent over, breathing hard, she reached the spot where the tips of her shoes could scrape solid ground again, and stopped.

"Natalie!" Doug called hoarsely, enunciating each word, though they were hard to make out from here. "You're. Going. To. Have. To. Stand. Up!"

Natalie stared out at the breach, and understanding settled dizzily over her.

If she didn't do this, then Doug was going to come back and try to help her.

She could see him poised to set out, his body readying itself as he lifted one foot. That would make three trips for him total, and he'd be faltering, weakening with each one. Doug was as thirsty and hungry as she; he might not have the strength to make it.

"*Stop!*" she screamed with the deepest breath she could drag in. She fought to suppress another coughing fit. "I'm coming! I'll come!"

She waited until the heaving of her chest had quieted before she got up unsteadily, first kneeling, then standing, the insides of her thighs quivering.

Then she raised one foot and took a step out over the open maw of trees.

Natalie shuffled at first until she saw that was only slowing things down, plus making her wobble. The space along which she had to walk was no narrower than the area demarcated by the yellow line in the subway. If not for the gaping chasm on either side, she could've gone at top speed, even shouldered someone standing in her way aside.

Natalie inched forward, focusing on what lay ahead, and keeping her face lifted to make sure that sky, versus the militia of trees below, filled her peripheral vision.

Doug loomed before her; she was close to him. Her stride leveled out, grew more sure. She was walking now, nearly strolling along. Her heart planed evenly.

And then the log shifted on its mount in the earth.

Just a slight movement—but enough to cause Natalie to teeter, and have to throw out her arms to get situated again. A skitter of rocks and dirt cascaded into the gully, their sound like cymbals clanging in her ears.

Natalie and Doug's combined weight on this end of the trunk had changed something. The tree couldn't remain planted where it had come to settle after whichever cataclysmic event—a lightning strike, an earthquake, the shove of some mythical beast—had caused it to topple.

Natalie was still several feet from where the slope became gradual enough to scale; if she fell now, she would land all the way at the bottom of the chasm, or be skewered on the way down by a tree.

The log was still slipping, groaning as if waking up after a long quiescence.

"Doug!" Natalie said, a helpless, useless plea. There was nothing he could do for her from there. If he tried to reach her hand, he would miss; walking forward would only hasten both their fates when the trunk let go.

Doug looked at Natalie, his gaze strong, reassuring as always, but filled with something new, a deepening born of this trip.

Love.

Then he jumped.

CHAPTER TWENTY-EIGHT

Natalie's scream was so sharp and sudden that her body wavered on the log. She didn't take time to steady herself, just broke into a run, as if she hadn't been fifteen feet off the ground. She was hardly aware of crossing the remaining section of trunk, nor of feeling any fear, except for her husband's fate. Natalie reached the place where the earth rose up to meet the tree. Holding on to the trunk, pull-up bar style, she dropped as close as she could to the place where Doug had come to a rest.

He had dug the fingers of one hand into the ground when he landed, but that move wouldn't have been sufficient to hold him. What was keeping Doug aloft was a slim root, over which his arm had hooked itself. Doug's body dangled, a large portion of its weight dependent on the crook of his elbow.

"My arm," he grunted when Natalie reached him. "I think I broke it." His face had gone waxy with pain; the words were barely audible.

Natalie bit back a shriek of pure rage. How much more could they stand? A broken arm out here meant that if they'd had any chance at all before, they wouldn't for much longer.

"I'll pull you up," she told Doug. "Let go when you feel my hand."

After a second, he nodded.

Natalie locked her fingers around Doug's good wrist, using both her arms to pull. Doug worked his hand free from the ground, holding on to Natalie so tightly that she feared he might drag her over. She dug her heels into the soil, bracing herself, and yanked with all her might. Heaving and gasping, she managed to get Doug up to more level earth. When his arm slid free of the root, he let out a roar of pain.

They fell backward, lying at a slant, their bodies coated in sweat, unable to climb any higher. When she had breath enough to speak, Natalie sat up and faced Doug.

"Let me see your arm," she said.

Doug pressed his lips together.

Natalie made her fingers as light as possible, but when she reached the bend in Doug's arm, his whole body bucked.

Natalie frowned. "I don't think you broke anything," she said. "You must've wrenched it awfully hard. But that spot where I just touched— there's not even any bone there."

Doug was breathing in hitches, uneven gasps that dampened his face with perspiration.

"We need to make you a sling," Natalie said. As a little girl, she'd wanted to be a nurse. She had never pursued the career, perhaps because it was her sister's, and the prospect of allowing Claudia to lead Natalie through life any more than she already had was unwelcome. "It will hurt less if your arm isn't dangling free." Natalie raised her arms over her head and took off her T-shirt.

"No," Doug got out. "Use mine."

"We can trade later," Natalie said, turning the fabric inside out so that no dirt and grime would lie against Doug's injury. "I don't want you to have to lift your arm." She twisted the cloth into the proper shape. "Let's get to where we can stand." She cast her gaze upward. "Ten feet. Do you think you can climb one-handed?"

The maneuver must've been agonizing to judge by Doug's face and suppressed grunts, and they didn't make it all the way to level ground, stopping once the incline grew gradual enough not to have to fear sliding.

Natalie stood behind Doug, a little higher up, and helped him ease his arm into a resting position before supporting it with the sling. Then she sat down on the slight slope, patting the ground beside her.

The lines of pain on Doug's face finally began to fade. "Thanks, Nat," he said. "That feels better."

She looked up at him.

"What's wrong?" Doug asked. He gestured with his good hand. "Besides the obvious."

The reply emerged with the force of something sicked up. "You would've left me!" Natalie cried. "Out here alone! Without you!"

Before they set out walking yesterday, Natalie had doubted her decision to marry Doug. Just for a fleet second, but still, in the moment that he'd leapt from the log, she'd realized how unfeeling that was of her, careless of the love she had been given. You didn't question a bond like theirs just because things had gone horribly wrong. Look at what Doug had been willing to do for her when it came down to it. She didn't want to be out here without him. She didn't want to be anywhere without him.

Doug lowered himself onto the forest floor, gingerly positioning his arm. "I was trying to save you," he said mildly.

"Oh, Doug," Natalie said. Tears stung her eyes, though there didn't seem to be enough of them to fall. "If you had died, I don't think I could have gone on without you." She said the words with more certainty than she'd spoken her vows just six days ago.

"Shh," Doug said. He touched the fingers of his good hand to her face. "Don't use up any bodily fluids. I'm here. I'm all right. My arm barely even hurts anymore."

The last was an obvious lie, as Doug's careful motions and pale complexion proved, but they both lay back on the dirt, blinking up at the blue-washed sky.

Suddenly, Doug rolled onto his side. "Is that a—" He broke off.

"What?" Natalie asked. "What do you see?"

Doug didn't respond, but began to scrabble up the final few feet of hill, using one hand and both feet to move like some demented creature, monkey-like in his excitement. "Nat!" he shouted over his shoulder. "Come see!"

The ground flattened out, and Doug straightened up and started running.

Natalie followed.

"Look!" Doug called out again. And—was he *crying*? Yes, his voice was thick with it, his face shiny. Natalie was about to urge him to save his tears—same reasoning he'd just applied to herself—but then she saw what he did.

A blaze on a tree, signifying a hiking trail.

Not the blue metal ones from the trail they had been attempting to find—this was a painted splotch—but it was a blaze nonetheless, pink in color, unmistakably man-made. Blazes demarcated trails, and who cared if this one ran through a completely different part of the wilderness, its origin and terminus unknown? A trail, any trail, meant the end of bushwhacking. A trail meant a return to civilization.

They both began turning—spinning almost, as if on a carnival ride—while they scanned the woods around them.

"There!" Doug shouted, and loped forward.

It took a while to find the next pink mark, but the ground was tamped down, appearing to delineate a path. Natalie found another flag readily enough, though pale and indistinct, then Doug the one after that, until they were both giving way to each other, trading places in a gleeful, expansive pantomime of politeness: "You go." "No, you."

They started running, Doug cradling his bad arm, in a race to find more blazes, as if the trailhead might lie just ahead.

It was Natalie who thought to stop them. Panting, she said, "We're probably farther than it feels. We shouldn't exert ourselves this much."

It was so hot out—more like the city than the mountains—and they were both perspiring. The truth was, they could be many miles from egress yet. The direction in which they were traveling might lead them to the end of the trail versus its beginning, and then they would have to turn around, retrace their steps. Still, there was no denying that being on land where human beings were meant to tramp had changed everything.

They walked until it grew too dark to see the marks, especially given how faint most of them were. Afraid they'd miss one and veer off course, they stopped beneath a sheltering tree, its boughs lending coolness after the heat of the day. Doug sat leaning back against the trunk's broad base, and Natalie settled down beside him.

"I hope this heat breaks soon," she said. "It can't be helping our thirst." A vicious vise had clamped itself around her skull, a headache that a whole bottle of Motrin wouldn't touch.

Doug's lips looked swollen, and there were whitish scales around his mouth. It made Natalie recall that a part of the rhythm of their days had gone missing. For how long? When was the last time Doug had crept off to seek privacy behind a tree? A gush, a spatter, even a trickle would be an indication of health.

"Honey?" she ventured. "Have you been…peeing?"

He appeared to consider. "Not since yesterday. You?"

Though it hurt to do so, Natalie shook her head.

He lowered his gaze. They both knew what this meant, Doug from his wilderness training, Natalie from her amateur interest in health and medicine. Twenty-four hours without relieving oneself constituted a warning. Forty-eight would signal dire danger.

Natalie resisted the urge to lick her lips, which must've resembled Doug's. She was ghastly, a witchy husk on her honeymoon. Would Doug ever again be able to see her as that pickup at the bar, or as a bride, consumed with her appearance? Both women seemed so frivolous now, yet their replacement was hardly appealing.

As if reading her mind, Doug gave her a look up and down. "Looking good, Mrs. Larson," he said, aping the voice of some classic TV show character whose identity now escaped Natalie. Her thoughts had grown sluggish as they followed the trail. Spotting the next painted marker had been challenge enough.

"It's the bra," she said, something vaguely clever coming to her at last, and was gratified when Doug let out a faint laugh upon catching sight of the grimy, dust-streaked lace cups and nylon straps that served as Natalie's only cover.

"I was supposed to give you my shirt," he said. "But I don't know if I have the strength to take it off."

"It's okay, I don't want it," Natalie said. "It's so hot out." She sounded whiny, querulous, and wasn't sure why. What she should've felt was a deep and abiding sense of relief. They would be out of here and back home soon.

"We'll be back home soon," Doug said softly, an eerie echo of her thought, minus the malcontent mood. "Bet you I spot the first trail marker tomorrow."

"You're on," Natalie murmured.

The nocturnal noisiness of the forest posed a wilderness counterpoint to the nighttime soundtrack she'd lived with all her life in the city, and Natalie felt herself start to drift off.

CHAPTER TWENTY-NINE

A tornado began to whirl inside Mia's chest. She couldn't take a single step away from the men who now had possession of her phone, let alone fight or pull free.

She knew these men. Recognized them anyway.

One had a weird, lopsided walk as he steered her over toward the side of the stoop. And the other was the scowler who'd been sitting on the hood of that shiny new car when Mia had gotten here earlier.

"We just want to talk to you," the one who walked funny said.

His friend couldn't seem to stop scowling—his face looked like it was formed that way—but he nodded in agreement. "Then you can have your phone back."

Like they were her mom, taking away phone privileges. Mia faced both men challengingly. "What were you doing in my aunt and uncle's apartment?"

The one with the weird walk stared back at her, not refuting Mia's charge, but not offering an explanation for it either.

"Funny," said the one who scowled all the time. "That's what we wanted to ask you."

The man's brows hung low over his eyes, and even the corners of his mouth turned in, but the other man, the one with the short leg, had a pleasant enough face. Mia wondered if he'd gotten teased a lot as a kid. That would be sad.

Her own face felt red and blistery beneath the sun's strong rays. She had forgotten to put on sunscreen. Mia whipped her head to the left. No police were around, not even the kind that gave parking tickets. People walked by on the sidewalk, caught up in the slipstream of the subway crush and entrances to stores. None of them seemed to notice what was happening on the stoop a few feet above them, but they were all comfortingly close by if Mia decided to scream. Unless they wouldn't hear her, connected as they were to iPods or chatting on their phones.

"Did you come here to visit your uncle and aunt?" asked the man who limped.

"Of course not," Mia said in a *duh* tone. "They aren't even home."

Both men exchanged looks.

"Where are they?" asked Scowly.

Mia frowned. If these men didn't know that Aunt Nat and Uncle Doug were on their honeymoon, then perhaps she shouldn't be the one to tell them.

Scowly and his friend must've been the people who entered the apartment—they looked like the type who would know how to pick a lock—and why would they have done that? To check and see if Aunt Nat and Uncle Doug were there? Had they left upon catching a glimpse of Mia, when she hadn't known anyone had been watching her? Creepy crawlies started to slither against her skin.

The man with the short leg took out his own phone and began using his thumb to scroll. He tilted the screen in Mia's direction. "Do you know this man?"

Mia looked down. The person looked to be about Uncle Doug's age, but he wasn't like Uncle Doug or his friends. This guy looked edgier. His hair was buzzed, and he had a bunch of piercings and tats.

"No," Mia said, shaking her head.

"His name is Craig Reynolds," the nicer man said. "That ring a bell?"

Mia shook her head again. "Who is he?"

The nicer man glanced at his friend or partner or whoever he was. Scowly was clearly the one in charge.

"Friend of your uncle's," the nicer man said. "Which brings us back to—"

"Why did you come down here?" Scowly interrupted, impatient. "If you knew your aunt and uncle weren't home?"

Mia had no answer for that.

The nicer man said, "Let's go. She doesn't know anything."

Even though Mia wanted nothing more than for both men to do what the nice one was suggesting, his words made her mad.

Scowly took a step closer, crowding Mia on the stoop. "When do you expect your uncle back?"

Mia thought fiercely. Aunt Nat had told her their plan. "In four more days," she said. "Wait, no, three. No, it *is* four."

The nicer man began shaking his head, looking almost fearfully at Scowly. "That isn't true. So long as they stick to the plan, Larson—or Reynolds, at least—will be back from the mountains today. Tonight at the latest."

Well, if he already knew the timing, then why had he asked her about it? Mia thought crossly. Besides which, he was wrong. No way were Aunt Nat and Uncle Doug coming home today. Their honeymoon was only half over; Mia had complained about its length. A whole week plus one day for travel! The city was boring without Aunt Nat.

Scowly twisted, wedging his body close enough to Mia's that she could feel the heat coming off him. Fear suddenly clenched her like a fist, and she reacted on sheer instinct, pushing past both men. Mia took all three stairs at a jump, then raced off down the sidewalk, ignoring the startled shouts of pedestrians she brushed against.

She was six blocks away when she remembered her phone.

Mia swerved into the first bodega she came to. She asked the man behind the counter if she could use his phone. She couldn't think of the number she was supposed to call to reach her mother at the hospital, but her father's she knew by heart. That was probably better anyway; Mia couldn't imagine what her mom would do if she got this news. Hunt the men down herself maybe, knock on every door in the city.

Her father didn't recognize the phone Mia was calling from and answered with a cautious "Hello?"

"Daddy," Mia said. Tears caught her off guard, and she gulped back a sob.

"Mi?" His voice rose in alarm. "What is it? What's wrong?"

The encounter felt creepier and creepier the further Mia got from it. Plus, she'd lost her phone, when she wasn't supposed to have been out of her apartment in the first place. Her mom was going to ground her for life.

"These men… They—" She broke off.

"Mia!" her dad cried. "Are you all right?"

The store owner took the phone gently out of Mia's hand. "Sir? My name is Ravi Patel. It is my phone that your daughter is using. She is all right. I am looking at her, and she is perfectly fine. But I think you had better come down to my store."

Mr. Patel also called the police. They arrived before Mia's dad— Mia figured there were usually police at the ready in a neighborhood like this—but held off talking to Mia until her father could get there. An ambulance came too—slow day in Alphabet City—and one of the EMTs gave Mia a once-over.

Her father ran into the store, red-faced and sweating, moons of moisture beneath the arms of his shirt. In the air-conditioned chill of the bodega, Mia had forgotten how hot it was outside. Her dad looked like he had run the whole way, or at least hopped out of the cab to finish the trip. The streets were clogged with traffic; the sound of beeps and honks and tires squealing entered from outside.

Her dad held out his arms, and smelly and sweaty as he was, Mia rushed at him. "What happened, Mi?" He stroked her hair away from her face with a damp palm.

One of the cops stepped forward. He was unnaturally tall, like an NBA player. "Sir? We've been waiting to take your daughter's statement. Do you think you could come with us to the back of the store? No one will bother us there." The cop took a closer look at her dad, peering down to do it. "And it's cooler."

Still holding on to each other, Mia and her father followed the tall cop, moving like some conjoined creature toward the refrigerated cases of soda and beer.

Mr. Patel came back and placed two water-beaded cans of Coke into Mia and her dad's hands, free of charge. Mia cracked hers and drank the whole thing down without stopping.

The cop asked Mia what had happened, and Mia heard her dad take in a sucked breath when she got to the part about the men approaching her on the stoop and asking a bunch of questions.

"What is there to be done about this, Officer?" Mia's dad asked when she'd finished.

The cop had been bending down to listen to Mia; now he straightened. "Probably not much," he admitted. He tapped a spiral-bound notepad against his palm. "In the end, what we've got is a voluntary conversation between your daughter and two strangers. The men do seem to have an interest in your...sister-in-law, is it? And her new husband?"

Mia's father nodded.

"But since both of them are currently out of town," the cop said with a glance at his pad, "the suggestion I would make is for you to warn Mr. and Mrs. Larson upon their return. They can keep an eye out and call us if they see anything strange."

"That's it?" asked Mia's dad.

"Well, your daughter's cell phone was technically stolen," the cop said. "My partner and I will take a walk around the neighborhood, see if we can find anybody who saw something. But my guess is that the men themselves are long gone by now."

Mia's father wiped his hand across his brow; it came away gleaming. "Christ." He sounded angry, and Mia looked up at her dad, fresh tears wobbling on the rims of her eyes. But then her father said, "You got away from them, Mi," in a marveling tone, and Mia felt her whole body go tingly with pride. Even though the men had never actually made a move to hold on to her. "Thank God, you got away."

Mia followed her dad and the tall cop back to the front of the store. Her dad walked over to the counter, extending his arm.

Mr. Patel reached out, and the two men shook hands.

"I wanted to say…" Mia's dad began, then stopped and cleared his throat. "I wanted to say thank you. For being here for my daughter."

Someone entered the bodega then, causing bells to jangle as the door was banged open. It was Mia's mom. Mia felt overcome by an utterly childish desire to run over for a hug; she was scared she might've whimpered the word *mommy*.

Her mother wrapped Mia in her arms, her skin still carrying the chill of the hospital. She spoke to Mia's dad over Mia's head. "What happened?" she asked in an accusatory tone. "You barely said anything in your message."

"I just wanted to make sure you knew Mia was okay," her father replied, his voice also unpleasant. Snippy. If Mia had sounded like that, she would've gotten scolded.

Mia lifted her head. The top of her mother's ducky scrubs felt clammy, sticking to her cheek, and she saw the tall cop watching her parents.

"If I can make one more suggestion?" he said.

Mia's parents both nodded.

"You might want to keep a closer eye than usual on your daughter for a while," the cop said. "It's likely that this will turn out to be an isolated incident, but a little extra caution never hurt."

CHAPTER THIRTY

Natalie and Doug woke up shivering against each other, legs intertwined, bodies pressed so close there was no space in between. The heat had broken in the night, and Natalie's half-naked state had become a real problem. Her flesh looked three-dimensional, polka-dotted with minuscule, raised white bumps.

Doug moaned, moving stiffly to separate their bodies.

"Your arm," Natalie said, through lips she had to pry apart. "How is it?" The answer was obvious, and Natalie winced at the sight of his pain. Her myriad discomforts were nothing. Doug needed Motrin. No, he needed morphine.

He blinked blearily until his gaze landed on her. "Oh shit," he said, startled. "You're cold. Natalie, you're really cold. You need this."

She was shaking so hard that she couldn't refuse, although the sight of Doug trying to get out of his shirt would've brought tears to her eyes, had she any left to cry. She helped untie the makeshift sling while Doug cradled his injured arm with his good one. Letting the right arm hang loose seemed an intolerable proposition.

"Just keep your shirt on," Natalie said through chattering teeth. "I'll be okay."

Doug shook his head, gritting his own teeth. "Pull it over my arm. I'll do the rest."

The maneuver seemed to take hours as Natalie inched the cloth toward Doug's shoulder, her hands trembling too hard for precision. "I'm sorry!" she cried tearlessly when she jerked him for the third time. "I'm so sorry, Doug!"

Finally able to refasten the sling around her shirtless husband, Natalie patted dry his perspiring face and slick chest. The sweat was a good sign. Still, she was frightened by how shrunken Doug had grown after only two days, his chest hollow and sunken in.

Natalie pulled his shirt over her head and slid her arms into its sleeves. Filthy and stinking as the material was, it delivered instant warmth and comfort.

They found the next tree with a blaze on it, this one nice and new looking, red instead of pink. Their moods brightened along with the flash of color. They had to be getting closer to the trail's outlet; the well-maintained blazes seemed proof. Natalie and Doug linked hands and set out walking.

"Look," Doug said, after maybe an hour had gone by, as indicated by the rising sun. With his arm in the sling, and the warmth generated by walking, Doug's voice sounded more normal. "We really need to look for something to eat."

"Sure," Natalie said over her shoulder. She had taken the lead because she seemed better able to spot the blazes. "I'll let you know when I see a food cart. Maybe we can"—she tried to chuckle, but wound up coughing—"review it."

"I'm serious," Doug replied. "Even unripe blackberries or raspberries would do. We have to get some nutrition into us—and fluids."

The idea caused Natalie's belly to start rumbling like an engine. She and Doug had seen some hard, white-green berries earlier on in their trip, before they had gotten lost. Bypassing them when they had a backpack full of supplies had been a no-brainer, but now the pimpled fruit stood out in Natalie's mind like nuggets of the purest ambrosia. Her mouth began watering, a hot rush of saliva that she swallowed down thirstily.

She started turning her face, peering into the dense brush on either side of the trail. Berries grew in wide, bushy thickets; they should be easy to find.

"Anything besides berries you can think of?" Natalie asked. There was some kind of bark you could chew on, but she didn't think it was nutritive. Doug knew more about this topic, though.

The sun seemed to be creeping upward by mere millimeters in the sky. Having something else to focus on would help pass the time and also take her mind off her feet, which had started to ache. Norlanders weren't meant for miles of trekking. Natalie's cheek hurt too, the injury radiating outward from its original spot until her whole face had become a fiery field.

"Not the right season for fiddleheads," Doug called back. "And I don't think the ferns themselves are edible. We might be able to find some wild onions, though."

"We might!" Natalie responded, almost joyfully. "I remember reading something about that in one of our guides." The thought of the guides made her start trembling again, even though she felt warmer now. Once, the idea of foraging without text and photos to keep them safe would've been unthinkable. Now the risk seemed glancing against its alternative. How long could they keep pushing their bodies like this—roaming through hectares of untraveled land—with no sustenance, and not even any water?

Water.

If she let that notion take hold in her mind, she would start cater-wauling like an infant.

The trail swerved abruptly, leading them into a dry creek bed, like some cosmic joke, a finger taunting them as they lowered themselves over rocks devoid of moss, their Norlanders scuffing through dirt as waterless and silty as powder. Natalie winced to see Doug favoring his arm, although the injury must have been improving. At some point, her husband had removed the sling, cramming the wedge of cloth into one of his pockets. His bare chest and back were sunburned, ruddy with an illusion of health.

A blaze appeared, slashed across a rock. Natalie and Doug aimed for it, then continued steadily descending.

"Hey, look over there!" Doug pointed to a brambly patch lurking amidst a second-growth forest high above the confines of this former river.

The tree trunks Natalie and Doug had to make their way between were meager by a stouter forest's standards, yet still sufficient to cinch their clothes and clip their limbs.

Natalie cried out, "I see them!" and they both broke into a run.

"Doug," Natalie said, her voice trembly once they'd arrived at a mass of thorned plants. "These don't look like blackberries. Or raspberries."

Doug plucked a nubbin off its stem and began rolling it around between his fingers, studying the stain left behind on his skin. "They might be thimbleberries."

Natalie's stomach gave a hard, painful wrench. Her hands, as she extended them, shook with longing. "Thimbleberries," she echoed, relieved. "I've heard of those."

Doug continued to examine the fruit in his hand.

"Can we... Should we eat one?" Natalie asked. Her voice sounded hesitant, but her mouth was already puckering in anticipation of the sour juice, a fibrous bite to gnash between her teeth.

Doug moved deeper into the tangle of green. "Remember the taste test," he cautioned. "We have to do this right."

Natalie's heart sank, and she quelled a spike of rage, not quite sure who it was directed toward. Doug was right, of course; he'd told her all about this. The taste test, with its ladder of steps, each posing slightly greater risk while ensuring the opportunity to see how the body reacted to a particular substance, was the only way to ensure edibility. But the test necessarily took time, a whole day's worth of excruciating, unbearable hours.

"We can't stick around here long enough for a taste test," she complained.

If they stayed much longer, they would die in this berry patch, ten feet from the trail. She felt suddenly, coldly convinced of it.

"We'll take some with us," Doug answered reasonably. Natalie realized that the anger she felt was at him. She pushed past her husband into the tangle of green, plucking one berry after another off its stem. She had just lifted a handful to her mouth—brushing the questionable ingredient against your lips was the first step of the taste test—when Doug batted her hand away and all the berries went flying.

She turned on him, eyes blazing, her dry mouth singed.

"I'll do it," Doug said softly, raising a single berry to his lips. "Really. Let me be the first in case they're no good."

Hunger had catapulted Natalie into a completely irrational place. Doug wasn't trying to deprive her; he was taking the risk upon himself.

They picked as many berries as they could, stuffing their pockets till the fruit bled through. Then they wound their way carefully back to the trail, making sure to identify a blaze before setting out again, not trusting their memories to settle on the right direction. Their vision had grown dull, cloudy from focusing so intently on the fruit, and for the first few minutes of walking, it was difficult to see much of anything.

Midway through the afternoon, a leaf from a tree overgrowing the trail brushed against Natalie's cheek, and she screamed.

Doug spun around. "I'm okay, Nat!" he called, as if she had asked after him. "Touched two of those suckers to my tongue and still standing. We'll be having fruit salad for supper."

Natalie placed one palm on the trunk of the tree that had assaulted her, and stood there, panting. The pain was so excruciating that she couldn't imagine ever moving again, adding to the agony in her face by lifting her throbbing feet. Her feet had done all that they could for her now. Taken her as far as they'd go.

"Nat," Doug said. Clarity returned to his voice as he walked toward her. "What happened? What's wrong?" He looked at her face and cringed.

"Is it bad?" Natalie asked.

Silence.

"Please tell me," Natalie said. "We don't have a mirror. I can't see my own face. It can't be worse than what I'm imagining."

"The cut looks infected," Doug said crisply. "You'll need antibiotics when we get back. And there might be a scar."

Doug had taken field medicine courses as part of wilderness preparedness, and the rational quality of his assessment did almost as much for Natalie's state of health as medicine could have. "All right," she said quietly. "Thank you for telling me."

Joining hands—Natalie shocked by how dry Doug's skin felt, scaly, like lizard flesh—they walked on side by side.

At least the blazes were now reliably easy to spot. There were no more of those deteriorated ones, sparse freckles or mere slits of pink paint, nearly invisible between the rutted lines of tree bark. The marks Natalie and Doug followed were crimson and glossy, propelling them onward with confidence.

Twilight besieged them—coming on fast after the endlessness of the day—and they had to stop for the night, unable to see even bright-red flashes on the trees.

The falling temperature posed a new problem. It had been cool and gray all day, although movement kept them warm enough. Now as they positioned themselves on the ground for sleep, taking painstaking care to avoid Doug's arm and Natalie's cheek, another night spent exposed to the elements seemed impossibly long, a bridge to morning that couldn't be traversed.

"We can use dirt," Doug said, his words slurred, hard to make out.

For a moment, Natalie thought that he meant for them to eat the substance, and she wasn't sure whether to laugh or cry.

"To cover ourselves," Doug went on. He was shivering, his body racked with spasms. "It will keep us warm. Leaves too."

Understanding dawned. Reassured not only that Doug was thinking straight enough to have come up with a plan, but also by the prospect of cushiony, blanketing soil, Natalie cried out agreement. She plunged both hands into the ground and began to scoop up fistfuls of earth.

CHAPTER THIRTY-ONE

Kurt bent over a battered tin pot full of fiercely boiling berries. It looked like a cauldron of blood. Smoke from the fire drifted into his face, causing tears to stream down his flushed and heated skin.

These berries were poisonous, but that didn't matter; Kurt didn't plan on using them for food. Sufficiently reduced, this mixture, plus a little resin, would be indistinguishable from paint.

Kurt's senses were alert to many aspects of wilderness life that passed most people unnoticed—edibles, signs of water underground, scat that determined where to build a blind—but he was still a novice in a lot of respects. A babe in the woods, he thought, with a quirk at the corners of his mouth that didn't feel familiar.

He wished he'd had time to learn tracking from members of his would-be utopia, skills that would allow him to be certain that the lighter of the campfire remained in the region. But Kurt had to believe that anyone coming through here would've been stopped, at least waylaid, by that canyon. Which meant he couldn't have gotten too far away yet.

Crossing the canyon seemed possible only at its narrowest chute, and not coincidentally, that was where Kurt had stumbled upon the defunct hiking trail. Such a trail probably no longer existed on maps; the flags on the trees were reduced to mere streaks, some worn almost completely away. But the surrounding forest floor was still flattened down, which would provide welcome relief from the humps and hillocks of bushwhacking over the rest of the terrain. If Kurt brought the trail back to life, freshening the painted blazes, ensuring they led in the right direction, wouldn't a hiker making his way through these rough and unforgiving woods be liable to follow it?

The marks would require monitoring; the lightest rain capable of washing this concoction away, while blasts of direct sunlight would fade it. But that should prove to be enjoyable work, as Kurt found most chores out here to be.

He fashioned a paintbrush from pine needles, bound together with vine, and lashed the bundle to a stick. Too eager to wait for the substance he'd created to cool, Kurt wrapped the cuff of his shirt around the hot pot handle and set out walking, scarlet liquid sloshing in the basin.

Kurt kept a hawk's eye out for eroded flags, some faded to a barely detectable pink, the washed-out color of a Band-Aid. He likely missed a few of the less visible ones, but found plenty during his trespasses, pausing at a wandering succession of trees to dip his homemade brush.

Applying the intense focus of an artist, Kurt made the blazes young again, creating the semblance of a pathway with dab after dab of brilliant, eye-catching red.

CHAPTER THIRTY-TWO

Natalie and Doug buried themselves beneath layers of dust and soil, like children playing in sand on the beach. Before fully encasing his arms, Doug performed the third stage of the taste test, clamping one of the berries between his lips and letting it stay there for half an hour, or as close to it as they were able to estimate, lacking a clock and given the fuzziness of their heads.

Dirt sifted from Doug's body as he lifted himself out of the shrouding blanket to stow the berry he'd spit out beside the rest of their stash, temptingly arrayed on a place mat made out of leaves.

"We can't afford to lose any," Doug explained, lowering himself again. "I'll chew one for real in the morning, and if I'm still okay by afternoon, then we can feast."

Natalie stared greedily at the tinge of berry juice on Doug's lips. She had trouble keeping herself from wriggling sideways and licking off the stain.

Warmth from the earth enfolded them, and their bodies grew heated against each other. The dry gusts of dirt became feathery duvets in Natalie's dreams, the crackly leaves turned into crisply ironed sheets, and she sank deeply into sleep.

It was charcoal dark when she awakened, too hungry for further unconsciousness. How many hours had passed? Any notion of time had become as loose and ungraspable as vapor. Natalie might have been sitting here for days; she might continue to remain in place forever, until the dirt solidified with her body fossilized inside.

Her stomach felt like a wild dog, ripping and clawing at her guts. She wanted those berries, needed them. The taste test took too long—so much time was unnecessary. Look at Doug, sleeping peacefully. He was fine. And he had gotten to eat, or at least accomplish a vague semblance of the act. She deserved no less.

Natalie raised herself on weak, shaky arms, soil shroud sifting off her as she craned her head to locate the berries in the dark. Doug had fashioned two separate piles on the leaf mat. One big, one small. Did he mean for her to eat the larger amount? Or, Natalie thought darkly, had he allocated that one for himself?

She stretched out her hand.

Doug's dirt-coated fingers landed on hers.

"Don't," he said.

The word sounded entombed, as if coming from someone no longer alive.

Natalie twisted around. Her mouth felt arid, every droplet of moisture wrung from what had once been spongy flesh, her lips a spider's web of painful cracks. While Doug's own mouth looked juicy, puffy with fullness and life.

He'd meant to take the larger portion of berries. If she hadn't woken up early, gotten to them first, that share would've been gone.

"Nat?" Doug croaked, recoiling. "Why are you looking at me like that?"

Natalie squinted in the blackness. The swelling around Doug's mouth wasn't an indication of health. He had a rash on his lips, like a grating of freshly ground red pepper.

"The berries aren't edible," he said dully. "Thank God you didn't try one."

Natalie felt a sob roll up from her belly. Her empty, gaping belly. Starvation was driving her mad. In that moment Doug had become a monster to her, a thief. She would've fought him for the berries, maybe even killed him for them.

She gripped her temples with her fingers. "What about you?" she asked, grating the words out. "Are you sick?"

"I don't think so," Doug said. "Just a tingle on my lips."

"That should go away," Natalie said, head still in her hands and hoping she was right. "You were right to be cautious. Oh, Doug, I'm sorry. You were right."

"Pays to be a chicken." Then he groaned. "I had to go and mention chicken."

Natalie laughed, the sound of it shocking in the night.

"Fried," Doug went on, upon hearing her laughter. "Can you imagine how amazing fried chicken would taste right now? Remember that place we gave five stars to...the one where they coated wings in Korean hot sauce?"

Natalie leaned closer to her husband, dirt a paste between their bodies. "Thank you for trying the berry first," she whispered.

Doug's fingers wormed through the soil, and they clutched at each other's hands.

Natalie swallowed a dry mouthful, devoid of saliva. "Frosting," she said. "That's what I keep thinking about. The bakery on Charlton Street that kept asking us to write a review. I could eat a whole tubful now of that frosting we thought was so awful."

Doug didn't answer.

"And a toothbrush," Natalie went on. "I want one of those almost as much as I want food. And not just because of the frosting." She tried to lick her teeth, but they were so tacky that her tongue stuck to the enamel.

Doug finally stirred himself to reply. "Remember when they introduced that weird kind with colored flecks in it?" he mumbled, falling back toward sleep, or some other lesser state. "What was up with that?"

"It was supposed to be like Funfetti," Natalie replied, also sleepily. "But it wasn't as good."

Neither one spoke after that.

Time passed as the planet circled ceaselessly and senselessly onward.

Doug looked like he belonged to another life form when he rose from his dirt coverings, skin powdery and beige, bits of leaf matter sticking to his flesh. Natalie wasn't sure whether the sight should've triggered laughter or a shriek of horror. In the end, she didn't have strength enough for either.

The sun hung in place overhead, a lemony lozenge in the sky, failing to provide much warmth. Shivering so hard that debris flew off their bodies, Natalie and Doug struck out to find the next blaze, aware that motion would be their only source of heat.

Doug trudged along, pointing out a succession of plants he thought might be edible. His behavior stood in direct contrast to the caution he'd exerted while overseeing the taste test, as if he were throwing off binds, giving up the need for vigilance. Natalie, duly chastened after their near miss, deterred each suggestion. But after a while she started to ignore Doug's mutterings, needing to concentrate to spot the shocking-red streaks amidst the foliage. The going seemed rougher today: obstacles in their path that they had to avoid, or shift out of the way with great effort, multiple obstructions requiring a change of direction altogether. Thirst thickened their throats and glued their lips together, as miles accumulated beneath their aching feet.

Late that afternoon, another whole day gone by, they finally ground to a halt. They had come to neither trailhead nor endpoint. Whatever trail this was, they weren't going to be able to keep going on it long enough for it to save them.

"We're due home tonight," Natalie said, her voice heavy with sorrow. "I think. Maybe it's tomorrow. Soon though."

Doug didn't seem to register what she'd said. He opened and closed his mouth a few times as if he had to get a running start before speaking. "Nat?"

She looked up from the matted leaves on the ground. "What?"

"I don't think we've been following a trail."

Doug sounded more lucid than he had all day, but the cloak of clarity didn't reassure her. Whether they died with their wits about them, or utterly scattered, what did it matter? They were still going to die.

"At all?" Natalie asked. "I know those earliest marks were pretty worn away. But the ones we've been seeing lately are in good shape."

"Probably all of them were this red color once and just faded over time," Doug said. "But that's how I know it must be a decommissioned trail. The DEC wouldn't allow variability in the blazes. And anyway, they use metal tags for trail markers now. I didn't remember that the other day. I wanted so badly to find a way out."

Natalie couldn't take another step and sank down against a tree, clasping both dirty knees with her hands. "You mean these marks aren't in use anymore? I guess that makes sense." She found she couldn't work up the strength to care. She'd moved past the shock of it already, without even feeling the impulse to deny it. Instead she was grieving for herself and Doug, for all they could've been, together.

Doug dropped down beside her. He turned his head in her direction, though it looked as if he couldn't quite bring her into focus. "We can keep following the blazes," he said. "I could be wrong. But I think we'd just succeed in tiring ourselves out." He let out a laugh, coarse and broken. "Even more than we already are."

Natalie lowered her face, attempting a nod, but was unable to bring her head back up again.

"Unless someone's out here with us," Doug said abruptly. His voice rose on an alarming note. "And painted those flags himself. To fuck with us. To get us worse lost."

Natalie mustered breath. "Oh, honey, I don't think so—"

"Sure!" Doug broke in raggedly. "You don't think anybody could be that malevolent? You don't know shit, Nat. You never did." He jerked his head around as if the hypothetical villain might still be there, observing their plight with glee.

And indeed the branches swung and stirred, as if somebody was lurking nearby. Natalie narrowed her eyes, trying to see. There couldn't be anyone there, could there? This was a delusion on her husband's part, contagious in Natalie's own weakened state.

The desperation of their situation had caused something to become unfettered inside Doug, uncorked a fury that had until now lain dormant.

He got to his feet, looming over Natalie while she hunched like a turtle on the ground. She felt so frail, and her husband's voice was so loud. That suspicious toss of his head—his gaze shooting behind every tree, into every cleft of rock—made her hesitate to so much as look up.

What she really wanted to do was scream.

Stop it! If you have this much energy, use it to come up with a plan!

But she didn't have enough strength herself for such a riotous display, neither to yell at him nor to say something that might result in them taking one more step.

"You don't know shit," Doug said again. He lowered his face into his palms. When he took them away, his features were smeared with streaks of dirt, like war paint. "How can you be so naive, Natalie?"

Allusion, she thought. *Naive, Natalie.* Or no, that was alliteration.

That she was thinking about the terms at this moment frightened her more than the fact that she had gotten them wrong.

"We already know there's a murderer out here!" Doug raged on. "We were the ones who found Craig's body, remember? We know that he was killed!"

It took Natalie a few seconds; she was still cringing away from Doug's anger and warrior-like stance. But then his words drifted back to her on a current of breeze.

"Craig?" she echoed, and paused to catch her breath. "How do you know his name?" She finally lifted her eyes. "Did you know the man who got shot?"

CHAPTER THIRTY-THREE

Mia's parents weren't talking to each other more since the *incident*—as they had taken to calling it—four days ago with the skeezy men outside Aunt Nat's apartment, but they sure were trading a lot of tight, angry texts, making plans, coordinating *logistics*. If Mia had been making progress on the whole get-to-stay-on-her-own thing, then the *incident* had screwed it up big time.

Today, since her mother was still working extra shifts—that Shelley person was really sick, like with something that lasted—Mia had to go with her dad way the heck up to the wilds of the Bronx while he led a scrimmage. Might as well have been Australia. Mia would act as manager, record goals and penalties and the final score. Too bad her dad coached field hockey in the fall. No cute boys to watch run around on the field.

Mia's mother stopped her in the kitchen, smoothly lifting the coffee carafe out of Mia's hand. "This wasn't supposed to become a habit, Mi."

"Fine," Mia said. "I'll have tea instead. It has just as much caffeine."

"Have herbal," her mother said, the kind of suggestion that was really an order. "Hey, Mi?" her mom added. "Your father says you told the police that the men—you know, the ones from the incident—asked about another guy. Craig Something."

"Yeah," Mia said. "I can't remember his last name though."

Mia's mom began studying her, but finally she nodded, as if satisfied Mia was telling the truth. Which really ticked Mia off since she basically never lied, at least not directly. Maybe an oversight once in a while, something left out, or an exaggeration. Still, did her mom have to act so *distrusting*? In a way it was flattering, like Mia had a way bigger life than she did, the kind where stuff actually happened.

"And you never got to tell me what you were talking about last week, what Uncle Doug's groomsman said," Mia's mother went on. "The thing he didn't tell anybody else."

Mia felt her face fire. Still not a lie, but Mia knew she'd made what Mark had talked to her about on their walk back to the hotel sound like a big deal, when in truth, it had been too meaningless even to mention.

"Mia? I'm just trying to clear up some loose ends, if I can. Things seem to have gotten kind of…out of whack since the wedding."

Mia could see her mother gearing up. She wasn't going to let this go. "Mark just wanted to make sure the canoe stayed a surprise." She shrugged. "He asked me not to say anything to Aunt Nat about it."

Mia's mother looked relieved, and Mia flushed again. She wished there was something she could do that really would startle her mom, make her stop and take notice.

Then again, there had been something weird, not about what Mark had said, but how he had said it. He'd seemed on edge, awkward kind of, and Mia had wished that it'd been her making him feel that way. Why would a *boat* make anyone nervous?

"Oh shoot," her mom said, glancing at her phone. "I'm late. Can't keep this new schedule straight." She began writing a text so fast that it practically sizzled, and then Mia's mother was gone.

Her father showed up a few minutes later—buzzing to be let in like some kind of guest—and asked with this I'm-so-sorry-you're-dead kind of sympathy how Mia had been doing. Meaning since the *incident*. The two of them rode the subway uptown in silence, swaying and swinging and grabbing on to separate poles.

The truth was, Mia hadn't thought very much about the *incident* at all, at least not once her phone had been found. One of the people who hung out in front of the apartment building saw when it got dropped in the gutter—a brand-new iPhone—and went to retrieve it. Steal it, more likely. But whoever it was admitted to having the phone when the police questioned them, which Mia had to admit was pretty decent. Maybe the neighborhood wasn't as bad as all that.

When they got to the school, Mia's father handed her a clipboard.

"I'm going to call every foul, so keep a close eye out, okay? I need a record because the parents get irate when I make cuts." He jogged onto the field where a group of girls in micro shorts swarmed him.

Mia glanced at the sheet of paper clipped to the board. There was a grid of boxes that didn't make much sense. She lifted her eyes—the sun glaring, even this early in the morning—to see what was taking place on the field. How complicated could this game be? Just a bunch of girls around Mia's age running between two goals. But she felt distracted, unable to focus. Mia let the clipboard drop to the ground. This was just practice. She probably didn't really have to concentrate until the scrimmage started.

She drew her phone out of the pocket of her not-so-micro shorts and swiped at the screen. In addition to the fact that she'd had no life without it, Mia was glad to have her phone back because of the pictures she had taken of Mark and Brett. Her phone was the only place they existed, unless if she went back to Aunt Nat and Uncle Doug's apartment. And with her parents acting like jailers these days, that wasn't gonna happen.

After the super-tall policeman had brought her phone back—giving it to her mother instead of Mia, which had to be like a violation of her civil rights or something—Mia had downloaded an app that compared photos to faces online. Mia had searched through her mom's stuff, but couldn't find a copy of the wedding program. Unlike Aunt Nat, her mom was not the scrapbooking type. So now, instead of having to scroll past hundreds of links, with only a guess as to Mark's last name, Mia had a way to hone in on exactly the right guy—and hopefully Brett too.

She felt pretty clever to have thought of this, almost like a cop herself.

Mia bent over and placed her phone on top of the clipboard so that she would catch sight of any notifications. The sun climbed higher in the sky, Mia roasting beneath it. Sweat glistened on her bare arms. It'd been hot ever since they'd returned from the wedding, even though the weather people kept forecasting an end to the heat wave. Out on the field, the girls were swigging out of water bottles, but Mia had forgotten to bring hers. Had the scrimmage started already? A couple of shouts rose up from the field, and then one girl was suddenly surrounded by the others, like a gazelle by a pack of lions. Probably she'd scored a goal.

Mia crouched down and checked off a box on the grid.

Her phone dinged, and she snatched it up. She had to walk away from the field, find some shade beneath a tree in order to see the screen.

The calls and cheers from the field grew distant.

No one else was on campus; the school grounds had the graveyard feel of summer. With the rays of sun blocked by branches, the temperature dropped, and Mia actually shivered.

She could make out her screen, and what had popped up didn't have anything to do with the photo app. Instead, it was a reminder on her calendar. Aunt Nat and Uncle Doug were coming home tonight. Mia's heart lifted with gladness. She could go downtown and see them tomorrow. She wondered if Scowly and his friend with the weird walk were still looking to find her aunt or uncle, or that Craig Whoever guy. Mia definitely didn't want to run into the men from the *incident* again.

There was a shrill whistle from the field, and Mia jumped, scraping her arm against the tree trunk. Her eyes had to adjust as she left the dimness and protection of the leaves. Still nobody around, but shouts of protests rose through the air like smoke. Mia trudged in their direction. It wasn't only the shade that had caused the temperature to drop—the sky was graying over, and it seemed to be growing cooler in general, the heat finally releasing its grip on the city. Hey, the weather people had been right for once.

Mia saw her father standing at one end of the field, not looking at the play but casting his gaze around impatiently.

"Mia!" he called when he saw her. "Did you catch that foot foul?"

Some of the girls on the field stopped playing and looked over at her.

Mia caught a glimpse of the clipboard, abandoned on the grass, and broke into a jog. She felt a pinch of anger in her stomach. Didn't she have her own life to lead?

Her phone dinged again, and she ground to a halt, forgetting about the scrimmage, the girls, even her father.

The sun was gone from the sky, and so she could see.

She'd been sent a link, which she clicked on.

PhotoSearch has found a match for your entry.

CHAPTER THIRTY-FOUR

Doug didn't speak for what felt like hours while Natalie stared up at him. She clambered onto her hands and knees, then lifted herself off the ground. The motion ate up the final reserves of energy she had.

"Did you know the man whose body we found?" she repeated.

At first it seemed as if Doug had no memory of what he had said. He didn't appear to understand what Natalie was asking him. He stared at her, trying to lick his lips with a tongue that contained no moisture, flopping out of his mouth like a dead thing.

But then the cool light of descending evening lit his eyes. "Of course I knew him, Nat. He was my best friend."

"Mark and Brett are your best friends," she whispered.

Doug shook his head. "You know how there are always people you're closer to, and then others you're less so?" he said. "Or maybe you don't know," he added, his tone taking on a knife edge. "Your bridesmaids had to be dug out of a vault. You haven't seen Val or Eva since we announced our engagement."

Natalie tried to swallow, but couldn't. The reflex had been lost. She had never experienced this side of Doug before—a careless cruelty that left her skinless, flayed.

"Mark and Brett were part of my gang, like I told you. But they weren't the guys whose backs I really had, or who had mine. Not the ones I—how would your former girlfriends put it—clicked with. Nope. That was Craig. My bestie, as your niece might say."

Doug was losing it; he hadn't been making sense off and on for a full day now. This announcement sounded like it could've been delivered by someone in the last stages of delirium, or a particularly mean drunk. If Doug had had such a good friend—someone Natalie not only hadn't met, but had never heard a word about—then why wouldn't he have been at their wedding? She had no idea what was real, true, to be trusted, and what might've been the product of hunger, pain, and dehydration.

Except that the things Doug was saying did contain a certain note of truth. They cast light on a stack of events that in hindsight seemed just a little too ordered, poised to fall like a row of dominoes. The river eating their GPS, and Doug's sudden suggestion to hike out early, when he'd never given up on an outdoor challenge in all the time Natalie had known him. And a trail being conveniently located right nearby.

Not to mention Doug's earlier scythe-sharp statement that Natalie didn't know shit. She'd had no idea. Of anything. She still didn't.

Betrayal began to crawl across her body like a swarm of flies.

"Doug." Natalie raised her head, meeting her husband's gaze in the low, lavender light. "Why did we come here?"

Again he seemed to have lost the ability to answer.

Fury and confusion gusted through Natalie, and she ran at her husband. "Doug!" she shrieked. "Tell me! What have we been doing out here? What are we doing?"

The wound on her cheek pulsed with every word. She had to stop shouting, or it would burst through her skin, leave it open and caving.

Plus, yelling at Doug was accomplishing nothing.

It was like screaming at an animal struck down in the road, succeeding only in making Natalie feel even worse about herself.

How easily fooled was she? How hungry had she been for someone to love her that she would have settled for a love as full of holes and craters as this?

Doug stood there, blinking and uncomprehending.

Was this Craig guy real, and even if he was—a best friend Doug had lost touch with—was he the murder victim they had found, or had the two simply become linked in Doug's mind, the result of some hallucinatory, compromised state?

Her husband leaned forward to grab Natalie's hand, and she screamed.

Doug's fist felt like burlap, or hide. Something so slick and impenetrable that water would sluice right off its surface, accounting for its arid touch.

"Do you hear what I hear?" Doug demanded.

Wasn't that the start of a Christmas carol? But the notes rising in Natalie's head sounded more like Jack Nicholson. *Heeeere's Johnny.*

Doug began dragging her toward a stand of trees.

Tiny hearts blurred before her eyes as she fought to keep up—the dimpled hoofprints of deer on the ground—amidst other less-identifiable depressions. All headed in the same direction, toward some destination.

Natalie and Doug followed the tracks like bread crumbs.

It began as an inky black line, winding and writhing like a snake through the undergrowth before widening out. The sound Doug claimed to have heard seconds earlier finally became audible, her husband's senses so uncannily heightened that Natalie feared anew for his sanity.

A burble, a rounded chuckle like the giggling of many children.

Water.

Doug reached it first. He dropped to his knees, plunging his arms into the stream, and began splashing handfuls over his face.

"Careful," Natalie wheezed as she caught up. Every breath cost her now. "Don't get any in your mouth." She too got down on the ground and began scrubbing the accumulation of dirt and dried sweat and grit from between her fingers and underneath her nails. It was too cold to slide all the way into the creek, though the notion was tempting: the thought of washing off her entire body. But hypothermia was a risk at these temperatures, especially in wet clothes after the sun went down. Besides, just seeing clean, pink skin on her hands again was mind-altering.

Doug stared at her.

Craig. Natalie heard the name in her mind. *Of course I knew him, Nat.*

"What?" she asked, though Doug hadn't said anything out loud.

"Did you just tell me not to get any in my mouth?"

Natalie frowned, then nodded.

"Are you nuts?"

"Am *I* nuts?" Natalie rose to her feet. "This from the man who proposed a whole menu's worth of inedible foodstuffs today as if he'd never even heard of the taste test?"

Doug's hand shot out, pointing like an archangel up to the heavens, toward some distant alpine summit where the stream had its source. "This is the clearest, purest water I've ever seen. It's like God put it here in front of us. To save us. Before it was—"

He didn't finish the sentence, but he didn't have to. *Before it was too late.*

Still, Natalie shook her head, confounded. "Doug, we just rinsed about four pounds of dirt into this water. I've got news for you. The things in here that will make us sick are very, very small. As in microscopic." She glared at her husband, fuming. "In other words, you wouldn't be able to see them!"

Doug drew back. Natalie had never spoken to him like that before, and she wondered if her tone wasn't born of the widening gap between them. Was there a connection between them taking a honeymoon and a murder victim being found in the same place? Did Doug really know the dead man? Because if he did, then one thing was for sure. Her husband had had some reason for leading them into these woods.

Doug continued to point at the creek, avoiding her eyes.

Natalie knelt down beside the streambed. The water leaped over mossy rocks, silvery sheets forming miniature cascades. It looked like something out of Eden. But appearances could be deceiving. Especially out here.

"Doug," Natalie tried again. "There's a reason why we were so careful to pack in water from home—and backup batteries for the purifier—and iodine tabs for if we really got stuck." She knee-walked over to her husband, placing both hands on his grizzled face. A coppery scruff had grown in to cover his cheeks and chin. "You know as well as I do. Some creature could've died miles upstream and fallen into the water, polluting it. There's runoff from animal waste. The soil harbors spores our bodies can't tolerate. There are a billion reasons not to drink this water. Literally."

Her stomach lurched, and she used a newly cleaned hand to rub strands of dry skin off her lips. They floated like feathers to the ground, her body ridding itself of layers, paring itself back to its core. Before too long, that core would start to disintegrate too. You needed water to survive. They'd already made it an amazingly long time without any, and Natalie wanted to scoop up a handful from this stream as badly as Doug did. She could feel the silvery wash on her throat, taste its cold, clear nothingness. She got to her feet and stumbled away, not trusting herself.

"Goddamn it!" Doug shouted.

She blanched mid-step, and turned.

"I'm going to die if I don't get a drink," he told her. "Is that what you want? For me to die? Do you know how much my fucking head hurts?"

Natalie felt a tearless sob rise in her throat. "You'll die if you do." How easily, seamlessly they had come to acknowledge the proximity of death.

"Maybe," Doug replied. "But it'll take longer."

His eyes met hers like blazes, and Natalie knew she couldn't oppose him any longer. She'd never been able to oppose him really—Doug had always overpowered her. He'd even gotten her to come out here to complete whatever wicked task had wound up getting his friend killed.

Doug must've seen the fight wilt in her eyes for he lay down on his stomach, flattening himself out on the ground. He angled his face beneath a spot in the creek where the water tumbled over a series of stones, flowing through open space as if from a faucet. Liquid coated his hair and beard in silvery droplets, and Doug tossed his head back and forth, welcoming the torrent.

Then he opened his mouth and drank.

Natalie watched her husband with a feeling of impending doom, as if the judge's gavel had just slammed onto the block.

It took minutes for Doug to slake his thirst. Natalie could hear him slurping and glugging, and the noises triggered spasms in her own belly, sharp and painful. She had to turn away from the sight of the syrupy water. She could feel its slippery unctuousness coat the insides of her cheeks as if she had actually drunk. Her mouth cramped, agonizingly.

Doug gulped until the water began to overflow and bubble out, till he appeared to lack the strength for one more swallow. His face slackened. Water flooded over his lips and teeth, dripping back into the stream, an abundance sufficient enough to waste. Then he jumped to his feet, shaking moisture from his head like a dog, and laughing.

"Natalie!" he called out. "You've got to have some! It's the most delicious thing you ever tasted! It's nectar! The elixir of the fucking gods!"

Natalie watched him, her eyes stinging with unshed tears.

Doug lay down again on the ground, spent and wiping his mouth with the back of one hand. "Oh God, that was better than sex. Don't deprive yourself, Nat. Nothing that good could be bad for us."

She wasn't sure if he registered the lack of logic in his words. A heroin addict might've said the same thing. She averted her face, hoping to spare Doug the knowledge in her eyes.

It was now full dark. Her husband was going to start to get cold. Natalie went to him, dabbing at his wet hair and flesh with the hem of the shirt he had given her to wear.

Doug looked at her as she dried him. There was a sharpness to his vision that hadn't been there for days. The water had revived him, restored him to life. Natalie was a fool to avoid the same thing.

She'd viewed Doug's hysterical ardor as he drank with a feeling of disgust, behavior akin to gluttony. But in this moment Natalie envied her husband the self-indulgence. He had given in, done what they both knew not to, and for Doug all the aches and pains of a desiccating body were gone.

Although even without experiencing the benefits of hydration, something had enlivened Natalie too, at least a little bit. The doubt she now harbored about her husband was injecting its own brand of alertness, a jittery buzz through her veins.

There on a bed of pine needles, sitting beside Doug in the dark, Natalie found her husband's hand like a targeted missile, while she met his gaze precisely.

"Tell me the truth," she said.

The pause ambled out, as if they had all the time in the world, though for Natalie the silence seemed ready to snap.

At last Doug said, "There were drugs in the hull of our canoe."

CHAPTER THIRTY-FIVE

Natalie half turned in the blackness. She wondered if Doug could make out her expression: the tight folds of her face, a stitch between her brows. "What?"

Doug took a breath. "Maybe I'd better backtrack."

Natalie leaned against the trunk of a tree, while Doug scooted to follow her. "Yes," she told him. "Maybe you should."

Doug's bare chest rose and fell steadily. Even his breathing was easier since he'd drunk from the stream. "There were five of us growing up," he began. "Me, Mark and Brett—who you know—Luke, and Craig."

So there really was a Craig.

"Actually," Doug said. "You met Luke too."

Natalie frowned, going back in her mind over their guests.

Doug seemed to read her thoughts. "Not at the wedding. In that town you liked. Wedeskyull."

"The outfitting place?" Natalie asked, and Doug nodded. "One of your childhood friends is a river guide in the Adirondacks?"

Doug stared off into the distance, although his vision couldn't have penetrated far. Clouds had slid in, threadbare and diffuse, but sufficient to blot out the thin hook of moon. The starless, lightless sky was a bubble all around them, as if they were floating underwater.

"Not a real one," he said.

A chill washed over Natalie that wasn't borne of the night.

"You don't know what it's like," Doug said. "I was being an asshole earlier, the way I talked about your friends, and I'm sorry for that, but I was also getting at something. When you're part of a group, it becomes like your family. Closer, in our cases, since our families were all so screwed up." He threaded their fingers together. "When we were little kids, the five of us would've done anything for each other. We had an unspoken pact: if one got in trouble, the others got him out. Like soldiers who won't leave a man behind."

Doug's renewed vigor was amazing—his voice strong, his mind and memory operating at full bore. "I hadn't seen Craig or Luke for years— since we graduated high school—which is why they weren't invited to the wedding. But still, when Mark and Brett told me Craig was in trouble, I knew I didn't have a choice."

What had happened was still murky; Natalie felt as if she were swimming in a thick gruel of questions. "Why did you have a falling-out?" she asked, settling on just one of them. "With two of your friends, I mean."

Doug stared into the darkness again. "It was for the same reason that Craig needed help now. Back when we were in high school, he and Luke began getting into trouble. I mean, all of us were kind of acting out at that time. I spent more days in suspension in tenth and eleventh grade than I did in class. I've told you about that."

Natalie nodded.

"But Craig and Luke got into some serious shit. Hard drugs, gambling. A bet on that night's game to pay for their next fix, dealing to schoolkids so they could pay off whoever they'd just lost to. It was a mess. *They* were a mess. Mark and Brett and I had to cut them loose or get dragged down even further than we already were."

Natalie felt herself drifting, away from the truth Doug was holding out. Had this distance always been there between them, even if she hadn't known about it?

Doug didn't appear to notice her waning attention. "It hurt like hell to cut my best friend out of my life—like slicing off a piece of my skin," he said. "I always felt guilty about it, especially because Craig never really got himself back on track. I should've done something to help my friend instead of just abandoning him."

"You were just a—" Natalie thought to say, still from very far away, as if this story had nothing to do with her own life at all.

"Kid. Right," Doug replied. "But that's why when I learned the trouble Craig was in again—he owed money to these really bad dudes—I knew I had to step up. We weren't just kids anymore. And Craig's life was in danger."

She was floating back now, like a balloon without a string. "The men who came to our wedding," Natalie guessed.

Doug shook his head. "They only supplied the product. Luke found them—a contact from his past because Luke did manage to go straight. Kind of. He lives in a monastery somewhere in New York State, rarely sees other people."

Natalie was having trouble keeping up, and she didn't think that was due solely to thirst and hunger. Her whole identity felt shifted. Who was this man using terms like *product*, who had friends that got into life-and-death trouble?

Doug compressed his lips. "Hold on," he said. "I want another drink."

Natalie heard him make his way through the dark: elbowing branches aside, leaves crinkling underfoot. The sounds continued even after his departure. Whispery breezes, sudden, sharp cracks, the burr of insects. A bird's insistent caw. Natalie jumped and swung around, sure that somebody else had appeared, but saw only Doug returning from the stream, droplets glistening on the stubbly hairs on his chin.

Natalie tried to lick her lips, and failed. Her words tasted chalky on her tongue. "So the body we found was Craig's."

The statement thudded like a stone.

No wonder Doug had become unhinged when he first saw the body, even more so than such a discovery would've normally warranted. Natalie could still hear how his high, yowling screech slit the silence, recall Doug stumbling across the forest floor, his loss of control greater than any dose of whiskey could've imposed.

Her husband turned away, but not before Natalie saw his eyes begin to shine. He could cry again; he had tears. The water was bringing him back to life—but what kind of life? Natalie had known so little about it, about him, this man she'd married. Their outdoor excursions, the obscure restaurants they took such joy in finding, nights they'd spent drinking, talking, having sex, all felt as if she and Doug had had stand-ins for their roles, two other participants put there in their places.

He lowered himself down beside her. "Guess what we tried to do for Craig didn't wind up working," he said, bitterness coating his tone.

"What *did* you do?" Natalie asked. Was she always this slow and stupid? God, how she wanted to make a trip down to that creek herself, drink from the same devil's fountain as Doug had.

He let out a shaky sigh. "So Craig needs money, right?" he said. "The kind of sum that isn't easy to come up with, even illegally."

Doug seemed to be waiting for something. Natalie gave a nod.

"And he needed it fast," Doug said. "The men he owed weren't exactly patient types. I didn't think there would be anything for me to do. It's not like I had access to that amount of cash."

Natalie nodded again.

"But then Mark told me a fact about drugs, and New York State, that became important. Provided I didn't mind the prospect of altering our route."

CHAPTER THIRTY-SIX

Natalie turned her head, and Doug caught her eyes in the dark.

"Altering our route," she repeated. She realized with a quiver of shame that beyond the name of their put-in at Gossamer Lake, she'd never made it her business to know which direction they were traveling, or much of anything else about their itinerary. Maps again maybe, her lifelong aversion to them. It wasn't like she would've been following along. Or perhaps her hands-off attitude stemmed from an even worse weakness. Her tendency to defer to Doug, relinquish responsibility when he was around.

"Yes," Doug replied. "We had to go due north instead."

Natalie waited.

"So, Mark's a teacher, right?" Doug went on, taking in a breath. "He picks up stuff from his kids. You wouldn't believe what eleven-year-olds get up to these days."

"Okay," Natalie responded.

"In Canada, drugs carry twice their U.S. street value," Doug told her.

"Any drugs. All drugs. I purchase half a kilo of horse for $50K here in the good old US of A, get it across the border somehow, and boom, I can sell it for 100 thou."

Doug was sounding less and less like the man Natalie had married—or any man she would have wanted to marry. She moved her tongue around in her furry mouth. Her hands curled into fists she was surprised she had the strength to make.

"Ah, but getting it across the border," Doug continued. "That's the rub. Customs, drug-sniffing dogs, and those aren't the only ways to get caught. There are video cameras along the highway whose tapes Homeland Security scans, looking for indicators of illegal activity. They profile. Two guys traveling together, a guy alone, who knows what looks bad to someone, sets off an alert?"

And with those words, things finally came clear, a whole new reality appearing out of the gloom. "Getting something across the border where it isn't manned, though, would be much easier," Natalie said. "Say, in the middle of the wilderness."

Doug dropped his head. "Exactly."

"But we weren't supposed to be anywhere near Canada," Natalie said. "I would've asked why you wanted to go that far when there was plenty of backcountry to explore here on our side."

"That's where Luke came in," Doug told her.

"The guide."

Doug nodded.

"The *fake* guide," Natalie bit out. This lie was a swelling body, extending outward, its boundaries uncontained. "I knew he was too good to be true. That new-age crap about everybody paddling their own river. He was straight out of central casting."

"We prepped him," Doug muttered.

"And that's why he led us to the lake to talk," Natalie said. "Instead of meeting in the building. He didn't really work there."

Doug studied her in the dark; Natalie felt more than saw his eyes.

"Why did he come find us that first night?" she asked. "On the island?"

"You weren't supposed to see him," Doug said, still low. "I had been planning to meet Luke in the woods. We had that great sex, and then I fell asleep—"

He broke off as Natalie sent him a stare.

"—so he had to come look for you," she finished. "I heard him from the water."

Despite his renewed vigor and health, Doug looked miserable. "Up till then, I wasn't sure if I'd have to go through with it or not. Craig was still trying to come up with another plan. We arranged for Luke to give the signal, yay or nay."

"And obviously it was yay," Natalie said. She was finding it hard to breathe. "So Luke put the drugs—heroin, was it?—in the canoe that night."

Doug shook his head. "Mark and Brett took care of that at the wedding. What Luke did was mark the right route on the map for after I dropped the GPS. I did that deliberately," he added, with the air of relief that accompanies someone outside a confessional. "The route took us to a spot a few miles south of the Canadian border. I knew you might follow our progress on the GPS, but maps you'd leave to me."

Slick, slimy deceit enrobed her. The mud at the bottoms of the rivers that had gotten them here. "And did you arrange for those... those drug dealers to show up?" Natalie raked air into her lungs. "Before our *wedding*?"

"No!" Doug said. "I swear. They were supposed to meet Mark and Brett earlier. They were late. We all got pissed off about it."

"Imagine," she bit out. "Drug dealers not keeping reliable hours."

Doug's mouth hiked a smile, which vanished when he saw Natalie's expression.

Shards of understanding—each a sharp sliver of glass, stained bloody red and lurid—were finally filling in to form a whole picture. It wasn't water Natalie lacked now, but air. She was unable to catch her breath. "So this is why we're on a backcountry honeymoon," she said numbly. "To accommodate your friend's drug deal."

Doug faced her. "We're on this honeymoon because I love the outdoors," he said, taking both her hands in his. He moved easily now, rejuvenated, all prior injuries and wounds healed, or at least unfelt. "And I wanted you to love it too. I wanted to show you all the majesty and greatness there is out here. You have to believe that. We've been preparing for this trip almost as long as we were planning the wedding." He swallowed, a smooth, easy ripple of his throat. "That our plan happened to accommodate what my old friend suddenly needed… Well, that was just luck."

"*Luck?*" Natalie breathed, hardly able to force the word out. She tried to lean back against the tree, but didn't have the strength to lower herself in stages and wound up hitting it hard. Her eyes burned with unshed tears.

Doug's gaze gripped hers. "It wasn't supposed to go this way, honey. The getting-lost part. This was supposed to be simple. Easy. Two days in, two days out."

"The Craig-getting-killed part," Natalie offered. "I assume that wasn't supposed to happen either."

Doug flinched, and she felt a savage gladness.

"There's one more thing I haven't told you," he said after a pause. "About why I had to help Craig."

Paralysis was settling into her limbs, her lips, her entire being, and Natalie's eyes fluttered shut. "One more thing," she repeated flatly.

"You're just…so unquestioning, Nat," Doug said. "You accept stuff. Maybe that worked for me. For us," he added with a flash of insight that struck her as significant, although she lacked the strength to explore it. "But did it ever occur to you to wonder…"

"What?" Natalie asked in a barely audible monotone. "Wonder what?"

"That huge apartment my mother lives in," Doug went on. "You know I didn't grow up rich. How did we pull such a thing off?"

Natalie frowned. She'd thought about it, of course—such a grand apartment with an address to match—but only vaguely. "So?" she asked, her anger directed as much at herself as him. "What does that have to do with helping Craig?"

Doug shifted on the ground. "Remember I told you how my mom and I nearly became homeless?"

Natalie shrugged one shoulder in sharp assent.

"Well, Craig is the reason we never actually did. The eviction notice had been slapped on the door and everything. My mom planned to go to a shelter… I think she thought they'd take care of things for her. But I knew what shelters were really like. I was planning to live on the street, with or without my mom."

Natalie felt a mass blocking her throat, and fought to swallow.

"And then Craig stepped in," Doug concluded. "He had this big win one weekend—the biggest of his life. And he was really close to my mom. Craig's own mother is a complete whack job, used to go on retreats to Nevada, leave Craig alone for weeks at a time. She got herself renamed… Blossom, Flower, something like that. Total flake." Doug scrubbed the hair out of his face, but not before Natalie caught a sheen of fury in his eyes. "Compared to her, my mother was everything a boy could want. Always around, so grateful for anything anyone did for her. You can imagine what Craig buying the apartment— saving her from abject disaster and freeing her up for the rest of her life—accomplished."

Even in her disintegrating state, the scope of the act stunned Natalie. "I can."

"So then you can probably also see that when the chips were down in Craig's life—when he was as desperate as I once was—I couldn't turn my back on him again."

Natalie got the two words out once more. "I can."

"Craig was going to take care of the really illegal part: floating the canoe across the border. All I had to do was get close, navigate the tricky terrain. Craig's lived in the city his whole life. Until this week, he'd never..." Doug broke off, rolling his hands into fists. "He'd never even been on a hike."

Natalie stayed silent.

"If we'd gotten stopped," Doug went on, "we would've pretended we had no idea anything was inside the canoe. It wouldn't even have been pretense in your case. That's part of why I kept you in the dark."

Branches crackled to their left. Natalie squinted, trying to bring them into focus.

"I'm sorry, Nat," Doug said softly. "I'm so sorry for everything." Then he added, "I just want you to understand. Why I did it. Even if it wasn't the right thing to do."

She still didn't answer.

"Hold on," Doug said, and rose.

"More water?" Natalie asked sarcastically.

"Um, no, not now," Doug said, but he sounded distracted.

He walked off into the woods.

CHAPTER THIRTY-SEVEN

Not one, but two.

    After the dearth of company Kurt had suffered since staggering out of the river and into these woods, the number promised plenty of a level he'd never dared hope for.

Two, the first even integer, the amount comprising every pair, the magic threshold needed to create human life.

And two, the number of hikers headed toward Kurt's camp.

They'd been lured by the false hiking trail, just as Kurt had intended. Since painting the flags, Kurt had taught himself the rudiments of tracking, and he was able to monitor his impending visitors' progress, crouching to trace sets of footprints in the soil, finding indicators of disturbance in the woods. Who needed the pseudo-utopians to teach him anything, when Kurt was capable of such mastery on his own?

The duo wore strange shoes given the treacherousness of the terrain, a curiosity Kurt could scarcely wait to investigate. He gauged the pair's height by examining broken stubs of branches and leaves torn from the trees after they stumbled through a stretch of forest. A man and a woman, Kurt guessed, though he hadn't caught sight of them yet.

That singular joy would come tonight.

With the pair contained, Kurt had decided to hold off on making contact.

He had determined two reasons behind his failure the first time he'd attempted to bring someone to his camp. First, he hadn't fully utilized the power of his mind, his insight and skills of persuasion. And second, he had forgotten to account for a key element that would characterize anyone Kurt decided to take.

In hindsight, it was obvious.

Such a person would be desperate. He or she might not understand that Kurt was offering salvation, a different, better sort of life. The person would fight, his or her muscles would balloon with adrenaline, nails would become skewers, and teeth, daggers. A hiker or outdoorsperson, someone in his prime, would possess especial might.

A trapped animal could chew through its own limb—or the limb of the person attempting to keep it captive. Similarly, people in the full flush of youth, at the peak of life, were going be difficult to take down. This couple certainly fulfilled that description, Kurt observed, when he finally allowed himself a glimpse of them, his body a black outcropping of the boulder he hid behind.

Luckily, the solution was also obvious.

Kurt needed for the pair to become less robust.

Which they were doing all on their own—growing weakened through futile lurching around, failing to take advantage of perfectly apparent resources.

They were veering toward camp by a circuitous, haphazard route that suggested just how badly disoriented they must be, helped along by the blazes Kurt had provided.

Now it was time to hasten the process.

Kurt dragged downed logs into place and moved rocks so that the couple would walk in circles, exhausting themselves. He scattered debris to make them turn and head in different directions, effectively corralling them, drawing the pair closer and closer to his encampment without them ever knowing they were being steered.

And then the man did something so foolhardy that Kurt could hardly believe his luck. In a matter of days or even hours, the man would be helpless to muster a protest, let alone fight, and the woman would be out of her head with horror and disgust.

Kurt could sit back in delicious anticipation and await their arrival.

CHAPTER THIRTY-EIGHT

The truth was before Natalie now, an amorphous, bilious pool. It had finally started to slow in its spreading, its boundaries beginning to set. The contents were darker, ranker, denser than she could've imagined. Bilge and ash and ruins versus the spun sugar and ivory taffeta of wedding dreams.

Her husband had lied to her during the days leading up to their honeymoon, at the wedding, and for every moment of this trip. He'd acted out a charade—in that town she'd all but fallen in love with, on the river after purposely dropping their GPS, while convincing Natalie to abandon the canoe. Even once they had discovered his friend's body, Doug still hadn't told her the truth. If they hadn't gotten lost, if all had gone as planned, Natalie might have lived the rest of her life without knowing she'd been well and truly fooled.

Secrets were like dry rot, invisibly eroding the floor beneath you and the walls all around. Natalie stared off into the woods, realizing she had no idea where her husband had gone. If he didn't come back, what would she do? She wasn't sure what was more horrifying in that moment—the idea that Doug might not return, or the fact that she wasn't sure whether she would go and try to find him.

Leaves began to break and crunch nearby, then the sound of shoes stumbling across small stones could be heard. The ground around Natalie felt like it was shaking; she had to splay out her hands and brace herself as the footsteps came nearer.

Doug settled himself down beside her, using the tree trunk for support.

Natalie forced herself to speak. "Everything okay?"

"Yeah," Doug replied. "Fine." He offered her a smile. "Bodily functions just getting back up to working order again."

He had left to pee. Natalie felt a vile slash of envy. How long had it been since she'd gone herself? Every passing hour served as some sort of ticking countdown.

"So what went wrong?" Natalie asked, feeling only scant interest in the answer. "How did Craig get killed?" The flat quality of her voice frightened her. She sounded as if she were already partway dead.

"I don't know," Doug replied, equally tonelessly. "I assume the guy Luke found in Canada—who was going to be responsible for unloading the supply—got greedy, decided there was no reason to pay a lone man walking around in the wilderness. Why not just take the stash? Which means those dudes from our wedding have got to be pretty pissed right now, wondering where Craig is with their money."

Natalie gave a nod.

"I thought I could help my friend," Doug said, swiping at his eyes with the back of one hand. "Pay off a debt, and make up for walking away from him all those years ago."

"Why didn't you tell me?" Natalie asked.

Doug looked at her; she felt his body turn toward her in the dark.

"Maybe I could've helped," Natalie said. "At the least, we would've been on the same page. Handled things together."

Doug let out a short, hoarse grunt, and for a moment she went weak with shame. Of course Doug wouldn't have thought to rely on her for any sort of assistance. It was Natalie who sought out assistance, guidance, and direction—and had for all her life.

But then Doug said, "You would've married me, Nat? If you knew all of this? Where I had come from, and what I was going to have to do about it?"

"That's not giving me much credit—"

Doug jumped to his feet, so agile that she experienced another stab of envy. Natalie didn't know how she herself would ever make it to a standing position again. She canted her head, peering at her husband to the extent that she could. Her head felt too heavy to hold up, like a sandbag.

"Look what I did in high school," Doug said, looming over her. "Just turned my back on my best friend when he couldn't pull himself out of the muck. What if you had decided to do the same thing to me?"

Natalie stared down at the ground. It was only inches below her hanging face, but the darkness was so complete, she couldn't see anything. "It's too bad that you didn't trust me," she said softly. "Because you made it so that I could never trust you."

"Don't say that!" Doug dropped back down beside her. He reached to stroke her arm, but she pulled away. "Nat, honey, of course you can trust me. I did what I had to do. I was loyal, I lived up to the demands of the past. And now it's the present. It's *our* present. We can move on and never look back."

Natalie waited for the irony to occur to him—quite literally they had no way to move on—but Doug simply continued to sit beside her in the dark, awaiting her reply.

"You can't tell lie after lie, Doug, then expect a do-over, like life is an Xbox game. You don't get to start from scratch just because you confessed, which, by the way, you might never have done if circumstances hadn't forced it!" She finished, breathless.

"Okay," Doug said. "I get that." He took a deep breath. "I've been used to doing everything on my own for a long time now. You know why… You see how my mother is."

Natalie waited, in part because she lacked the energy to do anything else.

"And that doesn't work in a marriage. I'll have to change," Doug went on raggedly. "Because one thing I know—one thing that has no part of a lie in it—is that I love you, Natalie Larson. And if we get out of this, and we will, then I promise. I will never lie to you again."

She stared off into the night, where she would've sworn she saw a form moving, her vision wavering in and out, her eyes playing tricks on her. "How do you know if a liar is lying?"

Even in the dark, she could see Doug's eyes blaze.

"Don't tell me a riddle, Natalie! This is our marriage! This is our life!"

"I know that." Her retort came out low; she could no longer muster much volume. "And you know what, Doug? Maybe my past is at work here too. Does my father seem like a strong guy, someone you can count on? How did I manage to trade one man in my life for another who would only let me down?"

She feared she had pushed Doug too far, that he would simply stalk off and leave her in these woods. Instead, he seemed to calm. He reached through the dark for her hand, holding tightly when she tried to withdraw it.

"See, Nat?" he said. "These are the kinds of things we can talk about now that we're married. We can have deep conversations like this. And they'll bring us even closer together."

For just a second, the spark that had nearly been snuffed out—by betrayal, starvation, thirst, pain, and exhaustion—kindled. This was the reason she had really fallen for Doug. Not their mutual enjoyment of relatively surface things like restaurants, drinking, or even sex, but because from the moment that they'd met, they had spoken to each other from the deepest, partially empty recesses of their souls.

Then she slid her hand free. "They would have once," she said sorrowfully. "That was the kind of marriage I always wanted to have."

"Okay, then—"

"But not anymore, Doug," she went on, speaking over him. "Now it's too late. We can't exchange confidences when there have been so many lies. It'd be like trying to build a house on a rotting foundation."

Doug faced her. "Nat, please, that's not true," he said. "It isn't too late. I love you, and that's what matters, honey. Don't you believe me?"

She was sinking back down, or maybe the ground had risen up to meet her. It seemed to take forever to settle into a prone position, and once there, she couldn't tell if her eyes were open or closed. Had Doug stayed? Would he hear what she said, presuming her words were even audible?

"I'm sorry, honey," she murmured, or mouthed, or maybe just thought before she began floating away. "But I don't. I can't. Not anymore."

CHAPTER THIRTY-NINE

In the dead of the night, despair settled like a cloak over Natalie. Her marriage was over. There would be no divorce, but that was only because they weren't going to make it back to the land of such things—courthouses and paperwork and second starts for anybody who wanted one.

Their bodies would be found, and the story would be tragic: newlyweds who'd perished before they had even gotten a chance to begin their lives together. Her own sister wouldn't know the truth about Doug's betrayal, or that if he and Natalie had lived, they would've failed to survive in an altogether different way.

Natalie could feel her body shutting down. For a while now, certain functions had been curtailed—no tears to cry, or trips to the bathroom, difficulty swallowing—but these changes were deeper, more profound. They took place at her very core. Natalie's heart beat at a strange, uneven pace—terribly fast, making her twitch and turn on the ground, then hardly at all. She would start to drift off only to come to with a gasp, realizing she had forgotten to breathe. One of these days, hours, minutes, would she just stop, her body no longer taking care of what she'd never had to think about?

She wondered whether Doug was experiencing the same issues. He was stronger than she because the water had rejuvenated him. He had gotten rid of the headache they'd both been suffering from for days; Natalie could tell by how freely Doug moved his face, without wincing or cringing. She should drink too, but aside from the risk she knew such an act to entail, Natalie also lacked the will for it now.

What would it matter if she hydrated herself? Once they left this spot, they would be waterless again. And where was there to go? Even if right this very second the two of them had been plunked down on a real trail, they wouldn't possess the strength to follow it out. They had already tried that approach, and succeeded only in wandering deeper into the wilderness, depleting their final resources.

Certain of her symptoms had gone away at least, rendering Natalie a little more comfortable. Her sore cheek was numb, the flesh deadened. It might've been that she had no side to her face at all. Also, Natalie no longer felt hungry. That animal inside her gut had stopped scavenging, seeming to accept things and curl itself into a little ball. Natalie cupped her hands around her belly, quietly stroking the flesh.

Doug's voice sounded out of the dark. "The creek."

"I already told you." She was surprised that her voice still worked. "I won't drink." Hers was the stance of a petulant child, one who should just give in already.

"That isn't what I meant," Doug replied, moving toward her through the shadows. "I mean, now that we know where there's a creek, we can follow it out. Just like we talked about doing before. Water finds an outlet. And so will we."

"Doug." If she'd had the strength, Natalie would've laughed. "You think I can hike? Climb over rocks? For miles and miles? Have you looked at me lately?"

Silence.

Natalie shifted effortfully onto one side, the knob of her shoulder poking into the ground. It hurt, but she was too weak to turn over again. After a while, that pain blended into all the others and disappeared, like a drop of dye in the sea.

The idea snuck up on her from behind.

"You go," Natalie said. She had fallen asleep; she wasn't sure for how long. Was Doug still lying beside her? "You drank. You have strength. Follow the creek out on your own. Send back help."

"No," Doug said.

So he was still here. How sure his voice sounded, how strong.

"I won't leave you."

It took a while for Natalie to pry her lips apart again. So much work just to get a few words out, one small bunch at a time. "Doug. I can't walk. At all. I think you know that. I'll wait here. You get help."

Doug stood up and walked off into the woods, his footsteps fading out.

When he returned, Natalie realized she must've dropped off into unconsciousness again. Her eyes had crusted over, she couldn't open them. She was blind.

"I can't do it," she heard Doug saying.

"Yes, you can," she whispered, hoping he might be looking at her and see the resolve in her face. "It's our only chance."

"Not without you, Natalie."

Her eyes smarted stingingly, this new pain particularly offensive since her vision had been stolen away. Then the lids came unglued, and Doug's face swam into view.

"I won't leave you alone," he told her.

Two tears slipped out, the last leakage of her body. "You already did."

Something got decided, wordlessly, silent, in the untold amount of time that followed her statement.

"Okay," Doug said at last.

He would depart at first light.

He helped get Natalie situated a little more comfortably: a mound of pine needles for a pillow, a gnarled root for a bedstead.

The woods closed in as sleep crept close and closer, a character out of some fairy tale of old, coming for the weak, the small, the helpless. Then the forest itself began to transform, turning into a malevolent creature, dangling leaves for hair, touching Natalie with long, reaching branches. She fought to shy away, but her muscles lacked all strength. She couldn't move. Then it was upon her.

CHAPTER FORTY

Kurt's camp had grown from its meager beginnings into a place suited to the care and keeping of guests. But that didn't imply by any means that he was ready. There was an array of things left to take care of, as well as the myriad tasks that accompanied social endeavors to attend to. First up, his appearance.

After two years of hermit-like, mountain man existence, Kurt had stopped tending to what he looked like. There were no mirrors out here, and what would it have mattered if there were? Painful as the fact was, there had been nobody around to see him.

That wasn't true anymore.

He knew that he must be unfit for meeting new people, and Kurt was well aware of all that went along with making a good impression. His parents had both been doctors—psychiatrists—and as a child, Kurt had been required to attend hospital fund-raisers and other functions, his mother coolly observing her son's demeanor and behavior.

Because he had been so well-spoken and charming at a young age,

Kurt had learned to count his primary appeal as cerebral rather than physical. The way he talked—and more importantly, listened—to people drew them in, especially as he grew older.

But the construction of the stick-and-daub hut in which he now resided, the constant lugging of water up from the creek in a vessel he had fashioned out of sunbaked mud, not to mention racing after prey—and twice, away from predators—had rendered Kurt pleasing of body too. His arms were humped with muscle; his shoulders formed a broad ridge; his stomach had been whittled into six flat plains. His eyes were bright with a look of alertness and command, while the sun had added colors to his dark hair and beard, reds and bronzes and coppery shades. Kurt's ruddy hair flowed down his back, his beard formed a lion's mane around his face.

Ah, but his hair and beard. Those were the primary culprits, along with the state of his clothes. Kurt tended to stay in garments for a while, the only alternative being to don the sole pair of replacement pants and shirt he'd managed to come by, until both outfits stood up stiff with dirt on his body. When the weather allowed, Kurt preferred to wear nothing at all, which meant that his entire naked form was sun-bronzed along with the more customarily exposed parts.

Kurt had raided the cabin that fell down after his first winter for supplies and implements, but a scissors hadn't been among what he found. Thus, for this trim, it was either to be the machete he had stolen from a long-ago backpacker or else a dinner knife, which Kurt had patiently honed into something sharper, trying not to thin its blade.

He cocked his head, checking on the sun in the sky. Before it sunk too profoundly, he would have to look in on the couple, assess their precise whereabouts and declining state of health.

He sat cross-legged on the ground in front of his hut, combing out his freshly washed hair with his fingers. He began sawing the knife back and forth through the mass. Hair fell in a glossy pile around him. Kurt scooped up every strand; the material would provide insulation and cushioning come wintertime. It would be important to offer warm lodging to his guests, plus nothing could be wasted out here.

Kurt wished he could see what his newly shortened hair looked like, whether it'd been hacked off unevenly, or formed a cap he could slick into some sort of shape. He wanted to look nice when company arrived.

But there was still much left to do.

He needed a supply of sand for filtering—the small camp pot he'd been able to lift from the hiker's pack wouldn't provide enough water for three, particularly when two were badly dehydrated—as well as poplar bark, ground and ready to be ingested. Poplar made a good substitute for aspirin, and the man and woman were sure to be in some pain. Kurt would have to be careful that neither of them was bleeding before offering relief—poplar thinned the blood—but he wanted the remedy on hand. He remembered what relief it had provided when he'd chewed the bark himself. He had since learned to grind it with a pestle fashioned from a small stone; the procedure increased the bark's potency.

The nearest stand of poplars was a good four miles away, a trek Kurt could make in forty-five minutes if he pushed himself, the strength of his conditioning undermined by the difficulty of the terrain. He decided that he would check on his visitors prior to setting out, but before that, he chose to take care of prettying up the hut. The crudest of structures felt like luxury to Kurt after the first winter he'd spent here, but that didn't mean anybody else's expectations should be set so low. His new residents could have no reason to be dissatisfied with their dwelling.

Everything always took longer than expected without the shortcuts of man-made existence, and it was dark before Kurt finally got a chance to go in search of the couple.

He moved lightly, almost weightlessly, through the woods. He knew to pick his way over sticks without snapping them, and how to let the balls of his feet come down before slowly lowering his heels so that leaves were pressed into a mat instead of crunching. He could approach prey so silently by this point that he was able to hunt with no weapon at all.

When he reached a boulder a few yards from where the couple had lain down to rest, Kurt mounted it with the same ease as he would have climbed a ladder. Scuttling across the stone, Kurt got close enough to smell the sick, unwashed stink of the pair.

They were in worse shape than they'd been just that morning, the woman all but unconscious, while the man strode around on that high, thin edge of false strength that portends a collapse. Kurt observed them from his post, crouching upon a muscled hump of rock while he worked to subdue his every breath and motion.

The man lay down beside the woman, speaking in softer tones, and Kurt jumped noiselessly to the ground in one leap.

They were making a plan to leave. The notion would've been laughable, given their state, except that after a few moments of largely nonsensical back-and-forth, the man agreed to a solo attempt. While he didn't stand a chance of succeeding either, Kurt couldn't let the pair be separated.

He nearly grabbed both of them right then and there, two against one less of a problem when the one was Kurt, and the two were in this condition.

But Kurt didn't want to take the risk. Something unexpected might occur.

Nonetheless, there could be no more delays, nor last-minute chores taken care of.

He was going to have to act fast.

PART THREE
TRAPPED

CHAPTER FORTY-ONE

Natalie dreamt of water flowing downhill, of drops dripping from unstoppable faucets and bathtubs filled to brimming. Of the lakes and rivers she and Doug had crossed, their surfaces dewing the bottom of their abandoned canoe.

Her lips cracked when she tried to open them. They bled, and Natalie lapped thirstily at the liquid, spitting ferociously upon tasting salt.

She couldn't have imagined thirst like this. It was a beast borne of the devil, punishment for some act so evil it lay outside nightmares, wartime, and prison cells.

Her head throbbed as if a steel wire had been cinched around it and was being drawn tighter and tighter.

Doug had been right. Natalie should've drunk from the creek. Now she was too weak to make it there, though it lay only a few yards away.

Doug.

Where was he?

He'd left, she remembered. It must've been a while ago already. They had planned his departure for daybreak.

The sun sat high in the sky, its rays pale and watery, providing hardly any warmth—or at least none that Natalie could feel. She was shaking all over, and a twisted scrap of cloth slid off her. It took Natalie a while to realize what it was. Doug had used the sling she had fashioned from her torn shirt as a sad approximation of a blanket. He must have draped it over her before leaving.

Her eyes ached with wanting to cry.

She had slept half the day away. How far had Doug gotten? Was he almost out?

Then she began to hear moans.

They were so loud, howls of sheer pain, that they could only have been made by a creature of great size, and one close to death.

A bear perhaps, or a coyote.

Wounded animals were dangerous, but Natalie had no way to protect herself from this one. She didn't even have the strength to clap her hands over her ears to muffle the noise. If this beast came for her, it would spell the end, and perhaps that would be a relief.

How long could suffering like this go on? Her own or the animal's?

Hurry hurry hurry was the chant inside her head. *I'm dying, Doug, I'm dying.*

The woods began to shape-shift, mutating around her. The forked fingers of branches started to shed—no, pluck off their own leaves—as they reached in Natalie's direction; lichen-covered rocks turned into enormous, scaled lizards.

Then she realized that she was actually staring into the beady black eyes of a reptile. A small snake lay utterly still, inches from her face. Natalie looked at it for some time, lacking the will to feel either revulsion or fright. After a long delay, it occurred to her that she could eat this creature.

If she just lifted her hand—oh, for the time when lifting her hand was a *just*—and pinched a spot behind the tiny triangular head, she could chomp from the tail end until her mouth met her fingers. Hot, pungent saliva flooded her mouth, a concentrate so undiluted, it couldn't be swallowed.

Natalie willed her hand to move, but it seemed to be paralyzed.

She bore down, grinding her fist into the soil, unable to get it off the ground.

The snake slid away, its unhurried wriggle and sibilant rustle seeming to say, *It's too late, it's too late, it's too late.*

It was too late for anything now. She'd be dead by the time Doug returned.

She lay back, staring up at such an enormous swath of stars that it looked like the entire New York City skyline had been transferred to the heavens. *What matters is not the number of breaths you take...*

Natalie wished she were back home in her apartment, surrounded by bromides and homilies. She loved her collection. Other than those little plaques and paintings, she'd never had much in the way of guiding words and wisdom in her life.

The moans began anew, or perhaps Natalie just became aware of them again.

Bellows and bleats of sheer agony. Whatever kind of creature this was, it was being tormented. By what?

A shriek, then another moan, the latter somehow familiar sounding.

That was no animal.

It was Doug.

Adrenaline triggered Natalie's voice to work, jolted her limbs into motion.

"Doug?" she called out, and got onto her hands and knees in the dirt.

How long had it been since she'd been able to stand?

She crawled in the direction of those terrible yowls.

Doug hadn't made it out. He wasn't partway back to civilization, using the creek as a compass. What had stopped him? What went wrong?

The answer hit her seconds before she saw him.

The *smell* hit her, making things clear.

Natalie used low-hanging branches to pull herself along, maneuvering around a stubbly young tree. At her usual level of fitness, she would have simply crushed the slim trunk beneath her feet as she walked. As it was, the tree posed an obstacle nearly too significant to bypass. A few more feet and Doug came into view, squatting on the ground, hunched over and clutching his stomach, a pool of filth around him.

Natalie stopped just short of him. She felt a sob fill her throat. "Honey?"

A shudder racked Doug's body, and he wrapped his arms around himself and let out a scream. The spasms continued, one after the other, seemingly unending, until Doug finally leaned over, spent, gasping, and covered in thick, oily sweat.

A trickle of sludge added itself to the waste.

Natalie bent over, retching, though there was nothing in her stomach to lose.

"Guess—"

A sound so familiar, she lifted her head. It was Doug's voice, threaded, despite everything, with humor.

"—you were right," her husband said, and collapsed.

Natalie extended her hand, trying to reach him.

They lay on the ground, not quite able to touch, until footsteps began to thud nearby. Something was coming through the trees.

"Easy now," said a voice—or what sounded like a voice, though Natalie knew it to be just another hallucination, like trees that could strip off their own leaves, and lizard-turning rocks—before somebody stooped down beside her. "Easy does it."

Natalie was lifted by the strongest pair of arms she'd ever felt and lofted away.

CHAPTER FORTY-TWO

Standing beside the field, Mia clicked on the link that PhotoSearch had sent her.

The app displayed two pics side by side: the one Mia had entered and the one the app had found, which appeared on a school blog. Uncle Doug's friend was a sixth-grade teacher at Brierly Academy named Mark *Harden*. It was kind of refreshing to see her mother be wrong, even if it was just about a name.

Mia entered Mark's name in the search bar, and let the little wheel spin. A few Google references to teacherly things came up. A fund-raiser at an off-off-off-Broadway theater company, some honor awarded by the board of trustees at the school. No Instagram account for Mark Harden, or Snapchat either. He *was* on Facebook and, unlike Uncle Doug, might see a friend request right away—this very second even.

She could chat with him, at least see what he was up to. How cool would that be? *Of course I'm on Facebook*, Mia would tell her friends. *All the hot older guys hang out there.* She looked up from her phone.

The scrimmage had just ended, and the girls were running off the field, trading high fives with Mia's dad.

Mia sent the request, then texted a *welcome home* message—with the cutest emojis: bride, groom, wedding cake, even a boat—to Aunt Nat.

A few minutes later, her phone pinged and she felt a rush of happy anticipation. Mark Harden, accepting her request? Or could Aunt Nat have gotten home already? Mia wondered if she would comment on the adorable emojis Mia had sent. Probably not—Aunt Nat had been in the woods for a week and probably felt pretty tired and gross.

But the text was from Mia's mom.

What are you up to?

not much miss u, Mia texted back fast, both to end the exchange and because it was true, she did miss her mom when she spent time alone with her dad. Her parents made more sense together, as far as Mia was concerned. She looked out at the field again.

It was clear of people, a broad, empty stretch of grass. Where had her dad gone?

Mia's phone buzzed again. Another text from her mom. Mia ignored it—and the next one too—so she could continue looking for matches for Mark.

A hand dropped down on her shoulder from above, and she yelped.

"Mi, it's just me," her dad said. "Boy, you're on edge." He hesitated. "I'm sorry. It's perfectly understandable that you would be."

"No," Mia said, slipping her phone into the pocket of her jeans and hoping her dad hadn't seen either the photo of Uncle Doug's friend or the unanswered texts from her mom. "I'm not edgy, I'm just cold." She wanted this whole *incident* business behind them. It was like the fourth most important thing on her mind these days.

Back at the apartment, her father hung around. Her mother had agreed to cover another shift, which meant she wouldn't be back till after dinner. Only once she and her dad had eaten did he finally start getting ready to go. "You'll be okay for a half hour?"

Mia gave him a look. "Sure I will, *Mom*," she said.

"Don't bad-mouth your mother," he said automatically.

Mia rolled her eyes, but inside she felt like smiling.

"I know you don't need a bodyguard," her father added.

"More like a prison guard," Mia replied. She kissed her dad goodbye before running to her room. It'd been hard to sit still all afternoon, visiting with her dad like he was some kind of guest, making conversation so the *incident* wouldn't come up. Now she could go online, watch videos, do whatever she wanted by herself for a while. It was so peaceful, she lost all track of time.

The front door banged. Mia heard the clack of all three locks, and then her mother called, "Mi?"

"In my room!" Mia shouted back. She slid her thumb across the screen on her phone one last time before shutting it off. No new texts. *Hurry up, Aunt Nat*, Mia thought.

Her mom came in to give Mia a hug. "Sorry I missed your father."

Mia fake coughed. "Yeah, right."

Her mom looked hurt. "It's not like the two of us hate each other," she said.

Mia stared down at her phone. Darkened, it made her feel so lonely. No reassurance or company from it at all.

"When you start looking at your phone in the middle of a conversation," her mother said in the voice that meant she was serious, "is when I know to take it away."

Mia couldn't lose phone privileges now of all times. She had to come up with something that would justify what only her mother would describe as a major transgression. "It's shut off, Mom. And anyway, normally I wouldn't while we were talking, but Aunt Nat hasn't texted me yet. She's coming home today."

"Already? My, that went fast." Her mother gave a nod. "Fine. Text Aunt Nat to say welcome home. But nothing else, okay? You've probably been on that thing all day."

How did her mom even know? "I already texted her," Mia said sullenly. "I told you, she's not responding."

Her mom headed toward the door. "She probably hasn't gotten within range."

Mia jumped off her bed, putting out a hand to stop her mother. "It'll be dark soon, though," she said, glancing out the window. "They wouldn't leave the woods this late."

"The signal is terrible up there, remember?" her mom replied. "And their phones were left in the car so they probably need to be charged. Give Aunt Nat another hour or two. Then we can give her a call."

"How old-fashioned," Mia said sarcastically, although the idea actually comforted her in a way, the prospect of hearing her aunt's voice.

Her mom turned around at the doorway to give Mia a smile. "I didn't exactly suggest sending a telegram."

But two hours later, Mia had postponed bedtime as long as was allowed, and her aunt still wasn't responding to texts.

"I'm kind of worried," she told her mother before she went off to bed.

"Mi," her mom said, sounding exasperated. "Maybe they're having a wonderful time and decided to camp out an extra night. Maybe they extended their honeymoon with a room at some bed-and-breakfast and don't want to take calls. Maybe their phones went on the fritz from being unplugged for a whole week. Maybe—"

"Maybe you don't care about your sister anymore, just like you don't care about Dad!" Mia broke in.

"Mia," her mother said, her breath all whistly. "That isn't true."

"Which part?" Mia muttered. "About Aunt Nat? Or Dad?"

Her mother didn't answer.

Mia's phone buzzed then, and both their gazes shot to it, Mia almost as glad for the chance to look away from her mom as she was to hear from Aunt Nat. She snatched her phone up, out of view, realizing instantly that it was lucky she had.

"Where are they?" her mom asked.

"It isn't Aunt Nat," Mia said, frowning at the screen.

She clicked on the message she'd received before her mother could reach for the phone.

Mark Harden had accepted her friend request.

CHAPTER FORTY-THREE

Natalie assumed she was dead.

Heaven was a warm, soft mat with a pillowy top draped over her. And a trickle of the most delectable substance she'd ever tasted being dropped, silvery molecule by silvery molecule, into her open, waiting mouth.

A sleeping bag.

That was what she lay on. A bright-red synthetic fold of fabric enclosed her.

Did they have sleeping bags in heaven?

And the liquid she was being fed came from a spoon, its base broad and dented, not a bejeweled vessel of gold as she'd pictured.

It was water. Plain, old tepid water, with a slightly tinny aftertaste. And so delicious that Natalie thought she might cry.

She began to struggle and strain, gulping the contents of one spoonful before looking wildly around for the next.

"Careful," a voice told her. "If you drink too much at once, you'll get sick, and we can't have that. You can't afford to lose the salts."

Natalie sensed the legitimacy of the warning, even if she couldn't quite understand it. Glints of meaning arrived, propelled along by singleton words. *Electrolytes. Shock. Dehydration.*

Memories swam to the surface of her mind.

She'd been terribly, dangerously dehydrated. Still was, to judge by the sandiness in her eyes, and the tissuey interior of her mouth, which didn't secrete any moisture. How had she gotten to such a state? She couldn't think back.

"Here's another," the voice said, and tipped the spoon.

A man was ministering to her. Natalie tried to bring him into focus as she obediently swallowed a second sip, blinking and looking around. It felt strange for some reason to be inside. She was occupying a structure for the first time in—days? Weeks? Months? She had no idea. How long had she been here, wherever *here* was, while this man brought her back from the brink of death?

He wore a faded shirt that fit snugly on his well-muscled body. His hair was badly cut but had a beautiful sheen, hanging well past his collar. And his face, his eyes, plus his voice, his whole demeanor, in fact, were the most placid Natalie had ever known.

Her belly gurgled, and the man set down his spoon.

"Ah," he said. "That's our sign. Enough for now."

Natalie wanted to protest—she felt as though she could have downed the contents of an entire pitcher, if not a whole water cooler, without pausing for breath—but the man possessed a wisdom and expertise that wouldn't be denied.

She settled back among the folds of fabric. Her head had been raised that entire time, she realized. She was regaining strength, just from a few sips of water. She wondered if she had eaten anything yet. Probably not, to judge by the yawning emptiness in her belly. Her sense of hunger had been deadened, but was coming back to life.

Sleep exerted a more powerful pull, though, dragging Natalie away with nowhere near the gentleness and care that this man had shown when he'd helped her to drink. She slipped underneath, and was gone.

The next thing Natalie became aware of was some kind of slippery, viscous balm coating the ravaged ruins of her face. The injury had reawakened itself mere seconds before the substance was applied, a fiery rush of feeling returning to the area, like a volcano erupting inside her cheek. The balm, though, was wonderfully soothing, quieting the nerve endings as they came back to life.

Some kind of Native American remedy perhaps, boiled root or slippery elm. Something that befit such a man, whose unevenly chopped hair might until recently have been worn in a rich, glossy braid down his back.

"It's Neosporin," the man said.

She must've been mumbling aloud without even realizing it. She hoped the man wasn't insulted, that she hadn't been culturally insensitive.

"Sometimes hikers pass through, leave things behind. Or else we barter," the man explained. "Make some sort of trade."

How nice, Natalie thought, images of another land and time coming to her. Smoke-filled huts and vision quests, tepees made out of corn sheaths. Men with feathers on their chests and arms. It *is* like the Indians.

Then she was hurtled once more into sleep.

CHAPTER FORTY-FOUR

Natalie woke to the glorious smell of food and some kind of snapping, popping sound: meat being cooked over an open fire. Squinting outside into shadowy darkness, she saw sparks shooting into the sky.

Her cut throbbed, and she started to bring a hand to the side of her face, before promptly dropping it back down. Something deep inside told her what would happen if she touched her cheek right now.

"We have to be sparing with the Neosporin," the now-familiar voice said, speaking as calmly and evenly as ever. "But I'll apply more before you fall back asleep."

The man squatted beside her, holding out a battered cup. "Here. Try some of this. It'll cure what ails you even better than antibiotic ointment."

Natalie accepted the cup. She tilted it toward her mouth, flinching as soon as the contents struck her tongue.

"Careful. It's hot."

Natalie took a more judicious sip. The liquid rolled down her throat and hit her belly, triggering a clamor so great that she thought she would pass out.

"Can I...can I have some of whatever's on the fire out there?" she asked.

"Oh ho," the man chortled. "Getting greedy, aren't you?"

Natalie felt her face flush, making the wound in her cheek throb. "I'm sorry..." she began. But she couldn't help a moan from forming and working its way out, unbroken, almost sexual in longing. Her face heated again. To hide it, Natalie gulped the rest of the contents of the cup, lapping up drips with her tongue.

"That's broth," the man said. "From the meat I'm cooking. Broth is much easier to tolerate when you first return to eating."

"I'm just so hungry," Natalie said helplessly. "Can't you see how hungry I am?" Company manners—not to mention gratitude for her rescue, although she didn't yet recall what it was that she'd been rescued *from*—were beyond her right now, luxuries of a life she'd been forced for some reason to abandon.

"I do see." The man reached out and gave her shoulder a pat. "And I know that you are. You've been through hell, I think."

Natalie nodded, feeling like a small child. "I think I have too," she said. If only she could remember. "And now I just want something to eat—to really chew, I mean. I want that so badly."

"All in good time," the man replied. He was studying her face, peering directly into her eyes with an expression of curiosity and scrutiny.

Natalie blinked.

"You're crying," he informed her. "That's a good sign."

Natalie reached up, shocked to realize he was right.

"Once certain other bodily functions have returned"—the man turned, letting out a discreet cough—"then we can think about giving you some solid food."

Natalie shook her head, not understanding.

The man looked back at her. "You'll have to let me know," he said. "When you experience the urge. I wish I had a bucket to give you, but there's nothing like that here. So I'll have to carry you outside the hut and offer whatever assistance you might need."

Now Natalie understood. She still hadn't used the bathroom. In how long?

And what did it matter? She wanted a hunk of that broiling meat whose scent continued to drift in from outside so badly that Natalie thought she'd be willing to claw right through the man to get it.

He continued to examine her. "Shh," he said soothingly. "It's okay to be angry at me. That's only natural; your emotions are all over the place right now. But I'm just trying to exercise appropriate caution."

His words triggered something Natalie was forgetting, or failing to think of. Whatever the matter might be hovered foggily at the edges of her consciousness. Try as she might, she couldn't get hold of it.

The man stooped to take the empty cup out of her hand, walking off and leaving Natalie to the tantalizingly near aroma of meat.

In the middle of the night, Natalie was seized by a spasm in her lower back and groin, and she let out a scream.

The man was at her side almost instantly, and wordlessly helped Natalie outside where a cloudy lid of sky obliterated the moon.

She tripped over a rock—her feet seemed to have forgotten the mechanics of walking—and the man righted her. She couldn't wait another second then, and though she wasn't near a tree or hill or any sort of apt spot, Natalie dropped into a squat, yanking at her shorts without a glimmer of modesty.

Her body voided itself in a hot, gushing stream.

Natalie wobbled, too weak to remain crouching, and the man steadied her, politely averting his face.

She finished, and he silently handed her a clump of leaves.

"Don't worry," he said. "They're safe."

She dabbed.

"Now," the man said. "Let's get you something to eat."

He watched as she feasted. Natalie sat on the ground, resting against a rock and devouring morsels from a tin plate. The act of chewing caused her mouth to cramp viciously and her cheek to throb, but she hardly registered either source of discomfort. She licked the plate clean: stray threads of stringy meat, little burned dabs of its skin.

"What kind?" Natalie asked.

The man understood. "Chipmunk," he told her. "These woods are thick with them, and will be until winter."

"Is there any more?"

"In the morning," he told her. "It's best to go slowly. And you need some greens too. Roughage is crucial if you want to get your system back to normal."

Chipmunk should always be served as part of a balanced diet, Natalie thought.

"What's funny?" the man asked, watching her.

She shook her head, politeness having returned along with that one shard of humor—she didn't want this man to think she was criticizing his lifesaving offering—when another part of her mind kicked into gear as well.

Her memory.

"My husband!" she cried out.

The man looked at her through the dark. He reached for her plate, then stood up. "Best not to leave dirty dishes," he said. "They attract wildlife less pleasant than chipmunks." The smile he offered was bland and benign. "Don't worry about any washing up or chores yet, of course. I'll take care of everything for now."

Natalie was about to respond to his statement when a slipstream of memories suddenly took hold. "We were here together." She reached up and grasped the man's wrist. It was strong enough to pull herself to standing. "On our honeymoon."

"Is that what it was," the man said. He gave a polite shake of his head when she made a move to follow him into the trees. "Please don't feel the need to come. The creek's too far for you right now. Do you need my help getting back to the hut?"

Natalie felt tears well in her eyes, and whisked them away with the flat of one hand. "Is there something you're not telling me?"

Silence from the man.

"Did you find my husband too? Is he all right?"

"Perhaps in the morning," the man began, "you'll be better equipped to hear what I have to say."

"Please!" Natalie cried, and at the moment that her shout floated up to the sky, a barrier of clouds parted, sending down a silvery streak of moonlight. "Tell me where Doug is."

"Doug," the man said, bowing his head. "I wish I had known his name."

"Why?" Natalie asked, whimpering with fear. "Why do you wish that? What happened to him?"

The man set the plate on the ground and took both her hands in his. "I'm truly sorry," he said, "to have to tell you this, especially right now. I wanted to wait for you to recover more fully first."

His face became slightly less serene, focused intently on her. Then he opened his mouth to speak.

CHAPTER FORTY-FIVE

Your husband was suffering from an intestinal bacterium," the man began.

Was, Natalie heard. A tear ran down her face, joined by a flood of others, and the salt stung her still partially open wound. The ability to cry was both a blessing and a curse. She knew that now.

"Giardia probably," the man went on, "or its ilk. A killing malady. Few people survive it, especially out here without access to medical intervention."

"Where is he?" Natalie asked.

"I have him in a comfortable spot," the man replied. "A sacred spot even."

"I need to see," Natalie said. "I need to see him."

Recollections were coming back to her now—the moment when Doug had collapsed and she'd been too weak to reach his hand—but she still couldn't believe that her vital young husband could be dead. Even though she knew that vital young people died all the time.

The man gave a hard shake of his head. His thick hair, dark enough to reflect the moonlight, rearranged itself over his shirt collar. "You're not strong enough yet."

Did he mean physically? Or emotionally?

The man studied her, and his eyes reflected compassion. Though they were dark and hard to read, Natalie saw in the man's eyes a mirroring quality, like pools of water beneath a night sky. He seemed to truly want to know and understand her.

"I know how hard this must be," he said, his voice pitched low, as if to lessen any need for alarm.

Still, Natalie felt fear climb to a teetering peak inside her.

"Even if things between you didn't exactly amount to newly wedded bliss."

Natalie whirled on the man so fast that she swayed. Using a tree to brace herself, she cried, "What do you mean? How do you know anything about us?"

Oh God, what might Doug have said in his final moments? What had his dying words been? Natalie was going to have to live with what the end had been like between them. So ugly, stripped away, two people at their worst and weakest selves.

The man took a step forward, palms out-turned. "Doug didn't tell me a thing," he said consolingly. "He was in no condition to speak. But you both wound up in the woods, half-dead in your case, and in his—" He broke off. "That's all I meant. That this wasn't exactly your typical start to a lifetime of togetherness."

The night had grown cold. Goose bumps dotted Natalie's skin, and she wrapped her arms around herself and shivered.

The man gave his leg a light punch. "I knew I didn't want you to have to hear this news now. Getting chilled will set back your recovery. Let me help you into the hut."

They walked together, Natalie so exhausted that she found herself hardly able to lift her feet. At the entrance to the hut, she shuffled inside and collapsed.

The man zipped the sleeping bag snugly around her, squatting on the dirt floor and appraising the small structure with his eyes. "I hope you'll be comfortable here."

His words struck an odd note—as if he was looking for something Natalie wasn't quite sure how to give—but she offered a nod.

"You good?" he asked, and she looked up at him. He gave his leg another smack of reproach. "Given the circumstances, I mean. Do you at least feel warmer now?"

Natalie turned her head. There really wasn't anything strange about his queries; the man was just trying to make sure she was okay. She had no right to take out her grief and anger on him when he'd done nothing but try to help.

Sleep, that dashing temptress, came and beckoned Natalie away. Down a dark tunnel to a place where the fact of her loss, her aloneness, had no way to follow.

Sometime before consciousness stabbed her, Natalie began to mourn Doug, and woke with the sleeping bag soaked beside her face, its loft flattened by tears.

She'd thought that her marriage had come to an end after Doug confessed his lies, but now she realized that only death could act as a permanent sever. The two of them might've gotten past their shaky start. Gone to counseling. Explored the themes they had both raised about their childhoods and families of origin. Just as Doug had proposed on the night he'd finally told her everything.

But Natalie had spurned his suggestion. She'd told him it was over—that *they* were over. That was what her husband had to take with him of

Natalie at the end of his life. An assertion of abandonment. Her statement that they were through.

Natalie shifted on the sleeping bag, the fabric emitting a rustly sound. Otherwise, it was silent in the hut. The noises she had grown used to while camping—cricket song, rattling wind, small disturbances in the woods—were damped by the walls and roof.

She had to make it to wherever Doug lay in rest; she needed to see him for herself. Until that moment, his death wouldn't feel real. And then she had to figure out how to get the two of them out of this place. Would the man hike out, bring back help? Some kind of search-and-rescue team perhaps. A helicopter with a body bag.

She shuddered.

The man stooped to enter the hut, as if summoned by her troubled thoughts. He held out the battered tin cup, a curl of steam rising from it, and what could only be described as a wilderness salad: a tangle of jagged-edged green on the metal plate.

Natalie downed every mouthful, cursing her voraciousness. How could she feel hunger when Doug would never eat again? His death should've halted the needs of her body, made it so that all appetites ceased. But her stomach sang a different song from her heart's ballad of loss, and she gulped and gobbled and licked up every shred of leaf.

The man watched her carefully. "Tea made from raspberry leaves," he said. "And foraged greens. If they go down well, later on you can have some more meat." He leaned closer. "Your eyes are swollen. Are you experiencing any difficulty with vision?"

Natalie shook her head rapidly. "I have to go see my husband," she told him. "Please. Even if you have to carry me there."

He continued to examine her, then said, "Tears. You've been crying," as if realizing something.

But he had already noted that her ability to cry had returned. Natalie felt a sense of mounting impatience. "Yes," she responded. "I'm much better. Please, will you take me to my husband now?"

Still, the man hesitated. "I don't know if that's best. You're weaker than you may realize."

Something about the words made Natalie sit up a little straighter, the sleeping bag slipping down around her waist. She set the tin plate and cup beside her, registering for the first time that the floor of the hut was bare ground. Then she began to rise, breaking the move into discrete parts. First onto her knees, with a momentary pause for rest. Then, one foot on the earthen floor. She pushed down, trying to get the other leg under her, but failed and flopped back, panting.

The man watched the series of maneuvers, staring down at her from what seemed a great height, his face calm and serene.

"Please," Natalie whispered. She didn't even know if he could hear her.

At last he gave a nod. "We'll take a walk around the yard. You can lean on me and drink some more fluids. If you seem okay after that, then all right. I'll take you."

"Thank you," Natalie said. She couldn't believe the gratitude that suffused her, her driving need to—if nothing else—at least kiss her husband goodbye.

They covered the area the man had referred to as the yard: a plain of cleared dirt and open space. There was another hut propped against the one in which Natalie resided, somewhat bigger in size. And a cage made out of wooden sticks, with a family of chipmunks scampering around inside. An area fenced off by taller, thicker sticks was home to a few rows of limp, straggly plants, nothing recognizable like lettuce or peas, although what appeared to be a single stalk of corn was fighting for life.

The man who had saved her appeared to be some kind of society dropout. Judging by this uncertain array, the endeavor was harder than it appeared on TV or in books.

He studied her face as he guided her along. "It's not as meager as it may look."

"What?" Natalie asked. She glanced at the man, whose normally tranquil expression seemed to have slipped, a certain upset behind it. "Oh, no. I wasn't thinking that. I was actually imagining how hard it must be to have created all this."

"Please don't lie," he said mildly.

Natalie looked down at the ground, concentrating intently on her steps.

"Has it seemed difficult to you?" he went on, steering her nimbly around the cage. The chipmunks ceased their darting and held still. "Staying here? I was hoping you'd have everything you needed. That you'd feel well tended to."

"I do," Natalie responded truthfully, though it occurred to her to wonder why this mattered to him. "When I first arrived…well, it seemed like paradise."

"That's good to hear," the man said, still eyeing her closely. "Why don't you have a little water now? Then we can take our walk to go see your husband."

She'd forgotten her loss for a moment, and the return of grief was crushing, like a tidal wave slamming against her from behind.

They set off into the woods, the brushed-clear dirt of the yard giving way to uneven terrain beneath Natalie's feet.

"Stay right at my side," the man instructed. "That's very important."

As if his words served as some kind of trigger, a barrage of images assaulted Natalie. She was dipping her paddle into the sweep of white-water; the high-up log she and Doug had walked across jutted out over its chasm; the two of them were running, racing, breaking through the woods. Natalie became aware of a high, keening sound and braced herself for a strong wind, but no wind came. The air didn't so much as stir. Then she realized the noise was being made by her.

"Shh," the man said. He patted her with a strong, plank-like hand.

"I should've realized. Of course. This is the first time you've reentered the woods."

His voice was the comfort she sought; she turned to its source as if imprinted upon it. She held on to him, sobbing into his shirt.

"I was so scared," she cried.

He didn't answer for a moment. Then, "Yes. Of course you were."

She let out a sob. "I didn't know if I was going to survive."

Another reply uttered after a small delay. "You must've been so scared."

Natalie became aware of what she was she doing—breaking down in the embrace of a man she didn't even know—although she noted that he wasn't exactly holding her in return. His arms hung like poles by his sides. Natalie breathed in deeply, then made herself straighten. The man offered her the corner of his shirt to wipe her eyes.

Natalie sniffed in a rattling breath and braced her shoulders. She didn't want to enter the place that had robbed her of Doug. But nor could she stay out of it either.

The man repeated his order to stay close by his side. "You won't get lost again," he reassured her. "I won't let that happen. But these woods hold other dangers."

Now that they had broken the barrier of brown and green, Natalie's feet felt surer, and her strength seemed to be returning.

She had to see Doug. It was all she wanted in this world.

The creek began to burble audibly before they saw a glint of water. Natalie fought to hurry, the man easily matching her stride.

"Right there." He pointed. "I thought by the creek made the most sense. Given his condition. Don't worry, I've kept him warm."

Natalie realized she had closed her eyes, and forced them to open. A shaft of sunlight momentarily blinded her. Then Doug's fallen form came into view.

He was lying beside the creek on a raised cushion of dirt. A second sleeping bag had been placed over him and drawn up to his chin. A few scraps of cloth lay on a nearby rock, drying in the sun beside a rough piece of bark. They smelled clean and fragrant, pine scented as if the bark had been used as a scrubber. Natalie realized that the man must've used them to wash Doug's body.

Like a ritual bathing, as if the man were preparing her husband for burial.

Not here. Natalie would never let this loathsome wilderness have Doug. They had to get home.

A long, high cry escaped her, like a whistling wind. It was the sound of pure loss.

Doug's face twitched, and he blinked.

CHAPTER FORTY-SIX

"Doug?" Natalie said faintly, disbelieving.

He blinked again, though he didn't lift his head or make any other move.

"He's alive!" Natalie cried out. Her knees buckled under her, and the man grabbed her arm to keep her from falling. Natalie wrenched herself free. Her gaze shot back and forth; it couldn't seem to decide where to settle. There was the man who had appeared to be nothing but savior till this very moment when she realized that he'd lied to her; her husband, lying prone by the side of a rushing creek; and her own feet, newly planted with firmness on the ground. "He's alive," Natalie said again.

"Of course he is," the man responded. He regarded her as if he had only now thought to question her grip on sanity. "I've been attending to him very carefully. It wasn't easy when you needed so much care yourself."

"But...I thought you said—" Natalie broke off, unable to complete the thought, and ran for her husband.

She knelt, hands carefully seeking some part of Doug's body it might be safe to touch beneath the puffy sleeping bag.

"Be careful," the man said from behind. "In addition to the intestinal distress, he seems to have hurt his right elbow."

Natalie had forgotten all about Doug's injury. She looked at her husband, whose eyes appeared to be trying to stay focused, but kept falling shut.

The man spoke again, from a little closer, to judge by the sound, although Natalie didn't turn around and look. She couldn't take her eyes off Doug.

"He was better off here rather than at the hut," the man explained, "because I could keep him clean. It was easy to use creek water to wash him, and I laid the sleeping bag on top to keep his core body temperature up."

"I don't understand," Natalie whispered. "I thought he was…" She trailed off, not wanting Doug to hear what she had thought, how easily—it struck her now—she had given him up for gone. But when she looked down again, her husband had drifted into a deep, peaceful sleep: regular breaths and soft, ruffled snoring. Natalie rose more agilely than she had in days. "You said 'was,'" she charged the man. "That Doug *was* suffering from giardia, or something like it."

"He was," the man said, frowning minutely. "He seems to be over the worst of it now. He took in a few ounces of water this morning, and has so far kept them down."

Natalie shook her head. This couldn't just be a simple misunderstanding, yet she had no idea what other explanation there might be for it. "But…you called it a killing malady. Whatever Doug had. You said few people survived."

"Few do," the man agreed.

Natalie stared at him, looking for signs of duplicity or malice in his eyes. There were none. No signs of anything bad at all; only rapt, avid concern and a reflection of her own upset.

"Why didn't you want to give me the news then?" she asked. "You said you wanted to wait till I was stronger to tell me what happened to Doug."

"Look, I don't know how to put this delicately," the man said, blinking at her blamelessly. "I figured few women would want to hear that their new husband was lying unconscious by a creek bed, covered in his own filth. I felt that it'd be better if you were a little stronger by the time you had to take that in."

Natalie had no idea why she was continuing this interrogation. Doug was alive—saved by the man—and she should be nothing but grateful. But it was as if her world had been given a hard spin on its axis, a lifetime-sized change taking place in a nanosecond.

Speaking loudly enough that Doug stirred on the ground, she said, "You referred to this spot as sacred. Remember?"

"It is," the man said calmly, gesturing to the silvery creek. "Can you imagine a more peaceful place in which to heal?"

Natalie finally subsided. "I'm sorry. I don't mean to give you a hard time. You've been so good to us. To us both."

"No apologies necessary," the man replied. "You've been through hell. It's understandable that you wouldn't be acting quite like your normal self."

Natalie let her head drop, staring down at the ground. "I think it's time you told me your name."

"Kurt," the man replied. "Kurt Pierson."

"Kurt," Natalie repeated.

"And you're Natalie," Kurt said to her.

Again, she felt curiosity extend to a touch of suspicion. "How did you know—"

"Your husband," Kurt said. "He kept muttering your name. Doug was so worried about you. Even when standing at death's door himself."

Natalie felt tears prick the corners of her eyes. A wind rose up, and the fir trees soughed all around them. The breeze stirred Doug's hair, moving the ends on his scalp. His hair looked clean; the man must've washed it. His newly grown-in beard was bristly with life.

"I hope he understood when I told him you were all right," Kurt went on. "He hasn't regained consciousness long enough for me to assess his mental state. His reaction when you arrived just now was the most awareness I've seen him show."

"Are you some sort of doctor?" Natalie asked.

Kurt let out a sharp bark of what sounded like surprise. "No."

"You said 'assess his mental state,'" Natalie said. "Sounded professional."

Kurt didn't answer, staring at her for long enough that Natalie began to feel uncomfortable. She took a look over her shoulder. Doug continued to breathe evenly and steadily beneath the sleeping bag.

"Should we zip him inside?" she asked. "Instead of just laying that over him?"

Kurt broke their stare at last. "Not a good idea, in case he does get sick again," he said. "It's easier to keep both him and the bag clean this way."

Natalie felt her cheeks heat. The things this man had done for them as they returned to the land of the living! They both owed a debt it would be impossible to repay.

A whisper rose up from the ground, so faint that Natalie mistook it first for a rustle of leaves on the forest floor.

"Nat-a-lie?"

She dropped down. "Doug, yes, honey, I'm here."

"You're—" Doug's mouth fell shut as if hinged, the effort of opening it clearly too much for him.

"Alive, yes, I'm fine, or at least I'm getting there," Natalie said. "And so are you, Doug. So are you!" Her voice hit a joyful note. "Thanks to this man."

She sent a look of sheer gratitude up toward Kurt. He was handsome, she realized. Why did he choose to live out here all alone? The thought occurred to her—perhaps he didn't. Perhaps Kurt had a wife, or a partner, and had already sent that person to the nearest town for help. Perhaps she or he was headed back, right at this very moment while Natalie reunited with her own spouse, whom she had believed to be lost.

Doug began dropping back off to sleep. Natalie smiled, laying her head gently on her husband's chest, making sure to steer clear of his belly, which she imagined to be tender and sore. "He'll thank you, I'm sure," Natalie said, aiming her promise up toward Kurt, who had remained standing. "When he wakes up."

Kurt replied briskly. "No thanks needed."

"Do you think we can give him some broth?" Natalie asked. "I mean, he seems so weak. He needs calories, right?"

Kurt appeared to consider. "Another cupful of water first," he said. "If that stays down, then yes, some broth."

Natalie nodded. "But we didn't bring any with us. Water. Or one of your cups."

"I only have one," Kurt said, giving her a brief smile. "I've been boiling and washing it so the three of us could switch off. I'll have to make another couple out of clay. I've just been too busy to get to that yet."

"I'm sorry," Natalie said, flushing again. "Of course you wouldn't have dishes for company. You weren't exactly expecting guests."

"Not expecting," Kurt agreed. "But I'm certainly glad you've come."

Natalie gave him an uncertain smile. There was nothing in this situation to be glad about, although living out here in the wilderness must get lonely, of course. Kurt likely didn't have a partner then. The three of them would have to figure out how to summon help, or some other way for Natalie and Doug to return to civilization once Doug had regained more of his strength.

"Should I go back for the water?" Natalie suggested. "Where do you keep—"

"Don't be silly," Kurt interrupted. "You can't make the trip by yourself."

"I actually feel pretty good," Natalie replied. But she settled down on the ground beside Doug, letting out an exhalation of relief. "Though maybe I shouldn't overdo it my first day up." A faint ghost from the past drifted in on a wisp of wind. Their mother issuing a caution after Claudia had been out sick for a week, missing big-girl school, and staying home with Natalie. A warning that Claudia needed to take it easy, in the form of a word from their mother, one whose meaning Natalie hadn't known. *Relapse.*

Kurt watched her, his eyes studious and intent, as if assessing her claim of renewed health. Was he a doctor, and hadn't wanted to admit it for some reason? He'd acted odd when Natalie had asked.

"I'll wait here with Doug," Natalie said, stating the obvious once the silence had spun itself out. "While you go for the water."

"I'm sorry," Kurt said softly. "I can't leave you here by yourself."

Natalie frowned. "I'm not going anywhere without him," she said. "I'll sleep here tonight, I don't need the hut. I'm feeling almost normal, just incredibly hungry." Who would've thought the day would come when she'd crave a nice, juicy bite of chipmunk?

Kurt squatted down beside her, speaking right into her face. His breath smelled of pine and green things and the cool, crisp air around them. "It's not safe for you to stay on your own," he said, "now that you can walk. I'm afraid you'll have to come with me, and we'll both return with the water."

Natalie rose on unsteady feet, and took a look around. "Why isn't it safe here?"

"For many reasons," Kurt replied, guiding Natalie in the direction from which they had come, "that you don't need to worry about now." He paused. "So long as you and I move about together, you'll be fine. We'll all be fine."

Natalie turned back just once. Doug was still sleeping quietly.

Then she followed Kurt into the forest.

CHAPTER FORTY-SEVEN

Natalie couldn't have imagined an appetite like this. She would never again claim to be "starving" upon skipping a meal. That night, Kurt built a fire near the creek where Doug lay resting, using a dented pot to make broth from the carcasses of the chipmunks he and Natalie had consumed. Kurt had eaten just one of the small animals, taking judiciously paced bites, while Natalie had devoured hers before gobbling another two.

"I'll have to catch more," Kurt said, crouching by the fire to tend his soup.

He'd started the blaze without benefit of matches. The act seemed so seamless, so natural that Natalie had hardly registered it. Kurt had spun a stick between his palms until a second stick ignited. The handmade taper lay on a rock, ready for its next use.

A curl of fragrant steam rose from the pot, while the campfire contributed its own smoky essence. Natalie settled back against a rock, her hand quietly stroking her still-sleeping husband, and felt a glimmer of an emotion she couldn't identify. The right name came to her after a moment. It was a feeling of well-being.

"Chipmunks," Kurt elaborated when Natalie didn't say anything. "This is the time to capture them. Come autumn, they go into hiding and become much harder to find."

"I'm actually licking my lips," Natalie said, feeling a soft laugh build inside her, then bubble out. She looked down at Doug, who didn't stir. "Who would believe that chipmunk could ever sound tempting?"

Kurt studied her, and she had a moment to regret her unchecked words.

Then he gave her an uneven grin and said, "It ain't steak on the back-yard grill, that's for sure."

The exchange felt a little awkward, but Natalie smiled back.

"There's venison as well," Kurt said. "A deer was killed last night. Tomorrow I can make a stew."

Natalie's stomach started making noises, although satiation eased them from a growl to a mumble. A deer was killed, Kurt had said. What did that mean exactly? How had it been killed? "What made you decide to do this?" Natalie asked, using a waving hand to indicate what she meant.

Kurt's smile vanished as if a mask had been removed. "That's a long story."

"I have time," Natalie said, and giggled again. The food in her belly, the warmth from the fire, and the weight of her living, breathing husband beside her had all combined to lull Natalie into a state she thought she'd never experience again. She felt the same light, frothy tipsiness the champagne had bestowed on her wedding day. Kurt's dark cascade of hair, the way his eyes gripped hers with such comprehension, made Natalie feel nearly flirtatious. "Tell me," she urged.

Kurt looked at her across the high, darting flames.

Natalie sought to hold his stare. It had a penetrating, knowing quality about it; perhaps having been brought back from the brink of death by this man connected the two of them with a degree of intimacy belied by how long they'd been acquainted.

Natalie's face reddened in a way not attributable to the heat of the fire, and she was finally forced to look away. She squeezed Doug's hand, warm and vital inside hers, squinting through the dark to confirm the rise and fall of his chest before daring a glance back toward Kurt.

"Look up there," he commanded, pointing.

A convex bowl of sky, studded with white pinpricks, sheltered them from above. "I know," Natalie said softly. "It stunned me the first nights of our trip. So different from back home. In the city, you can go weeks without seeing any stars at all."

"You both must be quite the outdoorspeople, though," Kurt said. "To have gone on a trip like this for your honeymoon."

Natalie positioned herself nearer to Doug. She wasn't sure how much her husband was taking in, given his ongoing state of repose, but didn't they say that even comatose patients could hear things, possibly detect emotion? If she sat close enough to him and spoke very distinctly, then Doug might register some of what she said.

"Doug is," she said.

"Not you?" Kurt asked.

She let out another laugh, although this one didn't feel mirthful. "I can't even read a map. Like, literally."

Kurt appeared curious. "No?"

Natalie shook her head. "Doug took care of the navigating. And a lot of other things besides." She didn't want to think about what Doug had done, not when he'd just been restored to her. And she certainly wouldn't open up about this topic to a stranger.

"Did you have a dollhouse as a little girl?" Kurt asked.

The question took Natalie aback, but she felt a sad smile toy at the corner of her mouth. "My older sister did," she answered. By the time Natalie had been old enough to want her own such plaything, her mother was long dead, and her father didn't buy toys—or much of anything else—without direct instruction. "I used hers sometimes. Why?"

Kurt shifted on the ground, his eyes catching the shine of the moon overhead. "Maps are just like dollhouses. A scaled-down version of the real thing. A map is to these woods"—he gestured around, indicating the border of forest where the ivory glow of moonlight didn't extend—"as a dollhouse is to a real dwelling."

Natalie frowned. Kurt's explanation delivered little more meaning than a map did whenever she looked at one.

"Minus a few details, of course," he went on, reading her confusion. "Your dolls didn't need plumbing, for instance. Or heat. Similarly, a map won't show every tree and rock. But what it does reveal is enough. Does that make sense?"

"Yes," Natalie said, and it did, sort of, though she was sure any increased understanding would evaporate the next time she held a map in her hands.

Kurt's eyes lit, or perhaps the moonlight sparked in them. Still, Natalie had the strangest feeling that he sensed what she'd been thinking. The knowledge he seemed to have of her was at once comforting, and unsettling.

"You might surprise yourself," he said. "Still, it is too bad."

"What is?" Natalie asked. "What do you mean?"

Kurt leaned in through the dark, his breath quick and delicate upon her. "Doug did the navigating on your trip, you said? And not only on your trip…other times as well."

Natalie gave a nod. Had she said that? She couldn't recall. There was a strange hypnotic quality to the conversation they'd been having.

"You're still playing in your sister's dollhouse, Natalie," said Kurt. "In someone else's world. You haven't yet taken possession of your own."

Natalie pressed down so hard on Doug's hand that even in sleep, he flinched and pulled away.

Kurt stood up and began scouting around on the ground. He picked up a chunk of wood and positioned it amidst the flames, fanning them to build up the fire.

Natalie blinked as the smoke entered her eyes, stinging them like bees.

"I've angered you," Kurt said, prodding the blaze.

The fire soared higher, a bright-orange helium balloon. Kurt stood up and filled the cup with water from a hand-formed jug, offering it to Natalie.

Natalie gulped down the contents. Today's temperature had been lower than yesterday's, and the water consequently colder, tasting of the mysterious depths it'd risen from.

"I'm not mad at you," she said at last.

Kurt peered at her. "At Doug?"

Natalie stared off into the night. "Yes. But maybe even more at myself."

Kurt refilled her cup.

Natalie looked down at Doug. "Can I... Should I trickle some into his mouth?"

"You can try," Kurt said. "Start by wetting his lips."

Natalie was able to moisten Doug's mouth and slide a few drops down his throat.

"What happened?" Kurt asked. "Why would you be angry at yourself?"

Kurt seemed less to be prying than trying to ease her mind, allowing her to share. There was a blurry, swimmy quality to the evening—the dark, Doug sleeping so deeply, Kurt's ardent interest—that encouraged confidences.

"Doug was in trouble," Natalie began, checking her husband for a response. But he slept on, undisturbed. "In over his head. Actually it was his friend, Doug's former friend, whom Doug felt he had to help. And I didn't know about this," she concluded.

"That's a hard way to start a marriage," Kurt remarked.

Anger and betrayal, still set to ignite, blazed through Natalie. "If we hadn't nearly died out here, I don't know that we would've made it as a couple." She looked down at Doug, stroking a lock of his hair. "Despite all the things that brought us together. And even though, so many times out there, Doug tried to help me, save me even. It's a cliché, but almost losing my husband showed me that I didn't want to live without him."

Kurt's intent stare bore into hers.

Natalie dipped her head, feeling tears well. "I was ready to give up too soon, though. On our marriage. On Doug himself. I always..."

"Give up too soon?" Kurt asked when her sentence flagged.

Natalie managed a nod. The black-magic quality to the night had swelled, expanded. Kurt as sorcerer, extending his wand. Memories started to mix together in her head in a furious brew. Val and Eva, and how Natalie hadn't even tried to make amends after they'd communicated their hurt. And the job she'd just taken, the latest in a string that didn't come close to being what she really wanted to do. Even the way Natalie had chosen to settle in the city, less out of love for it than because that was all she knew.

Kurt kept silent, watching as if her thoughts were somehow being shared.

"I lost something very important at a young age," Natalie said hesitantly, feeling her way. "Some*one* very important." Another realization hung there, vague and unformed, though Natalie couldn't catch hold of it.

"And so you didn't learn how to hang on," Kurt said. "Even when you needed to. Because you're used to things disappearing on you. Or being taken away."

It was exactly what she had been thinking, but hadn't been able to put into words.

The whole world seemed to come alive then, in a way she'd never experienced before. Vibrant and forceful and exciting. The constant drone of the forest separated into distinct sounds: trickling water, a needful hoot from an owl, rustles in the leaves. Natalie let her eyes fell shut, and when next she took a look around, moonlight painted every detail, and the smells were overpowering: pine needles and loamy earth, the coppery rush of creek water, a metallic stink of bugs. She opened her mouth, and warm, humid air filled it.

Doug stirred on his bed of cushioning, darkness softly settled, and the sensory urgency of the night began to recede.

"We should get some rest," Kurt said at last. "We don't know when your husband might awaken and need our attentions."

"But…" Natalie suddenly realized. "You never told me about you. We began talking about why you decided to come live out here, then got onto me instead."

Like a pied piper, Kurt had led Natalie along a different path. Had that been deliberate? Kurt seemed genuinely more interested in others than he was in himself.

He positioned himself horizontally, lying upon the bare earth at a discreet point of remove. It seemed considerate of him, not to encroach on Natalie's personal space.

"Ach, me," he said. "That's a story for another time."

Natalie lay down on the ground, nestling against Doug. "Good night, Kurt," she said quietly, but fell asleep before hearing his reply.

CHAPTER FORTY-EIGHT

In the dead of the night, Natalie woke to a great, thrashing sound, then Doug sat bolt upright beside her.

He let out a moan.

"Honey?" Natalie whispered. *The sickness, it's come back*, she thought, envisioning a river of that sludge running down to meet the creek.

Doug moaned again. "I'm so hungry."

Natalie's vision began to adjust to the lack of light. She lifted her eyes and met Doug's. They were the clearest she had seen them in days, lit by a violent, rapacious need that Natalie recognized.

"Right here," Kurt said, and he was beside them, holding out the tin cup.

Its contents were warm, the metal pleasant to the touch in the chilly night.

"Go slowly now," Kurt cautioned.

Natalie held the rim of the cup to her husband's lips and helped him to drink.

Life seemed to seep back into Doug along with the soup. He finished one portion before downing another.

"Enough," Kurt said. "We have to be sure that stays down."

"My stomach feels like a rock," Doug said, thumping it with one fist. "It's a miracle. What did you give me?"

"Berberine," Kurt said. "It grows in the vicinity. Without it, I don't know if you would've survived. I had to make use of the same plant myself when I first came here and drank from the stream as you did."

Doug shook his head, his expression creasing. "That was lunacy, I know. I was just so goddamned thirsty." He gave Natalie a look of remorse, and she shook her head. "You weren't acting rationally, honey. Neither of us was."

"You managed not to drink," Doug said.

"I nearly died," she replied.

He touched her arm, as if making sure she was really there. "Me too. And my death would've been a whole lot grosser."

Natalie laughed out loud. She couldn't believe she had her husband back, joking around, referring to both their mortal ends. Gallows humor after a brush—no, not a brush, more than a nodding acquaintance— with the dark side.

She nearly forgot Kurt was there, so caught up was she by Doug's gaze and the warmth of his body next to hers. She looked around in the darkness.

Kurt's eyes glowed as he gazed at them, like some creature of the night. He was observing their exchange, his head turning back and forth.

Natalie took her husband's hand and squeezed it. "Honey. Meet Kurt Pierson. The man who saved our lives."

CHAPTER FORTY-NINE

K urt waited until Doug and Natalie had both fallen back asleep to rise from his spot on the ground. Theirs was the deadened rest of recovery, a sleep that said its participants had nearly entered the state past this one and been stationed there for good. It was lucky both slept so deeply because Kurt had a lot to do.

Still, he took a moment to look down at the couple. Higher in the mountains it must have started to rain, for the creek rushed by at a roar, droplets escaping their banks and dappling the sleeping bag Natalie and Doug shared. Kurt felt curiosity curdle his features, an expression he'd often seen on his parents' faces when they watched him. Passing a mirror one day, he'd been stunned to catch an identical glimpse of the look on his own visage.

Kurt was nothing like his parents. He understood people, knew what made them tick, in a way that his parents couldn't begin to approximate. And they'd both been psychiatrists! But that was the crux of the difference. His parents had accrued book knowledge, medical degrees, and clinical hours, while Kurt zeroed in instinctively on people's most hidden parts, taking out their secret, bloodied guts and examining them, holding them up to the light. Making them part of himself. Take Natalie, for instance.

She had aped surprise upon realizing that she'd spent the entire night talking about herself instead of Kurt. But most people chose to talk about themselves upon finding a listening ear. Natalie had little interest in Kurt, and every desire to prattle on about her own wounded parts and raw places, going over them repeatedly, like a tongue pressing a sore spot on the gum.

She'd lost someone when she was young. Her father almost certainly. The loss of a parent imprinted itself upon a child—one of the few carried into adulthood with little of its emotion discharged—and in Natalie's case, the willingness to follow her new husband into these woods made the pattern seem obvious. She was looking for a male to cleave to and had unconsciously placed a second unreliable man in that role. Doug had been involved in helping a friend with something disreputable or possibly illegal; Natalie's father had become undependable by dint of his death. It might've been the mother who died, but because women tended to marry dear old dad, Kurt's bet was on the father.

He could've debated the two possibilities for endless, joyful hours. Happiness at having people to ponder and peruse suffused him, flushed his skin, made his nerve endings stand up. It was a pleasure more intense and satisfying than sex. Kurt would sooner have had someone whose depths he could probe with his mind than a series of luscious concubines to bed. Even now, with both Doug and Natalie in a state of repose, capable of no confidence nor revelation, Kurt had trouble drawing his gaze away from the pair.

He needed to get moving however.

Only the thought of what might happen if he didn't check on his stations, shore up the ranks, forced him to turn and head off into the deeper stretches of the woods. He needed everything in tiptop shape around here, especially with guests just arrived. He also wanted to see what his holes might contain in the way of future meals—Doug's appetite would be returning, while Natalie's was already enormous—and he had to make sure that weather and topographical shifts hadn't caused any damage to the traps.

Normally Kurt enjoyed these tasks, but tonight his thoughts were focused only on the couple and the burgeoning relationship between the three of them.

Kurt had told the truth when he recounted being afflicted with the same malady that had beset Doug. During his first winter here, the wilderness had gradually unfrozen—a patch of bony brown here, a dripping icicle there—and vanishing snows revealed what seemed a great boon. A sign that Kurt had wound up in the Panglossian best of all possible places, the perfect spot to make his homestead. There was a brook at the end of a winding path, crystalline and seemingly pure. Kurt would have access to fresh water three seasons out of the year!

But the bounty had turned on him. He'd lapped up a melting trickle that ran between two remaining tracts of ice and immediately become ill. He could still feel the dangerous slipperiness of his innards, how not even the tiniest morsel would stay down. Lying prostrate on the ground, hardly able to move, he'd recalled a remedy. Crawling like a worm through snow and exposed earth, Kurt had made his way past numerous shrubs and bushes until he found a thatch of berberine.

It took weeks to fully regain his health, and Kurt had never again drunk a drop from the stream without boiling it first. Creek water made a better biological weapon than any that the armed forces currently possessed.

It had nearly killed Doug; Natalie's fear had been a natural one. Kurt hadn't planned to mislead her, although he did detect the moment she'd jumped to her conclusion and hadn't chosen to disabuse her of it. It had intrigued Kurt to see Natalie's grief start to take form, to imagine what keeping her here as a widow would be like. There was more interest and material to be gleaned with the two together however.

As the sound of the creek began to retreat, Kurt made sure to tread carefully, his eyes on the ground, examining every step he took. He changed the locations of his traps frequently enough that it was difficult to internalize a map of precisely where he'd placed each one. Whenever he reset a trap, its position always altered, however minutely. This was an ongoing process because Kurt had to continually hone wood, replenish poisons, and harvest the animals that fell into the holes he had dug.

Since the idea first came to him, Kurt had fitted out the woods with various armaments he took joy in producing, laboring over each one with a lover's intimate attentions. Sticks whose tips he'd whittled into spikes were thrust deep into the forest floor, poised to penetrate the sole of the thickest boot, and then the foot inside. Swaths of brush lay over deep pits impossible for any creature—even one as big as a man, or a bear, or the deer Kurt had recently butchered—to escape. A tincture distilled from stinging nettles, then boiled until it was hundreds of times stronger, painted various patches of greenery. One swipe against such a plant, and the victim's skin would burn as if roasting over a thousand-degree fire, requiring repeated dunks in the creek. If contact with the distillation took place on the leg, walking with any speed would become impossible. There were also lengths of wire-thin vine strung between tree trunks, low enough not to be seen, sharp enough to slice open a shin.

If anyone came to these woods, Kurt would know about it.

And if anybody tried to leave them, they would be stopped.

Kurt repositioned a run of sharpened sticks, placing them in an array that seemed suited to catching two people walking side by side, as he suspected this couple would do. Even with Doug not yet able to stand upright, he and Natalie were pawing at each other like a couple of horny teenagers. Which, Kurt supposed, they weren't far from being. He wondered how old they were, how they had met and decided to marry. So many nuggets of connection, of a more personal knowing, lay before Kurt. He felt himself shudder with anticipation. He had to place his knife on the ground, lest his trembling hand miss the tip of the stick he was honing and nick his own flesh.

He had hoped to keep the couple separate for longer, the better to get to know each of them well. Isolation had a way of encouraging revelation, made secrets come out. But the woman had proven remarkably strong-willed when it came to her husband.

It didn't matter. Strong-willed or weak, both types were equally fascinating to Kurt. And nobody had might or perspicacity enough to best him. He would revel in the complexities of this couple, their confused love for each other. It could play out in different ways depending upon the conditions Kurt set. Such occupation would keep him busy for years. Living in isolation all this time, Kurt felt as if a banquet had been laid out before him.

The bond Doug had to Natalie seemed as strong as hers to him, Kurt mused. It was true, as he'd told Natalie, that her husband kept saying her name while caught in the throes of delirium. What Kurt hadn't chosen to reveal was that Doug had gone on to offer countless other mutterings and vows, delivering a fertile bed of speculation for Kurt.

Don't hate me, please don't hate me.

I can't bear to lose you, Natalie.

The going will be free and clear from now on.

There's no price to pay, Nat, I can make it up to you.

And best of all—

I never meant to put him over us.

The friend Natalie had mentioned, whom Doug tried to help? Kurt wondered deliciously. *What fun it would be to make use of that particular tidbit.*

Kurt saw to each one of his installations, checking the tilt and angle of daggered sticks, laying fresh thatches of leaves over pits, painting swaths of foliage with blistering tincture. He walked in concentric rings around his camp, starting from the huts and moving outward until he came to land far enough away that no intruder or escapee could avoid encountering one of his traps. Then Kurt turned and headed back toward the creek, his jaunty whistle lost beneath the wind. A storm was picking up, making its way down the mountain like a great coiling snake, ready to wrap itself around Kurt and his guests.

He shivered, more from delight than from the falling temperatures.

What deepening wells of intimacy awaited him today?

Perhaps Doug would open up as Natalie had been so eager to do. It'd been vanishingly simple to effect: just a word of false praise, and the woman's lips parted like petals, exposing her deepest wounds. Natalie and Doug were the opposite of outdoorspeople, wasting away with an abundance of nourishment around, stumbling in circles instead of making use of natural landmarks, committing every beginner's mistake in the woods. To her credit, Natalie had rebutted the compliment, sending it in Doug's direction—who deserved it little more than she—just as she always gave him the prowess and control.

Kurt sensed that Doug might not be quite as easy a mark, although he did have access to one weak spot in the man. Doug felt guilty about something, the issue Natalie had referenced surely. Depending on the exact nature of the situation, might Doug have the impulse to flee or escape, either himself or whatever sort of reckoning awaited him back home? Kurt could use such a need against him. Perhaps offering up a secret of his own would allow him to coax further revelations from the male half of the couple.

The notion was tantalizing—to hear more of Doug's truths, while also laying bare his own.

Confession was akin to cleansing, and Kurt ached to wash himself in the waters of this couple's understanding. How he'd come to these woods with a small band of people, and when one of them behaved in a way to threaten the whole, inviting someone in who hoped to see their society destroyed, Kurt had no choice but to dispatch the intruder. The fact that said intruder happened to be the mother of the utopia's youngest member didn't matter to Kurt. He had to get rid of the mother lest she convince her daughter to leave with her. Kurt didn't want to lose one single object of study.

He had killed once already as a younger man—the time he'd spent incarcerated had produced his fierce fear of solitary confinement—although that crime had been accidental. This had been a deliberate undertaking, designed to preserve the sanctity of their group. He'd expected to win the approbation of every member—after all, he had acted to save them—but instead they had turned on Kurt. He was cornered, had no choice but to flee. He'd leapt into a river whose current dragged him away.

If Natalie and Doug heard this tale, surely they would view Kurt as a worthy protector, someone who could safeguard their needs and interests as well.

The prospect of being seen for who he really was lit a fire inside Kurt.

Nobody ever wanted to know the true Kurt.

Not the folks with whom he had journeyed to these woods, or the first hiker he'd tried to keep here, his son who'd been pulling away, his wife who had decided to leave him, or his parents, who'd sought only to confirm the things they read in books.

But now Kurt had a fresh start. A whole new opportunity.

He intended to make full use of it, to hold no part of himself back even as he mined the couple until there was nothing of them left.

He sensed something amiss before he got back to the creek. This was his home, and he knew every inch of the land, could perceive its slightest change. A flurry of movement, shifting air currents, disturbances in the dirt, all invisible to less probing eyes, were to Kurt no different than a door pushed open in a house, furniture overturned.

He had strayed too far in his efforts to batten down the hatches, roaming over acres of weaponry and traps. The remainder of the night had slipped away, and now it was dawn. He'd been silly to have gone to such lengths, since the couple was in no condition to cover anywhere near the terrain Kurt just had.

Although clearly they were regaining strength faster than Kurt had expected.

He'd underestimated them, and the misjudgment enraged him nearly as much as the prospect of having to hunt them down all over again.

He swore inwardly, striking his thigh with a rocklike fist till he felt the flesh turn pulpy and begin to bruise. Then he picked up his stride, breaking through a barricade of branches with an arm impervious to the clap of wood, his gaze sweeping the ground for signs of passage as he broke into a run.

He was sweating and panting by the time he arrived at the sleeping bag, neatly folded on a spot beside the creek. Fear rigidified Kurt's body. He began to stalk, Frankenstein-like, in the direction of camp.

Natalie and Doug were nowhere to be seen.

CHAPTER FIFTY

Doug pushed the sleeping bag aside and got shakily to his feet while Natalie watched. She offered a hand for balance, and he took it.

They stood beside the creek together, water darting and laughing over rocks, drops glinting like crystals in the moonlight.

"Just like old times, huh?" Doug said wryly, squeezing her hand.

Natalie's mouth lifted in a brief smile.

"Your cheek," Doug said. He started to reach out, but stopped himself.

Natalie swallowed. "Bad?"

"The cut is nearly closed," Doug said, a partial answer at best. "Does it hurt?"

Natalie shrugged, then shook her head. "How about your arm?"

Doug didn't answer that; he seemed preoccupied. "Think we'll ever be the same, Nat? How we were in the beginning?" His voice was filled with loss. "This land seemed so different then."

Natalie thought about what Doug had come here expecting to

get—salvation for his friend, a start for the two of them—and all that the place had instead taken away.

"I don't think so," she replied. "We can't be. We know what's important in a way that we didn't before. And we know how easily those things can be lost."

The temperature was dropping, and the banks of the creek lay bleakly beneath a cold and inhospitable moon. She and Doug were different, and the woods were changing too. Wind electric through the trees, leaves jangling, nocturnal birds chittering out alerts to their brethren. She recalled the moments she and Kurt had shared earlier, when all of the outdoors came to life. How wondrous it had been, like Dorothy waking up in Oz. But the flood of sensory input had taken on a menacing hue.

"Let me show you where I've been staying," Natalie suggested. She had the urge to get away from this spot. "We can go inside and warm up."

Doug raised his eyebrows. "Inside?"

"Don't expect the Taj Mahal," Natalie said, and led the way between the trees.

The huts appeared before them in a patch of ivory light just before the moon was blotted out by a field of clouds.

"This one is mine," Natalie said, surprised to hear in her statement a feeling of ownership. She ducked through the smaller hut's opening, turning around when Doug didn't follow.

He had crouched beside the row of slim branches that made up the outside wall of the hut and was touching each one, a frown on his face.

"I think he built this by hand," Doug said.

"I told you it wasn't the Taj Mahal," Natalie replied.

"No," Doug said. "I mean that I don't think he used any tools. These branches are too irregular. I can't believe this is even possible."

Natalie nodded. "Come to think of it, I haven't seen any tools around."

Doug pointed to the wall again. "There aren't any nails, so I wouldn't expect a hammer. But how about a saw or an ax?"

Natalie shook her head. "He collects wood from the ground for his fires. There's no chopping block even. Yet he gets those blazes to rage."

Doug let out an admiring whistle. "Who is this guy?"

Natalie rubbed her arms; they'd gone prickly with cold. She wanted to share the impressions she'd been accumulating about Kurt, but feared it might be too early in Doug's recovery. Her husband needed to build up strength. Anyway, it wasn't as if Kurt had shown anything besides caring and attentiveness toward them, and been generous with his sparse possessions.

"Do you know how long he's been living like this?" Doug asked.

Natalie thought. "Two or three years maybe? I think he made a reference to this being his third summer."

Doug whistled again, shaking his head. "So the two of you have spent some time together, it sounds like?"

With a burn to her cheeks that she hoped was imperceptible in the dim light, Natalie said, "Well, not a lot of time. Most of yesterday I was watching you sleep."

"How long was I out?" Doug asked.

Natalie paused. "You know? That's a good question. I don't know how long it's been since Kurt found us. I was in and out for a while myself."

A look passed between them, the shared strangeness of where they had been, the fact that they very nearly hadn't returned.

"I came to a few times." Doug's voice sounded tentative. "I don't think Kurt even knew I was awake. And when I did, I saw him..." He trailed off.

"You saw him what?" Natalie asked.

Doug changed course, emitting a dry chuckle. "He was probably just watching to make sure I was still alive. Kurt has this kind of penetrating gaze, you know?"

Natalie cast her eyes around, checking that they were alone. "I've noticed."

"But he'd also say things," Doug went on.

"Like what?" Natalie asked quickly.

"Maybe I'd been talking in my sleep, I don't know, but Kurt would murmur these phrases. As if he was trying to offer me comfort, except they were things he really shouldn't have known. *Don't worry, you haven't lost her.* Pretty intimate stuff."

Natalie felt a momentary flurry of goose bumps across her skin.

"Nat?" Doug said. "Kurt didn't... He hasn't tried anything with you, has he?"

Natalie shook her head, fast and hard. "No! If anything, the opposite—"

Doug looked relieved. "I don't mean to be a jerk here. We don't want to act ungrateful. I mean, the guy saved our lives."

"I know he did," Natalie said. "He had to take care of some pretty gnarly tasks too." With a flush, she recalled the first time she'd gone to the bathroom. "And Kurt seems genuinely invested in our recovery. I think he might be some kind of doctor."

"He sure cured me," Doug replied. "That plant or whatever."

They both nodded, looking at each other.

A sudden, loud crashing came from the woods, and the wind stirred up a cyclone of leaves. Natalie and Doug both jumped, then moved closer together. A branch broke off with a brittle snap, and they spun in that direction, dizzy on their feet.

"There you two are!" said Kurt with a ringing cry. "I've been looking for you."

CHAPTER FIFTY-ONE

I was worried about you," Kurt said, ushering them inside the bigger hut, which Natalie realized she hadn't seen until now. "There's a storm coming, and I don't think either of you is up to getting soaked and chilled."

Natalie spoke casually. "You know, we thought of something."

"Oh yes?" Kurt said. He pointed to a pad on the floor—this hut boasted a crinkly tarp covering a section of the bare ground—indicating that she and Doug should sit.

"Neither of us knows exactly when you found us," Natalie said. "How much time have we spent here?"

"Not much," Kurt replied. He busied himself beside a wooden crate that looked half-demolished, coming out with a protein bar, which he extended in their direction.

Natalie and Doug both gasped. It was like looking at an obsolete yet essential instrument, a relic that had been feared forever lost.

Kurt sent them a look of understanding. "A rarity out here, I know," he said. "I think I mentioned that hikers sometimes pass through and leave offerings. Today you'll be the recipients of their generosity." He unwrapped the bar and broke it neatly in half.

"Please," Doug said. "Take one of those. Natalie and I can split the other."

Kurt placed one of the halves on Doug's palm, then reached for Natalie's hand, cupping it to deposit the remaining piece of bar. "I wouldn't think of it," he said.

Natalie took a nibble. The taste was so overwhelming—manufactured flavors and ingredients intermingling at a hundredfold rate compared to anything Kurt had fed her—that her mouth cramped in a spasm. She had to hold off eating the rest. Only the site of Doug gnawing, his Adam's apple jumping up and down as he swallowed every bite, enabled Natalie to proceed cautiously again.

"Thank you," she said, licking her lips for any lingering trace of bar.

At the same time Doug said, "Not much...so like a couple of days?"

Kurt considered, dropping down beside them on the tarp. "Something like that. Possibly as many as three."

"Yikes," Natalie said. She looked at Doug. "So we're overdue by... how many?"

Doug paused to calculate. "I'm pretty sure we stopped walking on day seven. Which means we would've been expected... Shit. Two days ago."

Kurt watched them.

"People are going to be worried," Natalie told Doug. "My sister. Mark and Brett."

"Zach and Naomi too," Doug said.

Their bosses. Doug would be fine, but Natalie's new job meant she hadn't accumulated much time off yet. She'd been forced to ask for unpaid days for their honeymoon as it was. "Not to mention Mia," Natalie added. "She'll be leading the hunt."

Kurt spoke up. "Who's Mia?"

Natalie turned to him. "My niece," she said with a rueful smile. "We're very close. And she's at that age where she thinks she's the only one who can take care of anything."

Kurt sent her a similar smile back.

"This probably sounds stupid," Natalie said, "but do you have a radio? Or any means of communicating with the outside world?"

Kurt shook his head. "That's kind of the point," he said. "To be out of touch."

"How far are you from the nearest town or road?" Doug asked. "Trailhead even?" When Kurt didn't reply, Doug added, "Where are we?"

"As best I can tell—from hikers who have passed through—I now reside in what's called the Turtle Ridge Wilderness Area, some seventy-five miles south of the Canadian border," Kurt said. "So named for the way in which the many mountains resemble humped turtles lying on the ground."

Did Kurt not know exactly where he lived? Natalie sent Doug a look of surprise and dismay. This meant that they had covered seventy-five miles since discovering Craig's body. More probably, since a certain portion of the distance had surely been spent crisscrossing and doubling back.

"It's a five-day walk out," Kurt went on. "But that's at a good clip. For people in tiptop shape. And under near-perfect conditions, seasonally, weather-wise."

As if to drive home the point, a clap of thunder shook the thin walls of the hut. Rain slashed through the air outside, while lightning throbbed in a greenish-yellow sky.

Kurt rose, standing at full height beneath the slatted roof. "Today we stay put," he said. "Nowhere to go in the likes of this. You two can get at least another full day of rest. Time enough to discuss options after that." He paused, then nodded at them. "Unless of course you decide it's so nice and cozy that you wish to stay."

Doug offered him a grin in response. "Yeah, right."

Natalie's accompanying smile felt forced.

Kurt gave them both a nod, holding up a hand when Natalie started to rise, before crossing to the doorway and peeking outside. "Stay here. The mat is comfortable, and the tarp will keep you dry. I'll just run over to the other hut… I don't mind a little shower."

He ducked through the opening and was gone.

Natalie didn't expect to need a great deal more sleep—certainly not the heavy, drugged daytime sort that had so muddled her sense of time—but she didn't open her eyes again until purple twilight was filling the hut.

Then she rose from the mat and tiptoed over the tarp, trying to keep the material from crinkling so as not to disturb Doug.

She sensed when he came up behind her.

He ringed her waist with his arms as they stood at the threshold. Endless layers of mountains made up the vista before them, violet light pooling in creased valleys between. Off in the distance, they caught a glimpse of a shimmering lake.

"Wow," Doug said. "Some spot."

"See?" came a voice.

Natalie hadn't registered Kurt's presence till then. He'd been snapped into existence like a magic trick, appearing out of nowhere beside them. He had traded one set of clothes for another, and his damp hair smelled of pine.

"You like it here," Kurt added, a tiny smile pulling at the corner of his mouth.

It occurred to Natalie for the first time how rarely Kurt smiled. Even on those occasions when he had, the expression didn't seem to connote the same happiness that this one did.

"Let's just say I can see why you stay," Doug said, rocking Natalie against him. His body felt stronger already, although he still seemed to be favoring his right arm. Natalie made a mental note to ask about the injury again.

Kurt regarded them. "There's nothing like it," he agreed. "You know, I contemplated going back at first, like you two are. But when I started thinking about the things that I missed, they all seemed so trivial. Turning on a tap for hot water. What's wrong with fetching some from the creek and building a fire to heat it? Or ready access to convenience foods. As Natalie here will tell you"—he paused to nod in her direction—"things you never would've imagined eating taste mighty good out here."

"You can say that again," Doug responded.

Kurt looked at him. "When I started picturing—really picturing—going back, well, that was what did it for me. Because what I saw were bars clanging shut. Shackles pinching themselves around my ankles. Everything I didn't want to face. That's what life is like out there when you get right down to it. No one truly knows the meaning of *free*."

Doug looked mesmerized, entering some state conjured up by Kurt's words. "Hey, man," he said. "I totally get where you're coming from."

Natalie dug her finger into the scant flesh at her husband's side. He'd lost enough weight that she could feel his skeleton. But at least the touch seemed to snap Doug out of it. He turned to her and frowned. She thought to mouth a warning, but wasn't sure what it should be. Besides, what if Kurt proved to be as adept at lipreading as he was at intuiting other forms of nonverbal communication?

He spoke into the pause. "I have to gather firewood, then start tonight's meal. I'm sure you're both famished." He gave a clap of his hands. "Either of you like to help?"

Doug took a step forward, but Natalie caught his hand and pulled him back, allowing Kurt a head start.

"What's up?" Doug asked. He looked eager to get going.

"I guess you didn't get what I did out of that little speech?" Natalie asked.

Doug lifted his eyebrows. "What are you talking about?"

"I don't think Kurt was joking before we went back to sleep earlier." Natalie spoke hurriedly. "He's not a kidding-around kind of guy."

The picture had been forming in Natalie's mind, taking shape like a paint-by-numbers kit. Kurt stating that Natalie didn't have to worry about helping with chores "for now" after she'd first gotten back on her feet. His promise to make more clay cups. Why would he need to do that for temporary residents? He'd also referenced the future at least once— autumn, when the chipmunks would go into hiding.

Doug nodded Natalie on, no less impatient.

Kurt called out from the edge of the forest, raising his arm to summon them. "Coming, you two?"

Natalie gave an enthusiastic nod and wave back. Then she lowered her voice, speaking intently to Doug. "I think he means for us to stay."

CHAPTER FIFTY-TWO

Her parents kept Mia so busy, shuttling her back and forth between them, barely giving her any unsupervised time, that she didn't get to go onto Mark's Facebook account—page, whatever it was called—and poke around for another whole day. She still hadn't heard from Aunt Nat, and by then her stomach felt like she'd swallowed a porcupine—like the time she'd been in the school play, only worse—so that when Mia tried to log on, her fingers were shaking so hard she could barely hit the right buttons.

Even though he was hot and a teacher, Mark Harden only had forty-seven Facebook friends. Duh, it wasn't like his students would be friending him. They were all hanging out on Snapchat and Instagram, and Mia hadn't been able to find Mark there.

She scrolled over the grid displaying each of the friends. Uncle Doug, Brett, Aunt Nat...and then Mia came to another face she recognized. She let the tiny hand icon hover over the stamp-sized square. It showed the guy Scowly had asked her about.

Craig Reynolds.

That was his last name. Now she remembered, as if Scowly were right there, hissing in her ear. Mia shuddered.

She clicked on the photo and got a *to see what Craig shares, send him a friend request* message, which she did. But there was a post on Craig's public page that Mia could read. Someone named Flower, of all things, had written an update.

Still no word from my boy. He's never been gone this long before. If Craig contacts you, please! Tell him I need to hear from him ASAP. Another please! And then a number, an actual phone number. Posted right there on the home page for anyone to see.

Mia's stomach went even pricklier inside her. Her mom was acting like it was perfectly normal that Aunt Nat and Uncle Doug would be late getting back from their honeymoon—and Mia had almost bought it—but now a third person was missing too.

Was Flower Craig's mother? His girlfriend? Mia was leaning toward the former as she sent a text to the number on the screen.

think i might have info 4 u abt craig

A response came like two seconds later, a real live call. It was late, and Mia had put her phone on vibrate so her mother wouldn't hear it if it rang.

She slid her thumb across the screen and answered in a muted voice. "Hello?"

A pause, then, "You're so young! Oh Christ, you sound so young."

Flower had to be Craig's mother. Mia felt a flush of success at having guessed right. "I'm thirteen," she replied sharply.

Silence.

Mia felt the need to talk fast, prove she really had something to say. "Craig is friends with my uncle. Doug Larson."

"Doug?" Flower demanded. "Doug doesn't have any brothers or sisters."

290

"He just married my aunt," Mia said.

"Oh, right," Flower said. "Makes sense. Sorry. My mind is just about blown right now."

Mia wasn't sure what to say. "I'm sorry" was all she could come up with.

"Where are you?" asked Flower suddenly. "Home with your parents?"

"Well, my mom's asleep," Mia said. "She doesn't know I'm calling. She doesn't think there's anything to be worried about."

"What *are* you worried about?" Flower asked.

Mia realized she had better backtrack. "My uncle's missing," she explained. "Along with my aunt. At the very least, they're late. And I guess your son is too?"

There was silence over the phone, then the sound of a nose being blown loudly. "Jesus, what did you boys get yourselves mixed up in this time?" said Flower.

"I don't think they're all together though," Mia said. "I mean, my aunt and uncle are on their honeymoon."

Flower didn't seem to absorb that. "The cops barely even agreed to take my report," she told Mia. "Said a grown man can pretty much do what he wants, less there's signs of...how did they put it? Foul play."

"Foul play," Mia repeated. Scowly and his friend. They definitely seemed capable of something foul.

"Little girl?" said Flower. "You still there?"

"I'm here." Mia took a deep breath, then told Flower about the men, how one of them had shown her a picture of Craig and demanded to know if she knew him.

"Jesus Christ," Flower said, almost whistling the words.

Mia didn't expect what happened next, but she burst out crying.

"So why are you calling?" Flower asked when Mia's tears finally started to subside. "I can't help you find your aunt. I didn't even know she existed till now."

"I don't know," Mia replied miserably. "I just thought maybe the reason my aunt and uncle haven't come back yet has something to do with why your son's gone too."

"They'll be home soon," Flower replied, her tone certain. "Craig always comes back. And I bet the same goes for your aunt and uncle. Those boys—Craig, Doug, all of 'em—well, they're mixed-up breeds. Craig's daddy was the same way. Hard to tie down, hard to keep straight. And real hard to walk away from."

Silence after that.

Mia looked down at her phone.

Call ended.

When she hit the number again, it went to voicemail.

Mia got an Instagram alert from her friend who'd just finished camp, and the dinging tone jarred her into realizing. Why was she trying to track down Uncle Doug's friends and calling their rando relatives? Uncle Doug had only been related to Mia for like a week. But Aunt Nat she'd known her whole life.

Mia navigated over to Aunt Nat's account, scrolling back to find the women whose photos her aunt had shoved into a drawer. Mia requested to follow them, then fell asleep with the phone cradled between her pillow and her ear, hoping to be awakened by a penetrating ding of a text.

It took a second day, Mia still getting passed from her mom to her dad like a five-year-old in need of a nanny, before one of Aunt Nat's friends finally accepted Mia's request. Did these people not live on their phones or what? By then, Mia's insides were swarming with worry, and the response she got from Val after Mia introduced herself and explained the situation, made things a thousand times worse.

not surprised to hear it didn't exactly go smoothly

what do u mean? Mia texted, her heart punching a fist in her chest.

your new uncle isn't a good guy, sweetie, came the response a minute later. why do you think i wasn't at the wedding?

Because you're a stone-cold bitch and my aunt didn't want you there? Mia thought. She stared down at the screen, at a loss for what to say back.

Val texted again without waiting.

> he tries to control natalie he's a control freak of
> the highest order i could tell the moment i met him

And then another.

> or maybe she just wants to be controlled

A split second later, before Mia had even gotten a chance to start texting her reply—

> or both

Mia pictured Val's fingers jumping all over her screen, so fast she wasn't even taking time to breathe. *She's jealous*, Mia thought. Classic frenemy where one person couldn't stand the other being happy. Except then Mia's mind skittered to that moment at the wedding underneath the tree. Uncle Doug had been pretty—what was the word—*dominant* with Aunt Nat. Trying to get her not to ask questions and the like.

A final text dinged.

> if natalie insisted on going off into the woods with
> that guy, and now she isn't back when she should be, i
> don't know about you, but i'd be seriously concerned

Mia threw her phone aside on her bed and ran to find her mom.

"How late are they?" her mother asked, once she'd made sense of Mia's overlapping sentences and pleas to stop working. Her mom had been doing all her paperwork at home since she'd started covering extra shifts. She set her laptop beside her on the couch, closing it to hide treatment plans or something else confidential. "How long was their trip supposed to be again?"

"A week," Mia said instantly. How did her mom not know this? She always made it her business to be on top of everything. It was like Aunt Nat getting married had changed something, like her mom had lost a job. "They were supposed to finish canoeing after a week and come home the next day, but it's a long drive, so maybe not till night."

Mia's mom frowned. "So that was…what? Two days ago. How did I lose track?"

"That's what I've been trying to tell you!" Mia said, plunking down on the couch.

Her mother reached for her phone and thumbed it to life. She began clicking on email after email from Aunt Nat, then their old texts, scanning the screen closely at first, but soon going faster, barely reading before scrolling over to whatever she wanted to look at next. Mia scuttled closer to her mom, watching over her mother's shoulder. She had some web page open with FAQs about wilderness exploration, and was staring at it with the most bizarre expression on her face, all wide-eyed and kind of dazed.

Finally, her mother dropped the phone and let her hand fall to her lap. She muttered something and Mia said, "What?" But her mother didn't repeat what she'd said. Could've been *I told her so* or *I told her not to go.*

When her mother spoke next, her voice was a little clearer, but strange still, like a little girl's. "I've taken care of your aunt Nat her whole life." She didn't exactly seem to be talking to Mia, though, didn't even have her within sight. "But what is there for me to do now?" Her mother extended one arm, gesturing toward the windows that looked over the skyscrapers and the street. "I don't know anything about rivers or woods or land that empty. I have no idea what to do out there."

Mia slid down off the couch, getting onto her hands and knees in front of her mother, and laying her head on her lap. "Mom?" she whispered.

Her mother looked down as if she hadn't quite realized that Mia was still there. "Yes, Mi?"

"Why don't you just call the police?"

CHAPTER FIFTY-THREE

Natalie and Doug helped Kurt collect armfuls of wood, staying in a tight radius whose boundaries Kurt laid out, reminding them not to wander. Once they had enough kindling and sticks, they started to head back toward the huts—Natalie noting that she now needed no guidance, could navigate this part of the woods on her own—but Kurt held up a hand to say *wait* before ushering them in a different direction.

"Follow the trail I break," he said, forging a path toward a group of boulders bunched like a cluster of enormous grapes. "I've got a surprise for you both."

The sky was so soft, it looked brushed. Kitten-fur wisps of cloud melded with the lavender blue of descending night as the three of them walked. After a while, they came to the lake Natalie and Doug had glimpsed from the hut. Darkness flashed on as if cued, all remnants of daylight suddenly gone. An indigo pool of water sat in a bowl so deep its sides were the mountains, sparkling like a prism beneath a million stars.

Natalie caught her breath.

Kurt noticed, his ears pricking in the darkness. "Location, location, location. Isn't that what they say?" He pointed toward the water, regarding Natalie as she turned. "This would've sold me on my camp even if I'd had to deal with Realtors. Thankfully I didn't."

Doug reached for Natalie's hand, and they started walking toward the edge of the lake. Doug stripped off his shirt and shorts as he went, looking over at Natalie. She glanced down at her clothes. The prospect of slipping into that silky smooth water—the chance to really get clean for the first time in what felt like months—was hard to resist.

Doug shrugged, gesturing toward the boxers he wore, which looked just like swim trunks, then indicated Natalie's own undergarments. "No different from a bikini, right?"

What decided Natalie was the oddest, yet utterly certain conviction. Kurt would show no less interest in Natalie if her entire body were swathed in robes than if she'd stood naked before him. She tossed her T-shirt and shorts onto a rock before running beside Doug down to the water.

Her husband's renewed strength was reassuring, although Natalie felt aghast at what had happened to his body in so short a time. His ribs stood out like a fan, barely encased in flesh; there were grooves at his sides and hollows in his chest. Still, Doug's grip was firm as he tugged her into deeper water—up to their thighs, their hips, their stomachs—until they both plunged, laughing, beneath the surface.

Doug came up, shaking water from his head, while Natalie surfaced a few yards away. She dolphin-dove and swam underwater back to her husband. He caught her around the waist and pulled her close. Their gazes caught, then slid away, flicking to the shore before their eyes were drawn back together like magnets. Helplessly, Natalie lifted her face while Doug lowered his. Their lips met with a flutter of newness, a feeling Natalie had only experienced once before—on the night they had met, when it was hard to believe that two strangers could want the same thing with such equal intensity.

They both seemed to remember at once that they weren't alone, and twisted back around toward shore.

Kurt stood there, facing them. When their gazes met, he didn't turn away or avert his stare, but simply continued to look as if the moment was his as much as theirs.

Despite the cool swish of water against her, Natalie's skin grew heated, uncomfortable.

Doug grinned down at her, but there was a stiffness, a falsity to his expression compared to the intimacy that had united them just moments before.

Smile at me, he mouthed, and Natalie did.

"Look," Doug said. "I've been thinking about what you said."

Natalie took her eyes off Kurt on the shore.

"And I'd be a fool to dismiss it. I've learned that by now." Doug paused. "It's hard for me to get used to listening to anybody else."

It would be hard for Natalie to get used to saying things that people listened to, but she decided to hold on to that for right now.

"But it's understandable, right?" he said. "I mean, it must get lonely, living like this way out here. Kurt wants companionship. And he has it for now. It's not like he's going to argue when it comes time for us to go, even if on some level he might prefer that we didn't. I mean, he's got to realize that most people can't just trash their real lives."

Natalie nodded slowly. Cool lake water swirled around them.

"Hey, you two!" Kurt called from the shore. "Getting hungry?"

Doug continued to look at Natalie, one eyebrow cocked.

She gave a surer nod. "Okay," she said. "Tonight let's just be friendly, not even talk about the prospect of leaving. Tomorrow we can figure out a plan."

Doug squeezed her hand beneath the gray skin of water. They swam back to shore underneath the star-pricked sky.

Kurt had made a circle of rocks on the banks of the lake,

depositing the wood they had collected. A blaze was just starting to catch when Natalie and Doug emerged from the water, dripping and gathering up their discarded clothes, which they pulled on under cover of the darkness.

"Come dry off by the fire," Kurt called.

"I haven't seen you use any matches," Doug remarked, settling himself on a flat rock and tugging Natalie down beside him.

"That's because I don't have any," Kurt replied. "Or not many at any rate, and those I do must be saved for emergencies." He displayed a whittled stick.

"That can start a fire?" Doug asked.

Natalie glanced at him. He must've been going along with what she'd said, donning an easy amicability, because they had both watched the matchless-fire trick done on YouTube a dozen times before setting out on their honeymoon.

Kurt demonstrated the rapid wheel of the stick between his two palms, how touching it to a dry leaf ignited a flicker of flame.

Doug whistled. "Amazing."

Natalie leaned back against him, staring off at the distant mountains.

"I have a treat for us," Kurt remarked. He laid a pair of glistening fish upon a crosshatch of wood in the fire. "We'll take them off before the sticks really start to burn," he said. "Fish this fresh doesn't need much cooking. Just a nice sear of its skin."

"They from this lake?" Doug asked.

Kurt nodded. "Swam into my trap earlier today when you both were asleep. Doesn't happen very often." He turned a bright expression on them, although there was something cold and empty about it, reflective of the moonlight. "I think they came just for the two of you."

A chill wind swept through the mountains, causing the leaves on the trees to rustle like a nest of rattlesnakes, and wrapping itself around Natalie. Her clothes were damp from her body, and she shivered. Because with those words she'd realized something. She and Doug had both underestimated the forces at work here, the strength of Kurt's desire.

He was wooing them. His nicest locale, the choicest treats.

Leaving was not going to be easy.

CHAPTER FIFTY-FOUR

The wind continued to blow with that dry, corn-husk sound while Kurt poked the fire to awaken the flames. Embers sparked, giving off a smoky essence. Kurt served the fish, slicing one in half for him and Natalie to share, and giving the other to Doug.

"Unbelievable," Doug said, sucking a sliver of flesh off a translucent bone. "Best fish I've ever eaten." He shot a grin Natalie's way. "Five stars."

Natalie tried to smile in return. "We'll have to write our review in the dirt."

"Or when we get—" Doug began.

Natalie slid her hand over his, locking their fingers together.

Kurt licked the tips of his own fingers, catlike and somehow appealing. "When it's this fresh, you don't even need any butter or lemon."

The thought was a sharp shard in Natalie's head. *What I wouldn't give for some butter or lemon.*

Kurt's gaze rested on her. "It can take a while to shed the last vestiges of the old world," he said. "You probably want nothing more than to run into the nearest Stop & Shop right now. But I found such penchants didn't last long."

She hadn't said it out loud. How had he known? Natalie's skin prickled despite the heat of the fire, and she struggled to get down a last morsel of fish. "Gristedes," she said a little hoarsely. "That's where we go in the city."

Kurt offered her the cup, but Natalie shook her head.

"No?" Kurt said without lifting his gaze. "Not thirsty? Or in need of a drink?"

Natalie felt a breath of resignation leave her body. There was no use trying to conceal anything from Kurt; he seemed to sense everything. She accepted the cup from his hand, chugging the contents until the fish with its bit of bone slid down her throat.

Kurt gave a satisfied nod.

"So," Doug said, settling back. "We've been thinking about what you said."

"Oh yes?" Kurt replied.

"Be impossible not to," Doug said smoothly. He traced a finger along Natalie's arm in a gesture he probably thought would look affectionate, but which Natalie knew to be a warning. "Nights like this. But I gotta ask. How do you make it through the winter?"

A mental siren blared. *Don't do this, Doug. Hold off till tomorrow, like we decided.* They needed to come up with a plan before presenting their exit strategy to Kurt.

Kurt laced his hands together, as if warming to the topic. "It's not easy, I'll grant you. But when spring finally peeps its head...my, what a sense of accomplishment you have. In a way, you can't appreciate the seasons that give themselves to you more gently until you've survived their brutal sibling."

"I can see that," Doug said. He coughed and reached for the cup. "This full?"

Natalie poured him some water.

Doug drank, then gave Kurt his best smile. "Whiskey, though. I mean, you gotta miss that."

Kurt didn't smile back, his face smooth and implacable.

"Do you go into town?" Doug asked once the pause had drawn itself out. "Before winter sets in, I mean. To stock up on supplies?"

"No need," Kurt replied. "Summer and fall bring a new crop of hikers, and as I've said, they tend to leave things behind."

He means that he takes them, Natalie thought with a sudden stab of fear. Why would a hiker give up any of his equipment or rations?

"But if you did want to…" Doug said. "You know, say you ran out of something, or a backpacker didn't happen by. Then you would have to pick stuff up, right? Didn't you tell us it was a five-day hike?"

Natalie gave her husband's hand a firm squeeze. When he looked at her, she met his eyes and tilted her chin, a reminder.

Doug placed an arm around her, drawing her close. "Which way would you head?" he asked. "Do you come to any sort of marked trail, or is it all bushwhacking?"

Silence from Kurt, so heavy that it finally seemed to strike a blow.

Doug began to scramble in retreat. "Because I was thinking that if we were to settle in here—Natalie and I—then we could divide up the work. I could make a trip to town, while you two stayed back, getting things in shape for the winter."

"All that snow," Kurt said in a musing tone. "And ice."

"Must take a ton of preparation," Doug said, nodding.

His nod looked a little frantic to Natalie. This was the Doug who drank from the brook, not the measured incarnation who administered the taste test or directed their canoe through the rapids. Doug was straying from the strategy he and Natalie had come up with in the lake, and Natalie thought she knew why. For all the beauty of this spot, Kurt's description of winter made clear how utterly isolated the three of them were. Natalie and Doug had no more knowledge of how to find their way out than they'd possessed before. It was hard to go slowly, try and manipulate Kurt, when the woods were closing in like a cell.

"Two extra sets of hands," Kurt went on, "would certainly be a boon to me."

"That's what I'm trying to say," Doug replied, nodding vigorously some more. "We'd want to pull our weight around here. Not just impose on you, making use of all you've created without providing anything in return." He paused, Adam's apple rolling in his throat. "And if you did happen to run out of something and needed someone to make a quick run to town—"

"Well then, you'd be happy to help with that too," Kurt supplied, so smoothly it almost concealed the edge in his tone.

Doug shut his eyes for a moment, admitting defeat. He balled his hands into fists. "Look," he said. "We can't stay, Kurt. Tempting as the prospect may be." Doug gestured toward the lake. "Tempting as the prospect *is*—you really sold us. But we have friends and family waiting back home. Jobs to go to. Lives to lead." He glanced at Natalie for support.

Natalie gave a nod, but Kurt's gaze stayed fixed on Doug. "I can understand that." He offered a pleasant smile. "Really, I can."

Doug leaned back, a barely perceptible frown forming. "It's not like we're ungrateful," he said. "You saved our lives." There was a flatness to Kurt's expression, the smile a mere overlay, and Doug glanced away quickly. "Or even that we haven't enjoyed ourselves. It's been, well, kind of great."

"All good things must come to an end," Kurt said.

"Right." Doug reached for the cup, but it was empty. He licked his lips.

"Scott's Dash," Kurt said.

Doug looked as confused as Natalie felt.

"No need for whiskey—Scott's Dash is a natural soporific that grows in these parts," Kurt explained. "I dry the leaves and steep them into tea. One mug of that, and you'd better be ready to cart me away."

Doug gave an impatient jerk of his head. "Great."

"I should've prepared some for this evening," Kurt added. "As a relaxant. Because there are a few things I need to tell you. Before you make your final decision."

The frown on Doug's face became visible. "Look, I told you, man. It isn't really a decision at all...more like an inevitability. But whatever it is, we've made it."

"Still," Kurt said agreeably. "Hear me out."

After a moment, Doug nodded.

"That five-day hike you so blithely referred to?" Kurt said, and again Doug nodded. "It could be a ten-day trip. Or a two. You have no idea whether a single thing I've told you since we met is true. Turtle Ridge." He tilted his head. "What a quaint name for such a toothsome part of the world. Why, it sounds positively made up."

"Now, wait just a minute—" Doug began.

Kurt held up a palm to stop him. "Not that it matters where you are or how long it would take to get out, because you don't know which way to go. You'll wind up as lost as you were the day I pulled your sorry ass out of the woods."

Natalie felt the earth, their spot in this basin of mountains, suddenly tilt. Reality, as it had presented itself from the moment she returned to consciousness, started to slip away, exposing something else entirely.

Doug's mouth had stayed open. "You think you can make us stay— keep us here against our will—just by threatening us with getting lost?"

"No," Kurt said. "I don't think that. That would be crazy."

"It sure would," Doug said. "So then we're back to—"

Kurt leaned forward. The heat from the fire seemed to have infused him, radiating outward so that it enveloped Natalie and Doug as well. Leaping flames sparked in Kurt's eyes. "Have the two of you ever wondered why we tread so carefully here, the reason I keep ensuring that you both trail in my footsteps and don't wander off?"

Doug didn't speak, turning to look at Natalie, who frowned.

"I'm not surprised if you haven't," Kurt went on. "Most people are happily unaware of what takes place around them, content to live as if muffled by an infinite number of layers that prevent them from really seeing, hearing, understanding."

Doug's anger was apparent, but Natalie made her expression blank, giving nothing away.

"I didn't want it to come to this," Kurt said. "But I suppose I should tell you both something else." He paused, taking a look around the lake and shaking his head, as if its beauty stood in stark contrast to what he was about to reveal.

"Just come out with it," Doug said, his tone bristling.

Kurt waited a moment before speaking calmly. "These woods are armed," he said. "As lethal as if I had actual soldiers. There are so many weapons and traps and pitfalls spread throughout the land that nobody could make his way out without risking maiming, dismemberment, or worse."

Doug lifted his eyes, and what he felt was starkly visible, as clear as if he'd painted it. Refusal. Denial. "Yeah, right," he said.

Kurt shrugged. "Try me," he said. "You won't get ten yards before winding up in a condition that makes you wish you were only lost."

Doug stared at him blankly.

Kurt's lips lifted, not in a grin, but something worse. He extended a hand downward, mimicking the sharp snap of an ankle, then placed his hands around his own neck, pantomiming a choke hold.

The performance made no sense, which was the really frightening part.

It obviously meant something to Kurt.

Natalie reached out and took her husband's hand, for a new expression had begun to bloom on Doug's face.

The first mounting hints of horror.

CHAPTER FIFTY-FIVE

Doug acted without pause.

Natalie watched with her own feeling of horror as he drew back his arm and went to throw a punch, fast and forceful, his fist bunched like the end of a club. At the last second, though, Doug winced, and the blow wavered in midcourse. He would've toppled into the fire, propelled by his own momentum, if Kurt hadn't grabbed him by the wrist.

"I wouldn't," Kurt said in a *tsking* tone, before restoring Doug to his feet. "Your right arm doesn't seem to have completely healed. You're not functioning at maximum capacity. And even if you were—"

"You fucking bastard—" Doug began.

Kurt went on as if there'd been no interruption. "—you must see that it'd be a hard fight to win." He displayed his own muscled arm, appearing genuinely motivated to edify as opposed to preen.

Doug went for Kurt again, using his left arm this time to hook around Kurt's midriff and drive him toward the fire. Kurt spun out of the way of the flames, grabbing hold of Doug at the last second and yanking him clear.

Doug bent over, panting.

Kurt was barely out of breath. "You won't best me," he said. "I've prepared long and hard for this fight. In a way, every day since I got here has been preparation." He cocked his head, long hair flowing. "You think those huts erected themselves? They took muscle to construct—and not the kind young bucks like you build up at the gym."

Natalie spoke before Doug could do something foolish. He was outmatched by Kurt physically. That much was clear. "Why?" she asked. "Why would you want to keep us here, if we don't want to stay?"

Kurt appeared to consider the question. Then he leaned over and placed his palm against Natalie's uninjured cheek. Doug started forward, but Kurt held up his other hand in a cautionary gesture. "I think you know the answer to that," Kurt told Natalie. "Even if you're not yet aware that you do."

"Cut the bullshit, Buddha," Doug bit out. "We're not staying."

Kurt let out a patient sigh. "I've laid out the parameters for you as best I could," he said. "What you do from here is really up to you." He paused. "But I will say this. Winter's ugly bite aside, life in my camp can be quite idyllic, as I think you've seen. The two of you might want to consider whether you'd rather go on as we have so far, or push me into behaving in a way you might enjoy far less."

Doug's mouth hung open, gaping, but Natalie felt the opposite of surprised: needle sharp and focused. Kurt was right. She had sensed all along that something like this was coming. His references to the future, a longer-term stay. Even Kurt's deep and abiding interest in all the details of their lives. What did he want with them? Why would he wish them to be here? He hadn't hurt them in any way—the opposite, he'd healed them. And Natalie had never feared the slightest sexual encroachment from Kurt; indeed he seemed sexless, neutered. She thought back to how he had first presented the hut, a place of abode in which he hoped she would feel welcome and tended to, without making a move to come near her. It was as if he merely craved their…company.

The most terrifying desire of all.

Because it went on and on forever, no way to end or satisfy it.

Neither she nor Doug had responded to Kurt's threat.

"Plenty of water," he elaborated. "Enough food to eat. Fires. A roof and walls around you. The sleeping bag. Maybe even some other items—novelty or luxury—that I'll be able to procure in the manner I've described." He leaned forward, speaking right into Doug's face. "Now imagine living here without any of those things."

Silence descended.

Natalie and Doug moved closer together, reaching for each other in the dark.

Kurt looked from one to the other, avid, observing, and Natalie found herself taking a step away. She didn't want to give anything to Kurt—not one intimate detail of her mind or body or heart—including the fact that she'd turned to Doug for solace.

Kurt led the way back to camp.

The conjoined huts appeared, leaning against each other in the clearing. Kurt went into the larger one but immediately came back out again, holding the clay vessel, freshly filled and brimming with water. He took the lead into Natalie and Doug's hut, gesturing for them when they lingered outside. In wordless agreement, without exchanging a look, Natalie and Doug entered the smaller structure. They yawned broadly and lay down atop the sleeping bag. After a moment, Natalie wriggled sideways, pulling the fabric over them both.

"Sleep well, you two," Kurt said, crossing to the opening. "And try not to be angry. We're going to have fun here together, I promise. Tomorrow we'll build you a door." He cocked his head. "Newlyweds need their privacy, am I right?" He strolled out of the dwelling, and the confidence with which he left—administering no warnings, not seeking to erect a barricade—was more chilling than any other exit could have been.

It said that Kurt had nothing to fear.

They wouldn't succeed in leaving even if they tried.

CHAPTER FIFTY-SIX

Doug threw back the sleeping bag and began to pace around the confined space. He barked a laugh. "Out of the frying pan and into the fire, huh?"

"You keep bringing up fried chicken at the worst times," Natalie muttered. "What if we never taste a bite of those skewers from that amazing Indian place again?" She expected Doug to smile—at the randomness of her association, if nothing else—but instead, he pulled her up to standing, using his good arm, and settled both hands on her shoulders.

"We're going to taste them again," he said, and the words sounded like a vow. "And everything else too. You hear me?"

Natalie nodded. Then she said in a small voice, "How?"

"That I don't know yet," Doug replied. He strode to the opening and braced his forehead with his arm, taking a look out at the moonlit yard. "You believe him?"

"About the obstacle course or whatever?" Natalie asked. "His traps?"

Doug glanced at her over his shoulder and gave a nod.

"As I said before, Kurt's not a joking-around kind of guy," Natalie reflected. "And he didn't seem worried about leaving us in here on our own."

Doug turned back to the exit. "That's what has me convinced too."

"This is Kurt's full-time job," Natalie said. "No…it's his life. He's lived out here for years without anything to do except lovingly tend to this hypothetical garden of booby traps."

Doug gave another nod, jaw clenched so tight it seemed to interfere with speech.

"I don't know that we stand the best chance if we fight," Natalie ventured. "Or try to oppose Kurt head-on."

"What then?" Doug asked, regarding her seriously.

Natalie lifted her shoulders. "Something more…indirect."

Doug crossed to the clay pitcher and took a swig of water. He wiped his mouth with the back of his hand, then offered the vessel to Natalie. "Have some," he said. "We're going to need our strength for whatever might lie ahead."

Natalie drank deeply, tilting the jug.

Doug asked, "What kinds of traps do you think he means?"

She licked her lips, catching the last droplets. "I have no idea. Something that would break your ankle? Or choke you? What was he acting out back there?"

Doug shook his head, appearing as lost as she felt. "Tripwire could do some damage. Slice your legs or your neck, depending on how high he placed it. And Kurt could make that himself. He also told me he rescued items from this cabin he stayed in during his first winter. He might have a bear trap for all we know."

"But not…lots of them," Natalie said hesitantly. "I mean, no one would have a dozen such things. So what are the chances of us stumbling onto the exact wrong spot? And if we kept a close eye out…" She began to trail off.

Doug grabbed her excitedly. "Right," he said. "In a way, Kurt undermined his whole strategy, didn't he? By telling us what he's done. Now we're prepared. Just how well could he conceal something big enough to maim?"

"Very well." Natalie began to backtrack. The prospect Doug was raising, or which she had raised and he'd glommed on to, began to seem reckless and foolhardy. "Kurt's smart, honey. And able. If he says these woods are dangerous, then they are."

"Nat." Doug pulled her closer to him. "We don't have much of a choice. It's not like I'm going to kill the guy in his sleep."

That the suggestion bore uttering out loud said something about the depths to which they had descended. Natalie lowered her head. Options cycled through her mind like cars on a racetrack, each one going nowhere. They could hunker down till a hiker came through, then signal that they needed help. But who knew how long that might take, and the chance of Kurt intercepting any such message was high. Natalie's sister would get in touch with the proper authorities soon—although their father would dilly and dither, never getting around to it at all—but how successful were search operations way out here? Natalie and Doug were the proverbial needles in a haystack.

"Nat?" Doug urged.

"We need to be quiet," she said. "What if Kurt's listening?"

Doug sank down, cinching himself into the sleeping bag while making room for Natalie. He gestured for her to join him.

"What about what Kurt said?" Natalie whispered, letting Doug take her in his arms. "About us just getting lost all over again?"

Doug spoke in a low tone. "We know where the creek is now, and it isn't just wilderness lore. Every guidebook—even those instructions the DEC puts out with their maps—says that if stranded, you should follow water out."

Natalie quieted, momentarily satisfied. "We'll need supplies," she said suddenly, lifting her head. "Kurt has iodine tabs—he must've gotten them from one of the hikers he mentioned—and a clay jug will add weight, but might be worth taking."

Doug twined his fingers through hers. "Some food too. We don't know how long this will take, and we'll need energy to stay ahead of Kurt. I wonder if we can find something portable that won't spoil right away."

They lay back, considering. The night grew darker, folding itself around them, stars sputtering out, until their next step appeared out of the gloom.

"We have to get into Kurt's hut," Natalie said at last.

Doug remained quiet.

"A guy who basically never leaves us alone, certainly won't be going anywhere by himself right now, and even if he did, seems to have an almost spooky ability to sense when any part of his territory has been changed or disturbed."

Silence.

Natalie shifted toward Doug in the dark. "I know how we can do it."

Doug sat up, blinking and rubbing his eyes. "Jesus, it's dark out here. Can't see a damn thing." He paused. "What's your idea?"

Natalie's own eyes had adjusted, the hut taking shape before her now. She saw the roof made of sticks, the gaps between the walls and the dirt floor, the rectangular slit that served as both entrance and exit. Airtight the place was not. She tried to imagine what it would feel like come winter, or even late autumn, when icy air would slither in through each passage and opening, and shuddered.

"We can't do it straightaway," Natalie said, her thoughts pick-sharp and focused in the darkness. "We need a little time."

"For what?" Doug asked.

She turned toward him, burrowing close as his arms slid around her.

313

The most comforting feeling in the world.

Would she ever have known how comforting it was if she and Doug hadn't faced such extremity and duress together? If embraces like this had been hurried, peremptory, following long, exhausting days at work, life in the city with all its associated hassles, Natalie and Doug grumpy and wearied by first-world problems, living out their unexamined lives without any appreciation of true hardship?

Natalie spoke quietly in the dark. "There are things we can take care of around here before we try to enter Kurt's hut. Ways to prepare and also lull him a little, make him think we've resigned ourselves to staying."

"That makes sense," Doug said.

Natalie lifted herself on one elbow. "Do you think we can get Kurt to show us around the camp a little more? Give us, I don't know, like a tour?"

Doug frowned.

"Because if we can," Natalie went on excitedly, "then we'll basically have a ready-made path out. All we'll have to do is remember where we walked and follow the same trail tomorrow. Kurt's not going to lead himself into one of his traps."

Doug began nodding. "And once we make it past his perimeter, we'll know we're home free."

Natalie lay back down. "Let's get a little more sleep, we're going to want to be rested. In the morning, just act like we saw the wisdom of Kurt's words, and we've decided to go along with everything he says. Make our lives here."

She rolled over, Doug's arms enclosing her from behind. Silence seeped up from the woods and settled over the tiny dwelling.

They were both still asleep when Kurt rattled the wall.

CHAPTER FIFTY-SEVEN

In the middle of the night, Mia woke to a sound she hadn't heard in forever. At least it felt that way, although in reality it'd probably been a year ago at most. The sound cast her back to a time when Mia was a whole different person, a little girl, falling asleep to the murmur of her parents' voices, the most comforting sound in the world.

She got out of bed and tiptoed to her door, which faced what used to be her parents' bedroom and now was just her mom's. She listened, her hand cupped to her ear.

"You think I didn't try?" her dad was saying.

Maybe not so comforting then. In fact, this was more like it—what Mia had gotten used to whenever her parents were together these days. Arguing. Angry voices. Fights that turned into all-out wartime battles.

Footsteps sounded back and forth, lighter than her dad's. Her mom must be pacing. She murmured something that Mia couldn't entirely hear, but which sounded snippy. *I have no idea what you did.* And they said Mia had an attitude problem.

"I wanted to take care of you," her father said. "You never let me."

Her dad's voice was louder; Mia could hear it distinctly. While her mom's replies were frustratingly hard to make out. *You know the reason for that.* Was that it? It must've been, or something like it, because her father said, "That's the point. *I* knew it. You didn't tell me. Didn't share your past with me in a way that would've brought us closer together. Instead you held me at arm's length. You've always been an army of one, Claude."

Something else from her mom.

"Life is about more than just being strong all the time!" her dad roared. "Maybe I didn't want to be the only one who needed things!"

There was a sharp hiss, her mom warning her dad to *shh*.

"But now you need someone," her dad said at lower volume. "You've got a situation and no way to handle it. You can't just step in and solve everything yourself for once. This time that isn't going to work."

Unintelligible murmurs from her mom.

"I'm sorry," her dad said. "I misspoke."

Mia couldn't hear any response. She cracked open her door and peeked through a slit.

"*We've* got a situation," her father said. "If you'll let us, that is."

He lowered his voice; after that, Mia couldn't hear either of them anymore. But she saw a shuffle of motion, the shadows of her parents moving closer together.

Her heart began to sing inside her.

When her father spoke again at his normal pitch, the sound of it was every bit as comforting as Mia remembered.

"Let's hear what you learned." Her dad led the way into the hall.

Mia took a quick step back, and her shoulders thumped the wall. Next she heard footsteps approaching. She jumped into bed, but couldn't get her head onto the pillow or her eyes closed fast enough.

The door opened wider, and both her parents peered inside.

"You still up, Mi?" her father asked.

"Worried about Aunt Nat?" said her mother.

Mia nodded, her face against the sheets.

Her mom sighed. "Why don't you come to the kitchen with Dad and me? I can share what happened when I called the police. You've been more on top of this than I have. There's no reason to leave you out."

Mia felt the fizzy rise of a feeling she had almost forgotten.

Happiness.

She leaned her head on her mother's shoulder as they walked together down the hall.

"Coffee?" her mom asked Mia's dad once they reached the kitchen.

Her dad nodded. "Thanks."

Her mom looked at her, speaking before Mia could. "Not at night," she said, her voice swift and sure as always. But then she took a deep breath. "Okay, Mi? I mean, even decaf has *some* caffeine."

Her father looked back and forth between them. "Since when does Mia drink coffee?"

Both she and her mom burst out laughing, harder than the comment deserved.

"Can I have peppermint tea?" Mia asked once they'd stopped.

"Good choice," her mom said, turning her back and facing the stove.

Mia's dad let out a cough, then asked, "So what did the police say?"

"They were very helpful," her mom replied. "I spoke to the chief himself. He's going to call the New York State Federation something. They're responsible for search and rescue. It's a little complicated because Nat and Doug are paddling so they didn't have to fill out a trail register or file a route plan."

"Did the police chief sound concerned?" Mia's dad asked.

"Not overly," her mom replied, giving Mia's hand a squeeze. "He said the rivers and lakes change constantly because of rising and falling water levels, so what looks to be a portage—that's when you have to get out and walk with the canoe—on the map doesn't turn out to be one. Or vice versa. Paddlers often take longer to complete their journey than expected."

Her mom went to give her dad a refill, and when she did, her hand stayed on his longer than looked necessary to steady the cup.

Mia said, "So that police chief? He's going to look for them?"

"He's going to do everything's he supposed to at this stage of the game," Mia's mom promised. "Now. Finish your tea, which will hopefully make you nice and sleepy. I know I am." She glanced at Mia's father. "Elliott? Want to sleep on the couch tonight? It's pretty late to go back to the Bronx."

Mia's dad held her mom's gaze. "Sure," he said. "That'd be great."

"Or you could just stay in our room," Mia's mom added casually. "Save getting out a lot of extra blankets."

"Sure," Mia's dad said again.

Mia felt that bubbling inside her again.

She wasn't all that tired, but she went back to her bedroom and let her parents make their way to…whose? Was it both of theirs again? With questions cycling around in her brain, Mia began to drift off.

It still wasn't light out, the sun not even touching the air shaft outside her room, when Mia became aware of a heavy, insistent drumbeat across the hallway.

It echoed the gonging in her chest. She hadn't even realized she'd gotten out of bed; only the feel of the floorboards beneath her feet told her where she was. Then she remembered. She had reset the ringtone herself the other day, telling her mom she should go more gangsta. Somebody was calling her mother crazy early.

Mia tiptoed across the hall, her eyes adjusting as she entered the room. Her dad lay beside her mom in bed, their arms wrapped around each other. Her mom was wearing the nightie that Mia loved and her mom hadn't worn in forever. In the dim light, Mia could just see its straps—scalloped with little roses she used to pretend were a garden.

The phone was so loud that she didn't know how it hadn't woken them up yet. Finally her mother began reaching for it, patting around on her nightstand.

"Hello?" she said, her voice muzzy and low. "Oh. Oh yes. No, that's all right." A pause. "Hold on, let me put you on speaker. I'd like my husband to hear."

Despite her still-clattering heart, Mia smiled at that.

"Yes, go ahead, Chief Lurcquer," her mother said.

The police were calling. From the Adirondacks.

"I'm sorry for waking you," the police chief said. He had a nice voice, deep and level. It said to stay calm, everything was under control. With this man in charge, Mia suddenly felt sure that Aunt Nat was going to be all right. "But we put out an alert for your sister and brother-in-law's car. And one just came in matching the description, correct license plate, registered to a Douglas Larson."

"It did?" Mia's mom said. "So that's good, isn't it?"

"The place where the car was found isn't used all that often by paddlers," the police chief said.

The statement fell like a rock thrown into the sea. Mia felt her sense of reassurance recede, replaced by a cold fear. From the doorway, she could see her parents looking at each other.

"The only route to it requires some pretty arduous carries," the chief went on into the silence. "Places where they'd have to get out and tote along their canoe."

Mia's dad finally spoke. "You're saying their route was…suspicious somehow?"

"I wouldn't go all the way to suspicious," the police chief answered. "But it isn't where we'd expect your average pleasure-seeking paddlers to wind up."

Mia expected her mom to jump in, but she didn't say a word.

"We appreciate your efforts on this," Mia's dad said.

"I'll keep you posted," the police chief replied. "Again, apologies for disturbing you at this hour."

Mia's mother lowered the phone; it cast an eerie glow around her face. "Something's wrong, Elliott," she said, her tone a startling jab in the low light.

What happened next was even more alarming.

Her mom let out a long, lonely sob, like the wail of a train. "Something's happened to my baby sister. I know it. I feel it. And there isn't one thing I can do about it!"

Her father reached out and took her mother in his arms, and Mia ran for them both. Her mother folded Mia up in a hug.

"Are we going to go up there?" Mia asked. The words came out muffled because of how tightly her mother was holding on to her. "Where Aunt Nat's supposed to be?"

Her parents exchanged looks again in the dimness.

"There are experts working on this now," Mia's dad said. "Looking for Aunt Nat and Uncle Doug."

Mia's mom opened her mouth, then closed it.

"We would just get in the way," her father added.

"There's nobody looking who loves Aunt Nat," Mia said, biting her lip.

Her mother reached out to stroke Mia's face, but didn't answer.

Mia looked into her mother's eyes, and bits of things began to collect in her mind, like those pictures they showed in science class of space dust coalescing till it formed a starry cloud. "I know you can't make this better, Mom," Mia said. "You don't have to fix anything. Just let us be there. Let us be there when Aunt Nat comes out of the woods."

Her mother's eyes shimmered, and she dropped her head. "How did this happen, Mi? How did you get to be so wise and grown-up? And how did I not notice?" Then she turned to Mia's father, taking a deep breath as if slipping underwater.

"You don't have to say it," Mia's dad said. He was already climbing out of bed and tugging his shirt over his head. "We're all awake so we might as well not waste any time. The police will probably start searching first thing."

But Mia's mother sat there, clenching the sheets in her hands. "Shelley Parsons is ill," she said. "I've been covering her shifts. I'm on back to back today." She glanced down at her phone. "I practically have to be up now anyway to get on the subway."

Helpless tears started rolling down her mom's cheeks. Instead of feeling shock and upset at seeing her mother break down, Mia put her arms around her, and began stroking her back. She knew what it felt like to cry like that.

Mia's father crossed to the doorway. "I'll go get the car, bring you to the hospital," he said. "That way we'll be ready to leave from there. Mia and I can hang out at the other apartment—"

He hadn't said *my* apartment, Mia registered with a bolt of gladness.

"—and you work as much of the shifts as you have to, but let them know you need to arrange for emergency leave," Mia's dad finished.

Mia's mom nodded, slowly at first, then brisker. She went over to her closet and started throwing things into a suitcase, calling out as Mia left the room to make sure she put on a warm outfit and real shoes. "It can get surprisingly cold up there already, Mi. And we may be on some trails."

Mia had never been so glad to hear her mom giving instructions.

She dug around in a box that held her stuff from camp last year and found clothes to change into. Waterproof pants and a shirt that zipped into a jacket and even her boots. Everything felt a bit snug, but at least she looked the part. She grabbed some contraption for drinking—a pouch with a snaky straw—that she'd never once used.

At the last minute, she picked up her phone and thumbed in a reply to the unanswered text from Val.

thanks so much for your concern, Mia wrote, hoping the sarcasm would come through. but now the people who actually care about aunt nat are going up to find her

CHAPTER FIFTY-EIGHT

Tim Lurcquer decided to join the Federation boys at Crosch Pond where they'd planned to meet at first light to talk about the missing paddlers. Overdue by two full days, today marking the third, and every hour without contact like a stone in a fortress, sealing away the chances of the couple's safe return.

Crosch. What a crazy place to put-out. A beautiful system of trails spider-webbed the area, extending most of the way to Canada, but the water itself wasn't much deeper than a mud puddle. Tim hoped the search team might be able to shed some light on the implicated route.

Tim's own men were tied up right now looking for a group of Boy Scouts that had gone missing north of Lake Nancy, and it was lucky Federation resources were available for this second search. Tim wasn't feeling very lucky, though. Hadn't been in quite some time, if he were being honest, although search-and-rescue operations always put a particular weight in the pit of his stomach. And not just because they were notoriously unpredictable, with life and death inevitably on the line.

Tim climbed into the Mountaineer and headed up Freedom Pass—an unpaved road that was little more than an ATV track—mentally suiting up for the day.

Summer vacation. You had to love it. Long, light-filled nights, warmth, sun, lemonade, grilling…and dead vacationers. Sportsmen and sportswomen, even their kids. Parents taking children on expeditions once only trained experts would've attempted.

Which was the problem with search-and-rescue ops.

It was hard for the Federation team members, and Tim's men too, not to look down on folks who got into trouble in the wilderness. Not that searchers wouldn't do everything in their power to support, assist, and rescue—because they would, and with a level of success equal to or surpassing Tim's department's own solve rate. But in some silent, unspoken way, the missing and the lost would be held in contempt. It was one part the same gallows humor that made coping possible on the job, and one part something unique to SAR. There were no truly innocent victims in the wilderness. They had all gotten where they were voluntarily. They were folks who had enough skills and resources to put themselves into a bad situation, but in many cases, not enough to get them out.

There had always been a divide in Wedeskyull between natives and newcomers—probably going back to Indian times. Who was native and who was new changed, but the animosity between the two camps did not. The old-timers, whoever comprised their party at the moment, were not likely to climb a mountain for fun. Too busy trying to survive on this land to use it for recreation.

A second chasm had appeared lately. On one side stood former military, Forest Rangers, and law enforcement looking for supplementary work. Avid athletes, moving in from Boulder and Boise, the Sawtooths and the Cascades. On the other? Weekend warriors, extreme yet less experienced athletes who continually misjudged the three Ws—weather, wilderness, wet—and second-home owners. Folks with too much leisure, money, and hubris on their hands.

Outfitters had cropped up like mushrooms after a rain to cater to these people.

The new divide: folks who sought out danger, and those who saved them from it.

Tim hooked a sharp right into a lot that was slowly encroaching on the forest, borrowing from an eroded lakeshore. Two SAR members stood conferring by a Nissan Rogue. A hybrid SUV, the ultimate oxymoron. Tim imagined the endless fun this vehicle would provoke. *Let's save the planet by using a little less gas while launching a rescue with a carbon footprint the size of a third-world nation's.*

The Mountaineer's tires ate gravel, spat bits of stone. Tim climbed out.

He greeted the two team members, both of whom he recognized. Steve and Brad. Good men. The first had done three tours in Afghanistan, had seen enough hell to sizzle him, then had come back to be healed by the land, even if he wouldn't have put it that way. The second was a college kid, studying cooking of all things at Paul Smith's, but a hell of an outdoorsman, especially when it came to tracking.

"Chief Lurcquer," Brad, the college kid, said respectfully. He didn't look old enough to shave yet, his face smooth and pink with sun or anticipation, possibly both.

Searches contained a certain excitement of the hunt, especially at the start. There was no denying that.

"Tim," Tim told Brad, knowing that the next time Brad addressed him, it would be as *Chief.*

Steve strode forward and clapped Tim on the shoulder. He still kept his gray hair clipped military short, and the lines around his eyes turned into creases as he came up to Tim wearing a look of concern. "The Boy Scout troop?"

Tim shook his head. "No sign of 'em yet."

Steve gave a hard shake of his head. "Lotta worried parents."

"You can say that again," Tim replied.

"How many hours in, Chief?" asked Brad.

He was a little like a Boy Scout himself. "Expected back yesterday afternoon," Tim told him. "My men set out at six, completed the first pass before nightfall. Now they're on a second, trying to beat whatever weather blows in." He cast his gaze up to the sky where large clouds had begun blotting out the early-morning blue.

"I don't think those are gonna do much besides roll on by," Steve said, the hard edge of authority in his voice.

Tim nodded, accepting the salve. "I appreciate your optimism."

Brad clapped his hands together. "Let's talk about our lovebirds."

This was it. The part Tim hated. He could hear the line that would come next—its general tone anyway—and sure enough, Steve delivered it as if reading from a script.

"They couldn't have just gone to Paris," he said, a grin altering the arrangement of lines on his face.

"Much more romantic to get eaten by black flies and drown," said Brad.

"It's late July," Tim pointed out. "They knew enough to avoid black-fly season."

Brad had the grace to look chastened, but Steve simply narrowed his eyes. Then again, Steve had seen injuries and deaths no civilian could imagine.

"Let's get some facts down besides their marital status," Steve said, tugging at the brim on his USMC cap as the sun started its climb. "Timeline?"

"Today will be the third day past expected," Tim said, glancing upward again. Steve had been right, at least for now—the clouds were gone, any weather on hold for now, and the morning sky looked gentle. "They were supposed to finish paddling on the sixteenth, then take a day to get back home, returning in the afternoon or evening. That would've been the day before yesterday."

"So we're now at the start of day four post-paddle?" Steve clarified.

"That's right," Tim said. He rubbed his chin. He'd left too early for a shave, and the bristles itched.

"Who sounded the alert?" Brad asked.

"Wife's sister," Tim replied. He walked over to the Rogue, fingering a hank of rope on the roof that had secured the canoe. He leaned down and peered through a rear window. "No gear left behind."

Steve and Brad both nodded.

Tim studied the view across the pond. He wasn't any sort of boater himself, and didn't know the waterways except as they came up on the job. "Tell me about this route."

Brad spoke up. "Other than one nice spot—an island I can see newlyweds enjoying—putting-out here basically guarantees they came through a lot of petering-out creeks, one brief stretch of lowly rapids, and some pretty brutal carries. There aren't a lot of good, open stretches of water up this way."

"Which could explain why they're taking longer than planned," Steve noted. "Now, if you weren't paddling, you've got some incredible backcountry hiking. Crucifer Chasm is in there—so-called jewel of the Adirondacks, which hardly anyone gets to see because it's so remote. But would our pair just abandon their canoe?"

They all reached the same conclusion at once.

"Won't see much by air," Tim said. "Leaf cover is too thick right now."

Steve agreed. "Not worth sending a helo up."

Brad clapped his hands together again. "A two-man kayak is lying around our field office in Gumption," he said. "Steve, want to assemble some supplies and paddle after the happy couple?"

Steve doffed his cap, holding it out in front of him like a bouquet of flowers as he took the lead across the lot. "I do," he said, and Brad guffawed.

Tim left them to it.

Freedom Pass was the shortest way back to Wedeskyull, so Tim took it again, although its roadbed had proved a little gnarly, even for the Mountaineer. Winter ate at asphalt and gravel, sunk its teeth in and chewed, but the DOT had enough repairs to make on the paved thoroughfares and rural routes. These lesser roads seldom got any attention.

Tim was leaving the search for the newlyweds in good hands, and given the potential weather still set to come in over the mountain, he needed to return his attention to the Scouts.

Weather. The least predictable of the three *W*s. In the Adirondacks, balmy could be swapped for dangerous as if a switch had been flicked.

This Scout leader was experienced—six years with the same troop—but nothing could prepare a person for every eventuality he might encounter in the wild. Civilization was a jealous mistress, constantly demanding you value her rewards. Even though the leader had chosen a well-traveled route and was staying away from trouble spots—

Tim braked, hard and sudden. He stared through the windshield, a shaft of sunlight glaring off the glass, although that wasn't what had made him stop.

Something had been tugging at him like an insistent child ever since Steve and Brad began discussing the perils of the honeymooners' route. A hunch, nothing more, made up of sense and vapor. Gut instinct, hard to pin down, even harder to trust. But Tim knew from personal experience what could happen if you didn't trust your instincts.

When he got back to the barracks, he felt dazed, as if he'd been caught sleepwalking. It was a condition that often descended just before he put two parts together, started viewing things from a whole different angle. Pieces from an unsolved case a year ago were starting to come back, as if magnetically drawn to the situation they were up against now with the honeymooners. Was this going to turn out to be a search-and-rescue op—sadly standard for these parts—or something else altogether?

Dorothy Weathers—dispatcher and general point person for the department—delivered the news that the Scouts had been located, having gotten turned around after being confronted by an uncharacteristically friendly black bear.

Even this notice failed to fully penetrate Tim's haze. "Thank God," he said, valiantly trying to hide his state. "Tell everybody to go home and get some rest. They were up most of the night, and I may need 'em again."

"Chief?" Dorothy asked. She was an older woman, the wife of the prior police chief, and little fazed her.

This would, though, Tim had a feeling. If he was right. Dorothy had taken the lack of resolution in that other case almost as hard as Tim and his men.

"I'll explain if I need you to call anybody in," Tim told her. "But first things first. Have all the parents of the Scouts been notified?"

Dorothy offered a rare smile. "No one was out of range or in the woods searching themselves. More brains them," she added. "Everybody knew within minutes."

"Good work," Tim said. "Hey, Dot, think you can do something for me?"

Dorothy nodded her head with its thinning white hair and cotton ball of bun. "I just might could," she said, sending him a wry look.

"I need everything we've got on Theresa Valero," Tim said.

A momentary wince caused Dorothy's forehead to crease. Tim recognized it. This particular unsolved had pained them even more than most. There had never been a lick of hope to it, a time when they thought they were getting somewhere.

The older woman began striking keys on her keyboard.

"That form mention the location where she went missing?" Tim asked, leaning over Dorothy's thin, humped shoulder. "I want to make sure I'm remembering right." He knew he was remembering right. But he wanted to hear his dispatcher—the person he trusted in some ways even above his own men—say it.

Dorothy adjusted her glasses and bent over the screen. "Turtle Ridge," she read out loud. "We never got a single lead on that case." She clucked. "It was like that poor woman disappeared into thin air."

"You're right," Tim said. His focus had returned; he felt like a ship or a jet plane being steered by something, set on course. "It was."

Late last summer, a female hiker had disappeared from the Turtle Ridge Wilderness Area. No trace of her had been found, neither her body nor her belongings. The incomprehensibility of so complete a vanishing had given rise to all sorts of wacky conjectures. Abduction by space aliens. Turtle Ridge was an Adirondack version of the Bermuda Triangle. The land was haunted by the ghosts of all the outdoorsmen who had perished in the challenging terrain. Superstitious hikers started to stay away.

Experts claimed that Turtle Ridge was suited only to the most fit and accomplished backpackers, and guides began to refuse to organize trips there unless their clients could demonstrate fitness and prove experience, not trusting such rough land, miles from any outlet, to novices. In a few more years, the area would be the subject of local lore, scary stories passed on by old-timers, seen as sinister and malign.

The tract of wilderness was a fair shake from the honeymooners' intended put-out spot at Crosch Pond. But if the two had gotten tangled up in the territory Steve had mentioned, they could have wound up over there. In fact, given the nearly impassable chasm that dominated the land, shunting hikers toward its narrowest end, Turtle Ridge might even be viewed as their most likely position.

What if something besides the three Ws was at work in the region?

Amidst a host of other bad contingencies, it would mean that Steve and Brad were setting off to look in the wrong place.

CHAPTER FIFTY-NINE

U p and at 'em, you two," Kurt called. "Are you decent?" Daylight shone into the hut so that Kurt appeared to enter via a shaft of sun. "I made breakfast."

Natalie scrubbed grit from her eyes. Beneath the cover of the sleeping bag, Doug felt for her hand, and their middle-of-the-night plans came back to her. She had to look away, pretend to be searching for her shoes, in order to hide her expression from Kurt.

Kurt served berries boiled down to a sauce, which he ladled over some kind of flatbread made out of pounded acorns. It didn't taste half bad, in a paleo kind of way. Once they had all finished eating, Natalie proposed her idea.

"A tour?" Kurt said stiffly.

Natalie combated his tone with an easy one of her own. "Well, yeah," she said. "If we're going to live here, we should get to know the place, right?" She dipped her face in what she hoped was an appealing, coquettish gesture, even though she had the feeling that Kurt was impervious to female charms. "And I would guess that you've done a lot more with it than we've had a chance to see yet."

Doug nodded enthusiastically. "It's pretty amazing really."

Natalie gave his hand a grateful squeeze.

Kurt did seem to be responding to their ploy, his eyes keen, intent on them as he considered. "All right," he said slowly. "I suppose we can put off building your door. Let me just go get something out of my hut first."

When he reappeared, he had a broad, steel blade strapped to his belt, and Natalie felt momentarily struck still, as if she'd been sliced by it.

"A machete," Doug said faintly.

Natalie hoped Kurt would miss her husband's tone. She was finding it hard to speak herself, the sight of that lethal blade obliterating everything else.

"It'll help with breaking trail," Kurt explained.

Natalie and Doug fell into step behind him as they entered the woods.

As they wended their way through the trees, Kurt offered repeated reminders to follow in his tracks. He whacked at branches with the machete and tested the ground with the tip of the blade. The maneuvers put Natalie's senses, already heightened by the thought of tomorrow's escape, on alert. She cast her gaze around, tilting her head to listen, detecting faint odors in the air. Then she noticed an irregularity in the landscape.

It was a mere dip, a marshy spot, to her left. Scarcely noticeable, appearing amidst scattered leaves like a blemish on a perfectly made-up face, and yet something in the sight caused Natalie to swerve abruptly, overcorrecting before she veered right again and wound up, breathing hard, just behind Kurt.

His arm shot out to grab her. Doug stepped forward, about to intervene, but Kurt yanked him close as well.

"I told you to stay by me!" Kurt said. He was breathing hard.

Natalie and Doug looked down at the ground.

Kurt stooped and picked up a rock, seemingly too big and bulky for one man to lift. An icy tentacle of feeling reminded Natalie of Kurt's strength.

He dropped the stone onto the slight sag in the land.

It vanished.

Along with a cascade of leaves and dust, the ground ate the enormous rock.

It fell for long enough that they had time to wait before hearing the thud. Natalie's mouth felt as dry as the dirt disappearing into the man-made sinkhole, like sand through an hourglass.

Doug braced his shoulders. "That must've been quite a feat, digging that."

Kurt eyed him. "I live here alone," he said. "Without benefit of conventional weapons, a gun or the like. I need some means to keep people out, wouldn't you agree? From stealing what it's taken me such pains to create?"

Natalie continued to study the gaping hole in the ground. If somebody stepped on it with both feet, he or she would drop grave-deep. And stepping with only one foot might be even worse. His or her legs would splay out, drawing and halving the victim.

She emitted a dry husk of a laugh, caustic and angry, which fortunately Kurt didn't appear to hear. These traps didn't keep anyone out. They only kept people in.

The three of them continued to walk through the densely packed forest. Stands of brush grew in thick knots, impossible to untangle or push through, the only choice being to weave around the clumps. A heavy canopy of green enclosed them from above. The wilderness felt both endless and constricting, as vast as it was inescapable.

A circle of trees that had been severed at the stump, all their branches and leaves removed, appeared before them. The amputated trunks looked like a giant's set of checkers. They surrounded a beehive-shaped cone of rocks, which stood as tall as a person.

Natalie frowned in Doug's direction, but he shook his head, just as unwitting.

Mere pinpricks of sunshine made it through the parasol of leaves overhead, staining the whole world green, like the windows of a cathedral. The place had a confessional feel, and Kurt spoke in a hushed tone. "This is my smokehouse. You could call it a storehouse too. It's where the venison will go, after we've eaten our fill."

He prodded at a stone, lifting it out of the structure and setting it on the ground. A thick, meaty smell emerged, and despite everything, Natalie felt a clawing in her belly. Perhaps another deer had taken up residence inside; surely they must get killed often enough, stepping into one of Kurt's pits.

Kurt continued removing rocks until he'd formed a large enough opening for Natalie and Doug to peer through.

"Go on," he urged. "Look." The expression on his face posed a challenge.

Natalie took a peek, and her stomach gave a slow, heaving roll; she tasted bitter bile. She put the back of her hand to her mouth, stifling a scream. Doug grabbed her before she could spin away, jerking his chin toward the ground, then up to the green umbrella of leaves, and the reality of their situation slammed back at Natalie, full force.

Every step held danger out here, and its nature was worse than anything she had feared.

That was no deer in the smokehouse.

Within the stone walls hung lengths of meat, flattened out and preserved. Too big to belong to any animal except a bear or a buck, only these weren't the right shape for either creature. Instead, they were clearly of another shape, one whose form had been altered as the flesh was turned into…jerky. Yes, that was jerky, like you'd find in cellophane-wrapped sticks at a convenience store, only different from those, of course, naked and unpackaged, yet still terribly, horrifically recognizable. Like a poster from biology class, the musculature of *Homo sapiens* splayed out, its meat and fat and sinew exposed.

Natalie swayed, and Doug caught her. They stumbled away from the cone of stones, keeping to the tracks their shoes had already pressed into the dirt. Natalie couldn't get enough air into her lungs. She was going to hyperventilate. Her gaze went wheeling about the woods.

Kurt strode to her and held her steady. "Breathe," he commanded.

His arms formed a straitjacket; she had no idea how she'd ever found this man remotely appealing. He was flesh devoid of feeling, his hands like slabs of meat, his muscular form mummified and dead.

Natalie jerked free as Doug stepped between the two of them.

She hid her face against her husband's chest, her words emerging muffled. "The hiker...whose things you took..." Natalie forced herself to look up. "You...you..."

"Killed her," Kurt finished calmly. "Yes."

Doug clenched and unclenched a fist.

"Terry was her name," Kurt noted. "A stout, practical girl, like a farm woman or a pioneer. She would've done wonderfully here," he added. "I didn't want to do what I did." Kurt paused as if reflecting. "But Terry resisted me with every strong muscle in her body. I couldn't get her to spend a civil hour in conversation without attempting to flee."

Doug made a sudden lunge for Kurt, and Natalie hurled herself sideways into her husband's arms, where she huddled close, waiting for both their heart rates to slow.

"But that wasn't the only reason I dispatched her," Kurt went on without a hitch. "And you both should understand this. Because you remember, I think, the terrible grip of hunger. No, I didn't kill Terry simply because she opposed me."

Motionless now, holding on to each other, Natalie and Doug both watched Kurt.

"I did it out of necessity," Kurt informed them. "Survival of the fittest;

nature is red in tooth and claw." His voice had remained steady and level throughout his whole confession, but it began to waver under the intensity of his vow. "I will not starve during another winter out here. And neither will either of you."

PART FOUR

SAVED

CHAPTER SIXTY

Natalie and Doug made their way out of the woods in a straggling, beaten line. Following Kurt's lead, their shoulders hunched, vigilantly regarding the ground at their feet. In low murmurs, Natalie voiced the need for them to speak alone in private; returning on an even quieter note, Doug suggested they ask to take a nap.

They were cowed, Natalie realized. Scared in a whole new way from before. Now they knew what Kurt was capable of.

They spied the clearing and the huts.

"Do you still have water left?" Kurt asked once they'd arrived. "We'll want some with our lunch."

Natalie gave a single nod.

Kurt clasped his hands together, approval pervading his face as light does a chapel. "Good girl. You're learning to make resources last. How I loathe the idea of turning on a tap. The sheer waste! It's appalling. Why don't you fetch the jug I gave you from your hut?"

Natalie hung back to wait for Doug, but Kurt gave her a nudge with one of his plank-like hands. "Doug can stay here with me, don't you think? Share a little of the work? Those fires don't build themselves, you know."

The rest of the day proceeded in the same manner, Kurt never giving them one second alone. He demonstrated how to fashion cord out of vines, then set Natalie and Doug to work while he scoured the forest floor for firewood, keeping to a tight radius around them. Natalie and Doug helped with chores, going along with the schedule Kurt laid out. Kurt even turned a trip to the thicket of trees into a joint excursion, pointing out the perfect slope from which to relieve oneself. Natalie hardly noticed the invasion of privacy. She was focused on nightfall and the earliest moment she and Doug might be allowed to declare bedtime. At last, the sun began to droop in the sky, a mellow blotch of peach and gold over the endless layering of mountains.

Natalie yawned broadly.

Doug gave her a look that appeared loving and relaxed. "Tired?"

She nodded.

Doug turned toward Kurt. "Guess we'd better pack it in."

"I suppose so," he said.

A pause. "Thanks for dinner," Doug added. "That venison soup was great."

"Glad you enjoyed it."

Kurt made no move to rise from the campfire, so Natalie and Doug stood up, at which point Kurt got to his feet, and they all shifted awkwardly around each other. They bid good night at the huts, Doug ducking inside while Natalie turned to offer a final wave.

She waited until Kurt strode into his own dwelling before entering theirs and going to lie down. Buried within the folds of the sleeping bag, she and Doug began to talk, fast and low.

"Today was a warning," Doug said. "Kurt could've shown us where he forages for greens, he could've guided us to the best swimming hole, or taken us to the fucking berry patch. Instead he leads our parade straight to Trader Cannibal's."

"Stop," Natalie said, stone faced, feeling her stomach lurch again. "Don't even joke about it. That poor woman, Terry, did he say her name was—"

Doug drew her into an embrace, quietly stroking her arm. "I know," he said. "It's really sick. What kind of person is capable of something like that?"

Tears slid down Natalie's cheeks like molten lava. "I thought Kurt saved us."

"What else were we supposed to think?"

Natalie gave a helpless shrug.

"We need to consider that machete," Doug went on in a whisper. "I didn't realize Kurt had a weapon like that. It changes things."

Natalie felt a shiver jolt her, sudden as an electric shock.

"Let's get out of here," Doug said. "Now."

"Not without water," she whispered back. "We know where that leads."

"We'll take the jug," Doug said. "It's almost full. We'll have to ration."

Natalie shook her head. "That won't be anywhere near enough. We need the iodine tabs. And I bet Kurt has more protein bars. Think how helpful they'll be." She paused. "It's easy to imagine setting off when our bellies are full of deer and chipmunk."

Doug gave a short laugh. "You said you had an idea. To get into Kurt's hut."

Natalie nodded, then shifted to face him. "I want you to open the cut on my face."

Doug looked unsure whether to laugh again or not.

"I mean it," Natalie said. "I was thinking about how Kurt took care of me. Not just me... There were some pretty unpleasant tasks he had to attend to while you were out cold too. He seems to get something out of…ministering to people."

Doug flinched, although Natalie took a certain savage enjoyment from the thought of Kurt having to clean up her husband's bodily fluids.

"Anyway," she said, "if we can give him something to do, he'll be occupied for a while. You'll have a few minutes to grab some supplies. Then we slip out tomorrow night while Kurt is asleep in his hut."

"No," Doug said flatly. "I won't do that."

Natalie felt a flash of insistence. "Look, this is going to require something real. Authentic. Kurt's too smart not to see through a dodge. And what I'm suggesting is big, but not life-threatening, or even dangerous really. Just…painful." She winced. "I'll do it myself if I have to. But you'll be able to see what you're doing." She threaded her fingers through Doug's. "Please, honey," she said. "Do this for me. Do it for us."

"But your cut's healing," Doug whispered. The breath he let out sounded savage, like something that was being ripped apart. "Your beautiful face. How did I let this happen to your beautiful face?"

Natalie extricated herself from her husband's hold. "Don't say that," she hissed. "Don't even think it. You didn't do this. Even if Craig's trouble started us out along a bad path, there was no way you could've known where it would lead."

In the murky darkness, Doug's eyes gripped Natalie's. Their mouths met, salty and hot. For a moment, there was no divide between them.

Then the wall of the hut shook and Kurt entered, sleeping bag draped around his shoulders like a king's stole. "Hey, you two. Still awake?"

It took effort for Natalie to swallow.

Doug didn't speak.

"Nights are getting chilly already," Kurt said. "I know you're newlyweds and all, but it makes sense for us to bunk in together for the duration. Share the body heat."

Kurt couldn't have eavesdropped on them. They'd been talking quietly, and there was space between where she and Doug lay and the wall connected to the other hut. No, Natalie thought, with a sudden stab of conviction. Kurt hadn't needed to overhear their plans. Because he had sensed them.

She stood up, helping Doug pull their sleeping bag over to make room for three. She settled down beside her husband, moving as close to him as possible, although she could still smell Kurt's sharp, pine scent, hear the intake of his breaths.

She didn't think she would sleep, but she must have.

The next thing she became aware of was Doug on his knees, leaning down to peer at her in the tarry, starless night. He laid his hand against Natalie's cheek, probing gently.

Natalie sucked in air. She bore down, bracing herself, but when Doug at last began to tug, his touch was so tender that Natalie didn't even register it as pain.

Scream, Doug mouthed at her, the word as gentle as a caress.

CHAPTER SIXTY-ONE

Natalie felt blood flowing, a warm, red waterfall down her cheek, and leapt to her feet. She didn't have to fake her bleat of distress.

Kurt sat bolt upright in his sleeping bag, a wild-eyed expression emblazoned on his face. When he caught sight of Natalie, some of the flames died down in his eyes.

"Nat?" Doug said, a blowsy, dazed mutter worthy of an Oscar. "Whatsa matter?"

"I must've rolled over"—Natalie bent in half, and a ruby bauble of blood struck the ground—"in my sleep. Onto a stick or a rock—" A clutch in her throat gave way to a sob.

Kurt jumped up, his gaze homing in on Natalie through the darkness. Then he leaned over Doug, pulling him upright in one swift move. "Get going," he said, contempt coating his tone. "Can't you see your wife is hurt? The first aid kit is in the wooden crate next door."

Despite the pain pulsing in Natalie's face, a sense of hope sparked inside her. This couldn't have worked out better if all their parts had been scripted. She'd assumed Kurt would go for the first aid kit, and Doug would have to slip out undetected while Kurt started to tend to her. This way, Doug could grab the supplies during his assigned trip.

Kurt walked over to Natalie to examine her cheek, leaning so close in the dark that she could feel the flutter of his lashes. He dabbed at the wound with a length of cloth torn from his shirt. The newly opened skin stung as if submerged in salt water.

"You know, Natalie, it isn't entirely a bad thing that this happened," Kurt said. "Mother Nature is a clumsy healer, and when your cut closed in the wild, it took the path of least resistance, lopsided and irregular."

Natalie licked her lips, tasting iron and salt.

Kurt glanced at the doorway.

How long had Doug been gone? Pain was distorting Natalie's sense of time. She reached for words. "So you think you can treat it?"

Another blotting with the strip of cloth, another look toward the opening.

"It needs stitches, doesn't it?" Natalie asked.

Kurt balled up the cloth in his fist and strode off.

Natalie ran after him.

They ducked outside into the night. Chilly air enrobed them, the sky an ashy, lightless mix of grays.

Doug was nowhere to be seen.

Six or seven long strides, and Kurt would be at the entrance to his hut.

"Doug!" Natalie called out. With any luck, Kurt would think pain responsible for the frantic warble in her warning. "What's taking so long?"

Kurt took a step into his dwelling, then came out suddenly, walking backward, one arm braced over his eyes.

Doug emerged, aiming the bright beam of a flashlight right at Kurt's face. "Artificial light," he exclaimed. "Haven't seen this in a while." He flicked off the switch and extended the plastic tube toward Kurt. "I thought this might help with the surgery." He turned to Natalie. "You all right, honey? That cut looks painful."

Kurt regarded Doug levelly.

Doug lifted the red kit he held in his other hand. "Took a while to find. Hopefully it has everything you need."

Without a word, Kurt led their trio back inside.

He was a patient physician, and though the procedure, sans any sort of numbing agent, was agonizing, Natalie tolerated each meticulous stitch, imagining all the things Doug might have been able to stuff into his pockets.

"I wish I had a mirror," Kurt said with delight once he'd finished. "I've never seen such an even row of stitches."

"I don't suppose you have any Advil in that kit?" Natalie asked weakly.

Kurt frowned. "Unfortunately, those are long gone," he said. "But I do know a bark whose aspirin-like properties you won't believe till you've chewed some. I'll show you where it grows once the sun comes up."

Doug held out his hand, an easy grin on his face. "I don't think we'll have to wait that long to offer my wife a little relief."

Kurt raised his eyebrows.

A tiny clay receptacle, smaller than the cup they all drank from, sat on Doug's palm. It was filled with what looked like crushed, gray-green leaves.

Natalie frowned. Pot? Had that hiker—Terry—brought a stash into the woods?

Kurt's face was expressionless.

"I'm right, aren't I?" Doug said. "It's the stuff you use for tea. That has a relaxing effect."

"Scott's Dash," Kurt said evenly. "That will indeed help."

"Let's all have some," Doug proposed. "I could use a little medicinal assistance getting back to sleep myself."

Kurt took the cup. "Just have to start a fire," he said, maneuvering toward the exit.

Understanding and relief began to bloom inside Natalie. And it wasn't due to the prospect of the pain-alleviating tea. Because hadn't Kurt said that a cupful of this stuff knocked him out cold? If so, then Natalie and Doug wouldn't have to wait another day to escape. Their imminent departure roared at her like a train.

They would leave as soon as Kurt dropped off to sleep.

The three of them sat on flat stones around the fire. Kurt boiled water in a dented pot, sprinkling leaves across its surface for a makeshift kettle.

"Steep it strong," Doug suggested.

The flames crackled.

Careful, honey, Natalie thought. It wouldn't do to forget how smart Kurt was, especially not when they were so close to getting out.

"I need the sleep," Doug explained as if he had heard her. "That was a bit of a rude awakening—literally. Although…" He got onto his knees, illumination from the fire permitting him to study Natalie's face. "I have to say that your technique is superb, Kurt. Those stitches may not even leave a scar."

Natalie hardly felt the injury, how tightly her skin was stretched to accommodate the threading. Her nerves jangled, adrenaline placing her on a cliff's edge.

Kurt handed around a trio of cups, drinking from his own before anyone else could take a sip. The rim didn't entirely conceal a smile on his mouth.

"Our own cups," Natalie said faintly.

Kurt lowered his. "I put the finishing touches on them tonight. After you two fell asleep."

Cold air shot through Natalie. That meant that Kurt had been awake—walking around—while she and Doug were discussing their next move.

But Kurt's expression looked mild as he poured himself more tea.

Natalie took a sip of hers, letting it dribble back into the cup without swallowing. The last thing she needed tonight was to be drugged. She tilted the contents of her cup onto the ground when Kurt got up to tend to the fire. Then she braced her hands behind her waist, leaning back to stare at the sky. The moon had come out, and a million stars pierced the firmament, sharp as bits of glass.

"You know, it's really wonderful," Kurt said, sitting back down.

Doug gave him a curious look.

"How you two seem to have worked things out."

Natalie lowered her face to her cup without drinking.

She had grown accustomed to Kurt's tactics by now, how he liked to come up from behind with something no one was prepared for. But Doug looked as if he were warding off a blow. He reached for Natalie's hand, and she clasped it.

"I mean, that was quite the betrayal, wasn't it?" Kurt went on. "I imagine most marriages wouldn't survive. Particularly not when something like that takes place right at the start of your lives together."

Doug turned toward Natalie in the dark, and she looked away, ashamed. What was he going to say? Any amount of reproach at the way she'd revealed their secrets to a stranger—a madman—would be justified. *You told him?* she heard her husband ask.

Instead, the wariness slid off Doug's face. When he spoke, his voice hitched, but he faced Kurt squarely. "I learned something from it. About being honest with your spouse, even when it comes to the ugly parts. Maybe that's why we could get past it."

Natalie tightened her grip on Doug's hand. A single tear slipped down her cheek, stinging as it caught in the rigging that Kurt had assembled.

"Have you ever been married, Kurt?" Doug asked.

But Kurt seemed to have lost interest in the subject. He gave a yawn, the hinges of his jaw cracking. "I told you Scott's Dash goes to work on me. You two must be getting sleepy yourselves." He stood up, kicking ash over the fire before turning toward the huts.

Natalie and Doug lay utterly still beside their sleeping bag instead of inside it, ensuring there'd be no rustle of fabric when they stood up. Barely allowing themselves to breathe until Kurt began to snore: soft, ruffled expulsions of air that could be heard distinctly from the other side of the hut. Early light had just begun to filter into the structure when Doug sat upright, patting the pockets of his shorts for one final check.

He and Natalie rose silently, looking back once to make sure Kurt slept on.

Then they tiptoed outside into the barely broken dawn.

CHAPTER SIXTY-TWO

A full day's search of the area upriver from Crosch Pond yielded no signs of the couple. But Tim was up the next morning before the sun had cracked the horizon—in his office and surrounded by the topo maps he'd all but memorized before catching a few short hours of shut-eye—when a call came in that a body had been found.

"Male," Phil Wilbur said. Wilbur was the lead guy in the Search and Rescue office in Gumption, New York, and he'd been in intermittent contact—signal a problem as always—with Steve and Brad since they'd left to paddle upstream. "Looks about the right age for our guy."

Couple of easy solves this week, Tim thought. First the Scouts, now the honeymooners. How he wished the second case could've gone like the first. Douglas and Natalie Larson were two people at the start of their lives together—or at least they had been. They deserved better than this.

"Anything as far as the wife?" he asked.

"No sign of her yet," Wilbur replied. "If my boys don't find one, what's the chance of getting a dog into those woods?"

A flintlike flicker lit inside Tim despite the reference to HRDs—animals trained in the detection of human remains. Maybe the wife had survived. "I'll put K-9 on alert." He paused. "You got a cause of death?"

"My boys tried to send a photo," Wilbur replied. "Not enough bandwidth. They're breaking down camp now, then they'll resend. They got lucky, were sleeping real close. Stumbled over this guy practically as soon as they had light."

"Right," Tim said, trying to reconcile the concept of luck with a man being dead less than two weeks after he'd gotten married.

"My guess is the usual," Wilbur went on. "Dehydration, exposure. Got cold out there the last few nights."

The map Tim had been staring at swam in and out of focus. "Was the body found near Turtle Ridge?" He realized he wasn't certain of the route Steve and Brad had taken.

"Only if you call eighty miles near," Wilbur said. "My guys are most of the way to the border. Place called Laughy Creek. Why? Turtle Ridge the PLS?"

"Any ID on this guy?" Tim asked, ignoring the question. Point last seen didn't matter if he had been wrong about the location. "We positive it's him?"

"No ID," Wilbur replied. "But that's not unusual on a backcountry expedition."

"Probably left behind in the car," Tim agreed.

Wilbur paused for a moment. "Hey, Tim, I've got that photo. Just synched up."

Something in Wilbur's voice. Tim felt himself straighten. The lines and squiggles, depressions and hills on the topo map he was staring at suddenly grew distinct, as if the scene had come to life and Tim had been airlifted into it. He'd felt this kind of energy before, like the thrumming that came when you stood too close to a power line.

"And?" he said.

"Looks like there's been a fair amount of decomposition, especially around the midriff. Could be a coyote or a cat had at him." An audible breath. "Face is intact."

"There a reason you're noting the face?" Tim asked, even though he was pretty sure there was. Even via satellite, he could sense the change in the climate.

Another intake of breath. "I think so. This is more your territory, though."

"Describe what you're seeing," Tim said.

"There's a hole…through his forehead… Tim, this guy has been shot."

Tim headed for the Laughy Creek recreation area, driving north toward Canada, going ninety, lights on, the whole way.

The DEC had provided a makeshift war room in a building they operated, a wooden structure out on Highway 30. Information center, museum, gift shop, all exploring the region's history and approach to conservation. A map encompassing Vermont, the Adirondack Park, and southeastern Canada had been taken out of its glass case and tacked up on the wall. A thumbtack indicated where the body had been found.

Steve and Brad, plus other searchers from the Gumption office, were setting out on successive passes around the site in the hopes of locating Natalie Larson.

Tim looked over the photo they'd been sent. A bullet in the forehead appeared to be the cause of death, although confirmation would have to come from the medical examiner. In the meantime, Tim cropped a headshot off the partially decomposed body and fuzzed out the patch on the forehead where a hole could be discerned. He left a message for Natalie Larson's sister, apologizing for the grisly email she'd be receiving.

The Wi-Fi was supposed to be decent in this building, but when Tim began a search online for Douglas Larson, hoping to confirm his identity, the links took forever to download, the little disk spinning.

Claudia Redding called back, listening as Tim issued his warning.

"Oh no," she said. "But it's a… I mean, they just found a…"

"The victim is male, yes," Tim said, as gently as such news could be delivered.

Claudia swallowed hard enough to be heard over the patchy signal. "I don't see any email. It must not have downloaded yet." She said something under her breath, then added, "We're in your area actually. We decided to come up."

It was Tim's turn to swear inwardly. Even with a typical search and rescue, there was little the family could do to help, although understandably, they often tried. But this was a whole different territory now. Claudia Redding shouldn't be here if it turned out that her sister had shot her new husband, which statistically was the most likely explanation, newlyweds or not.

Plus, Claudia had said *we*. Who all had come up?

He thumbed a text to Dorothy, asking her to reserve the apartment they used for such circumstances. It had decent connectivity and was above a small market and café, which made up for the fact that its inhabitants were essentially trapped, one of Tim's men stationed outside, preventing a bad situation from becoming worse.

"Chief Lurcquer?" Claudia Redding said, her tone light enough to float. "Your email just came through."

Tim replaced the phone by his ear. "And?"

"That isn't my brother-in-law."

Tim was gathering up printouts of both photos—the original and the one he had doctored—then rerolling his maps when a member of the Force, Canada's finest and good men to work with, came into the war room.

"Looks like your honeymooners weren't Mike and Carol Brady," he told Tim in faintly accented English. "Or maybe they were. Didn't Mike keep a few secrets?"

Tim remained silent.

"We located the canoe on our side," the other man informed him. "Its hull had been opened. We sent out the samples, but it's a fair bet they test positive. There were traces of powder in the compartment we exposed."

Tim paused in packing up.

The gentleman concluded, "I think the Bradys had a reason for heading up to fair Canada. And it wasn't to try poutine."

Tim held a secret conviction that the reason he was a good cop was because he allowed himself to be surprised on the job. Like right now, for instance.

He aimed a wordless double check—cocking one eyebrow—at the member of the Force, who nodded confirmation before offering a brief salute in goodbye.

Tim returned the gesture.

As soon as he'd pointed the Mountaineer south toward Wedeskyull, Tim put two of his men on the drug angle, attempting to match the photo of the unidentified corpse with known traffickers, as well as tracking down footage to see if Larson's Rogue had ever been noted crossing the border. Then Tim began trying to reach Phil Wilbur again, ruing the spotty signal for his thousandth time on the job.

Funny thing about living in a border state. Borders were often surrounded on either side by miles of untracked land, and they afforded the explorer willing to trek through that wilderness a few key opportunities. Here in the United States, drugs could make a guy rich. Across the border in Canada, they could make a guy richer.

Twice richer, to be exact.

Make a $10,000 buy in Poughkeepsie or Albany or Troy, manage to get it across to a contact on the other side, and you'd return home with $20,000 in your pocket.

Useful if you needed to turn a profit fast, or get your hands on a large amount of cash in a hurry. Tim didn't suppose the honeymooners to be drug kingpins, more likely just caught up in something bad, but the sorting out was going to keep Tim's men busy for a while.

He glanced down at his phone, rejoicing when he saw bars. Tim placed a call to Wilbur, keeping both eyes on the curving road and speaking into the Bluetooth. "How would you feel about lending me two of your best to take a look in a different location?"

A pause while Wilbur took that in. "What's on your mind, Tim?"

Tim swiveled the Mountaineer's steering wheel, tires skidding on the gravelly shoulder as he took the turn toward the Turtle Ridge Wilderness Area.

"I don't think this couple is near Laughy Creek," Tim said. He rubbed yesterday's stubble, feeling his Adam's apple move in his throat like a stone. Leaving behind policies and procedure, the cold, hard, lifeless facts of evidence, was like entering an unknown land. Anything could be there. Including the answers.

It had been a while since Tim had relied on instinct. In the wake of the old chief's departure, Tim had schooled himself to ignore his gut. But that hadn't gotten him anywhere. And, he suspected, it wouldn't get him to Natalie and Doug Larson.

"So where are they?" Wilbur asked. He spoke carefully but not dismissively.

"In or around Turtle Ridge, if I'm guessing right," Tim said. "And in case I am, I'd sure appreciate having your guys at my back." Tim's own resources would be tapped, given the drugs and the Redding family's arrival.

Tim had grown up in Wedeskyull, hadn't left these mountains for more than a few days at a time, and even such short excursions as those could be counted on the fingers of one hand. People said that searching the woods was like looking for a needle in a haystack, but that wasn't accurate, unless it was a haystack that spoke. For the woods offered clues, if only a searcher could hear them, was fluent in their language.

In this Tim had an advantage over the SAR guys, whose work required them to look for people who wanted to be found. If Tim's hunch was correct, he'd be hunting somebody trying to stay hidden, a man who'd already killed at least once.

"I've got to keep my boys at the site. I mean, come on, Tim. The canoe has been found a hundred miles north of where you're talking."

"I'm asking you to trust me here," Tim said.

There was a long pause. "Steve and Brad," Wilbur said at last. "I'll divide my team. For six hours, no more. Then if whatever this is—your hunch—doesn't prove out, I'll yank 'em and send 'em back to Laughy." He paused. "And you'll have to know that we squandered half a day below capacity."

Tim kept silent. It was simple math: every pair of feet on the ground widened the area that could be covered. The more eyes and ears, the more signs would be detected.

"We've got a couple of clueless subjects out there," Wilbur went on. "Kids really, just starting out their lives together. I want them to have a chance to grow up. Become a little less clueless."

"That's what I want too," Tim said.

He told Wilbur where to send Steve and Brad.

They would start on the trail from which Theresa Valero had vanished.

CHAPTER SIXTY-THREE

If Mia hadn't been so worried about her aunt, this trip would've felt like a vacation. Falling asleep in the backseat as her parents drove out of the city before the sun had even risen—up earlier than dawn for the second day in a row, yawn—then waking up in a different world filled with trees, streams, and narrow, curving roads. Even when they came to a stop in a town with a funny name—*Weeds-kill*, her mom said it was called—the vacation feeling didn't dissolve. The GPS led them to a parking lot with a big barn on one side and a splashy brook on the other.

Wayside Market & Necessaries was looped across a painted sign. The place sold outdoor wear, fishing licenses, worms, and food. Mia had to suppress a giggle.

Both her parents turned around in the front seat.

Her mom had wound up having to finish most of her double yesterday, but arranged to take something called FMLA after that, just as Mia's father had suggested. They'd all gone to sleep for what seemed like hardly any time at all in the Bronx apartment, Mia on an ugly, thrift shop couch, and her mother and father squashed side by side on a double bed.

It'd felt so crowded, it'd been hard to breathe. Mia wondered how her dad had stood living in such a tiny place all year. Here where they'd wound up in the country was way nicer. Especially because Mia was near Aunt Nat now. She could feel it.

She looked out through the car window. "What is this place?"

Her mother spoke up first as usual. "This is where we've been told to go." But after that she paused, looking at Mia's father.

He looked surprised, then said, "The police are going to meet us here."

Mia figured her dad wasn't used to filling in information, not when her mom was around anyway. She noticed the gray police car at that moment, parked beside a draping tree, and felt a twist in her stomach. "The police have to talk to us?"

Her mother opened her mouth to answer, again stopping to look at Mia's father. He took a breath and said, "While you were asleep, the police chief called, Mi. He told us that searchers found a man in the woods."

Mia jerked upright, the seat belt yanking her back down. "Uncle—"

Her mother shook her head firmly. "It's not Uncle Doug. We don't know who this man is, or why he was there. But, Mi, he's dead."

Mia frowned.

"Looks like we're about to find something out," Mia's dad said, indicating a gray-uniformed policewoman who had just walked up to the car.

They all unlatched their belts and got out.

Mia liked that the cop was a woman. She introduced herself as Mandy Bishop while she walked Mia and her mom and dad into the building. The bottom floor was a café, which smelled of crumb cake, spicy and good. There was a circle of dented metal tables and chairs, plus an area with worn couches surrounding a bench, which spilled over with trail maps and guides. The place had a battered but homey feel—splintery wooden floorboards, notices tacked up askew on the walls—that in the city would've been artful and affected, but here seemed authentic.

Officer Bishop offered a hello to the man behind the counter, then led the way to a spiral staircase. The steps opened into the sweetest apartment Mia had ever seen: two rooms into which the scent of baking carried, both overlooking the brook.

Officer Bishop smiled as Mia and her mom and dad all got assembled inside. "We hope you'll be comfortable here. The market serves meals, and you can feel free to take out items and bring them up." She turned a neat half-step and pointed to a TV on the wall. "You can stream movies, and your phones should work. If they don't, I'll be right downstairs or in the lot outside, and can come up and troubleshoot."

"You mean you're staying here?" Mia's dad asked at the same time as Mia's mom said, "You mean we're staying here?"

Officer Bishop smiled. "Yes to both," she said. "This way we'll know you're in one place, and I can find you easily as soon as there's news."

The arrangement sounded okay to Mia—she never got to watch movies at home due to the limits her mother imposed on screen time—until she got a look at her parents, who seemed a lot less happy about it, her mom at least.

"I've been Googling SAR," her mother said, holding up her phone as if for proof. "The clips I've read say that volunteers often help with a search. Even family members. It allows more ground to be covered. And one thing I can tell"—her mother crossed to one of the windows and gestured outside—"is that there's a lot of ground up here."

That had never occurred to Mia, the idea that they could all go looking too. It should have, though—why else would her mom have made her wear boots and find all that other stuff from camp?

Mia's dad walked over to the window and took her mother's hand.

Mia looked at the policewoman.

She gave Mia a friendly smile. She was pretty: hair held back in a ponytail that peeked out from under her gray hat, barely any makeup.

"You're right, that does happen in some circumstances," she said to Mia's parents, who turned around to face her. "But you're going to have to trust us that such an approach isn't appropriate in this case."

Mia's mom frowned. "That really doesn't sit right with me," she said, freeing her hand from Mia's dad's grasp. "I'd like to help. This is my sister we're talking about."

Her mother had spoken sharply, and Mia's father took over. "My wife isn't exactly the wait-around type," he said. "And she's very close to her sister."

Officer Bishop's face looked no less pleasant. "I understand that," she said. "But the single best thing you all can do for Natalie right now is stay put. We have top people from two countries searching for her. You couldn't ask for a better team."

"And you're not making use of volunteers?" Mia's dad asked. "At all?"

Mia's mom sent him a grateful smile.

"Not at this time," Officer Bishop said.

Her tone made a phrase pop into Mia's head, something her mom used to say whenever Mia argued. *This is my last word on the subject.*

Mia saw her mother's shoulders settle.

Mia's father touched her mother briefly on the arm, then looked over at Mia. "I wonder if they sell pizza downstairs."

After a moment, Mia's mom said, "Family movie day?"

Four hours later, Mia felt woozy from food and movies. Maybe her mother's screen restrictions made sense. Her father had brought dishes up from the café, neatly packed in takeout containers and reheated in the small kitchen's microwave, and they'd eaten them in front of back-to-back comedies whose plots already escaped Mia's memory. Now her dad was reviewing summer reading assignments on his phone, while her mom watched some medical show on TV.

Officer Bishop had come upstairs twice to check on them, talking to Mia's parents, but not really—Mia realized upon reflection—saying much of anything at all.

After the policewoman left for the second time, Mia's mother dragged her father into the kitchen—which made the one back home in their apartment seem roomy—and they began to talk in whispered breaths.

"I don't get why they're just keeping us here," Mia's mom hissed. "It's not the norm in situations like this. I read about this one case where the sibling—they were twins—found his sister. She'd been gone for sixteen days, they'd just about given her up for dead. And that was in the salt flats out west. Far more dangerous terrain."

"Right…" said Mia's dad.

When her mom spoke next, there was a tremble in her voice. "This is my baby sister, Elliott. And there are lots of stories like the one I just told you, where family members are especially tuned in to their missing loved one, and accomplish what police and searchers can't."

"I believe you," Mia's dad said. "But there's a reason we're not supposed to be in those woods. Don't forget about the body. I'm sure the cops know what they're doing."

But to Mia's ears, her father didn't sound very sure of that at all.

Her mom looked mad—whether at the situation or at Mia's dad's response, Mia couldn't tell. All she knew was that she didn't want her parents to start fighting again, before Aunt Nat even had a chance to see them back together.

"They might know what they're doing," Mia's mother muttered, turning away. "But they don't know me."

She left the kitchen and came to sit beside Mia. The look on her face almost made Mia laugh, even though there was nothing funny about being stuck here like this, of course. But Mia's mom looked exactly like Mia always felt when her mother was taking away her phone or refusing to let her stay by herself.

Mia got to her feet, stretching her arms over her head. "Can I go downstairs?"

CHAPTER SIXTY-FOUR

Natalie and Doug entered the woods soundlessly, heels down, then toes, staring at the ground as if their eyes were soldered to it. Doug paused to stoop and pick up two long pine boughs, which they used to check the forest floor before taking a new step, then clear away the tracks they'd left behind.

It was a painstaking, excruciating pace to maintain, especially with the specter of Kurt rising from his sleeping bag and appearing beside them. They passed through stands of tangled, knotted brush and spied the stump forest, that giant's set of checkerboard pieces, a short distance away. There came a glimpse of the conical peak of Kurt's smokehouse; no time to think about that now. They'd made it farther than they had been since Kurt entrapped them. Natalie and Doug exchanged a single, silent nod of satisfaction.

Doug took the lead, and the camp receded farther into the distance, the bodies of the huts disappearing from view, then the rims of their roofs, until finally there was no more cleared land to be seen and trees closed in from all sides. Natalie allowed herself to take air deep into her lungs; she hadn't realized she'd been holding her breath.

A flat, golden pancake of sun lay atop the mountains, rounding into a dome and filling the sky. It seemed to bode well for the day ahead, and a giddy sense of excitement began to prevail as they shuffled along.

Doug relayed the spoils of his raid of Kurt's hut, speaking in an undertone of barely concealed joy. For their journey, they had snack bars, iodine tabs, even a plastic-shielded map that might cover the whole region; Doug would know as soon as he could take a good look at it. He had spotted the machete, lying upon a shelf, its blade glinting in the darkness. "I couldn't think of a way to hide it, though," he whispered. "And I thought Kurt would miss it right away."

Natalie nodded agreement, but she was lost in thought. Should they still try to follow the creek out? Or would the map point them to a better route? Water would conceal their tracks, allow them to put distance between themselves and Kurt.

Doug had gotten ahead. Natalie swiveled, hurriedly brushing the ground behind her to rid it of tracks before catching up to her husband. The wispy green branch Doug was waving back and forth got stuck in something Natalie couldn't make out.

Fast as a lightning strike, Doug barricaded Natalie's body with one arm, then came to such a sudden halt that he nearly pitched forward. When he turned back to look at her, his face was slicked with sweat and he was breathing hard.

She still couldn't see and mouthed, *What is it?*

Silently, Doug pointed.

A length of vine, viciously studded with thorns, was strung between the trunks of two trees. It ran at shin height for Doug, knee high for Natalie. Not only would the vine have snagged them, but when Doug probed the ground a few feet in front of the tripwire with the tip of his stick, the forest floor gave way to an ankle-snapping ditch.

They stood in place, squandering minutes they didn't have, unable to take another step. Kurt hadn't exaggerated: this land was laced with mines.

Finally Doug raised one foot, stepping to clear the taut length of vine before helping Natalie over. They veered to one side to avoid the hole. Then they continued on, stabbing at the ground with the ends of their sticks, using feathery needles to sweep away the signs they left behind.

They felt it before they saw, or even heard it. A fine, silver mist in the air that sprinkled their skin. They gasped and nearly laughed aloud. Proud, soaring mountains rose on all sides, but a slight slope in the landscape hinted at the creek's nearby presence. Shuffling forward, checking the ground no less assiduously, they started to descend.

Natalie's shoe slid, and she slipped at the same moment that Doug touched the tip of his pine bough to the ground. Suddenly, the stick was sky-bound, hurled aside, and Doug's strong hands landed on Natalie's waist. He lifted her clean into the air—Natalie felt the sensation of flying—and she bit back on a scream, knowing that her shout would've carried. *What the hell are you doing?*

Doug set her upon a hummock of moss-slicked rock, holding her there as if trying to glue her feet in place, while his own foot came down where Natalie's brief skid had been about to send her. The spike was invisible when it punctured the bottom of Doug's shoe, but Natalie saw it come up through the other side.

Doug's hands left her body as if they'd turned to liquid. Natalie swayed for a moment on the hump of rock before regaining her balance.

"I'm okay, I'm okay," Doug said, his tone relieved. "It must've missed me." He paused to swallow. "You were about to step on it. Thank God I spotted it first."

Shock, Natalie thought, diagnosing the condition so clearly and swiftly that she must've been experiencing a similar state herself.

Doug had prevented the spike from stabbing her, but getting close enough to move her away had brought him into direct proximity with the same patch of ground, while his momentum made it impossible to stop before taking that last lethal step. Had he known what would happen—the physics of the situation registering in some low-level way? Or had he acted on the purest, unthinking instinct to save her, giving no thought to his own fate?

She stared downward, tears blurring Doug's form into a series of wavering lines that were woefully, horrifically insufficient to block from sight the length of wood that protruded through the webbed straps of his shoe.

The long, whittled dagger had come to a stop with its tip a few inches above the top of his foot.

"Honey—" Natalie began, but her mouth was too dry and sandy for further speech. Fear flooded her, charged with unspent adrenaline. There was nowhere to run—not anymore—and no one to fight.

Doug's face had begun turning waxen, shiny, but his expression appeared merely perplexed. "What is it?" he asked. "What's wrong?"

Natalie fought to keep her gaze from traveling toward Doug's foot. She stared off at the sun-washed sky, biting her lip as tears overflowed.

Suddenly, Doug looked annoyed. "Ow," he said, as if a bee had stung him. "That really hurts." And he glanced down.

When his back dipped, Natalie moved to catch him, forgetting to check the ground for traps. What did it matter now anyway? She lowered Doug carefully into a sitting position, then sank down beside him. She cradled his head in her arms as pain finally caught up to consciousness and Doug's leg began to twitch.

"Christ," he groaned. "Son of a bitch. That bastard." He reached toward his foot, but Natalie caught his hand in the vise of her fingers.

"Don't touch it," she barked, and he lifted his eyes. "That stick—it's cauterizing your wound. Or sealing it or something. We have to leave it where it is. We have to leave it alone." She forced herself to look. The spike connected Doug to the ground, but only barely—most of its length had wound up in his foot.

Doug started shaking his head, slowly back and forth.

"Honey, we have no other choice," Natalie said. Salty tears stung the back of her throat. "Maybe we can submerge your foot in the creek. That would help with the pain. Although I'd be scared of infection—"

Doug continued to shake his head, wildly now.

"What?" Natalie asked. "What are you trying to say?"

He reached for her hands. "You have to go on, Nat."

"What?"

"Go on without me," Doug said. "Get out. Use the creek like we planned."

"No," Natalie answered simply.

"Natalie!" Doug shouted, and panicked, she cast her gaze about the woods. "You won't do me any good by staying. All you'll accomplish is that we both die or get trapped here for good. When Kurt comes looking, he'll find the two of us." His leg kicked out, seemingly involuntarily, and Doug let out a long, low bellow of pain before he was able to clamp his lips shut. The motion had separated the stick from the earth.

Natalie gazed at her husband, the familiar planes and angles of his face beginning to change now, altered by the burden of pain.

Doug began trying to lift himself off the ground, using his good foot as a lever while keeping the hurt one immobile, and clawing around beneath the waistband of his shorts. He came out with a fistful of bars, which he handed to Natalie, along with one of the clay cups, a pouch containing four clammy tablets, plus the map in its lacquered coating.

"Take this stuff," he panted. "And go. Find a way out. Now go!"

Doug's voice sounded different too, stripped of all that had once made it his. Natalie got onto her hands and knees. "We need to move you," she said. "You can hide beneath those branches." She gestured toward a tree whose trunk was draped with green.

Keeping the wounded foot motionless, Doug used the other one, as well as his hands, to lift his body a few inches off the ground. Natalie stooped and slid her hands beneath her husband's arms, then began to pull him toward the sheltering tree.

Doug's body slid, and he moaned.

"I'm sorry, honey!" cried Natalie. "I'm so sorry!"

Rivulets of sweat poured down Doug's face, hanging in droplets from his new growth of beard. He ground out words. "Just get me there."

She pulled him a few more feet, pushing branches aside when they came to the tree. Working together, they used the greenery to conceal him. Natalie ducked out from underneath. She couldn't see any hint of Doug, not even a flag of color from his clothes.

She bent over, peering inside to say—what? *Goodbye? I'll be back with help? I love you?* Doug's upper torso tipped, the trunk providing support as he leaned against it. "Go," he said, sodden and sleepy. "Don't think. You've got this. I know you do."

Natalie slipped out from under the embrace of the tree, and ran.

CHAPTER SIXTY-FIVE

Kurt chose to allow Doug and Natalie enough time that they might grow optimistic, imagine themselves truly getting away, but not enough that such a thing would become a real possibility. It wouldn't be likely, of course, no matter how much time Kurt gave them—he'd planted too many traps. But the couple might get lucky, weave a path that avoided the worst of his obstacles, and Kurt couldn't have that.

He had begun to suspect a certain rebellious intent on the couple's part as early as yesterday morning, when they had all taken their meander through the woods. Natalie had been suffused with hope and promise, glowing with it like a bad sunburn. Clearly she and Doug were up to something, and the prospect of ferreting out what it was had made Kurt's nerve endings tingle. He'd decided not to allow the two to sleep alone; what if they planned to attack Kurt under cover of the dark? He had even shown them his machete, all but put it on display, as if daring them to make such a move. The couple's true strategy, however, made more sense, given their lack of strength and skills.

What they were planning came clear to Kurt once the two began to treat him to their B-movie acting. Natalie's injury had been self-inflicted, or else inflicted by Doug. No way had she rolled over on the ground, opening that cut on her cheek. There hadn't been a speck of dirt in it.

Kurt wondered what had been stolen from his hut; he would have to make a thorough check later. His machete still lay in its spot on the shelf, but he suspected the map he had lifted from a long-ago hiker was gone, which would pose a concern, should the couple get far enough to flee. Natalie, of course, couldn't do a thing with the map, by her own admission. But that still left Doug. Kurt had observed some missing energy bars, although Doug had been judicious, leaving several behind. With a shiver of delight, Kurt wondered at which point the two would allow themselves a treat.

He felt at a peak of power, his senses sharpened, not a shred of fatigue. It pleased him how easily the couple had bought his drugged act. After several seasons, Kurt had come to conclude that Scott's Dash was apocryphal. Even if the plant did exist somewhere in the region, the leaves Doug had found were far more commonplace. Wild thyme, an invasive that made a spicy, pleasing tea, incapable of putting anyone to sleep.

The couple would head toward the creek surely, intending to follow it out.

Were it not for Kurt, such a plan might even have worked.

The sun began to rise in the sky, wrapping the land in its gauzy glow. Kurt emerged from his sleeping bag, picking it up and smoothing it out close to Doug and Natalie's place of slumber. They would all rest again together tonight.

He started walking south-southeast out of camp, concentrating intently in order to spy the first blotch of blood or other sign of trouble on the ground.

Kurt had enough insight and self-awareness to know that the anticipation he currently felt had its roots in his childhood. His was a focus inculcated by his parents. Their psychiatric backgrounds meant they were both fascinated by the human psyche.

Kurt's parents had studied him with acute attention born of their school training, observing his every word and action, and reflecting upon it all with admirable professional distance. It took Kurt a long time to understand that his parents' mode of relating amounted to an infinitely better type of love than the tempests to which lesser people fell prey. Ordinary love caused hurt and heartache; Kurt's parents saw that all the time in their practices. Child abuse, domestic violence, divorce. Still, as a younger fellow, Kurt could remember hungering after more typical parent-child interactions.

He had once asked his mother to read him a bedtime story, considering this a benign enough request. Didn't most mothers read their children books, especially intellectual ones like Kurt's, who placed a value on education and literacy?

Besides, Kurt's mother enjoyed reading herself—the only time Kurt had ever seen her display any sort of emotion was when she would pore over romances procured from the library or drugstore or supermarket racks. Kurt used to like to watch his mother read, because when she did, her face would lose its habitual smoothness. Her eyes would widen, her cheeks grow red, and her lips part as the stories swept her away.

Upon hearing Kurt's bedtime proposal, his mother had acquiesced, digging out a brightly colored picture book that Kurt hadn't known they owned, then sitting down on the seldom-used rocking chair. Kurt had perched rigidly on her lap, his back upright, arms held aloft, while his mother began to read.

The trouble ensued when Kurt sat back.

In his memory, his small body had molded itself to his mother's with a sensation he had never before experienced. So natural, so comfortable, his muscles relaxing from their customary guarded stance, which resulted, surely, from not knowing what about his behavior might provide fodder for speculation, as if Kurt were a specimen in a cage. He felt his mother's breasts flatten against his back—such softness!—and then smelled something he'd also never known existed.

His mother had a scent, flowery and sweet and warm.

Kurt breathed in deeply, cuddling against his mother's form. He forgot all about listening to the story. His thumb wandered up to his mouth, even though Kurt had stopped sucking ages ago, when his parents began charting each incident, trying to see what prompted the need to self-soothe.

Then his mother leapt up, whirling on him and fixing him with a look Kurt didn't recognize, and never once saw again in all the years after.

The storybook fell to the floor, while Kurt himself was rudely upended, landing beside the book. He thought for a moment that his mother must have smelled fire or sensed some other sort of danger.

But she remained in the room, calm and contained, staring down at him. Though she did open and close her mouth a few times, failing at first to speak. Finally she called out, her hoarse tone giving way to a smoother one, "George, do come here."

Kurt stayed where he'd fallen, sprawled out on the floor, registering the fact that his eyes and cheeks had grown slippery for some reason, and wondering what label his parents would apply to this affliction.

At the summons, Kurt's father came hurrying down the hall.

"Look at Kurt," his mother instructed. "I believe he has developed an age-appropriate aversion to crying."

Upon arrival in the doorway, his father looked down at Kurt, who was fingering the slipperiness on his face while he attempted to stand up.

"Trying to wipe away tears, is he?" his father queried.

Kurt's mother peered closer. "I wonder if this is a lesson learned from his peers? I don't believe either of us has ever chastised him for such behavior."

"Certainly not," Kurt's father said. "That wouldn't be healthy."

Kurt hadn't made it higher than his knees. Hands splayed out on the floor, he stared up at his parents, as drops turned into rivulets, sliding down his cheeks and filling his mouth until he began to cough and sputter and thought he would drown.

His parents looked on, nodding.

Kurt had walked farther than he'd expected, passing the deepest of the manholes he had dug, as well as several long lengths of tripwire fashioned from thorn-spiked vines. He began to feel a grudging respect for the couple—they had kept their eyes peeled at least—and also a growing sense of fear.

He couldn't lose them.

They must have kept turning around to brush their footsteps away or else swept debris over them. Perhaps Kurt wasn't following the same course as Doug and Natalie had, but when he looked left and right, he could find no indication of another path.

Then he saw something, and relief flooded his body, so great that his knees buckled. There appeared to be a stain on the ground. But how recently had it gotten there, and was it human or animal in nature? In these woods, carnage was routine, due to his traps. Kurt seldom took a stroll without finding evidence of some death or slaughter.

He spotted another wetter, slightly redder patch of brown against the russet leaves on the forest floor, and moved to examine it. That was new, fresh. And not far off lay a long, cleared swath of earth. As if something—or someone—had been dragged along.

But he could also hear the furious laughter of the creek now. His heart began clip-clopping, a wild horse inside his chest, for the creek spelled escape. The misty wash of vapor appeared in the air, chilling Kurt, while his thoughts sped up like an overwound watch. He forced himself to pause and take a good look around, leveling out his breathing. Sweat, potent and slick, began to dry beneath his armpits.

A kingly sense of confidence reigned inside him again.

He was going to locate his quarry; Kurt knew that as definitively as he knew his own needs and motivations. They couldn't have gotten far from here yet. He willed himself to contemplate the various potential outcomes, each one a morsel to savor. By now, Natalie and Doug would imagine they had made it. It'd be King Kurt, there to show them the error of their ways, while having the distinct pleasure of observing how it felt to fall from a pinnacle of desperation and hope.

He came to a bank of rocks as wide as a city block, taller in some spots than the surrounding trees. A barrier too immense to bypass, especially for anyone injured. There was nobody here, though, dead or alive. It was as if the couple had been airlifted out.

Kurt cast his gaze up to the sky, as if a helicopter might be hovering there.

Nobody searching was likely to have happened upon this location; it was but one prick in an infinite pincushion. And no part of the forest appeared to be disturbed.

If something had saved Doug and Natalie, it had been the hand of God.

A voice Kurt scarcely recognized as his own emitted a long, warbling howl of sheer deprivation and rage. He began to strike his leg with his fist repeatedly, the stony muscles in his thigh no match for the titanium knobs of his knuckles, until he roared with pain. Kurt's eyes blurred for a reason he couldn't understand. He fell to his knees on the padded forest floor, fingers laced in a position of prayer.

Squinting till his vision bleared, still on all fours, Kurt crawled frantically forward, headed for the enormous wall of rock. It was pockmarked and divided by crevices.

He knew what must have happened.

CHAPTER SIXTY-SIX

H ungry?" Mia's mom asked after Mia had made her request to go down to the café and market. "There's still some noodles. I put them in the fridge."

Mia made her tone casual. "How about if I got us some dessert? And drinks?"

"Good idea." Her mom handed Mia a daypack, heavy because it had the thing you drank water from inside it, the contraption Mia had found in the box back in her room. "Load up whatever you get in here. I'd like a Diet Snapple if they have one." Her mom reached for her purse and began to poke around.

Mia's dad stopped her. "They're not letting us pay."

Mia's mom raised her brows at that, and Mia left them to their conversation, slipping out the door and onto the spiral staircase.

The first floor smelled of coffee and other tempting treats. Mia ordered one of those sweet, frothy blends so unlike her mother's morning brew, while examining the baked goods to keep from being bored.

She'd left her phone upstairs and didn't have anything to do. As she waited for her drink, Mia looked around for Officer Bishop. She spotted her standing in a corner of the café, talking on her own phone.

Mia edged closer, letting a group of old men with fishing poles block her from sight.

"Chief doesn't think they're at Laughy," Officer Bishop said.

Laffee? Laughing? Mia wasn't sure. But it was more information than either of her parents had gotten so far. She bent over to study a case of energy bars.

"He thinks they might've wound up in Turtle Ridge," Officer Bishop said. A long silence followed. Then, "Yup. That's the spot. She vanished right off the trail."

It had to be Aunt Nat the policewoman was talking about. How many people could be lost up here right now?

But then Officer Bishop said, "About a year ago."

"Young lady?" The man behind the counter handed Mia an over-flowing drink, wiping his hands on his apron. They left behind smudges of chocolate. "Want a couple of those granola bars you've been eyeing? Go on, take as many as you like."

Mia thanked him, stuffing a fistful of bars into the pack. It was true what they said—people were nicer outside the city. Or maybe everyone just felt sorry for Mia and her family.

She went over to one of the comfy couches and sat down. The other couch was occupied by two girls, slouched over and apparently asleep. Mia wished again for her phone, although at least there were maps and guidebooks to look at here. She grabbed a stack of pamphlets, sipping at the foam on her drink as she flipped through pages. One of the brochures had a photograph of a beautiful, lonesome wilderness on the cover, all towering trees and spattering waterfalls. It was called Turtle Ridge.

The girls woke up at the same time, blinking and smiling in Mia's direction.

"Whoa," one of them said, indicating the brochure. "Turtle Ridge."

"You know it?" Mia asked casually.

"Who doesn't?" said the girl.

Her friend agreed. "Best backpacking around."

"That where you're headed, little sister?" asked the first girl.

Mia almost laughed, then stopped herself. Turtle Ridge was where the police chief thought Aunt Nat and Uncle Doug were. And what had her mom said about family members finding missing loved ones? If a niece could do such a thing, it would make almost as cool a story as the one about the twin. And while Mia's mom was trapped, practically held hostage by the police, no one had charge of Mia right now.

Plus, from the moment they got up here, Mia had felt like she was the one who was meant to find Aunt Nat. She loved Aunt Nat in a way nobody else did. She could just imagine Aunt Nat's face when Mia appeared to lead her out of the woods.

She glanced around the café. Officer Bishop stood chatting with the man who served drinks. Mia ducked her head, not quite looking at the two girls. Then she nodded.

"Cool," one of them said. She began braiding her long, dirty blond hair with a red bandanna as the third strand. When she lifted her arm, Mia saw a small tuft of hair under it, like a mouse. There was a smell coming from the girl's armpit, pungent and strong, as if she hadn't showered or used deodorant in a while.

"Setting out soon?" asked her friend.

Mia nodded again.

Both girls had taken off their hiking boots and were applying some kind of strips to their bare feet. The girl with the braid held out a fold of the stuff. "You ever use this?"

Mia shook her head.

"Oh, you've got to," her friend said. "Put it over blisters you've already got, or where you know you're going to get them if you haven't been on the trail in a while."

Mia extended her hand to take what the girl was offering—a thin, stretchy material that felt a little like the skin you peeled off a callous—then began to tug off her own boots and socks. After a few weeks spent wearing flip-flops, her feet felt like they'd been encased in concrete.

"Whoa," braid girl said. "You're a virgin."

Mia felt her face flame, and stopped in the midst of pressing some of the substance to the back of her heel. Was that where you were likely to get blisters? She had no idea. She'd only gotten blisters once when she'd borrowed (slash stolen for a night) her mom's one pair of heels, even though they hadn't been all that high.

The other girl dropped her gaze to Mia's feet, before nodding and saying in a dry tone that made Mia feel as if she was missing some joke, "Well, she is only, like, sixteen."

Mia didn't bother to correct her, examining her feet for whatever both girls were observing.

Braid girl pointed. "No blisters, no calluses even. Your feet have never gotten beaten up by a trail."

"We've done two thru-hikes ourselves," braid girl's friend informed Mia.

It was supposed to be an explanation, but of what, Mia had no idea. She tried to keep her face blank—you're sixteen, she thought, so act like it—but the girls clearly read her confusion.

"As in the whole length of the AT," one said. "Not this trip, of course—you can't leave this time of year—but we plan to make it from the Dacks to the Catskills."

Mia nodded, hoping she looked like she'd understood a little better.

"So, like, what I meant is your feet. They're unsullied." The girl's smile seemed to leak off her face. "You sure you're up for Turtle Ridge?"

"I'm up for it," Mia said while both girls looked uncertainly at each other. "I need to do this," she added, suddenly convinced. "It's like I have to go."

"Hey, we totally get that," one of the girls said at last. "Sometimes the trail calls to you louder than anyone else can hear."

"And there's nothing like hitting that dirt." The other girl directed her gaze downward. "Let's see how you applied your skins."

Mia obediently extended her feet. She'd have to fill the water thing from the cooler that stood in one corner of the shop. She hoped she could figure out how to strap it on correctly, or else these girls would get even more concerned.

"Good job," said one of them.

Mia twisted to look at the counter. Officer Bishop had just accepted a drink from the man in the apron. "I don't have a great way to get there, though." Mia held up the flyer. "I mean, I could walk, of course." The little square map on the back of the flyer put the trail several miles from here, but Mia figured hikers would be used to such distances. "It's just that I'm really itching to get going."

"You want to make some miles today," said the other girl, nodding.

Mia shot another glance toward the counter. Officer Bishop had begun walking toward the spiral staircase. Now she would go upstairs to non-talk to Mia's parents, and Mia would have a few minutes to slip out. She nodded emphatically at the girls.

"We can give you a lift," one offered.

"You can?" asked Mia.

"Sure," said her friend. "Trail sisters look out for each other." She presented her fist for a bump, then rose in her newly laced-up boots.

Both girls shrugged into framed backpacks before leading the way toward the exit of the barn. "Come on, little sis. We'll get you to Turtle Ridge."

CHAPTER SIXTY-SEVEN

The water felt icy as Natalie entered the creek. She could've stayed dry by maneuvering along the bank, but that path looked unreliable, climbing up and dipping down, as well as fraught with obstacles. Hooked elbows of misshapen tree roots, slippery patches, and pebbly stones. Besides, in the water, her tracks would be obscured.

She scrambled over rocks, her shoes sliding on their mossy surfaces, using her hands as much as her feet. Her legs grew numb; she felt only the occasional splash that landed higher up on dry skin, or when a pool caught her unaware and she sank to greater depths. Small stones shifted beneath her feet, sending up clouds of murky water clouded with plant life and casting tiny, fast-moving fish into disarray.

Natalie came to a narrows where the current grew strong, tugging at her knees and forcing her to throw out her arms to stay upright. In the sunlight, the water moved like quicksilver, splashes making little drops of mercury skitter over rocks. A huge boulder loomed, big enough to block passage unless she got out of the creek. She placed both hands atop the rock, throwing one leg up and trying to hoist herself over.

Natalie stopped so abruptly that she slid back down, the smell of wet moss rank in her nostrils, brown streaks like the goo from slugs smearing her body.

What was she doing, leaving her husband behind in the woods? Injured, his consciousness ebbing, and alone. The depths that had drawn her and Doug together had been largely unknown back when they met, unplumbed, nowhere near fully mined. They knew themselves better now, and their reasons for marrying amounted to far more than the light-hearted, enjoyable pursuits they'd once shared. However much life Doug had left, or she did for that matter, Natalie wanted them to live it together.

She turned her back on the enormous rock and began to struggle through the water, upstream this time, against the current. Kicking up splashes, stubbing her toes on rocks as she headed back the way she had come.

When she got to the place where she'd entered the creek, all the trees looked alike. She had no idea which one she had helped her husband hide beneath. It had been something deciduous, not a fir, she was pretty sure, and she began batting dark, fleshy leaves aside, snatching quick glances underneath before moving on.

Doug was gone.

They had been beside the creek when he got hurt. There were no trees left to check. She'd even looked beneath the pines.

A sob crawled up her throat. Had Kurt come for him? Should Natalie go back to camp? Or had Doug, like an animal, dragged himself away to die, abandoned and alone?

The word *drag* triggered something in Natalie's brain, and she saw what she had been missing. A long swath of dirt, cleared of leaf matter and debris.

Natalie began to follow it.

She came to a structure composed of rocks that made the one that had stopped her in the creek look pebble-like. These boulders had been positioned by giants, soaring outward and up to the sky so that the sun had to fight to find pockets to shine into.

The brushed bare patch of earth traveled into a crevasse between two monoliths. Natalie dropped down, crawling on all fours into the narrow tunnel. Doug's journey must've been unbearable—the space was tight even for her, and her husband was bigger, and injured. The slightest knock of his foot against a stone wall would've caused agony. Doug's decision made sense though. It was warmer in here, the edifice baked by sunlight.

Her husband lay, knees drawn up to his chest, with his arms wrapped around one calf, leaving the other alone as if even a glancing touch far above the foot would be too much to bear. Doug's body shook, flapping like a plastic bag in the wind.

Natalie curved over, shell-like, wrapping her arms around her husband's chest. It felt like there was less to him already. Pain had diminished Doug, stolen parts away.

"Nat? You're back... Did you find... Are we going to be..." Doug's voice was so fractured, it was hard to be sure he was talking.

"I didn't go for help, honey," Natalie said, swallowing a sob. Her own voice had to be firm and sure. She had made the right decision. The only decision she could live—or die—with. "I came back to be with you. I want to do this together."

Settling down beside Doug, the rock's surface rough and warm upon her skin, she didn't let herself think what *this* might mean.

One of Doug's arms fell like a weight onto her lap. Natalie picked up his icy hand and pressed it to her cheek.

Her husband's lips cracked in a semblance of a smile.

Natalie rotated his palm and kissed it, over and over, to try to heat up the skin.

"I..." Doug's voice wound down like the ticking hands on a clock. "...you. Nat."

"Shh," she said, speaking softly also. "I love you too. I always will."

She lay down carefully, positioning herself next to Doug's crumpled form and fighting to transfer some of her warmth. She must've been experiencing her own breed of shock, as if by taking on a share of Doug's, she could ease his suffering, because unbelievably, she dozed. In fact, she slept hard enough to dream. She dreamt that Doug could walk again, only not really, this was a zombie-like stalk, his arms extended stiffly while he explained that Natalie had to leave right now, not a moment to waste, she had to go, go, go, as if agony had turned Doug into some frenzied version of an athletic coach. Natalie came to, arms wrapped around the jittering body of her husband.

He was trying to tell her something, but couldn't get any words out.

Natalie heard a cannonball blast of successive, pounding footsteps headed right in their direction, and she knew.

Kurt was coming.

Natalie reacted on sheer instinct, scooting backward, deeper into the cones and runnels of rock, until she came to a cleft too small for Kurt to infiltrate. She had to wrap her arms around her torso, reduce her circumference, in order to fit. Straitjacketed, she wedged herself inside and out of sight, then worked to still her breathing.

The sound of Kurt's voice was so jarring that it laid waste to Natalie's best efforts, made her heart gong against her chest in a way she feared would be audible.

Luckily, Kurt's attention was focused elsewhere.

"Good Lord," he said. His voice came from close to the ground; he must have crouched down. "You encountered the worst of my traps, didn't you? You poor man."

A long pause, the sound of steady, measured exhalations. Kurt's, surely. Doug's fragmented breathing couldn't be made out at all.

"We seem to be missing someone," Kurt said after a moment. "Doug, I can see you're in pain, and deserving of my attentions, but tell me first. Where is your wife?"

Natalie shrank back behind the barrier of rock, pushing herself a few inches farther into the hollow column. Now the confines were so tight, they squeezed, pressing in on her from all sides. She felt the coarse, burlap texture of stone against her skin, smelled moss and oxidation. Then she could penetrate the ageless mass no more, its walls and floor and partial lid impervious to budging.

Claustrophobia delivered a python hug. Wrapped tightly on all sides, Natalie was unsure whether, when the time came, she'd be able to reverse her maneuvers and get herself back out. Her breath sped up, and dizziness overtook her. The narrow space began to waver. She was going to pass out.

Natalie forced her eyes to close, then open. The return of light—a laser beam of sun shining down from overhead, out where space was abundant—calmed her.

It was harder to hear from this deep point of remove, but Doug must've been trying to say something for Kurt spoke loudly. "What's that? I can't quite make out what you're telling me."

There came a slow, halting rasp. Doug's voice, shorn of everything. "She left..."

Kurt let out a shriek of sheer fury, then scurried out of the cave on all fours. Natalie could hear him moving about like an animal; she knew when he got to his feet and started to stride around the structure. He must have arrived at a point right above where she curled, for all light was suddenly blocked. She could no longer see a thing, not the humps of her shoulders, nor her fingers clasped against her sides.

"Natalie!" Kurt cried out ringingly. "Where are you? Don't lie to me! I know you would never leave your husband!"

How much did she want that to be so—to scurry out to Doug right now and stay by his side forever, or for however much time the two of them had left. Instead, she crouched and cringed inside her hiding space. Way back here, the stone itself seemed to be weeping, a slow, steady seepage that chilled her face and arms.

"Natalie!" Kurt screamed again. "I'm going to kill your husband, you know! If you don't come out right now, then I promise you. That spike will seem a mere splinter compared to the injury I inflict."

Natalie smacked a hand to her mouth—abrading it against the rock—feeling the flesh on her knuckles scraped raw. It was the only way she could keep from crying out in protest, telling both Kurt and Doug not to worry, she was coming out now.

Kurt would detect the smell of blood, sniff it in the air like a wolf, and so Natalie bent her head in the cramped space, cricking her neck painfully in order to lick every sticky, coppery drop from her skin.

Leaves began to flutter and fall outside the rock structure, making a noise like rain, creating shadows. Kurt, rattling trees, snapping their limbs in a rage.

"Are you here?" he shouted. "Did you climb a tree, thinking I wouldn't look up?"

Beating footsteps as he raced between the tree trunks, giving each one a forceful enough thrashing that the ground around it shook.

"Can you hear me, Natalie? You've been able to stay hidden longer than I would have guessed. You must not be thinking of all that I intend to do to your husband."

Kurt's footsteps retreated, the sound of his voice also fading away. He stayed gone for long minutes, enough of them that Natalie nearly crawled out to Doug.

Then Kurt arrived back at the maze of rocks, his tall shadow falling over its entrance, cooling the interior. He scuttled inside, low to the ground again, his panicked voice booming off the walls. "Doug? Wake up! Are you still with me, Doug? Doug!"

There was no response from her husband.

Still, Natalie hunkered down, her breathing finally slowing.

Because she had realized something.

Kurt wasn't going to kill her husband. He would never voluntarily sacrifice a companion, a specimen to study out here in the woods.

He was going to save him.

Only once Kurt was clearly occupied, intent on whatever maneuvers he might be performing, his breathing no longer labored and no more shouts forthcoming, did Natalie allow herself a peek.

Kurt knelt on the floor of the cavern, naked except for a pair of boxer shorts. His chest was covered with the same hair that formed his bushy beard. Veins on his neck stood out with exertion, and lengths of muscle bunched in his arms as he worked the clothes he had stripped off himself onto Doug's trembling form.

"Wha..." Doug began, and Natalie's heart fluttered with hope. "Are you—"

"Have to get you warm," Kurt muttered.

"Why?" Doug sounded like his mouth had been shot full of novocaine.

Kurt pulled one of his wool socks onto Doug's uninjured foot.

"Why?" Doug asked again, lips mealy and numb. "Do you hate us so much?"

"Hate you?" Kurt responded, his voice robotic and hollow. He continued to tug the sock into place with a series of automated jerks. Despite the passion of Kurt's next assertion, not even a film of emotion lay over it. "My God, I don't hate you, Doug. No, not at all. I love you. I love both you and your wife so very much."

Natalie shrank back inside her pocket of stone until she could no longer see and her breath was constricted, knowing that in some monstrous way, this was true.

"And now," Kurt said, "I have to bring you to safety before I go find her."

CHAPTER SIXTY-EIGHT

As soon as the sounds of Kurt getting Doug out of the rock formation diminished, Natalie began to wriggle free of the tight column behind which she'd wedged herself. Then something stopped her, as sure as a barricading arm, a cautionary command. The concave section of rock she'd been about to maneuver around served as a cup against which she could lean as she thought.

Kurt was smart. He'd guessed their intentions and seen through their ruses at every turn. What if he wasn't truly convinced that Natalie had left, but was just giving her a chance to reveal herself?

She couldn't imagine how she would delay, pass time that could allow for a head start while Kurt tended to Doug back at camp, without going insane. But what if Kurt simply put Doug down on the forest floor, while he himself lurked at the entrance, waiting for Natalie to squirm out, vulnerable as an inchworm, from the rock?

She became aware of something slicing into her waist, and reached down.

Here was a way she could ensure that Kurt was really gone while accomplishing what would be a necessary act if she intended to escape these woods.

Natalie pulled the map in its plastic sheath from her shorts, and there in the dimness of the chasm, began to unfold it.

The space was so tight that she had to look at one small square at a time, fighting to orient herself amidst what appeared to be a hopeless morass. The streaks, dashes, and squiggles were as incomprehensible as always—encryption she had no chance of breaking. She could've been looking at the thing upside down, or sideways, and indeed bunched up a clump in frustration, giving it a spin before trying to smooth the same section out again and examine it from a different angle.

If she squandered this chance, Kurt would win as surely as if she and Doug had just accepted his will, never even tried to escape. Except that it wouldn't be Kurt keeping them prisoner in that case. It'd be Natalie herself.

The night she and Kurt had spent by the fire before Doug woke up.

Kurt had pried insight and revelation from Natalie as if he had a tool, a physician's sharp implement designed to open up her deepest, darkest reaches, or an insect's proboscis that ate out the core of its prey.

But Kurt had revealed something as well, hadn't he?

Maps are just like dollhouses. A scaled-down version of the real thing.

The sun shifted its position in the sky, and a pinprick shaft of light shone down through the opening in the rock above Natalie.

There was the lake.

A pale-blue shaded area leapt out from the rest of the confusing symbols and muddied lines, as clearly as if the word for *self-contained body of water* had spelled itself out. That lake, surrounded by mountains—those faint triangles must indicate elevation—had been where Kurt had roasted the fish. Which meant that Natalie should be able to find Kurt's camp if she could only interpret the spaces between.

And that would lead to the system of caves and rock shelters in which she found herself now.

Her fingertip slid across the sheet of paper, a Ouija board coming to life. At first she was able to identify only the most recognizable landmarks, but slowly, she began making sense of orientations and configurations too, the way one unknown area fed into the next. A map wasn't linear, like a book or an article, and trying to read it as one had always confounded Natalie, stopped her cold.

Instead maps represented multiple dimensions.

Natalie found the creek, and pulled that part of the paper close so as to see what lay adjacent. She rued the narrow closet of rock in which she sat when what she really needed to do was spread this whole thing out and study it in full. Natalie made the map into a fan, drawing each fold in once she understood what it represented, until a brief scrawl of words clanged a bell in her brain.

Turtle Ridge Wilderness Area.

With a dashed line that indicated a trail.

About some things at least, Kurt hadn't been lying.

But he had indeed meant to fool her, in terms of his leaving. For Natalie could hear him now, coming back to the cave.

Kurt was clearly taking pains to keep quiet, but inevitable sounds jumped out, the same ones she and Doug had been unable to mask when they'd made this trip. Plants pressed into the earth by the weight of a heel. Air currents stirred so that dry leaves trembled on twigs, brushing their diaphanous bodies against each other. A songbird's light departure.

The light shining in from the front of the tunnel changed. Didn't disappear, but grew shadowed somehow, parts blotted out. Kurt was inside the rock structure.

Natalie glanced around the tight space to make sure she was concealed.

A tiny corner of map protruded, sticking out over her lap. A white slice glowing in the dim confines of the roofless cave.

Just a sliver, but enough for someone like Kurt to notice.

Natalie started to lower her hand—if she slid the map over by a fraction of an inch, that piece would disappear—but suddenly halted. The paper would crinkle, make a noise that might be perceptible to a man with senses as acute as Kurt's.

Instead, Natalie eased her body sideways, tilting it so her shadow fell across the paper. She was tucked in so tightly, the motion couldn't be seen.

The rock edifice stayed as silent as a monastery. Kurt's was an antipresence, a great, sucking vacuum of space that indicated he was still there.

Unless he hadn't ever really been here at all, and simply lived inside Natalie now, a being impossible to erase.

Then she heard a noise that told her not only had she been correct, but also that she'd hidden herself successfully. Kurt believed himself to be alone, had no idea that Natalie remained nearby. For he'd begun weeping, unashamedly, unselfconsciously, an echoing of pure loss and despair throughout the stone space.

Only after Kurt's sobs started to abate, and he made his retreat, did Natalie allow herself to count, a slow, hypnotic beat in her head. She enforced a wait of ten full minutes, six hundred seconds, before beginning the slow, effortful wriggle out from her hiding space. Clenching the precious map between her teeth, she fought to shimmy free, scraping her arms and shoulders against the rough rock walls until they widened enough to allow her to get down on all fours and crawl out.

She emerged into a changed day, the sky oppressively low, holding the promise of rain. With the sun hidden from view, Natalie couldn't be sure how early it was, but she sensed that no more than a couple of hours had passed and it was still morning.

According to the map, she had to cover fifteen miles; Kurt had been truthful about the name of the nearest trail, but not about its location. Given her current level of fitness and acclimatization to the terrain, this was a walk of hours, not days.

The creek would still be of use. That deeper section Natalie had come to earlier would propel her along, both concealing her passage and enabling a shortcut.

Beneath a gritty overhang of rain clouds, Natalie lowered herself into the cool, gray pool, and as the current of the water took her, it also rinsed her clean.

CHAPTER SIXTY-NINE

Natalie emerged from her dunking when the creek started to shallow out, then used the map to orient herself. She gobbled one of the energy bars as she set off into the woods, breaking through a fierce cage of branches. These trees had fangs, and they sunk themselves into her. She had to wrench herself free. Each tree stood so close to the next that their branches intertwined. Lower down, brush was snarled like long hair and snagged at Natalie's shins, requiring pauses to untangle it before she could proceed. At last the forest loosened up minutely, and Natalie began to half jog, half walk, desperate to be out of here and find help for her husband, yet aware of the need to pace herself.

Despite the pulse of impending rain, the day was warm, and Natalie was soon coated with sweat. It stung the new scrapes and scratches she'd accrued. She kept snatching glances at the map, reminding herself of the clarity she'd come to in the rock formation, until the crosshatch of lines became something she felt she could actually rely on.

The humidity felt spongy and thick. Natalie kicked aside a clump of brush while thunder muttered overhead. Her heart throbbed along with the sound; she was all but running now. The air wrapped itself like a woolen cloak around her. She wished the sky would just open up already, but the rain stubbornly held off.

Another quick perusal of the map, a second energy bar. She only had two left, but that was okay, she was almost out of the untrammeled part of the woods.

A section of third-growth forest appeared, the flora spindly and young. It made for easier bushwhacking, except that now Natalie had to trudge through a muck of leaves and forest debris, this land open to the sky. The ground sucked at her shoes, and Natalie forced herself on, aware of how each minute, each mile meted out danger for Doug. Her stomach churned—all those nuts and seeds from the bars—in time with the rumbling sky.

She came to a steep pitch and checked the map before starting to ascend. Her calf muscles complained as she forced them on, harder, faster, higher, but with every twang, her heart rejoiced. Because according to the map, this incline was the last before the Turtle Ridge trail should begin to unspool, perpendicular to where she was walking.

Natalie pushed aside a nothing branch—it split under the brunt of her assault—then stopped, her heartbeat ragged. Not because of the exertion, the way she'd run up that final hill, but because she could hear noises now. A body crashing through the woods. Kurt, in a fury, taking no care to be silent.

The roaring sound became discernible as Natalie started to back away. Was that Kurt, hollering out his rage? Or water somewhere, rushing past?

She began to whirl around, seeking a hiding place, but the branches on these trees were sparsely leafed, and all the boulders scattered. Natalie could think of nothing to do except crouch down, lower herself as close as possible to the earth, and pray that Kurt didn't stumble upon this spot.

She bent over, aware that she had begun to cry, frightened, hopeless tears of defeat. Were there no limits to Kurt's reach? Drops from her eyes struck the ground like the rain that refused to fall.

The crashing grew louder. Branches thrust aside, leaves dashed to the ground.

Also a voice. Calling out her name. And Doug's.

"Nat-a-lie Lar-son! Doug-las Lar-son! Can you hear me? Nat-a-lie! Doug!"

That wasn't Kurt.

Natalie rose so abruptly, she nearly fell over. Was the voice coming closer, or growing more distant? The sodden air distorted sound, turning shouts into watery echoes.

"Yes!" she cried out frantically. She ran in the direction she thought the noises were coming from, stopped, then spun in a circle, her gaze scouring the woods. The voice called out again, and Natalie started to scream. "Yes, it's me, it's Natalie, I'm here!"

The man who'd been shouting was middle-aged, his hair close-cropped and gray, but clearly in excellent shape. A United States Marine Corps cap sat atop his head, and he was swathed in waterproof rain gear, wearing boots whose grooved soles made short work of the slippery ridge he had to scale to reach Natalie.

As soon as he appeared, she grabbed him, yanking out the map and flapping it in his face. "There's a man"—she gasped—"in the woods... I mean, my husband—"

"Hold on just a second," the man said. He held Natalie in place, looking her up and down. "We know your husband is missing. We have searchers looking for him close to where your canoe was found. Did you get separated? How did you wind up here?"

Natalie didn't answer the question, immediately parsing what the information meant for Doug. However many searchers there were, it couldn't be an infinite number, and some of them were nearly at the Canadian border. This man who had found Natalie might be all that she had. What had made him look here?

He was peering into her eyes, shining a pinprick light while pressing one finger to her wrist at the same time. He kept count, lips visibly moving.

Natalie snatched at his hand. "We didn't get separated," she told the man fiercely. "My husband is here too."

"You stayed in one place?" The searcher regarded her. "That's great. That was exactly the right thing to—"

Natalie shook her head rapidly. "I'm sorry, I misspoke—" She felt suddenly confused and wished for a cold splash of rain to jolt her. "Doug isn't here, he's about fifteen miles away, I can show you on this map. But there's a man—who will try to stop you—and the woods there are booby-trapped—"

That seemed to get the searcher's attention. He paused in his examination, the next question he'd been preparing aborted on his tongue.

"Please!" Natalie's head felt like a centrifuge, her thoughts spinning. "We've got to hurry! My husband is seriously hurt!"

"Okay, Mrs. Larson, I understand," he said.

"You do?" It was more of a demand, a challenge, than a question. How could anyone possibly understand the bizarreness of this situation?

The man turned, one deliberate rotation of his body. "Yes, Mrs. Larson, I do, and I'm going to need you to calm down." He fished in his pack, coming out with a bottle of spring water, which he uncapped and gave to Natalie. Only after he'd watched her drink, did the searcher ask, "Can you describe the nature of your husband's injury?"

Natalie felt the water hit her stomach coldly. "I can tell you, but isn't it enough for now that he's wounded? I mean, the first part you have to deal with is the traps."

This hadn't occurred to her till now. If Natalie and Doug hadn't made it safely out of camp themselves, after living there and knowing Kurt's practices, how were rescue workers supposed to make it in?

The searcher continued to regard her oddly.

If she couldn't make this comprehensible—get the searcher to see what she was saying—then he wouldn't be equipped to find Doug. Nobody who hadn't visited Kurt's camp, seen the way he had militarized his land, could understand what invading it would require. Natalie backtracked, her insides roiling as she recounted all that had happened to the two of them, forming it into a narrative that at least to her ears made sense.

The searcher studied the ground for what seemed like a long time, then unclipped a radio from his hip. He depressed a button and spoke. "This is Steve, do you copy?"

"This is Brad," came a voice through the static. "Copy."

Crackling over the airwaves was duplicated inside Natalie, her nerve endings jangling, keeping her from standing still.

The searcher named Steve prevented her from walking off with one firm hand, before speaking into his radio again. "I've crossed the river an eighth of a mile from where we last triangulated. Wife found alive, in stable condition. Copy that?"

"Wife alive," the one named Brad burst out. "Copy."

"You'd better come fast," Steve said. "Copy?"

"Copy and on my way," Brad replied, briskness detectable in his tone even through the thready sound. "Over."

Natalie neither heard nor saw the approach of the second searcher. Brad appeared beside her and Steve as if he'd been dropped there.

He was dressed just like Steve, minus the cap, although Brad looked to be younger by decades. He greeted Natalie with an expression of joy. "I'm very happy to see you, Mrs. Larson."

Natalie tried to smile.

Brad turned to Steve, who talked swiftly, repeating what Natalie had told him. Then Steve raised somebody else on his radio—a policeman, from the sound of it—and gave the same report again. Steve and Brad both began talking—the logistics of getting a badly injured man out of terrain both impenetrable and dangerous—while the voice on the other end kept silent.

The dialogue proceeded after that at such a machine-gun-fire pace that it was difficult for Natalie to keep up. Without realizing it, she had grown chilled, her body quaking so hard that her teeth rattled. It must've finally started to rain—the sky opening with a whimper, not a bang, faint rainfall versus any thunderous clashing of clouds—for when Natalie sank into a crouch, the ground was sopping wet and the world had grown fizzy with moisture. She looked down to see her skin dappled by drops, and felt water sluicing her face. She wrapped glistening arms around slick knees while thoughts swam through her head like fish too fast to grab.

Steve and Brad had donned waterproof hats. They seemed to register her condition at the same time and snapped into action. Brad pulled a crinkly silver blanket from his pack, Natalie giggling because those packs were like circus cars, items spilling out in endless succession. Neither man appeared to find her reaction strange, merely regarded her with a look of close scrutiny while winding the space-age blanket around her body. Brad whisked out a small tarp—provoking renewed mirth in Natalie—and sat her down upon it. He helped her sip hot, sweet liquid from a metal bottle and gave her a piece of jerky to gnaw on.

The direness of the situation had clearly become apparent, however, because the second Natalie had been seen to, both men resumed their conversation via radio.

Options were raised and discarded. Thick leaf cover and no place for a helo—helicopter?—to touch down. The bumpy jouncing of an ATV. Hours of hiking over tricky terrain, trying to hold an emergency evacuation gurney steady. Both searchers shook their heads, clamping off muffled swears and frustrated breaths, before conferring with the policeman again.

Natalie felt a noose tightening around her neck. She couldn't have come this far only to lose Doug in the end. She whimpered and Brad leaned over, readjusting the silvery wrap. Natalie grasped his wrist, using it to pull herself to standing. The space blanket fell off her and onto the ground.

Brad's focus returned to his companion.

The air grew less hazy, the rain letting up, and Natalie suddenly thought to display her map. Snapping the sheet of paper into view, she whispered, "There's a lake."

The men continued talking, near misses and dead ends as they explored ways to access Kurt's camp.

"There's a lake!" Natalie said louder. She stabbed at the spot on the map.

They looked at her.

Natalie nodded, fast and urgent. "A sizable one. With a direct route between it and the area where we were staying. No traps. I'll just have to find the right path."

CHAPTER SEVENTY

Natalie's solution was relayed to the cop by radio.

"Raise Jim Huggins at the Boat & Fishery," came his crackling command. "See how soon he can get his float plane into the air."

"Copy that," said Steve.

"You and I will meet due east of trail marker twelve," said the policeman. "That way we'll both be making headway toward this camp, cutting a line off the triangle."

"Copy, and on my way," Steve said.

Taking a last look at his own map, Steve jogged off into the woods.

Natalie turned to follow. They couldn't get separated—Steve still wasn't remotely prepared for what lay up ahead.

From behind, Brad touched her gently on the arm. "This way, Mrs. Larson."

Although warmer and drier now, Natalie was still experiencing a few lingering shreds of disorientation. The woods spun, leaves making kaleidoscopic patterns against the sky. "What do you mean?" she asked. "We have to go get my husband."

Brad looked away from her, down at the ground.

Natalie frowned, tracking his gaze. Ferns and other plant life stood upright, no longer bowed by burdens of moisture. Puddles were soaking into the saturated earth.

"Come on," Natalie urged. "We have to hurry."

"Ma'am," Brad said awkwardly, "we would never let a subject back into a situation like the one you described. Our best searchers—not to mention law enforcement officials—are going to get your husband."

Brad began to walk in the opposite direction from the one his partner had taken, but Natalie planted her feet. "Then your friend is going to die," she said.

Brad's foot paused in the midst of rising.

"Or get seriously hurt," Natalie amended. "That policeman he's supposed to meet up with too. I already told you how my husband wound up in his condition. The land your friend's headed toward is so rigged with traps, it's impossible to avoid one."

Brad had appeared to be considering her words, but now shook his head. "When people have been through frightening experiences, their recollections are often cloudy. Uncertain." He sounded as if he were reciting from a book. *How victims behave after rescue.* As if to prove the point, Brad gave her a rote smile. "The men going to rescue your husband are professionals. They have skills to handle any terrain they encounter."

"Not this terrain," Natalie said.

Brad gave her the same distant smile, then set his sights on a swath of trees that appeared to lead to a clearing. He tried to turn them both, one hand planted firmly on her shoulder.

He doesn't believe me, Natalie realized, struggling to keep herself from being led. *He thinks I'm exaggerating, or maybe delusional with shock.*

If she let the rising hysteria she felt overtake her—like water in a capsized boat—Brad would never change his mind. Natalie had to stay calm, somehow convince this person who thought himself prepared for every eventuality that a completely outlandish situation was all too real.

"Brad?" she said. "I know that you and your partner are experts… trained in SAR. But the land Steve is heading into isn't like anything either of you has ever seen before. Whatever Steve tries to look out for will be a fraction of what he might actually face."

Her words sounded dramatic and overblown, even to her own ears, and she could see Brad coming to the same conclusion.

Natalie went on, grasping for an explanation that might make sense. "It's like when U.S. soldiers were sent to Vietnam. They weren't prepared for the jungle over there, or the way the Vietcong knew how to fight. Do you remember that—reading about it maybe?" He looked so young. Too bad Steve hadn't been the one to stay with her. He seemed to have a military background, which would render this more comprehensible.

Brad continued to regard her, the look on his face less certain.

"But I've been living under those conditions," Natalie went on, quelling a frantic note in her tone. "My husband too. Who's injured now, unable to walk, maybe permanently." A sob crawled up her throat, and she choked it back. "I got out safely," Natalie went on. Thanks to Doug, although she didn't distract matters with the fact of her husband's self-sacrifice, the way he had spared her from that spike. "And if we hurry—if we move fast enough to catch up—I can make sure that your friend does too."

Brad's face finally reflected the fear that Natalie had been suppressing. He depressed a button on his radio, and she could make out Steve's voice, asking for status.

"Have you come across the chief?" Brad said, ignoring the request.

Nothing but static and crackling over the airwaves—Steve must have traveled some distance already—before a few faint words came through. "I can't raise him." White noise overtook whatever Steve said next, then nothing could be heard at all.

Brad replaced his radio on his hip, his expression eerily calm. He began to stuff gear back into his pack, still clearly following some protocol. *Even in extreme situations, don't leave behind an item that may turn out later to be essential.* Brad yanked the zipper up with a high, screeching whine before squaring the pack on his shoulders. He paused to skid a finger across Natalie's map.

"This way?" he asked, and she nodded.

Brad grabbed her hand, and they ran.

CHAPTER SEVENTY-ONE

Kurt returned to camp with Doug cradled in his bare arms and laid him down on a mat. Doug's skin looked glossy and pale; his eyes were shut. The state inspired in Kurt a form of frustration he hadn't felt since Terry had ceased talking, or even looking at him. All other practical reasons for her death notwithstanding, in the end Kurt had been driven to strangle Terry simply to try to provoke some sort of response.

It was important to keep Doug warm. Kurt cinched the sleeping bag around him. Before rising from the floor, he felt around toward the bottom of the bag for the spot where Doug's foot had been bisected by the whittled wooden dowel. Kurt gave the flesh a vicious squeeze through the puffy material. Not to hurt Doug, just to jar him into consciousness. He nearly wept when the man didn't so much as stir.

Kurt had rudimentary knowledge of first aid, but an injury this grave would be beyond him—at least when he was in such a hurry. He had to go and get Natalie. Now. With any luck, the map would remain a funhouse mirror to her unseeing eyes, and she'd be stumbling around in circles, leaving obvious signs for Kurt to follow.

But he couldn't count on it.

He paused to elevate Doug's feet and slip between his lips the Advil he had withheld from Natalie after suturing her cut. The relief offered by the pills as they dissolved, scant though it would be, might be sufficient to return Doug to consciousness.

Kurt hoped so anyway.

He wanted Doug awake when Kurt came back with his wife.

Kurt slapped at branches as he strode through the woods. Leaves threatened to slice his face, and he angrily knocked them from their stems. He hadn't outfitted himself for this walk, a beginner's error the likes of which Kurt hadn't made since he'd first begun to fashion a life in the wilderness after his compatriots abandoned him. He could do without water and sustenance—fifteen miles was but a stroll around the block for him now—but his machete would've come in handy for breaking trail.

It wasn't like him to have rushed off unprepared. Overtaken, in a sense, by emotion rather than rationality. He was sad, Kurt realized, mentally examining the feeling, tasting its salty tang. Already mourning the loss that was to come.

He was going to have to kill Natalie. Not because she had excited his ire or caused in him any particular passion. Kurt didn't miss Natalie, nor feel anger at her for escaping. No, he was going to do away with her for one simple, bloodless reason.

She knew how to get in and out of Kurt's camp.

One of these days, the map she had surely taken—Kurt hadn't found it on Doug's person when he'd wrapped him in the sleeping bag, nor in either hut—would begin to make sense to her, and then she would know how to leave, the only person besides himself who did.

Natalie was going to join Terry in the pyramid of stones Kurt had constructed. His smokehouse. He stopped amidst a thatch of brambly branches to ponder. Observing Natalie's reunion with Doug would provide blistering fulfillment to Kurt. He could do away with her immediately afterward, certain that he had borne witness to a set of emotions as complex as any she would experience in her foreshortened life, like imbibing one sip of the finest aged wine.

Kurt pushed off through the woods again, anticipation heady on his tongue. After some time, a branch whipped his face and he tore at it, severing the wood from the tree and splitting it over his knee with one savage blow. The thinning flora should've alerted him. He had made it all the way to Turtle Ridge, unaware of the miles passing, or the amount of time he had spent striding along, lost in his imaginings. Only now did he register how close to the trail's outlet he had come.

With no sign of Natalie.

Kurt lifted his head to the yellow-green sky. It had started to rain, and he hadn't even noticed. His body was soaked, clothes wrapped around him like strips of plaster. Kurt let out a howl that startled nearby creatures seeking cover from the downpour into a scurry of motion.

"Natalie!" Kurt screamed. "Where are you?"

He began to race forward, eyes fixed on the ground, hunting any hint of human passage. But his raptor's gaze couldn't make out a thing; the rain had concealed whatever traces there might've been. Natalie had gotten away.

She would bring back help, send rescuers to his camp. Thoughts swirled in the basin of Kurt's mind. He could stand to forsake his homestead, start over again from scratch, surviving a winter without shelter or supplies. He had done that before. But what Kurt couldn't imagine abandoning was Doug. Forego the pleasure of observing his crippled captive adapt to life as a widower in the wilderness? That would be like turning down a breath of sweet oxygen while drowning.

Even if Natalie did return with assistance, wouldn't Kurt's traps make short work of any rescuers? Could he risk going back? Or should he take flight now, run for his freedom?

His eyes seized on a muddy track to his left.

There was a set of footprints sunk into the moist earth of the trail. Then came a trampled-on stand of brush and the end of a twig made jagged by the stumble or near-fall of someone unfamiliar with the hazards of this terrain.

The print didn't come from the type of shoe that Natalie wore; this one belonged to a not particularly good boot. But that was all right.

Only one thing could've quieted the frenzied debate erupting inside Kurt.

The promise of someone novel and new to bring to his camp.

CHAPTER SEVENTY-TWO

The two hiker girls were envious of Mia's water pouch, which they called a Hydro, and which apparently had a bunch of features their older versions didn't. Mia didn't see how anything with a straw attached could get very advanced, but she didn't bother asking. She didn't want to give the girls time to have second (or third or fourth) thoughts about taking her to Turtle Ridge.

Rain was starting to fall when they got there, what would've been a light, sweet rain in the city, but one that even Mia knew would feel icy and damp once she'd hiked enough miles in it. The girls gave her an extra waterproof poncho when they saw she didn't have one. Mia tugged the triangle of nylon over her head, fearful that this oversight on her part would set off alarm bells. But both girls seemed eager enough to head out on their own vision quest or whatever that they took only a few seconds to trade quick hugs and goodbyes with her.

By the time she was a few hundred yards along the trail, Mia had already begun to rethink her plan. Or her lack of one. Sure, doing this amounted to something gratifyingly bigger than the non-secret Mark Harden had told her about the canoe. But what if Mia got herself lost, in addition to Aunt Nat and Uncle Doug?

The farther she walked, the more such an outcome seemed likely. This wasn't hiking like Mia had done at camp or during school field trips to Bear Mountain. This was hard-core, requiring all the equipment the two girls had been lugging along and then some. The hills climbed so steeply that Mia was tempted to get down on all fours and crawl, then dropped at even sharper angles—although how could that be?—so that she really did sit on her bottom and slide along the wet ground, hoping her pants were in fact waterproof. She'd never gotten a chance to test them at camp.

The borrowed poncho helped keep Mia dry, but between its hood and the rain, she was finding it hard to see. When she reached a part of the trail that hugged a cliff, she got seriously scared. If you took too wide a step here, you'd fall into a canyon. Like the Grand Canyon almost, except with trees filling up all the open space. And even after Mia had managed to navigate the winding path without falling to her death and was in the woods again, the leaves grew so thickly, it was hard to spot trail markers pinned to the trees. All in all, Mia was nothing but relieved when she spied another hiker, the first person she'd come to in what seemed like forever. He looked even less prepared than she was for the woods, wearing a button-down flannel shirt and pants, like a lumberjack or something. He didn't have a pack and was standing a ways off the trail, parting the branches of a tree with one hand so he could study its trunk.

Mia hesitated. The other hiker hadn't seen her yet, and Mia had gone far enough by now to conclude that it'd be smartest just to turn around and reverse her steps. The thought of taking those hills and dips again made her want to cry—never mind having to maneuver past that tricky cliff face—but she still knew better than to flag down some stranger in the wilderness.

Except that the rules among hikers seemed to be different. Look how those girls had helped her out, even given Mia some of their stuff.

The thing that decided her was the sight of the man himself. Far from appearing frightening in any way, it actually looked like he was the one who was scared. Wet and scruffy, but those things were practically hiker chic. He had begun walking—almost running—from tree to tree and pulling back their branches. It was clear he was looking for one of the blue metal trail markers, and Mia knew how to find one.

"Hey!" she called, waving one arm. "Are you lost? The trail's actually over here."

He looked up, blinking rain out of his eyes, and when he caught sight of Mia, the expression on his face was so relieved that she almost laughed out loud.

"You're on the trail? A real one? You sure?" the man called back.

At that Mia did laugh. "A real one. I promise. It's called Turtle Ridge."

The man came hurrying through the trees, shaking rain from his head like a dog and smiling along with her. "Oh thank God," he said. "I never meant to be out here at all—my car broke down, and I thought I would take a shortcut through the woods—well, some shortcut that turned out to be. I've been walking for days."

All of which explained his strange attire and lack of gear.

"You made it," Mia said, and pointed. "If you go back that way, it won't be very far to the trailhead. Even if it feels like it," she added. "Far, that is."

"Thank God," the man said again. Then he paused to look at her. "Are you okay out here? I mean, I can tell you know what you're doing. But the rain's gotta suck."

Mia looked down at her dripping poncho. "You can tell I know what I'm doing?" she said. "Welcome to a party of one."

The man gave her a look of understanding. "I hated being... What are you, thirteen?"

No one ever guessed her age right. Mia nodded.

"That was the worst," the man said. "Nobody thinks you can do anything, even though thirteen was probably the smartest I ever was. After that, I started trying too hard to please everybody."

"I already do that," Mia said.

"Well, don't," the man replied. He took a step onto the trail so that he was standing beside her. He smelled piney, like the trees. "You're fine as you are. Better than fine. You practically saved my life."

"You would've been okay," Mia said, taking a slight step away, but only so no one would think it was weird that they were standing so close. She actually liked being next to this man. He made her feel protected, even though he hadn't done anything besides need help. "You're probably a lot better in the woods than I am."

The man gave a shake of his head. Rain flew off his hair and beard in droplets. His beard was pretty thick, probably from being out in the woods so long. "I doubt that. But thanks for being nice."

He seemed insecure, kind of like Mia herself. She wanted to tell him to act like he knew what he was doing—then one day the act might become reality.

He lifted his hand, giving her a wave before turning. "This way you said, right?"

Mia hid her smile. "It's actually that way." She reached out to touch the man on his arm, pointing to show him.

"Oh shit," he said. His face turned red beneath its coating of rain. "Sorry."

"It's okay," Mia said, a shrug in her tone. "I curse all the time." That sounded stupid, like she was the type to call all her friends *bitches* and go around swearing. It was her turn to blush.

"It's just..." The man peered around Mia, studying the trail ahead. "I can't go that way. You're lucky you're hiking in, not out."

"What do you mean?" Mia asked. "I actually was planning on turning around now myself. Hiking back too."

"You were?" The man gave a regretful shake of his head. "You can't. Not yet anyway."

Mia grew suddenly chilled beneath her poncho. A second ago, these woods had been massive; now they felt claustrophobic, as if she were trapped. She reached up to scrub rain out of her eyes, and her hand came away freezing. "Why not?"

The man took a few paces forward, nodding as he returned, like he'd just confirmed something. "I came from that direction a few minutes ago. I was too stupid to realize I was on a trail."

Mia offered him a tremulous smile and a headshake, contradicting the *stupid*. God, this guy was even worse with the hating on yourself than she was.

He smiled his thanks, although the smile didn't look too genuine.

"So what's the problem?" Mia asked after a moment.

"You remember that steep area? Where there's a cliff?"

Mia nodded. Of course she remembered that. Who knew trees could grow as sharp as daggers until you'd pictured falling on top of like a zillion of them?

"Well, it's all slid out," the man said. "The rain must've loosened the earth. No way to get past until the people who maintain the trails come through with their equipment. And who knows when that will be?"

The memory of that pitch, a sheer drop to a canyon, made Mia start shivering even more than the rain. The trail had been narrow as it was—unimaginable if a slice of it had fallen away. And without a path of some sort, there would be no way to make it out to the trailhead. She and this man were prisoners. Mia's parents were probably panicking right now. This was the stupidest thing she had ever done.

"Hey," the man said, taking a step forward. "Don't beat yourself up. It's not like you did anything wrong."

Mia looked up at him through a glimmer of rain.

"I bet we can figure something out," the man went on. "Maybe find a way to get around the pass through the woods?" He gestured toward dense forest. "Then we'll loop back to the trail where it starts running smooth again."

Mia took a look into the woods, crowded with trees. It looked almost as impassable as that canyon. She shook her head, doubtful. This man had been lost when she came upon him, after all. Following him out couldn't be a good idea.

"Or you could just keep hiking in the direction you were going," the man said. "Me, I'll take my chances in those woods. I want to get out of here as soon as possible."

"I do too," Mia said.

He looked to his right. "It's not that bad, really. I was just in there. Want to try?"

Mia hesitated, then took a step off the trail. It felt like she was leaving behind more than just the cleared path, abandoning solid ground to enter another realm.

The man reached in front of her to hold back a branch.

Mia thanked him.

"Hey, by the way," the man said, and she twisted around to look.

"My name's Kurt."

Hiking was easier with Kurt there to break off branches and go first to mat down clumps of soil with his boots. His boots were good ones, really well broken in. Kind of weird footwear to wear for the drive he'd been taking when he got lost, but Mia was grateful for his choice when he kicked aside a rock she'd been about to trip over.

The rain had finally stopped falling, or else the leaf cover from the trees was too thick to let much through, and the whole world seemed to be drying out. Mia shucked off her poncho, balling it up and stuffing it in her pack. She took a drink, noting that the water really did flow easily from the pouch into her straw, then sidestepped a log, its fleshy interior open to the elements and alive with insects. She shuddered.

"Gross," Kurt said.

She laughed that he'd said it aloud. "Think we can head back to the trail now?" she asked. "I mean, it feels like we've gone pretty far."

Kurt took the idea seriously, getting his bearings and looking around. "Not quite yet, I wouldn't say," he told her. "Let's allow for a little extra before swinging back."

Mia tilted her head. She thought she could hear the rushing course of a river somewhere not too far off. How long had they been walking? The endless rows of trees, the sameness of the landscape, had a way of making time morph. It suddenly felt a lot later than it had been. She was hungry, like she'd missed a meal.

There also hadn't been a river anywhere near the trail, if Mia was remembering correctly from the map on the brochure she'd looked at. "I really think we should go back," she said. "Things have dried up. I bet the trail is more solid."

"Solid won't matter if it's all been lost to a rock or a mudslide," Kurt said, walking forward and indicating that she should move on as well.

She didn't like how he was acting. Like he no longer thought Mia could make her own choices, decide things for herself.

"Look," she said. "We don't want to wind up lost like you were before. I'm going back, even if I have to go on my own." Let him try and stop her.

Kurt nodded sagely at that, taking her point, and Mia had time to regret her temporary change of heart. He wasn't like all the other grown-ups in her life. Kurt and she were more equals, kind of how Mia was with Aunt Nat.

Still, he spoke with authority when he said, "I think we should do it the way I'm suggesting, Mia."

Cold air laced through her. She hadn't mentioned her name after

Kurt had told her his. She knew she hadn't, because she had been heeding the warning she'd heard in her head from her mom—*don't tell a stranger your name*—then spent the whole hike trying to figure out a non-awkward way to get in the introduction.

"Come on," Kurt said, waiting.

"Like I'd listen to you," Mia responded, immediately regretting her words, or at least her tone, the one that always got her mother so upset. Something that hadn't been there just a few seconds ago told Mia she shouldn't jeer at this man.

But Kurt didn't get mad. He bent over, lowering his hands to the ground.

Mia tracked his movements, looking to see if his boots were untied or something. "What are you doing?"

Kurt straightened up, holding a good-sized rock in his palms, and jogging it up and down a little, as if testing its weight. Then he lifted it into the air.

Mia didn't have time to scream before he brought it back down.

CHAPTER SEVENTY-THREE

The trek back to camp with Brad felt far shorter than the journey out had been. It was another inexplicable paradox of wilderness life—distances didn't stay constant; they mutated. Different factors could change them: Conditions. Type of terrain. Knowledge of the area condensed miles, while sheer, unchecked need expanded them past all reckoning.

Natalie recognized certain features—a series of deep trenches in the ground, the thickening of the forest that seemed to beckon her through steadfast gates—and used them to mark their passage. They had to be drawing near, hours passing despite the fast clip at which they were hiking, the midday sun starting to droop in the sky. Natalie pictured her husband, alone and in pain—oh God, how she hoped he was alone—and sent a mental message. *Hold on, honey. We're coming.*

She continually referred to her map, which felt by now like an old friend, although Brad chose to use his GPS. They seemed to be on track; the ground felt known to her feet. But as they began to approach the creek, Natalie wondered if she'd been wrong all along, the familiarity of the landscape just one more wilderness illusion, which seemed designed to trick and deter the wanderer, almost with intention.

The creek that served as informal border to Kurt's camp was essentially a babbling brook. Studded with boulders in places, which sped up the current or made for pools, but not much fiercer than a stream. Whereas whatever Natalie was hearing sounded like a river, and a fast one.

Brad's rapid pace didn't falter—he didn't know this land, had no expectations, and so it didn't feel suddenly foreign and mistaken to him as it did to Natalie. She spied the water for a second, a quick slivery flash, before it was stolen away behind a macramé of leaves. Natalie's feet slowed; she paused to tilt her head and listen.

The white-noise rush of water grew louder, and the explanation occurred to Natalie just as she felt the soil change abruptly, turn cushiony and moist beneath her Norlanders. Rain had caused the volume of water to swell.

She began to hurry along again, confident that at least they were in the right place. The confines of Kurt's camp, its stick structures and clearings, should become visible soon after they crossed the creek. At that moment, the rushing of the water turned into a roar, filling Natalie's ears, making it hard to hear anything else, including her own startled yelp as a gully appeared before her.

The transformed creek had the strength and power of a silverback gorilla, muscles rippling as it raced along. Natalie's cry of fear was lost beneath its churning. The riverbank reared up, and Natalie realized she was headed straight for it. She fought to dig her shoes into the ground, but they started to skid; she wasn't going to be able to stop, would be washed away, downstream of Doug, wasting valuable time, and that was presuming she was able to climb out at all—

Brad grabbed a twist of her shirt, pulling Natalie up short.

A trail of rocks and dirt went skittering down in her wake and were lost amidst the thrashing water. She bent over, panting.

Brad used the pause to take a drink from his water bottle.

"Thank you," Natalie said once she could speak.

He inclined his head, then pointed. "We can make it across over there."

Natalie looked. The boulder that had presented such an obstacle before now protruded a mere foot or so above the surface of the water. It could be used as a bridge. She and Brad would leap from the riverbank to the top of the boulder, then from there to the opposite side. Natalie took the lead, crossing in a trio of nimble steps, and allowing herself just a few seconds to get oriented on dry ground.

Kurt's series of traps began here.

Natalie used the same method she and Doug had, back when they'd possessed the hope of escaping together and making it out unscathed.

Brad looked doubtful when Natalie found a long, sturdy stick and placed it in his hand, demonstrating with her own branch how to poke the ground. She proceeded cautiously enough that she feared Brad would grow impatient, following along behind her. Instead, when she turned, he was standing in place and staring downward.

"You see something?" Natalie called. They'd gotten separated by a few yards. She headed back toward him, tapping the ground with her stick.

"Yes," Brad said. "But I don't think it's what you were expecting me to see."

Natalie frowned, also peering down. She couldn't make out anything besides the usual surface of the forest floor, leaf matter and debris, rotting evidence of last year's flora becoming one with the earth.

Brad used his stick to indicate a spot on the ground. "That's a boot print."

Natalie squinted, but still didn't see anything. Brad traced an outline in the air, just a few inches above the shape he'd claimed to see, and the faint impression of a heel swam into view, all but concealed by the swampy soil.

"How did you spot that?" Natalie marveled.

Brad studied the ground silently, intent on finding the next.

"They must be close," Natalie told him, dropping her voice. Steve, maybe that policeman too, were somewhere up ahead. Had Doug been rescued? Where was Kurt? The air felt suddenly charged, electric, as if the rain might've been only temporarily resting, gathering force for the real storm to come.

Brad walked forward. He continued to stab at the ground with his stick, but in a perfunctory manner, his real focus clearly on identifying footprints.

Natalie took the lead, then cut suddenly in front of him, swift and precise as a knife blade. "Stop," she hissed.

Brad halted. "What?" He looked down. "Another footprint?"

Natalie edged Brad a safe distance aside before raising her stick and pointing.

A tripwire had been strung between two slim trees to their right. Natalie whacked at it with her stick, and a rock swung down from above, a deadly pendulum netted with vine. Brad's face paled as he cast his gaze upward. The stone came whistling, shrilling down, aimed right at the spot where he'd been standing a moment ago.

Its back-and-forth motion took a while to slow.

Brad looked as if Bigfoot had attacked, a mythical beast turning out to be real.

When he set out again, he walked with care, using his stick to check for traps on the ground while snatching nervous glimpses overhead.

Up ahead, Natalie spotted a difference in the forest floor. The dirt there looked darker, although as they approached, she saw that the color was an optical illusion, created by the fact that the earth had actually fallen away altogether. As if some giant claw had reached down and torn open a cleft in the ground, left it ugly and gaping.

Or else a pit had been dug, with a mat of leaves and brush lain over it, designed to crumble the moment somebody stepped.

The footprints Brad had been tracking ended right at the edge.

CHAPTER SEVENTY-FOUR

Tim leaned with his back braced by the wall of the hole he'd fallen into, one leg folded into an odd, unnatural angle, the other splayed out. The wall was studded with stones that had bruised his flesh, his spine, but his back wasn't broken. He had tested his fingers and toes; they could move, he wasn't paralyzed.

The real damage had been done to his leg.

The fracture was a compound one, his shin bone protruding through the skin on his calf. Tim could feel air entering a part of his body where it had no business being. Gave new meaning to the saying *blood ran cold*.

The rim of the hole ran in a lopsided oval several inches above the highest reach of Tim's hands. Tim had hoisted himself to a standing position already, keeping his weight on his uninjured leg. But that had cost him a fraction of an inch, and the lip of solid ground was tantalizingly close—less than an inch might matter. So he had placed the foot of his broken leg on the ground, then fought to rise on tiptoes, stretching the flesh around the arrowed bone so that a second shard pierced a section of untouched skin, and bellowing sounds he wouldn't have thought himself capable of making—ox-like, inhuman—before finally falling to the dirt again, completely spent.

He wouldn't have been able to reach anyway; his fingertips had scraped the shaft just below the place where higher ground beckoned, denying him a chance to heave himself out.

He couldn't raise anyone on his radio. It might've broken in the fall, or there might not be anyone with range. Which range? Tim wasn't sure of his exact location. If he could get out, he would be able to determine it, at least figure out how to reach—limping along, belly-crawling if necessary—some known site. But that assumed that he would, in fact, find a way out.

At least one other creature hadn't. Tim's shin bone glowed ivory in the vaporous sun shooting into the hole, as did the remains of a carcass, coyote-sized, or possibly a lion, pecked free of flesh by birds.

Vultures, leathery, wide-winged creatures of scavenge, had made it down here for a meal. It took a lot to give Tim pause, but as he lifted himself on his arms to look up at the sky, which had never seemed so remote and removed, a shudder took hold of his body, and he swore he heard the sound of flapping.

He sank back down to study the injury that was preventing him from jumping up and getting a hold on the circumference of the hole. His bone wasn't shattered, but split. One piece had come away, simply sheared off from the section it was supposed to attach to. Tim had enough first aid experience to know there was no physical way to reset this himself. It was going to require surgery, pins and the like.

Time started to swerve in and out.

Tim grew light-headed, deep in the chill of the earth. The pain in his leg had become a constant; he was growing accustomed to the sensation.

Then the hole above him darkened.

Tim blinked woozily up at it. Weather moving in again perhaps.

"Chief!"

Had one of his men fallen down into this well along with him? Tim took a look around the tunneled shaft. What a feat it must've been to build a well this deep in the wilderness. Wait, it wasn't a well. There was another explanation for what had happened to him, only Tim couldn't remember it at the moment. What other type of hole would be man-sized and of this killing depth? And how would a second member of the Wedeskyull force wind up inside?

"Chief!" called the voice again.

Not one of his men. Tim knew who that was, the searcher who could never manage to call Tim by name. And he also knew that he wasn't in a well. It was just as the missing wife—Natalie Larson—had tried to tell them when Brad had found her. This land was rigged with traps.

Tim glanced upward, where a second shadow had fallen, feeling a sense of mild curiosity. Then he reached down and probed the jagged sliver of his bone, chalk-rough and gritty beneath his fingers, an agonizing, brutal touch he endured with only one goal in mind: to wrest himself back from the brink of shock.

"Down here!" he shouted. "I'm down here! Here!"

Tim heard a female voice say, "He's alive."

Then Brad called down, "Is Steve in there too?"

"Sent him on ahead!" Tim yelled back up. He had to manually yank his voice into producing something resembling a coherent sentence. "To warn the pilot at the lake! Didn't want him walking into an ambush! And—" What else had Steve been supposed to do? In the aftermath of Tim's fall, both of them realizing that this land was more perilous than anything either had anticipated, Tim had refused to allow Steve to assist him in any way. Their responsibility was to the civilians. "—see if he can find the husband!"

The blotch made by the two bodies looking down with the sun behind them wavered, then thinned out. There was a patter of footsteps heading off into the woods, moving at a steady clip, not fast.

That had to be the wife.

"Brad!" Tim shouted. "Go after her!"

Search and Rescue personnel were trained to aid and support subjects, not deal with suspects. They protected civilians from nature, often from their own hubris and carelessness. But they knew nothing about madmen who rigged the land with traps.

Silence from the surface.

Brad had done what he'd been told, as was his bent. Now he was headed into an unknown, uncontained scenario, the likes of which might overwhelm trained LEOs. And Tim had given the order. But what choice did he have? The alternative was to allow a civilian to go on her own into the same situation.

Then an arm shot down, one hand reaching for him.

"Go after Mrs. Larson?" Brad called back. "She knows what she's doing better than any of us! I'm not going anywhere until I get you out, Chief."

Tim planted both hands against the dirt walls, and raised himself to standing. He rested his weight on his good foot so that he could lift one arm. Brad grasped Tim's wrist with his hand and pulled him toward the light.

"Go," Tim grunted once they were both back on solid ground.

"Chief, your leg…" Brad said. "It's pretty bad."

"I know what it is." Tim was sweating, his face beaded, even though it was cold out here, the temperature promising a resurgence of rain. "Don't worry about me."

"But I can splint the—"

Tim stood on one foot, unable to take a step forward. He knew Brad had assessed his compromised state, and he also knew that Brad was charged with applying his skills to stabilize Tim's condition. But there were more pressing priorities right now. Brad might not have experience in handling the circumstances that lay ahead in those woods, but from the looks of things, Tim and his own men wouldn't have much acquaintance with anything similar either. Steve, with his military background, arguably had the most relevant know-how. Either way, time couldn't be wasted back here.

Tim made his tone commanding. "You know your duty. Go after the wife, and locate her husband."

Brad gave a nod. Then he dropped his gaze, his head turning back and forth. After a moment, his posture changed, the set of his shoulders squaring.

He'd spotted the first of the wife's tracks on the ground, and as a hound or a pointer would be, Brad was poised to go. Tim was a decent tracker himself under normal conditions, but the ground looked like one muddy streak to him now.

Brad swiveled, sending Tim a last reluctant look.

Despite pain wavering around him, like the heat shimmer on a highway, Tim managed to signal Brad on.

Brad picked up a long tree branch. Focused, pausing to test each step, he moved off into the woods.

Tim let the pain reach a crescendo before patting around on the ground with his hands, feeling for his own stick, glad to have gotten the reminder. He wasn't thinking as clearly as he would've liked, but Brad would leave good tracks, so Tim figured he wouldn't need to look for additional holes or other kinds of traps quite so carefully.

First, though, he had to get himself mobile.

He had a loop of rope on his belt, and he cut off several hanks with his knife. A strong, stout branch lay within reach, roughly the right length. Tim lined up the branch with his leg and bound the two together, panting with the pain of shifting his limb, but not pausing to rest. He reached for two more branches, stripping their twigs off, then standing to test his weight on the makeshift pair of crutches.

They held.

Scouring the ground for the first imprint Brad had left, Tim started forward.

The pace he had to maintain was excruciatingly slow, but it enabled Tim to spot the snaking thread of a thorn-studded vine, twisted into a coil on the ground. Cut by Brad, surely, who could've simply stepped over the tripwire, but had instead rendered it inert in case Tim managed to make it this far.

"I'm making it," he muttered. "I'm making it."

The ground was uneven, humped with piles of dirt and rocks that threatened to trip him even without the added threat of booby traps. Tim swung himself along, relying on the crutches, and then one of the sticks split, just shattered into a bundle of splinters, and Tim went down, his broken leg beneath him.

His howl rocketed up to the sky, a shrieking, shameful sound. He lay on his back, breath coming in hitches, helpless tears coursing down his face. He had rolled some distance when he'd fallen and was now several feet from where Brad would have planted his next step. Tim couldn't imagine how he'd ever spy another print on the ground.

He heard a voice, shallow, light, female, and thought he might be dreaming. Was that his wife, come to assist him? Or an apparition?

Tim sat up. He began searching the ground for a replacement crutch.

The voice called out again, and this time it was accompanied by the faraway sight of an outline, a vague form glimmering in the sunlight.

Tim crawled forward, agony to be on his hands and knees.

A young girl sat concealed by a pile of brambles like some fairy-tale creature, hidden away. She was hurt or sick, her eyes glazy and unfocused.

"Please," she whispered, the one word mushy, indistinct, like a record album spun too slow. Her hand grazed Tim's wrist, light as a breeze. "He went that way."

On all fours, Tim turned to look toward the last print Brad had left.

"Not that way," the girl said. "There." She pointed off in the distance, at a series of tree stumps and what looked like a conical pile of stones. Her arm flopped and fell back to the ground.

Tim frowned at her, trying to determine to what degree she might be confused. The direction she'd indicated wasn't the way Brad had gone.

The girl nodded, a slow, pained motion. But her voice was insistent, and very, very certain. "Hurry. I think he's got my aunt."

CHAPTER SEVENTY-FIVE

Natalie's first glimpse of Doug in the hut caused her throat to thicken and turn solid. There was a barrier preventing air from passing into her lungs, and she swayed, throwing one arm out to keep from falling. Her hand struck the stick-and-mud wall, and she clutched at a rod in order to remain standing.

Being back here again had the strangest feel. As if the land Kurt inhabited was a magnet, exerting its own pull, impossible to escape.

And also as if in some bizarre way she'd come home.

Natalie ran to Doug's side, her flying footfalls beating like wings in her ears. Her husband lay on a brightly colored mat, padded despite its thin heft. Additional spoils from some ill-fated hiker. Perhaps it had belonged to Terry.

Natalie felt tears prick her eyes. She crouched down, staring at Doug's still face, the muscles motionless, his eyes shut without so much as a tremble beneath the lids.

Her husband lay swathed in the same silvery wrap that had been placed on Natalie after she was found. Steve must have been here with his emergency supplies. He was gone now though, the hut abandoned. Doug's injured foot extended from an opening at the bottom, transformed by gauze into a cocoon of white.

Natalie searched amongst the folds of stiff material for Doug's throat. His skin felt cool, but not icy. This blanket couldn't have been on for long; Steve hadn't had that much of a head start. Doug might simply not have warmed up yet. Natalie felt with two fingers for a pulse, even a weak and thready one, but couldn't make anything out.

"Doug," she said aloud, her voice echoing in the stillness of the dying day. "Honey, please."

Had Steve administered pain meds that knocked Doug out? Natalie placed her head lightly against her husband's chest, but the crinkly material made it hard to detect any activity.

"You always were frightened of the wrong things," said a voice.

The words had come from behind her in the tight confines of the hut. Natalie was on her feet without being aware of making a move.

Kurt's camp was impossible to escape, and so was he.

Her gaze shot to the rough wooden shelf at the same time as Kurt's did. But Kurt moved a splinter of a second sooner and snatched up the machete.

"Doug is going to be fine," Kurt said as he rotated the blade. "Relatively speaking anyway. I'm eager to see his reaction when he learns your fate, however."

Natalie's thoughts spun. If Kurt was willing to kill her, then it meant she'd become of no interest to him. Why? The question distracted her from the impossibility of preventing Kurt from doing what he'd clearly already decided on. He overpowered her physically even without a lethal weapon in his hand.

"Don't worry," Kurt added. "Physical suffering has never been of interest to me. I keep this blade so sharply honed, you'll hardly even feel it."

Natalie cast a sharp, desperate look around. Steve had been

here—would he come back? Or had that downed policeman sent Brad on to help?

Kurt shook his head, walking toward her with a reproachful expression on his face. "Still waiting for someone to save you, Nat?"

Her nickname sounded poisonous on his tongue. Natalie felt her fists fold.

"Maybe the small-town copper I passed on my way here will arrive just in the nick of time," Kurt suggested. "Although I don't know how much he would actually do, even if he wasn't down in a hole. The police chief is a by-the-book kind of guy, I could see it in every fold of his no-longer-clean uniform. A procedure patsy, trapped by his policies and protocols far more than by anything I dug in the dirt."

Natalie stared at him.

"I would've liked to see you learn one lesson, Natalie," Kurt said, his tone regretful. "That relying on anybody besides yourself is folly. But I will have to turn my attention to other things. Your husband. Your niece."

Hearing this madman mention Mia caused Natalie's fists to tremble, made her yearn for that machete or any other implement to carve out the knowledge she'd given Kurt about her family. He had even less right to take up residence in her life than he did to try to end it.

Natalie's throat felt dry, incapable of much sound, but she let out a grunt. "Your reach isn't that great, Kurt."

Kurt's expression perked up at that, reflecting a flicker of renewed interest. "You didn't come upon her then. Good. I hid her well."

Natalie's limbs loosened, overcome by doubt. Did this explain Kurt's sudden willingness to do away with her—that he'd found a replacement? She wouldn't give Kurt the satisfaction of further protest or denial. Why in God's name had Mia come here?

Kurt answered as if Natalie had spoken aloud. "To find you, of course. Beset by the misbegotten belief that she could serve as rescuer." Kurt paused. "Perhaps she didn't want to wind up like her aunt, years from now. A do-nothing, waiting around for someone else to call all the shots."

Despite being prepared for Kurt's mental grenades, Natalie recoiled at that one.

"I didn't put two and two together immediately," Kurt continued. "But the family resemblance is strong, and I recalled you talking about a niece caught in the throes of teenage self-aggrandizement. I took a guess, and watched Mia's reaction when I said her name."

Natalie pried her fists open, a gesture of surrender. "I'll stay," she said.

Kurt gazed at her.

"With you, in camp," Natalie went on, stumbling over, choking on the claim. "Just please. Let's get Mia out of here." She'd never tried begging Kurt, and had the feeling that doing so would simply provide one more interesting motivation for him to examine. But what other recourse did Natalie have? Kurt was right—she'd never been the master in any situation. While he was the lord of all his.

"You don't have to worry. Mia will do fine here," Kurt answered, gazing levelly at Natalie. "At least, I hope she will. Head injuries can be unpredictable, but I tried to be judicious with this one."

Natalie felt her legs fold as if two strings had been cut. She braced herself, flattening one hand against the stick wall and fighting to stay upright while her shout exploded in the small space. "What did you do to my niece?"

Instead of answering, Kurt whipped toward the slanting doorway, head tilted.

Natalie only heard it then, a sound that had been drowned out by the roar of her own scream in her ears.

She and Kurt raced from the hut in tandem. The machete whistled in the wind as Kurt ran with his hand wrapped around the blade's handle.

Outside, they stood with their faces turned in the direction of the lake.

The noise was unmistakable now.

The faintly beating rotors of a plane.

CHAPTER SEVENTY-SIX

For the first time, Kurt's face registered an emotion that didn't appear scripted, planned, decided on in advance. His features seized with what could only be described as panic as he looked up at the sky. Then he pivoted, turning his back on the lake. Advancing on Natalie, he raised the machete and sliced it down through the air.

Natalie felt the wind the machete made, caught a glimpse of ragged teeth, before spinning out of the weapon's reach.

She had to make it to the lake, where the float plane must be. Help had arrived, if only she could get to it.

Kurt's arm shot out, snakebite fast, and pulled her toward him. "Natalie," he panted into her ear, crooking his arm around her throat. "Didn't I promise this would be painless? Do you know how much uglier things will get if you persist in darting around?"

Natalie twisted desperately, fighting to look in the direction of the lake. She opened her mouth to scream, but Kurt's elbow was constricting her throat, and the sound she forced out was barely audible.

Kurt switched his grasp to the scruff of Natalie's shirt, holding her just far enough away to accommodate the swing of the blade. The choke hold of his fingers was too powerful to budge. For a second, Kurt's body stilled, and his long hair settled on his shoulders. Then he yanked Natalie's head back, exposing her throat.

With her face tilted upward, Natalie caught a glimpse of two distant bodies, moving with painstaking deliberation through the woods. Steve and Brad? The policeman? They were too far off to hear Natalie even if she'd been able to shout at top volume, and too far away in any case to make it here in time.

Kurt thrust his arm upright, like a tower over Natalie's head. The blade of the machete sparked before the sun was stolen away by a freight train of clouds. It was suddenly as dark as night in the treeless ring that Kurt had cleared. Then a clap of thunder shook the sky, letting loose a drenching fall of rain.

Kurt stood motionless, not even blinking, beneath the downpour. His hand didn't so much as quiver, rivulets of rain running down the blade of the machete. Darts and arrows slung from the sky sheeted over Kurt's body until he looked less like a human being than something that was part of nature itself. A waterfall, a river coursing.

Suddenly, his body pitched forward and he was thrown horizontally onto the ground. Kurt thrust his arms out in front of him, trying to block his fall, and the machete flew away, splashing into a newly formed pool of water.

Natalie didn't take time to try and figure out what accounted for Kurt's sudden dive. She'd seen a flash of light in the leaden sky, perhaps a lightning strike had been the cause. It didn't matter. She dove forward, landing beside the machete.

Natalie dug her fingers into the sloppy earth, wrapping mud-caked fists around the handle of the blade, extending it tremblingly as she rose.

The scene in front of her came clear, a curtain rising.

Doug's arms encased Kurt's legs. He'd landed on top of him, his weight driving Kurt to the ground. But her husband was so weak that Kurt had only to whip his body around, like an enormous fish on a dock, all thrashing muscle, to throw Doug off.

Then Kurt was free.

Natalie leapt forward, the machete held outward.

Rain continued to plummet, distorting the sight of Kurt in front of her, keeping her from seeing how close he might be. Natalie staggered toward him, blade thrust out. She could hear the suck of Kurt's heavy boots pulling out of the soil. Not far away then, but not yet within reach of the machete's probing end.

The veil of rain parted, and Natalie could make out Kurt, moving nearer to her, until they stood mere inches apart.

Kurt's face shone, his eyes were clear. The sky began drying up, and the emerging sun cast his form into sharp relief. "Natalie," he crooned. "What do you think you're going to do with that? You've never done anything in your life."

Doug raised himself into a sitting position. He didn't waste time struggling to his feet, but torpedoed his body sideways, arms poised to bring Kurt down again.

Kurt kicked him in the chest, and Doug flopped back onto the ground.

Natalie skirted her husband's body, drawing closer to Kurt as he lifted his boot to deliver another monstrous blow.

Natalie hefted the machete in her hands, folding both fists around the handle and tightening her grip.

Kurt's foot struck Doug again, even though he lay unmoving in the dirt.

Natalie stifled a screech as her husband's body bucked upon impact.

For the briefest slash of a second, Kurt paused, then took a step toward her.

He was close enough now that she could track every movement as he leaned in, focused on her face and nothing else, his nostrils flaring as he inhaled deeply. Kurt's lips parted, and an unfathomable expression crossed his face. Contentedness. Fulfillment. Joy.

Natalie wheeled around in his direction, a judo spin of sheer, solid rage.

"Leave my family alone!" she screamed. The machete formed an extension of her arms, her whole body, as she sank it into Kurt's immutable form.

It took seconds, minutes, untold amounts of time, before Natalie's eyes took in the damage she had wrought. The saw-toothed blade of the machete had landed squarely in Kurt's throat. The machete had embedded itself so deeply, it seemed fused with his body, part of the man himself, as a branch grows out of a tree.

A geyser of blood spurted forth in a great, garish red plume and Kurt dropped.

He reached up, and as he lay there, facedown, panting, it appeared as if he were trying to stanch the flow of blood from his neck, or maybe attempting to extract the machete from it.

Instead Kurt used both hands to manually rotate his head so that he was able to look in the direction he wanted. He caught Natalie's gaze and, for the last time, observed the expression on her face, viewed her reaction to his fate.

She watched Kurt register the blend of horror, and relief, and perhaps a single scant thread of satisfaction as blood jetted out from his body. It formed a penumbra on the ground while life slowly leached from his eyes, until finally they darkened, never to read another person ever again.

CHAPTER SEVENTY-SEVEN

Natalie bent down, needing to see that Kurt's back didn't rise, the lack of breath in his body. In some ways, she didn't believe that even death could claim Kurt. But he lay completely still. Even the circle of blood had stopped spreading outward and was slowly seeping into the earth.

Natalie yanked her gaze away, and ran for Doug.

Steve and Brad arrived in the clearing, the expressions on their faces as dazed and disjointed as Natalie assumed hers to be. They looked as if they'd been dropped on another planet. But both men leapt into action, Brad checking swiftly for Kurt's pulse, while Steve unfolded a portable stretcher and strode over to Doug.

"He's alive," Natalie said, the statement emerging on a sob. "He was unconscious before—and might be again—but he's definitely—"

"Can you move away for me, ma'am?" Steve asked, getting down on the ground.

Brad made sure Natalie steered clear, a fleeting look of gladness on his boyish face. *Good job*, he mouthed, and another sob swelled her throat.

Then the most improbable sight of all appeared in camp.

The last time Natalie had glimpsed the man now stumping his way out of the woods, he had been deep in a hole. The police chief kept his gaze pinned to the ground because he didn't have his hands free to check for traps. The reason he didn't have use of his hands didn't compute right away.

The chief dragged his left leg along behind him, messily splinted with a branch, a dagger of bone protruding from the flesh. Only the chief's densely muscled physique could've accounted for his ability to stay upright; he looked as if he shouldn't have been able to take a step at all. But he was walking—intently, methodically, placing his good foot down before pulling the bad into place, holding a young girl cradled in his arms.

"Mia," Natalie cried, or tried to, though the word came out a whimper.

The police chief warded her off with a single look, then turned his fierce expression on Steve and Brad, who were already moving toward him.

"Get that man off the stretcher and stabilize him here," the police chief barked, his voice so raspy, the command was hard to make out. "Got a teenage girl—started to go into convulsions three and a half minutes ago—probable head injury—"

Steve and Brad flashed each other looks, a complicated calculus of triage.

"Only one stretcher—" said Steve.

"Space in the plane is tight—" Brad said.

The chief's legs crimped, and he went down on one knee, although he kept his arms raised and his hold on Mia secure.

Steve swept Mia out of the police chief's grasp and carried her away.

Natalie whirled, caught between the twin magnets of her husband and her niece. If they couldn't be evacuated at the same time, who should go first?

Brad began the process of removing Doug from the stretcher and assisting him back into the hut, while Steve laid Mia down and buckled a series of bands across her body. Then Brad ran out again to hoist the stretcher with Steve.

Just as they reached the path that wound through the woods and led down to the lake, Brad stopped and called to Natalie. "Come on! We have to come back with another stretcher for your husband, but there's room on the plane if you squeeze." He gestured to the ground in front of them. "And you can show us the best way to go."

The float plane took off lopsidedly, rising from the sheer surface of the lake before banking abruptly. Natalie sat with her hand on Mia's unconscious form as the engine grumbled and the windows rattled and wind swept past the aircraft fast enough to make it sway in the sky.

Steve and Brad adjusted the oxygen mask on Mia's face and began another recording of her vitals. The sight of her niece so vulnerable and prone, looking like a small child again, made tears swim in Natalie's eyes. The lake shattered into a series of prisms, droplets sparkling beneath intermittent bursts of sun glare.

Natalie stared off at the blurring side of a mountain until her eyes smarted. Another mountainside appeared after that, then another, and another, to form a seemingly endless wall of green, just starting to be spattered here and there with gold.

But at last small signs began to indicate the approach of change. Blotches of land where no trees grew. Splashes of man-made color, a necklace of buoys floating on a pond. The dark gash of a long, paved road.

They were back.

Mia went into surgery immediately upon arrival at the hospital. Pressure had built up in her skull, and they were inserting a tube for drainage.

Jim Huggins, pilot of the plane, executed an immediate turnaround to evacuate Doug and the police chief, but Natalie wasn't permitted to go along. Instead, she sat through a series of tests, then a barrage of questions, ultimately being offered a consult with a plastic surgeon. He looked at Natalie's cheek, turning her head this way and that, before pronouncing that he couldn't have done a better job himself.

"You can have those stitches removed in a week," he told her, exiting.

Someone tapped on the cloth curtain, and Natalie looked up to see her sister.

Once, not so long ago, Natalie would've fallen into Claudia's embrace, sapped of strength and requiring her sister's unique ministrations. Claudia would have lent comfort as she always did. But circumstances had thrown both sisters into a centrifuge, spinning their needs and claims and roles around until everything was reversed.

It was Claudia who dropped into Natalie's arms, a sagging, boneless weight. She tried to speak, but for once could not.

Natalie's hand faltered as she lifted it to stroke Claudia's hair. "Is she..." Natalie began at a whisper. "Is Mia going to be..."

Claudia let loose a sob and started to go down. If Natalie hadn't been there to hold her erect, Claudia would've landed on the gleaming tile floor. Her voice when she spoke was shattered, mere fragments of its former strength.

"I don't know, Natalie. They said it's too soon to tell."

The surgeon who operated on Doug acted as if she saw patients with spikes through their feet every day. She informed Natalie that although her husband would have to stay off his injured foot for twelve weeks, and require rehab after, he was expected to regain complete and unimpeded mobility.

Natalie fell asleep, curled by Doug's side on the narrow hospital bed. His leg was raised in a harness, making for a little extra space.

A policewoman had been stationed outside the room; Natalie supposed she was there to guard them, although she wasn't sure what she and Doug needed guarding from now that Kurt was dead.

The police chief arrived the next morning, on crutches, his leg encased in a black ankle-to-hip contraption that scarcely seemed to inhibit his authoritative stride as he entered Doug's room. He'd come to check on them, he explained somberly, and also because he needed to take a statement from Natalie.

She felt a chill whistle through her as understanding hit. That policewoman wasn't there to protect them—she was making sure they didn't leave.

Natalie opened her mouth and began to tell the story, as much of it as she knew.

"So your husband was aware of the drugs in the hull of the canoe?" the chief said, laying his crutches aside once she'd finished. "Although you were not?"

Natalie stared off at Doug's sleeping form, tears shimmering on her eyes. "He was trying to help a friend out of a desperate situation."

"I understand that," the police chief said, and wrote a few lines on his pad.

How foolish Doug had been. Natalie turned back toward the chief. His face wasn't unkind, just intense, as it had been when he'd limped into camp, and it told her what she should've realized already. Even Doug's not-central role in the transport of the drugs amounted to a crime. Natalie swallowed past thickness in her throat. After all they had been through, all they had survived.

She forced herself to ask, "Is Doug going to be arrested?"

The chief began to make his way toward the door. "Once he wakes up and is medically cleared, he'll be brought in for questioning," he told her. "We'll have to take it from there."

Natalie stared down at the floor.

Around noon, Doug finally stirred, and Natalie leapt to his side. She felt as if she hadn't spoken to her husband for years.

Doug's eyes cracked open a millimeter. "Am I dead?" he asked croakily.

Natalie grabbed a plastic pitcher, filling a cup with a trembling hand.

"Well, this feels familiar," Doug said as she dribbled water between his lips. His voice cleared as the liquid hit his throat. "Are we still in the hut?"

Natalie gave a brief smile, but her husband's attempt at levity, which should've been reassuring, only made her feel worse in light of the police chief's visit.

"There was a plane..." Doug began. "I remember flying... How on earth did you get us a plane?"

"I'll tell you," she said. "But there's something we need to deal with first."

They were interrupted by a knock on the door.

Natalie looked up, frowning for a moment before it came to her. "Forrest?"

The guy who entered the room offered a rueful smile. "Luke."

Natalie's face heated. "Of course. Luke."

Doug reached for her hand.

"You okay, man?" Luke asked. Then his head bowed.

Doug gestured grandiloquently toward the bottom of the bed. "Aside from this new orifice in my foot, I'm just hunky-dory."

Luke flinched. His gaze traveled to Natalie, who moved closer to her husband.

"Listen, Doug," Luke said.

Doug raised his eyebrows, aiming an easy, lazy gaze Luke's way.

"I mean it, man. Listen to me."

Natalie sat forward, although Doug remained relaxed, leaning back against a stack of thin hospital pillows.

"The cops are out there," Luke said. He gestured with a thumb toward the door. "But my lawyer got permission for me to stop by and see you first."

Doug didn't respond, and Luke plowed on. "I'm sorry, man," he said. "I'm so sorry we dragged you and Mark and Brett into this. And I know—" He broke off, swiping a hand across his face. "I know Craig would be too."

Doug watched him without expression.

"That's why I came to tell you—" Luke broke off, fisting his eyes again.

When Doug spoke, he sounded annoyed and a little impatient. "Tell me what?"

"They're going to offer you the chance to testify against me," Luke said. "That's what my lawyer says. You and Mark and Brett were just accessories. You'll probably get off with probation."

Understanding began to shadow Doug's face, along with a trace of fear. "Never," he said. "I wouldn't do that to you."

Luke leaned down over the bed, speaking fiercely. "You will do it. It's what I want. It's what I deserve." He swallowed, a visible chug in his throat. Then he said, "And Craig would've wanted it too. Of all people, Craig would've wanted that for you."

Luke backed out of the room, whoever waited for him in the hallway descended, and then they were gone.

Doug's tears didn't start until they could no longer hear a last echoing footstep. Natalie turned toward her husband, startled by the sudden display, like a thundercloud erupting. She wrapped her arms around him, and he rocked and shook against her.

"We had a rough start, Nat," Doug said once he could speak.

"The roughest," Natalie agreed. "Probably who does the dishes will seem like small stuff after this."

Doug caught her hand, stroking it with his thumb in the way that he did, which set all her nerves to tingling. "Would you do it again?"

A series of images, too proximate to be called memories yet, streamed across the mental screen of her mind. Her cheek and its surgical stitching, Doug's speared foot and the escape attempt they'd made, the relentless march of Kurt through their lives. And then other images enabled her body to uncoil, stop preparing for the next strike. Water arcing in a silvery sheet from Doug's paddle, their lovemaking by the river, the curl of the rapids as they captured their boat. Doug eating the berries first, and jumping from the log. How their truest joining only took place after they'd nearly been separated for good.

"Every single day," she told him.

"Knock, knock," someone said, and an orderly walked into the room. "Here to get you ready for PT."

Doug was assisted into a wheelchair, but as the orderly began to roll the chair toward the bathroom to help Doug get dressed, Doug stuck out a hand and stopped him. "I'm thinking you can't get me out of this thing and onto my knees?"

The orderly frowned, as if unsure whether a joke was being made.

Natalie looked at her husband.

Doug gave a nod, answering his own question. "Then this may be the closest I get for a while," he said.

He scooted the chair forward, extending one arm toward Natalie.

She reached down and took his hand.

"Natalie Abbott Larson," Doug said.

Natalie caught her breath, inclining her head.

"Will you marry me?" Doug asked. "Again?"

ONE YEAR AFTER

Natalie didn't get home until after her family had already arrived.

Claudia and her husband were sitting on the front porch, where a row of chairs had been set up, looking out over the woods. It was the only finished portion of the house. Inside was a complete disarray of needed repairs, partially renovated rooms, and unpacking left to be done. Natalie loved every inch of it.

She waved as she climbed out of her new/used car. Couldn't get away with having just one vehicle up here—luckily the parking was plentiful—and Natalie loved her battered Subaru. "Sorry, I got held up. Welcome!"

It was the first time everyone was seeing their new home. Until now, Natalie and Doug had been making the trip down to the city for visits. They weren't really set up for company yet, plus Natalie's niece kept resisting the drive north.

"Nurse's hours," Claudia called back, smiling.

"Student's hours," Natalie corrected, mounting the porch steps. "I don't think I'll ever finish this rotation."

The front door swung open, and Mia emerged.

"Hi, Aunt Nat," she said in her new, husky voice, not the lighthearted, girlish whoop she once would've given, if not yet a woman's sure tone. Mia was holding an ivory-wrapped package in her hands. She walked over to Natalie and gave her a hug. Mia was tall enough now that she had to lean down to do it.

Natalie smiled. "What's this?" she asked, indicating the box.

Mia extended it. "It's from Val," she said. "She says she's sorry she missed some year deadline or something for sending presents. And sorry for a lot of other things too."

Natalie swallowed, staring down at the package as Mia put it in her hands. Finally, she blinked and took a good look at her niece. "You're beautiful," she said, and Mia was. Everyone had always thought that Mia looked older than her years, but that had been for relatively superficial reasons. Her height, her habit of borrowing her mother's clothes. But now Mia truly did look mature. Her eyes were shaded with a certain wisdom, and an overlay of wariness. She was someone who had faced the worst and survived.

"You too," Mia said, depositing a kiss on Natalie's cheek.

The cut Natalie suffered in the woods had indeed left a scar, although Mia's assessment of its cool factor was almost enough to convince Natalie: a minuscule arrow shot across the bow of her face.

"How was the trip up?" Natalie asked. Meaning, not the traffic out of the city, but what was it like to come back here?

"Easy," Mia said, holding Natalie's gaze. "Surprisingly easy."

She turned and opened the door to the house, allowing Natalie's father to pass through. Mia now carried herself with a hint of command. She was getting straight A's in school, and Claudia had told Natalie that Mia had her first boyfriend. They'd met through a hiking Meetup for teens.

Natalie's father stepped onto the porch, gripping a tray full of sandwiches.

Natalie stared at him in disbelief. "You cooked? In that kitchen?"

Her father smiled. "Well, it's not like I attempted anything as bold as the stove."

"You'll have to come up here more often. Doug and I have been depending on the kindness of neighbors and a paucity of restaurants."

She and Doug had already exhausted the menus at all three options in town—a diner, a wood-fired pizza place, and a retro bistro—giving them all five stars. Doug joked that they benefited by comparison. Nary a chipmunk dish in sight.

Natalie started to reach for the tray, but left the task to her father when Doug's SUV swung into the drive.

She took the porch stairs at a run. Even through the worst of a Wedeskyull winter, with snow piled up beyond the sills of the first-story windows, Natalie had run to greet her husband every day.

She'd been tired most of those days, fatigue the most enduring symptom of her ordeal. The fatigue was in part due to the nightmares that plagued her. In her dreams, Natalie was never in the woods; in fact, the woods were a sheltering parent, Mother Nature herself. They were the one place Natalie truly felt safe in this new life she and Doug had created. So Natalie would instead be inhabiting some spot whose danger hadn't emerged until too late—bars they used to frequent, the human resources office where she'd toiled a few scant months, a busy, crowded restaurant—and Kurt would suddenly appear, machete in hand. Natalie would jolt awake, covered in blood that turned out to be perspiration. The first dream-free night she spent didn't take place until after snow-melt in June, when Doug led the two of them on a short day hike to the summit of Jay.

The man who killed Craig had never been found, although the investigation was still ongoing, just one addition to a series of drug-related deaths of which Natalie had gained more than a passing knowledge, and more than she'd ever wanted to possess.

Doug had spent most of the winter serving out his probation, not physically ready for the kind of work he wanted to do. Luckily, the cost of living up here was sufficiently low that gifts from their wedding had given them a buffer, allowing them freedom not to rush into jobs that would only grind them down.

And by this point, Doug was back to normal—actually, more fit than ever.

He twirled Natalie around in his arms, lifting one hand to wave to everybody eating and rocking and chattering on the porch.

"Good day?" Natalie asked. "You're all wet." Doug's hair was glistening, and he smelled of the river he'd just come from.

Her husband scrubbed one hand over his head and wiped damp from his beard. "That couple wanted to test out a few whitewater runs before they put-in next week. Ben suggested I show them a few advanced strokes."

Ben was Doug's new boss at Off Road Adventures.

"Oh, right," Natalie replied, walking hand in hand with her husband back toward the farmhouse. "I remember."

Doug looked at her.

Natalie took a breath. "The ones who are going on their honeymoon."

READING GROUP GUIDE

1. On the day of her wedding, Natalie witnesses her soon-to-be husband, Doug, arguing with two strange men. If you were Nat, how would you handle the situation? Would you try to get to the truth, or let it go to enjoy the day?

2. Natalie and Mia are extremely close. What do you think draws them together? Do you have an older family member or friend with whom you have a special connection?

3. Natalie agrees to a backcountry honeymoon in the isolated Adirondack region, even though Doug is the avid outdoorsman of the two. If you were Natalie, would you agree to Doug's honeymoon plans? If so, why? If not, what would you want to do instead?

4. Describe Nat and Doug's relationship at the beginning of their honeymoon. What do you make of their dynamics? How does their relationship change over the course of the novel?

5. Doug puts both himself and Natalie in danger out of loyalty to

his friend, Craig, who is in financial trouble. Do you think this is a good enough excuse? Do you have any friends for whom you would risk anything?

6. Natalie and Doug must battle the elements, which ends up being almost as dangerous as the man stalking them in the woods. If you were in their situation, what would you do to survive? Do you have any basic outdoor survival skills? How did you feel while reading about Nat and Doug's struggle?

7. Describe Kurt. What makes him so dangerous? Why do you think he is fixated on Natalie and Doug?

8. Compare and contrast Natalie and Kurt. Do you see any similarities between them?

9. If you had to choose, which would you prefer to face: Kurt and his booby traps or the natural elements of the Adirondack region without any supplies or directions?

10. How does Natalie change over the course of the novel? What about Doug? Do you think their relationship will succeed once the story ends? Why?

11. Describe Mia. Why do you think she sets off on her own to find Natalie and Doug? If you were Mia and you knew a family member was in danger, what would you do?

12. Who do you think is the hero of the story: Natalie, Mia, the search-and-rescue team, or a combination of the three? How did you feel reading about Nat and Doug's rescue? Does any moment particularly stick out?

13. Why do you think, after the rescue, Natalie and Doug decide to change careers and move out to the Adirondack region? If you were in their situation, would you do the same?

A CONVERSATION
WITH THE AUTHOR

What was your inspiration for *Wicked River*?

For me, the wilderness is like a siren's call, beckoning with a whisper to write. What darkness hides in the woods? What secrets lurk there? That said, the first inspiration for *Wicked River* had to be my own backcountry honeymoon, which, uh, didn't go so well but didn't go *nearly* as bad as Natalie and Doug's journey did. My husband and I came home after one day of canoeing and promptly hightailed it to France, paying (or not paying) for the trip with the first credit card either of us had ever owned. I never stopped asking myself "What if we hadn't turned back when we did? How much worse could things have gotten?" The answer to those questions became *Wicked River*.

Your novel brings to life the dense, beautiful, and dangerous Adirondack region. Why did you decide to set Nat and Doug's story there?

The Adirondack Park consists of more than six million acres, and there's just something about that kind of vastness, that kind of space.

So many things can go wrong there. As I write this response, there is a seventy-seven-year-old hunter who's gone missing south of the park. A twenty-six-year-old ice fisherman just plunged through the ice on a pond near Lake George and died. I feel such sorrow for the missing and the families of the lost. These stories are so tragic and so untimely. People perish while trying to feed themselves or enjoying a little recreation. At the same time, the land we're talking about has to be some of the most majestic in the world. Jagged peaks and crystalline streams and alpine meadows. Each season of the year is beautiful in some way—wildflowers with petals soft as baby skin in the springtime, the green and blue and yellow of a brief Adirondack summer, the kaleidoscope burst of fall foliage, the hushed quiet of a land swathed in snow. Somewhere within those two poles, danger and beauty, lived Nat and Doug's story.

Are you an avid outdoorsperson yourself?

Oh gosh. See my first response. I am an *aspiring* outdoorsperson. I wish to greater skills than I have. I love the idea of a starlit night and a trip devoid of civilization. But when I actually get any distance away, or even begin planning such a trip realistically, I become aware of all the dangers and think, *Hey, what's so wrong with a real bed and air-conditioning anyway?* In some ways, I think that being able to write a book like *Wicked River* is mutually exclusive with being a true outdoorsperson. For me, the stories are all too real.

The story unfolds from three different points of view: Natalie, Mia, and Kurt. Which character did you relate to the most? Which was the most fun to write?

There's a theory of fiction that says every character has a piece of the author inside him or her. But I find it works in the opposite way for me. In order to write a character, I have to take a piece of him or her and let it live inside me until I become that person for a while. It's very method. So

I related to all three characters—Natalie, Mia, and Kurt—though none of them are really like me. They were all deeply gratifying to write. Not *fun* precisely—but it was exhilarating to become a young bride again, a teenage girl, both living in a world staggeringly different from the one I inhabited during those stages of life. Cell phones and GPS and texting, oh my! And learning where Kurt's hurt, hidden places were, why, despite the abhorrent things he did, he was really weak and wounded himself, was a revelation I felt privileged to observe.

Kurt is a psychologically complex and layered character. What kind of research did you do to bring him to life?

Here's a little secret about my writing: I do almost no research at all. I hate to admit this, because it seems like to be a Real Writer, you must do research, right? Yet many of the writers I admire most—Lee Child, Stephen King—don't do a lot of it, or warn against its hazards. In terms of Kurt specifically, he suffers from a narcissistic personality disorder, with grandiose features, and having worked as a psychotherapist, I gained at least a passing knowledge of how that diagnosis will manifest. But for the most part, he, like all my characters, arose organically, came to life on the page, and I sat back and watched him move. He told me about his parents and how their behavior shaped him into the man who terrorized Natalie and Doug, which was not his intent. Kurt worked against himself; he brought down on himself his deepest fear—solitude—by alienating everyone in his life until the only place left for him was in isolation.

What draws you to the thriller genre?

Time for another secret—I don't actually consider myself a thriller writer, although I love thrillers. In a way, I think the fast pacing of my stories, the fear and the stakes, serve to camouflage what's also there. The first elements to register in my work do bespeak *thriller*. And fear certainly drives many aspects of my life—the awareness that just a subtle twist of the knob could change it all, rid a person of everything, plunge her into a horrifying scenario she might not have the ability to survive. But what drives me in my writing is the potential and promise of triumph, the chance for a weak and flawed character to overcome her deficits and emerge victorious. More than anything, I would say I am a fairy-tale writer.

What do you ultimately want readers to take away from *Wicked River*?

A bookseller in Olympia, WA, once told me: "I feel a little stronger as a person myself when I am reading one of your books." That's what I hope every reader of *Wicked River* takes away—that in each of us lies the potential for strength we never knew we had.

ACKNOWLEDGMENTS

Every novel is a journey, and this book takes the reader on a literal one. It took its author on one too. Things didn't get *quite* as thorny for me during the process of bringing *Wicked River* to you as they did for Natalie and Doug, but…it was hairy there for a while.

For expert shepherding of my career, and passionate devotion to every book, my agent, Julia Kenny, deserves unending gratitude and thanks.

Everyone's tearing their hair out these days, wondering how best to publish books. I found an oasis of calm, knowledge, creativity, and enlightenment in the home I was given at Sourcebooks. Shana Drehs and Margaret Johnston saw right to the heart of what this novel wanted to be—and helped me get it there. Seven massive revisions. Each scene, every line of dialogue, almost every single word pored over. Their skill and devotion shine like suns. Lathea Williams, Stephanie Graham, Valerie Pierce, and the entire publicity and marketing team prove every day that there really is a method to the madness and a wisdom behind the wins. The art and design wizards deserve huge props for finding the exact perfect ornament to evoke rapids and creating one of the most eye-catching covers I've ever seen. Thank you, Dominique Raccah, for all that you've created in your authors' lives and the lives of booklovers and readers everywhere.

The independent publicity team of JKS Communications has been behind every book I've written and also behind Take Your Child to a Bookstore Day, the latter out of the sheer goodness of their book-loving hearts. There are no better independent publicists on the planet. Outside-the-box thinkers, with a Rolodex like a box of fine chocolates, Julie Powers Schoerke, Marissa Curnette, and Sara Wigal, I love working with you.

For investigation, research, and help figuring out how a man would survive in the north woods, everything from the stick-and-daub method of building to where berberine grows, thanks are owed to my son, Caleb. For expert and detailed advice on Search and Rescue, thanks go to Jake Keller of Multnomah County, Oregon—and thanks to author April Henry for putting Jake and me in touch. Author and pal in Minnesota Chris Norbury is my go-to for additional questions about outdoor pursuits. Thanks to my brother, Ezra, for the Forest Service catch.

Author, reviewer, and friend to the mystery/thriller community, Kevin Tipple, set a good thing into motion when he suggested just the right adjective to make the title click. Kevin suffered the loss of his beloved wife, Sandi, this year, and I hope she is somewhere smiling at how her husband's way with words had such a profound impact.

International Thriller Writers is the writers' organization nearest and dearest to my heart, and it's safe to say that this book would not be what it is without one of ITW's founding members. Author and legend David Morrell—you know when an ending flags and, better yet, why. Another of ITW's founders, Gayle Lynds, provided words of support on submission, as did ITW members Steve Berry, Carla Buckley, Lee Child, Andrew Gross, William Kent Krueger, John Lescroart, M. J. Rose, and

Chevy Stevens. That roster of names also happens to make one heckuva reading list for lovers of thrillers and tales of domestic suspense. Enjoy!

A shout-out for Sisters in Crime, whose speakers' bureau I am proud to be a member of and which has a long, illustrious history of supporting authors during every point of their careers.

Booksellers and librarians, for all that you do ushering my books to readers before and after they are on the shelves, I thank you. For all that you once did, growing the young me into an author, I owe you one of the best parts of my life.

My Patreons have made this year in the life of an author a little easier with support and assistance along the way, including much needed dinners out and some downtime. Patreon allows readers to connect with content creators. I have treats and goodies for both fans and emerging writers on my Patreon page and am so grateful to everybody there.

At the Iridium level, enormous thanks go to author Devorah Winegarten.

At the Gold level, great thanks go to Steve Avery, Julie Anne Valdez, and Julie Powers Schoerke.

At the Silver level, my thanks go to David W. Madara, Ron Barak, Mary Jane Frederickson, and Jonathan Kaplan.

At the Bronze level, thanks go to Joe Clifford, Lauren Sweet, Karen Boml, Lori Mohr, Elizabeth C. Main, and Dan McFadden.

I rely on different members of my family as trusty readers and here must single out my mother, Madelyn; father, Alan; and brother-in-law, James. Their enthusiastic reading of early drafts made me think I might be on to something. James, way to rearrange the books and make me a treasure I wear close to my heart.

There are three people without whom I can't imagine writing a book and wouldn't want to. Josh, this one is dedicated to you. You believed I would have a career as soon as Dorothy Whatshername flicked that light bulb in my mind and never wavered once in all the tough days and years to come. You get me through every plot snarl as if you had a fine-tooth comb or a crowbar—and a map. And yet you still believe, as I do, that a hefty dose of magic is involved.

Sophie, I know this was a tough one for you. My dearest hope is that you read it again one day with a feeling of freedom and light.

Caleb, thank you for sharing every frisson of happiness the story gave you, especially at the Twist. Thank you for loving it, almost as much as all the Erin Hunters combined.

And finally, my readers, dear to me all. Without you, I would be traveling alone through a dark and fearsome land. Thank you for coming back to Wedeskyull with me, and welcome, new readers, to a place I love as much as any real location on earth.

ABOUT THE AUTHOR

Photo © Franco Vogt Photography

Jenny Milchman is an award-winning, critically acclaimed novelist from the Hudson River Valley of New York State. Her debut novel, *Cover of Snow*, won the Mary Higgins Clark Award for best suspense novel of 2013, and her follow-up novels, *Ruin Falls* and *As Night Falls*, were both Indie Next picks. Jenny is vice president of author programming for International Thriller Writers, a member of the Sisters in Crime speakers bureau, and the founder and organizer of Take Your Child to a Bookstore Day, which is celebrated in all fifty states.